THE FIRST MOUNTAIN MAN: PREACHER'S PURGE

THE FIRST MOUNTAIN MAN: PREACHER'S PURGE

WILLIAM W. JOHNSTONE AND J. A. JOHNSTONE

THORNDIKE PRESS
A part of Gale, a Cengage Company

A Cengage Company

GALE
A Cengage Company

**LIBRARY OF CONGRESS CIP DATA ON FILE.
CATALOGUING IN PUBLICATION FOR THIS BOOK
IS AVAILABLE FROM THE LIBRARY OF CONGRESS.**

ISBN-13: 979-8-88578-961-5 (hardcover alk. paper).

Published in 2023 by arrangement with Pinnacle Books, an imprint pf Kensington Publishing Corp.

Printed in Mexico
Print Number: 1   Print Year: 2023

THE FIRST
MOUNTAIN MAN:
PREACHER'S PURGE

CHAPTER 1

"Them soldier boys are studyin' on us mighty hard, an' in an unfriendly manner, Preacher. So hard an' unfriendly my neck hair's standin' on end."

"I know it." Preacher sopped up the dregs of his stew with his last biscuit and devoured it.

The seven blue-uniformed soldiers his friend Lorenzo referred to had already caught Preacher's attention with their furtive glances and cold intensity. The tension had been building, and Preacher supposed he knew why that might be.

The soldiers sat around their table in the back corner of the Scalded Beaver Tavern. There were seven of them now, all wearing blue uniforms and all hard-looking men who looked like they'd been on both sides of the mountain. They drank heavily, but they'd been drinking before they came in. A couple of them had stumbled pretty good.

7

The time was just an hour or two past dark, and the meal was sitting well with Preacher. Or it had been. Most decent folk were back in their homes and only the night owls, gamblers, and those who had a taste for alcohol and soiled doves were out and about.

At another table on the other side of the tavern, a small group of men peered at a map and talked quietly among themselves. In their own way, the men seemed just as intense as the watchful soldiers. Preacher didn't know if these men would be considered "decent," but the men didn't pay attention to much outside themselves.

One of them wore a tall, brown D'Orsay hat. Although the hat had been obviously cared for, the distinctive curved brim was wilted in a couple places and showed a few scuffed spots. The hat had been through some tough times. Preacher supposed the young man sitting under it had too because he had a knocked-about look that showed in his rough clothing and wind-burned face.

An air of desperation clung to the man and his group that wouldn't be found in most folks in Fort Pierre.

The mountain man looked away from the group and focused on the soldiers. Their grumbling had gotten hotter and louder.

Those men weren't decent or quiet men. The scars and haphazard attention to their uniforms advertised that.

They were trouble. Or were soon to be trouble.

Preacher wouldn't claim to be decent, but he could be a bad man for those who had wronged him or others he decided to protect. He didn't hesitate when push came to shove, or when it was time to root, hog, or die. Tonight, he had no wish for aggravation.

He chased the last swallow of stew with a sip of beer and glanced over again at the group Lorenzo had called his attention to.

"They came in about an hour ago and have been watchin' us ever since," Preacher agreed. "I think they're workin' their nerve up to somethin'."

Across the table from Preacher, Tall Dog cut another bite of his steak with one of the knives he carried. The young Crow warrior was a walking armory, and that was only one of the things Preacher respected about him.

Like Preacher and Tall Dog, Lorenzo wore buckskin pants and a shirt, all of them recently made and in good shape. He carried two pistols shoved through the sash at his waist. His Hawken rifle leaned against the wall close to hand just as Preacher's did.

"We could go ask what they find so interesting about us," Tall Dog suggested. "I would be happy to do that."

He popped the bite of steak into his mouth and chewed like he had all the time in the world.

Preacher pushed his empty plate away. "No. I don't want to go on the prod. The major over the army here doesn't much cotton to folks disturbin' the peace. We'll lie low and give 'em leeway to figure out their own path. They can't surprise us. If those varmints are dead-set on confrontin' us, they'll come back later when we ain't expectin' it."

Lorenzo grinned mirthlessly. His skin was dark, but his hair was going gray these days, not black like it had been when Preacher had first met him years back. He was slimmer now than he'd been, wiry and tough. Time was creeping up on him and had worn away at any spare flesh he'd carried. Until he and Preacher had gotten reunited a couple months ago at a Crow camp on the Snake River, Lorenzo had been talking about seeking the easy life. Boredom had settled in pretty quickly and he'd wandered West again.

"Now that you know they're lookin' at us

10

lookin' at them," Lorenzo said, "any chance of you not expectin' them?"

Preacher grinned back. "Nope. But I'm not going to look at them too hard. I'd rather get this over with now if anything's gonna come of it. Before they talk themselves out of it doing something now."

"You afraid of scarin' them off?"

"There are seven of them. Seems like if they were really feelin' froggy, they'd have jumped by now. I'd rather see it comin' than be lookin' over my shoulder the whole time we're here."

Lorenzo pulled a face. "You're bored, spoilin' for a fight, an' we only got in late last evenin'."

"After all the excitement recoverin' those rifles and fightin' Diller and his men, the trip back to Fort Pierre was just a mosey. A fracas in this tavern might take the edge off of bein' back in civilization."

"All of these people constantly around has that effect on someone used to living in the mountains," Tall Dog said. "Their presence is most . . . irritating. I find myself weary of it as well."

Lorenzo shook his head. "My oh my, but the bloom fades quick, don't it? An' here you was all excited to see a big town."

"I still want to see it," the young Crow

11

warrior said. "I have heard many stories about large places such as this one. I just do not find the experience as relaxing or as informative as I believed I would."

"This ain't even big." Lorenzo snorted. "Fort Pierre don't hold a candle to the likes of St. Louis. An' if you really have a hankerin' to see somethin' of civilization an' society, why you should get yourself on down to New Orleans. Now that there is a big city, but it's got food the likes of which you ain't ever seen. Take you weeks to sample it all, an' there's a lot more to see."

"I think I shall have to limit my exposure to small portions," Tall Dog admitted ruefully. "I did not get much sleep last night."

"Them beds is soft," Lorenzo observed. "I found mine mighty welcome after campin' out along the trail gettin' here."

"The bed is too soft," Tall Dog said. "I slept on the floor, but all the noise from the tavern on the first floor and out in the street kept me awake."

The broad-shouldered young man was tall with dark blond hair shaved to the scalp on the sides and left long enough on top to make a braid that hung down his back. His heavily bronzed skin marked him as an Indian, and that made him an outcast in several places within the fort.

He wore a sword with a looped hilt sheathed in a scabbard down his back. A short dark blond beard covered his strong chin. He'd gotten the hair color and the steel-gray eyes from his Swedish father. His bronze skin and polite ways came from his Crow mother. She was soft-spoken and had insisted on good behavior from her only son. His Christian name was Bjorn Gunnarsson, but he generally introduced himself as Tall Dog, a Crow warrior, because that was more believable.

When Preacher had headed north from the Crow village beside the Snake River, Tall Dog had, with the blessing of his parents, accompanied the mountain man to return the lost rifles they'd taken back from the rogue Army captain Diller. The young Crow warrior had wanted to see more of the white man's world, though his father Olaf had promised him the visit would be disenchanting because he'd had enough of it himself.

Still, a young man tended to wander. Preacher knew that for a fact. He'd left home early himself because the mountains had captured his heart and imagination with their mystery and majesty. He'd never regretted going into the wilderness.

"If a bed is troublin' you," Lorenzo declared, "I can't promise you're gonna get on much better with anythin' else you're gonna find here."

Tall Dog considered his empty plate. "The food is good."

"Are you certain?"

The Crow warrior regarded Lorenzo suspiciously before answering. "I am."

"I only ask 'cause it took you two plates' worth to make up your mind. From the way you wolfed it down, I figured you never bothered to taste any of it."

"Well," Tall Dog said, "from my continued observation, which was necessary, I now know that the food here is both good *and* plentiful."

Lorenzo shot a sour look at Preacher, who laughed aloud because the older man knew he'd been one-upped.

"Why don't you make yourself useful an' get us another round of beers," Lorenzo suggested to Preacher.

"I can do that," Preacher replied. "Need to stretch my legs anyway."

"I'll watch your rifle."

Preacher stood and adjusted the gun belt he wore. Even though he'd worn it every day for a few months, it was still a new thing to him. Normally he'd carried his flintlock pistols in a sash at his back. He still carried

14

those there, but the new Colt Paterson revolvers he'd been given by the Texas Rangers rode in holsters on his hips. Those weapons had caught the eye of every man in the fort who knew armament. The repeating pistols were still new out West.

Tall and powerful from years spent living in the mountains and fighting Blackfeet Indians and outlaws, Preacher drew the attention of the men sitting around the Scalded Beaver. Some of them he'd met in passing while doing business at the fort. Others knew him by suspicion and reputation. He had a fresh haircut and shave, courtesy of the local barber, and his mustache was in fine fettle. With winter coming, he'd grow out his beard again soon, but for now being clean-shaven suited him.

The stout, red-bearded bartender was mostly bald on top. What was left of his hair was oiled into place and looked like a dead jellyfish spread out over his pink scalp. He dressed neat, though, with an apron and gartered sleeves. He spoke with a Gaelic lilt.

"You'll be having another three beers?" the bartender asked. "Or would you be wishing for something a little more powerful?"

"The beer's good. A man can't always get

15

good beer."

"Beer it is, then."

Preacher glanced at the mirror on the wall behind the counter as the bartender stepped over to the tapped beer keg sitting on the long shelf beneath the mirror.

Three of the soldiers got up from the group at the back of the tavern and approached the bar through the scattered tables. One of the soldiers wore a fringed yellow epaulette on his left shoulder that marked him as a subaltern, probably a lieutenant.

"You got company coming, mate," the bartender said softly so his voice didn't carry any farther than Preacher.

"I see them," the mountain man replied. "No idea what they want."

Warm excitement filled him. Since the soldiers had come in, he'd weathered the threat they had presented with their covert, at first, attentions, then their downright brash brassiness.

"You know the leftenant?" the bartender asked.

"Nope."

"That's Judd Finlay." The bartender placed a full glass of beer down and reached for another glass. "He can be a bad bloke."

Preacher nodded. "Thanks for the

The lieutenant was broad and heavy-faced with high cheekbones. His nose sat askew from its proper position. His brown hair was combed back from his high forehead, but a few unruly strands hung down over his bushy brows. His mouth looked small on that wide expanse of face, only a little broader than his nose. Dark brown whiskers covered his square chin. He was about Preacher's age.

The bartender filled the third glass. "He's a southpaw. Catches folks off guard with that. Hits hard enough most opponents don't recover."

"I'll keep that in mind."

The bartender placed the three glasses of beer in front of Preacher. The mountain man dropped enough coins on the counter to cover the beer, and added a nice tip.

"Thanks, mate." The bartender disappeared the coins and turned to Finlay and his two cohorts with a practiced smile that revealed nothing of the conversation he'd had with Preacher. "Something I can get for you, Leftenant?"

"Shot of whiskey," Finlay growled. He tucked into the bar to Preacher's left only inches away. The man smelled like a brewery. "The good stuff."

"All right then." The bartender turned back to the neat rows of bottles. "Coming right up. Shots for your mates, too?"

Preacher picked up the three glasses of beer. Lorenzo and Tall Dog watched him from their table. The four soldiers in the back moved toward the center of the tavern.

"Them, too," Finlay agreed and nodded to the men. He turned and focused his dark green eyes on Preacher. "Say, ain't you the one they call Preacher?"

Preacher returned Finlay's gaze full measure. "I am."

Finlay ran a finger alongside his crooked nose. "Story goes that you came in talkin' ill of Captain Diller."

"You're talkin' about the same Captain Diller who robbed Pierre Chouteau's shipment of rifles a few months ago," Preacher said evenly and loud enough to be heard around the tavern, "and blamed that robbery on Blackfeet warriors? That the varmint you're talkin' about?"

Everyone in the tavern stilled. Conversations stopped. Glasses quietly returned to tabletops. The man in the D'Orsay hat turned to watch with bright interest.

Finlay's face suffused with blood and he opened his mouth.

Before the man could speak, Preacher

18

continued. Maybe he was on the prod. A little.

"You're askin' about the same Captain Diller who also murdered the Army's replacement for the major in command of the soldiers here? And all the soldiers who rode with him? Is that the Diller you're talkin' about?"

Finlay's eyes narrowed. "They say you killed him."

"I did. Shot that varmint right between the eyes while he was drawin' down on me. He knew what he was gettin' into."

"He was my friend."

"I gave Diller a Christian burial out there in Colter's Hell. He didn't deserve it, but I try not to leave a man without buryin' him. Especially if I killed him. I marked the grave so he'll be easy enough to find if you're of a mind to visit and pay your respects."

"If you killed him, you backshot him!" Finlay roared. "Ain't no other way you could take Diller head-on! An' then you spun that story about rescuin' Chouteau's rifles just so you could lay your own claim to part of them! I heard all about that! You're a liar an' a thief!"

Preacher spoke coldly, the only warning he was willing to give. "Maybe you need to learn to pick your friends better."

Finlay spun and fired his big left hand straight off his shoulder at Preacher's face. The lieutenant masked the blow with his body till the last minute. If Preacher hadn't been forewarned by the bartender and his own observation of the soldiers' heightened interest in him and his friends, he might have gotten caught looking.

CHAPTER 2

The mountain man swayed back just enough to be out of range of his opponent's fist, then he set the three beer glasses on the bar. He spun to face Finlay.

"Hey!" the bartender yelled. He reached below the counter and came up with a wooden club. "No fighting in here! Get out of my — !"

Finlay threw another left-handed punch. Preacher caught the blow on his right forearm and turned it aside. The impact partially numbed his arm. The lieutenant was strong as a mule.

Moving quickly because both of Finlay's cohorts closed in, and one of them had somehow gotten the bartender's club, Preacher took a half-step forward and jabbed Finlay in the face with his left hand hard enough to drive the man back, then pummeled him with a roundhouse right that caught him on the jaw and sent him stumbling backward in a rush.

The man behind Finlay attempted to catch the lieutenant and became tangled with him.

The third man circled them. Lantern light glinted dully off the brass knuckles on his fists as he stepped toward Preacher. Before the man's lead foot planted solidly on the sawdust-strewn and beer-stained floor, Preacher kicked the man's ankle and knocked him off balance. As the man tried to recover his stance, the mountain man caught his opponent's left wrist in one hand and gripped the man's elbow in the other. When the man tried to yank free, Preacher used the motion to violently crank the captured hand down and back. He drew his hand from the man's elbow, then drove it back down as hard as he could.

Something snapped in the man's elbow or shoulder, possibly both, and he squalled in pain. He dropped to the floor and cradled his injured arm.

Preacher didn't care. He'd intended to break at least one of those joints to reduce the odds and let the brawlers know how far he was willing to go. Finlay and his men outnumbered Preacher and his companions, and this wasn't just a barroom brawl. The surprise attack and the brass knuckles proved that.

Beyond the fallen man, Lorenzo and Tall Dog squared off against the other four soldiers. Patrons of the Scalded Beaver, including the man in the D'Orsay hat and his friends, were vacating the premises, but several of them crowded the windows to peer inside. They were backlit by the scattered lanterns that kept the night at bay along the cross streets where the tavern sat.

"Don't kill them unless you have to!" Preacher bellowed.

He wasn't wishful for any trouble with the current Army major or Pierre Chouteau. Fighting was one thing, but killing a man would bring more problems. He'd only intended a couple days of respite before returning to the mountains he loved. Profits in the fur trade were growing thin, and it was too late in the season to find a wagon train to guide. Preacher would make do living off the land for the winter.

Returning the captured rifles after claiming two dozen of them as his own hadn't left Preacher in any good graces with Pierre Chouteau, but it had given him a small poke after selling those rifles. Losing those weapons had deeply cut into the French trader's profit margin.

Preacher turned his attention to Finlay

and the other soldier as they closed on him. He considered drawing one of the Colt Patersons and putting an end to the fracas. He might have done it if he weren't sure he would have had to kill one or both the men facing him to stop them. They were just mean-drunk enough to be stupid and stubborn.

Then again, if they'd tried to ambush Preacher in an alley, he'd have killed them straight off.

Finlay and the other soldier wore pistols and knives but so far hadn't seemed inclined to go for them. Evidently, they had been intent on just delivering a beating.

Growling an oath through his bloody lips, Finlay grabbed a chair and swung it at Preacher. The mountain man stepped toward his opponent to use him as a shield against the other man carrying the club, took the brunt of the chair across the thick muscles of his back, and slammed his right fist into Finlay's face.

The big lieutenant dropped the pieces of the broken chair and thudded to his knees with glazed eyes. Slowly, Finlay toppled onto his face and didn't move.

The soldier with the club swung over Finlay, but Preacher ducked, avoided most of the blow, and caught a glancing blow on his left cheek and temple. Even though he was a little dazed, he came up with a throat punch that temporarily shut off the man's wind.

Panicked because he suddenly couldn't breathe, the soldier stumbled back with both his hands wrapped protectively around his neck. His eyes were wide with fear.

Preacher grabbed the man by the hair, yanked him to the side, and kicked his feet out from under him.

"You're going to be all right," the mountain man told his opponent lying on the floor. "If you stay down."

The man rolled over onto his back and struggled to get his wind back. He made no effort to get up.

Tall Dog stood with folded arms in the middle of three unconscious men, two of whom had, at first glance, at least one broken limb. At six and a half feet tall, the Crow warrior towered over his vanquished foes.

Lorenzo struggled with one overweight soldier who was big as a bear and fought like a banshee. Despite the fat man's struggles, Lorenzo kept him corralled against the wall beside the tavern entrance. Lorenzo cursed like a mule skinner and sounded frustrated to boot as he huffed and puffed and swung his knobby fists.

The fat man hit Lorenzo in the ribs with a hard right that took the air out of the smaller man. Lorenzo responded with two hooks, a left and a right, that smashed into the soldier's face and caused his head to thump against the wall.

Preacher stood beside Tall Dog. "You ask him if he needs help?"

"I did. He told me he did not require assistance."

Preacher folded his arms over his chest and waited.

Lorenzo grabbed the man's ears and hammered his opponent's massive head against the wall with the stubborn intensity of a woodpecker working a new tree.

Preacher raised his voice over the thudding. "Lorenzo? You need a hand?"

"No, I don't need no help!" Lorenzo yelled and wheezed for breath. "I ain't some two-bit, wet-behind-the-ears greenhorn! This man is just too stupid an' onery to know when he's outhorsed!"

"You might need to blow for a minute," Preacher suggested.

"I'm fine," Lorenzo growled. "Leave me be. I've almost got him whupped."

"I think the man is mostly unconscious," Tall Dog said.

Looking at the ineffectual way the soldier swung his arms, Preacher agreed. "Hey, Lorenzo, just step back a minute."

Reluctantly, panting, Lorenzo stepped back with his balled fists in front of him. His opponent stood for a moment and jerked his arms. He never blinked. Then, slowly, he fell forward to the floor with a massive, meaty thump and remained still.

Lorenzo bent over and rested his hands on his knees. He drew in deep breaths.

"Told you I had him," Lorenzo said.

"You did," Preacher agreed.

"That's a big ol' boy," Lorenzo gasped and glanced at Tall Dog. "Wasn't no pantywaist like them you three were fighting." He shifted his gaze to Preacher. "Or them three you fought."

"I reckon not," Preacher replied agreeably. "You did fight the biggest one."

"I hope to shout," Lorenzo agreed.

"Maybe we should get out of here while the gettin's good," Preacher suggested.

"Lemme find my hat."

Movement out in front of the tavern caught Preacher's eye. Blue Army uniforms cut through the crowd and headed for the tavern.

"Might not get out of here after all,"

Preacher said and nodded toward the window.

Lorenzo glanced up and frowned. "Damnation." He bent down again and retrieved his hat. "You wouldn't think polecats like these would have friends." He shrugged and took a breath. "Takes all kinds, I suppose."

The front door banged open and a dozen soldiers ran into the room with their rifles raised.

Lorenzo waved a hand at them. "Preacher, you and Tall Dog go ahead an' dig in. When I catch my breath, I'll be along. Save me a few."

The soldiers leveled their rifles at Finlay and his men lying scattered on the floor. A few of those rifles covered Preacher and his companions.

A whip-smart young officer walked into the bar and stood in front of his troops. One of his gloved hands rested on the hilt of his military saber. A neatly trimmed blond mustache covered his upper lip. His blue eyes were hard.

"This fracas is at an end," the officer declared in a clear voice. "I am Lieutenant Kraft. I'm here to sort this mess out. Any continued hostilities on your part will result in you getting shot."

"Well," Lorenzo said like he was disappointed, "that plumb puts an end to things, don't it?"

CHAPTER 3

"I won't be taking you into custody, sir," Lieutenant Kraft told Preacher. "I was informed by the bartender, Mr. Ivers, that Lieutenant Finlay and his men started this brawl."

"They did," Preacher agreed.

He stood with the young officer at the front of the tavern. The turn of events surprised him. He'd expected to be arrested on general principle for disturbing the peace. It was no secret that Pierre Chouteau wasn't happy with him, and the Frenchman owned the fort. The Army was allowed to base there at his indulgence.

Of course, that favor to the Army was mutually beneficial and worked both ways. In exchange for their base of operations in the territory, the soldiers helped keep the peace in the fort and prevented rampant thievery, and they kept the Blackfeet and other hostile Indians at bay for wagon trains that passed through on their way to Oregon.

"An' we'd finished the fight by the time you arrived," Lorenzo declared.

He would have sounded more fierce had he not been leaning against the wall for support, though he tried to act like he didn't need it. He blotted a napkin at the blood trickling through the gray scruff on his chin.

"Saved you boys the trouble of wranglin' with them," Lorenzo went on. "Some of your young whippersnappers there, seein' as how they don't look too experienced, might have gotten themselves hurt in a little set-to like the one that was fought here. You could say we saved 'em from that."

"Yes, of course," Kraft said. He adjusted his saber hilt with authority and didn't look terribly impressed with Lorenzo's claim. "I'm sure Major Crenshaw will extend to you his appreciation for that service. Since learning of Captain Diller's involvement in the robbery of Mr. Chouteau's rifles, the major has held Lieutenant Finlay in disfavor. Finlay's actions with Diller prior to this latest debacle was suspicious at best, and criminal in my mind."

"The major might have extended his appreciation while Chouteau was squawkin' at us this mornin'," Preacher said sourly. The way he'd gotten dressed down after actually

31

doing the trader a good turn had rankled him.

Kraft frowned slightly. "I understand, but Mr. Chouteau's disappointment over the loss of those rifles is understandable."

"Not so understandable that Major Crenshaw gave up the percentage of those rifles that the Department of War had agreed on for the transportation of those rifles," Preacher pointed out. "He kept his fair share same as I did."

"That was not the major's decision to make. He was under the direct order of Joel Roberts Poinsett, the Secretary of War, to take those rifles as was agreed. The Army acted in good faith regarding delivery of those rifles, and Major Roger Voight gave his life while protecting them. The major only assumed ownership of that which was promised in good faith."

"I reckon Chouteau was a mite put out since it was the Army who caused those rifles to go missin' in the first place," Preacher said. He decided maybe he wasn't done being cantankerous for the evening.

Kraft reddened slightly. "Captain Diller was not working on behalf of the Army when he killed Major Voight and absconded with those rifles."

"Maybe not," Lorenzo said, "but I'll bet a

solid dollar Diller was drawin' Army wages while he was out stealin' them rifles."

"I wouldn't know," Kraft said, but his neutral expression and tight voice didn't fool Preacher. Kraft was a by-the-book Army officer. He was well aware of Diller's crimes, and they shamed him. He cleared his throat. "As I said, the bartender told me Lieutenant Finlay started the fight with no provocation on the part of you three."

"He did," Preacher said.

"When I heard about the fight, I suspected as much. I'm not surprised Finlay attacked you."

"Mighta been nice if you an' Major Crenshaw mentioned that was a possibility this mornin' while Chouteau was givin' us whatfor," Lorenzo said.

"Despite what Diller did, there are many men who looked up to the captain," the young officer said. "Diller was a trained fighting man and an experienced Indian fighter by all accounts. Lieutenant Finlay was a good friend of his."

"If Finlay was such good friends with Diller," Preacher asked, "why didn't he ride out with Diller after those rifles?" That question had come to mind while he'd waited to see what Kraft would do.

"When Captain Diller rode out of Fort

33

Pierre, Lieutenant Finlay was in lockup. Otherwise, I'm sure he would have gone with the captain." Kraft looked uncomfortable. "I'm afraid tonight's violence might not be the end of the matter, Mr. Preacher."

"Diller has more friends here, does he?" Preacher asked.

"I'm afraid so, sir. How long do you intend to stay at the fort?"

"We haven't decided. We were thinkin' on it over supper an' we got interrupted before we could decide."

The fact that other soldiers might want to champion the dead captain's cause didn't surprise Preacher. He'd known that when he and Lorenzo had decided to return the rifles to the Frenchman.

Diller had established a profitable little black-market trade in and around Fort Pierre. According to what Preacher had found out, hijacking the Hawken rifles Pierre Chouteau had bought in St. Louis to sell to hunters, trappers, and immigrants passing through on their way to Oregon had been the biggest enterprise Diller had ever attempted. If successful, the theft would have paid off well. By the time immigrants reached Fort Pierre, they'd learned the need of a good rifle.

Preacher and Lorenzo had picked up that

information from men they talked to while arranging care for their horses and during trades to upgrade their own equipment. A couple of the recovered Hawken rifles had helped finance those purchases. Once the locals discovered who they were, many of the men were happy to talk to them about Diller and the sorry business he had going on under Major Lawrence Crenshaw's nose.

Others had given them an earful about what a good man Diller had been.

The opinions weren't evenly split. Most of the folks around Fort Pierre who had dealings with Diller hadn't liked the man. Preacher suspicioned the few who had a knot in their tail about Diller being dead had been in business with him and were mad about losing their illicit income.

"Might I suggest," Kraft said, "with the hopes of not sounding too crass, that you make this a short visit to Fort Pierre and select a venture that will take place anywhere but here?"

"You can suggest," Preacher said, "but I'll be hanged if I get run off by a varmint like Finlay's group of thugs. That ain't my style. Never will be."

Kraft frowned.

Two soldiers yanked Finlay to his feet and pushed him toward the door. His hands were cuffed behind his back and his face was puffy from the punches he'd received.

"You better grow eyes in the back of your head, Preacher," the lieutenant warned. "One night I'm gonna be there an' you won't see me comin'."

Preacher grinned at the man. "Maybe if you ask the young Lieutenant Kraft here for a brief time-out from your trip to the hoosegow, we can step outside and take care of things between us. Gun or knife. Don't make any difference to me."

Finlay scowled and spat at the mountain man. The bloody spittle landed on the floor a yard from Preacher.

"Mr. Preacher," Kraft said, "I'm afraid you'll need to take that threat to heart. The Army will hold Finlay for a few days for this infraction and the damages, but he isn't known as a forgiving man. You embarrassed him tonight. He will come for you again."

"I appreciate the warnin'," Preacher said. "If you're done with us, I think we'll head over to the boardin'house where we're stayin' while we're here. If things break right, we might have a big mornin'."

Kraft nodded.

Preacher gathered his rifle and his pack and led the way to the door.

Outside on the street, Lorenzo asked,

"What do you reckon we'll do in the mornin'?"

"We'll have breakfast, and we'll think on it. We'll find something to do. Something will show up. Always does."

Preacher hoped that was true. He needed to stay busy. It wasn't in his nature to lay about. That was when trouble usually came calling.

"Long as it don't get us killed," Lorenzo said.

The open space in the middle of Fort Pierre was covered in narrow, sunbaked ruts left by the wagons that wound through them, and from the lack of rain in recent days. Preacher minded his step as he walked north from the Scalded Beaver toward the hostlers where he'd left Dog and Horse.

The cool breeze that held the promise of the coming winter raised dust flurries and sent them scampering to the northeast. Pierre Chouteau Junior had built his trading post on the west side of the Missouri River just north of the mouth of Bad River in 1832.

Joseph La Framboise Junior had established Fort Tecumseh a mile to the north on a small island in the Missouri River in 1817, and it had blossomed into a trading post. It had been named for Tecumseh, who had been a chief of the Shawnee tribe. La Framboise had worked as a fur trader for John Jacob Astor's American Fur Company.

After helping Andy Jackson at the Battle of New Orleans in 1815, Preacher had headed west. He'd seen Fort Tecumseh soon after it had been built.

Chouteau's new trading post had quickly put Fort Tecumseh out of business in 1832, and that had caused some hard feelings between some traders and trappers that still lingered even though the same company was behind the building of both. Two years later, Chouteau and his partner Bernard Pratte bought out Astor's fur company and concentrated as much on trade with immigrants as for furs because the lucrative nature of beaver pelts was ebbing.

Preacher lamented that loss. It was a way of life he'd enjoyed, and it would never be as robust as it once was. That was the primary reason he sometimes took on guide jobs heading folks who weren't smart enough to save themselves across dangerous territory.

Still, he'd work the fur trade and live in the mountains as long as he could. No other place or enterprise matched him quite so well or made him so happy. There was good money to be made in hunting buffalo hides, but the work was a lot more risky, and Preacher knew Indian families depended on the buffalo meat to live. He hated to take that away from the friendly tribes. Hunting buffalo in lands away from the friendly tribes put him smack-dab in the middle of Blackfeet territory. Since he'd warred with the Blackfeet nearly his whole life out West, he was a marked man to those warriors. They called him Ghost Killer and White Wolf.

Preacher pondered on things as he walked, and he kept an eye peeled for any of Diller's or Finlay's friends. He was pleasantly drunk and full as a tick, but he was completely alert.

Hiller's Stables was located near the boardinghouse that ran along the western wall of the stockade fence. Over the last nine years, the timbers had grayed with age, but they were still thick and stout and had withstood musket and rifle balls, arrows, and fire, in addition to the elements. Likely they would stand for a lot more years.

The Army headquarters was against the back wall, opposite the main gate that was constantly guarded. A large United States flag flew over the building in the daylight hours, but it was taken down at sunset. It would be back at the top of the flagpole come morning when a bugler blew "Reveille."

Chouteau's general store was opposite the boardinghouse and the stables. The building was the largest structure in the fort, second only to the Army barracks. The blacksmith's and the saddle shop were tucked in at the end of the general store. If Chouteau didn't have goods somebody wanted in his store, he had men who could make them. He even kept two seamstresses on the payroll to work on officers' uniforms and pretty dresses for their wives.

Hiller's Stables had started out as a long lean-to. Preacher had helped build it in the spring of 1832 when Chouteau had started constructing the fort. He'd been younger and, after having a bad run of luck involving a Blackfeet ambush, had needed money to buy traps, powder and ball, and pistols to go back into the mountains. As soon as he'd gotten enough cash together for a new outfit, he'd left.

Now, instead of a simple lean-to with a north wall and a roof to block off the sun, the stable had walls all the way around to protect against the brutal winters. During the summer months, part of the walls was taken down to allow the air to circulate.

They were up now.

A lantern hung by the door so late arrivals who were new to the fort could find the stable in the dark. Preacher could find the structure by the smell of hay and horse manure with both eyes closed.

The mountain man knocked on the door, and it rattled on its iron hinges.

"Who is it?" Dempsey yelled out in his gruff voice.

"Preacher. Come to check on my animals."

"They got feed and water. No sense in checking on them. That's what you pay me for." The door opened and revealed a skinny man with a large forehead and a nose that listed badly to the right.

Dempsey was in his forties, a good man with a horse, but he'd had his fill of trapping and living rough a few years back. He raked his hair out of his eyes and pulled at the ratty beard that hung to the middle of his chest.

The hostler raised the lantern he carried in his hand and peered at Preacher. Then he grinned.

"Somebody caught you a good one there on that cheek, didn't they?" Dempsey asked. "Should be purty tomorrow."

"This was courtesy of one of Diller's

friends." Preacher stepped into the stable.

"That would be Finlay," Dempsey said. "Diller didn't have many friends. A few bad apples in the troops, but most of them were no-account so-and-sos who like makin' their money the easy way. Takin' it out of somebody else's pocket or sellin' illegal goods to the Indians."

"It was Finlay. Lieutenant Kraft put him in lockup."

"Kraft's a good man. You don't want to cross him though." Dempsey made a production out of looking at Preacher's eye. "You might want to learn to duck. Just some advice."

"I appreciate it."

Dempsey laughed and the mountain man joined him. Preacher had enjoyed a good meal, a good drink, and even a fight that hadn't gone too badly — except for the eye. Things had gone well on his first day at the fort, and he felt buoyed.

Preacher walked along the narrow stalls to the one that held Horse and Dog. Dempsey followed to provide light.

Horse nickered gently and bobbed his head. The dark gray stallion stood tall and was well-muscled. His dark eyes showed intelligence.

"Hello, feller," Preacher greeted.

He reached over the stall gate and ruffled Horse's mane. The big animal butted his head against the mountain man's chest and whinnied hopefully. The horse didn't like being cooped up. He was used to the wilderness and preferred it there.

"No, we aren't going anywhere," Preacher said. "We're going to rest up a few more days. Then we'll see where we go. I know you're anxious to get back into the mountains, too."

Preacher stepped back and looked into the stall corner where Dog lay.

Gray-furred and large, the cur looked like a wolf at first glance. Dog yawned and his pink tongue lolled for a moment.

"Dog," Preacher said, "you're with me. I want an extra pair of eyes and ears with me tonight. Let's go."

The big cur got to his feet, took one lope, and hurled himself over the stall gate. He landed in the spread straw on the other side and stretched.

"I swear that animal gets bigger ever' time I see him," Dempsey said.

"He's coming into his winter coat." Preacher scratched Dog's ears. "Always makes him look bigger."

"Maybe so. I know he almost scared off some of those new fellers from back East

43

who haven't lived out here. They took one look at him and wanted to take their horses someplace else on account they thought he might eat 'em."

"There isn't any other place."

"That's what I told them. Then I told them Dog was just fine if you leave him be. He was just here to protect your horse."

"Horse can protect himself."

"I know it. I just had to tell them something. Don't know if they finally believed me or just gave up on tryin' to keep the horses anywhere else. It appears they're runnin' into some bad luck. Don't know what kind, but they've had some long faces the last couple days."

"What are they doin' here?" Preacher just had a naturally curious mind and tended to ask questions. That was how a man learned things, and it was how he'd taught himself nearly everything he knew.

"They're plannin' on settin' up a trading post over by Spearfish Canyon. I heard 'em talkin' about it."

Preacher shook his head. "Those are Sioux lands, though the Blackfeet contest them for it now and again. Trappin' there ain't safe for a white man."

"I mentioned that to them. Their leader is a man named Barnaby Cooper. Pure Easterner from Baltimore, Maryland. He's smart enough from the sound of him, just not when it comes to bein' out of doors. He's got twelve wagons full of trade goods an' more comin'. Says he figures he's sold a chief of the Sioux on the notion of a trade post goin' up there."

"One chief isn't going to speak for them all. There's seven tribes up in those mountains."

"I know it. Told him that myself. He said he only needed one chief."

Preacher rubbed his smooth-shaven jaw and stroked his mustache. "He's got one more chief than I would have expected."

"Spearfish Canyon is two hundred miles closer than Fort Pierre." Dempsey scratched his jaw. "I have to admit, I think Cooper's right. He might make a go of it. Those other chiefs might just agree with Cooper so they won't have to travel so far to trade. That'll save on Sioux trade parties the Blackfeet might be tempted to rob."

"The other chiefs might not like the idea. White men start buildin' civilized places, more white men usually follow along to fill up the empty places. Next thing you know, those places get all swelled up with folks." Preacher frowned. "I can't say as I like the idea myself. You been to St. Louis lately?"

Dempsey shook his head. "Not in six years. Place was getting too big then."

"Well, it's bigger now," Preacher said. "I wouldn't wish bad luck on a feller, but I don't know that I'd want a tradin' post that far into what is beautiful country all on its own."

"Me neither. But a man has a right to make what he will of things out here if he's willin' to work at it."

"I'll leave you to your evenin'," Preacher said. "Sorry to disturb you. I appreciate you lettin' me in."

"Always good to see you, Preacher. Wish I'd been over to the Scalded Beaver to watch Finlay get whomped. Of course, mighta been more fun watchin' you get that black eye."

Preacher smiled. "You'd have had to look quick. I didn't see it happen. C'mon, Dog."

Dog fell into place beside the mountain man and they left the stable.

"Watch," Preacher said.

The big cur pricked his ears and got extra watchful.

46

CHAPTER 4

"You say Mr. Gabbert is dead?" Barnaby Cooper asked in stunned disbelief. He was tired, and it was possible he'd heard that last part incorrectly.

He stood in the common room of the boardinghouse where he and his partners were staying while in Fort Pierre. The cheery blaze in the fireplace warmed him on the outside, and the glass of brandy in his hand warmed him from the inside.

The lanky mountain man standing before Cooper held his rifle by the barrel. The butt rested on the floor and the weapon pointed at the ceiling. The man's name was Hiram Kirkland, and he was reputed to be a good guide in these lands.

Kirkland was fifty years old if he was a day. His thick beard was gray and looked like piled snow on his chest. He wore a coonskin cap, buckskins, and calf-high moccasins that had seen better days.

Evidently the man hadn't spent any of his earnest money for his scouting on getting himself better outfitted.

"Gabbert's dead all right, Mr. Cooper. On the way back from Cherry Creek, we got rousted by a band of Blackfeet warriors out huntin'. They come up on us before we knew it. Arrows flew like blazes." Kirkland raised an arm and stuck a finger in a pair of holes through the buckskin shirt he wore. "Like to got me, too."

"You had six other men with you," Kent McDermid said. "Surely the eight of you put up a fight."

Blond and good-looking, barely into his twenties, McDermid was a banker in Maryland. Actually, McDermid's father owned the bank, and he'd been the one to put up money for Cooper's venture. The father had insisted on sending his son along to watch over that investment.

From conversations Cooper had had with the younger man on the steamboat junket from Baltimore to Louisville, young McDermid had lived an easy life in his father's shadow and had been content to do so. The young man talked of balls and clothing like they were the only things that mattered.

Kirkland's face hardened a little, and his eyes tightened. He turned to McDermid.

48

on hunts in his younger days, and he'd told all the trading post party of his adventures. Those hunts had been organized safaris with guides and men to beat the brush to force animals back to face him. Those creatures had had no chance at all. The man had brought back trophies from the animals he'd slaughtered. Cooper had thought the experience couldn't have been much different than running a hog onto a Chicago killing floor.

Humboldt was pushing forty hard, and had a little extra weight on him. His mustache was a fierce thing that followed the cruel curve of his mouth. His slicked-back hair fell over his shoulders and into his eyes upon occasion. He'd recently married a younger woman whose family had money and wanted more of it.

Opaline Humboldt craved adventure, so she had convinced her husband to come along with Cooper, then she'd dealt herself into the mix. Mrs. Humboldt had decided she was going to be a true pioneer woman and the best way to do that was to help build the trading post. She'd even brought along a young journalist to write up stories of their adventures in the West that would be printed in newspapers her doting grandfather owned back in Baltimore.

Cooper had lobbied hard to convince the woman that there was too much danger and too many hardships for her to accompany them. She had insisted. Then her grandfather, Ludwig Seitz, had insisted. The Seitz newspaper money was almost half of what Cooper had needed to make this trip, and Ludwig Seitz promised an even larger investment in the spring once the trading post was standing.

So Opaline Humboldt was in an upstairs room sleeping off too much wine.

After spending days with the woman traveling, Cooper halfway suspected her grandfather had agreed to the journey to get rid of her.

"Did you get the message to Chief Stands Like Buffalo?" Cooper asked.

"We went to where you told us to go," Kirkland said.

"Where the chief told you he would meet you," Cooper corrected.

Kirkland shrugged. "If you say so. We went to Cherry Creek an' followed it onto the Cheyenne River. Exactly where you said we was to meet. That chief never showed up. Ain't nobody showed up. We hunkered down and waited two days, then we left. We should have left sooner."

"Why did you leave? You knew the chief

was coming. I told you that."

"Me an' Bob didn't sign on to be out there more'n a day or two for this meetin'. You got both them days. We didn't short-change you, an' you even paid ol' Bob to up an' die for you. Ain't much more a man can give than that."

"I would have paid more if you had stayed longer."

Kirkland heaved a tired sigh. "Maybe you don't believe it, Mr. Cooper, because no-body mentioned it, but that's dangerous country. You don't keep an eye peeled, the Blackfeet will do for you the same way they done for us. An' the Sioux ain't gonna like you bein' out there neither. They might not be as quick to kill you as the Blackfeet, but if they decide you're goin', why you're goin'."

"This won't do," Humboldt thundered. He looked at Cooper. "You said this Indian chief would meet us with his warriors and give us safe passage through those lands to Spearfish Canyon. We're planning on hiring some of them to help build the fort."

"Something must have happened to slow Chief Stands Like Buffalo," Cooper said. "I'm sure if you'd stayed a little longer, Mr. Kirkland, he would have been there."

Kirkland shook his head. "Mister, ol' Bob

an' the rest of them done stayed too long. They're still out there stayin' on account I couldn't pack them on in an' give them a proper burial. I feel bad about that. Dyin' out there like that, they're gonna be there a good long while, an' none of 'em will be restin'. You best hope you don't run across them if you still plan on goin'. In case the ghosts of them men figure on evenin' the score with you for causin' their deaths."

An image of moldering bodies and ghosts wandering around like in Washington Irving's tales filled Cooper's head. He barely restrained the shiver that ran along his spine.

"Flummery!" Humboldt said and had a fierce countenance. "There are no such things as ghosts."

"Reckon a man don't believe in ha'nts till he up an' meets one," Kirkland said to Humboldt. "Me, I'd like as not have to do that again. Once was enough." He glanced back at Cooper. "I'll tell you somethin' else, Mr. Cooper, on account I got paid good money for riskin' my hair out there. Me an' Bob talked to some friendly Indians an' some trappers along the way who've been out there long enough to know what's what. Not a single one of them heard of this here Chief Stands Like Buffalo you told us about."

"Then you weren't talking to the right people," Cooper said. "I put an ad in the newspaper and said I was looking for a contact out near Spearfish Canyon. A gentleman in St. Louis answered it and told me he could put me in touch with Chief Stands Like Buffalo. He did. That's how I knew where to tell you to meet the chief."

"This fella in St. Louis have a name?" Kirkland asked.

"Stewart Pope. He was a guide into the western lands for years before the loss of his legs forced him to give up the wilderness exploration that he loved. He owns a tavern in St. Louis and helps people who wish to travel on to Oregon."

Kirkland shook his head. "I never heard of him, an' me an' ol' Bob know most of the guides an' trappers out here goin' back nearly twenty years 'cause we been out here that long."

"Well, Stewart Pope hadn't heard of you either," Cooper said. "Mr. Chouteau recommended you and your partner. He spoke highly of you."

"Me an' ol' Bob done some work off an' on for Mr. Chouteau. He's a tolerable man to work for. Every time he tells you somethin', it's true."

A sinking feeling opened in the pit of

55

Cooper's stomach. He suspicioned things were about to take a turn for the worse, and there was nothing he could do to stop it.

"Can you find someone else to help you guide us out to Spearfish Canyon?" Cooper asked.

"No sir," Kirkland said, "I can't."

"Surely you don't plan on taking us out there by yourself. Not after you've just offered testimony as to how dangerous travel through that country is."

"One man won't be enough," Humboldt assured Cooper with grim authority. The guide's know-it-all attitude sometimes irritated Cooper. "We need more guns. The Blackfeet will probably be looking for more easy prey now that they've spilled blood. Especially after they've had their way with you lot."

"Outnumbered four to one an' them on top of you?" Kirkland's face reddened and his voice tightened. "Likely they'd have their way with anybody."

"You'll be better prepared on the next trip," Humboldt said. "This time I'll be going with you."

"Oh, I ain't goin'," the guide said. "Me, I'm quittin' on it. Had me a belly full, an' losin' ol' Bob was just the last straw. Passin' through that rough country is risky enough for a wagon train outfitted to take on Indians an' keep on goin', but you're plannin' on stayin' the winter out there. That's just foolishness. Me an' ol' Bob agreed to carry a message to an' fro. That was it."

"I'm going to open a trade post in Spearfish Canyon," Cooper said. "Once I find Chief Stands Like Buffalo, I'm sure everything will be taken care of. If you throw in with us, you stand to make a not inconsiderable amount of money."

"Can't spend any amount of money if you're dead," Kirkland replied. "Even if you smooth things out with the Sioux, which I ain't none too sure of you doin', you got Blackfeet out there to contend with, too." The mountain man shifted his feet and glanced at the door like it was calling his name. "This here's the fork in the trail, Mr. Cooper. I'll wish you luck an' all, but I ain't goin' with you. Now, if you'll excuse me, I'm gonna go drink till I can't stand up. May do it again tomorrow."

The mountain man turned and walked out of the common room. His moccasins thumped against the wooden floor and echoed hollowly.

Aghast, horrified by the turn of the events, and the death of the man he'd hired to meet with Chief Stands Like Buffalo, Barnaby Cooper stared helplessly at the mountain man's back and tried to think of something to say that would turn Kirkland around. Cooper was a good salesman, one of the best in Baltimore. Everybody said so.

But he had nothing he could offer Kirkland, and the door closed with a note of finality behind the mountain man.

The fireplace had burned low, no longer so cheery, but the coals filled the room with enough heat to take off the winter's chill that had come with sundown.

That chill was enough to remind Cooper that his endeavor to establish a new trading post was going to face winter in a couple months. They had to hurry if they were going to make the timetable he'd established.

He was determined to succeed.

All his adult life, he'd lived in Baltimore. Winter up in the Indian lands west of the Iowa Territory was going to prove harsh, but he looked forward to the challenge with the same vigor Humboldt claimed to have employed while facing down wild beasts in foreign lands. Building while fighting the cold and blizzards would take all he and his men could do, but come spring, they would open that trading post he dreamed of.

That coming battle with nature left Cooper a little unsettled tonight, though, but at thirty-five, he'd only ever lived in Maryland and traveled to Pennsylvania to visit relatives. He believed this was his last chance to go adventuring.

He had a wife and young children who were depending on him being successful. Seventeen investors were counting on his eventual triumph as well. He had convinced them of his venture, and he was determined not to let them down. He would make everyone who had partnered with him wealthy. He had vision and he had backers.

He just wasn't having much luck these last few days.

Dark as a thundercloud with anger he was refusing to contain, Humboldt rounded on Cooper. "Well, this is a fine mess. How are you going to fix it?"

Cooper thought quickly. His other investors stared at him. "At this moment, I don't rightly know, Mr. Humboldt."

"You have got to make this right. I have come too far, and I'm not a man given to failing."

"I will. I'm a problem solver." Cooper stood as tall as he could and didn't show any of the fear he felt. That was how a man sold himself and whatever wares he was peddling. He had to stand right up and look the other man in the eye and tell him how a bargain was going to be struck. "This setback only now showed up. It will take a moment to correct. Let me talk to Pierre Chouteau in the morning. I don't want to barge in on him tonight, especially since he's been so gracious. I'm sure there is another guide we can find that he will recommend."

"What about Chief Stands Like Buffalo?" McDermid asked. "Are you sure he's out there?"

"Kirkland and Bob Gabbert, and I don't mean to speak ill of the dead, must have gone to the wrong place. That's all."

"What if the Blackfeet killed the chief, too?"

Cooper thought quickly. "Then Kirkland would have found his body, wouldn't he?"

Sometimes a question, a demand for a speaker to think for himself, was the best answer because most folks liked having someone make their decisions for them. That was something every salesman knew.

McDermid frowned, but he didn't say anything further.

"If those men did go to the wrong place," Tom Kittle asked from his chair by the fireplace, "how do you plan on getting to the right place?"

Kittle was a short, squat man with broad shoulders and huge, callused hands. His shock of red hair matched his unruly muttonchops and thick mustache. He'd made his money in warehouses along Fell's Point in southern Baltimore and worked alongside his stevedores. Most people would think him a brute and not a clever man. That was an incorrect assumption. Kittle owned a modest fleet of small sailing ships and sidewheelers that plied the Inner Harbor. He'd earned his fortune by working hard for it and by chasing a vision.

Cooper had drawn him into the venture by talking up the possibility of establishing a steamship service along the Missouri River like Captain Joseph M. LaBarge. After hearing about LaBarge in a conversation with Kittle at his favorite tavern, The Horse You Came in On, Cooper had researched the steamboat captain in the papers.

The easiest way to sell a man a dream was to sell him a dream he wanted.

Tom Kittle wanted to be a steamboat captain on the Missouri River just like the legendary Captain Joseph M. LaBarge. LaBarge owned steamboats that traveled up and down the waterway and hired out to the American Fur Company. Everything John Jacob Astor touched turned to gold.

Captain LaBarge had been touched.

"I plan on correcting our present setback by hiring the right guide who can take us to Chief Stands Like Buffalo," Cooper said. He spoke as though the matter was easily settled.

He hoped such a man existed in Fort Pierre. He thought of the mountain men and the young Indian who had fought the soldiers in the Scalded Beaver Tavern. Surely men like that would be boon companions on the grand adventure into the West.

Cooper just had to find one.

CHAPTER 5

"Finlay! Hey, wake up!"

Irritated, Judd Finlay came awake in the dark. His drunk had worn off enough that he was feeling the pain of the fight he'd had with Preacher. He was still drunk enough that he could sleep — if he wasn't bothered.

"Finlay," the insistent voice called again.

Gradually, cursing the fool who was disturbing him, Finlay opened his eyes and peered through the bars that made up one wall of the small cell he was in. He lay on the floor wrapped in a blanket that didn't keep him quite warm enough. With winter approaching, days were warm but the nights were chilly.

It took him a moment to remember he was in the stockade. He'd been there a few times and everything was familiar.

On the other side of the bars, Ian Candles stared down at him. Candles was a lean man and had boyish features. His ears were a little too long and stuck out. His dark blond hair was raked back and hung over his shoulders. The patchy beard that covered his pointed chin and dimpled cheeks was more blond than his hair. He wore a silver skull pendant at his throat. When the skull's red eyes caught the light, they gleamed with an almost unholy fire.

At first glance, Candles looked like somebody's kid, but that impression vanished when a man looked into those washed-out blue eyes. Candles was twenty-three years old and had killed forty-seven men. Many of them had been Indians, but almost half of them had been white men. Candles didn't count the women and children he killed because he didn't consider them a challenge.

"What are you doin' locked up?" Candles asked.

"What does it look like I'm doin'?" Finlay said. He sat up on the floor and pulled the blanket over him. "I was tryin' to sleep."

"I heard about the fight in the Scalded Beaver." Candles wore that stupid grin that almost looked innocent, but anyone who'd been around true killers knew the look for what it was. The cruelty beneath it was almost hidden, but it shined through. "Skinny told me some old guy laid you out.

That happen?"

"He wasn't that old," Finlay grumbled. "An' I was drunker than I should have been. I just gave in to bad judgment. Couldn't hold myself back."

Ian was Candles's given name. He didn't know his father. When he'd grown up, his mother had kept company with a succession of men. She'd been a soiled dove and traveled through a lot of camp towns. She'd dragged her son after her. The first man Candles had killed at age twelve was one of those men. When Candles was thirteen, his mother had gotten herself killed while thieving from a bank robber named Seymour Gilberd in New Orleans. Gilberd was the eighth man the boy had killed. After that, the boy stole a horse and left Louisiana.

He took the name Candles as his surname because that was what he considered himself best at: blowing out another man's candle. Finlay counted the younger man as a friend, but he never much turned his back on him. A friend was one thing, but trust was another. Candles had a sobering history of shooting friends he thought had wronged him.

Candles sometimes rode as a scout for the Army. No commanding officer at the post would sign him on as a soldier or even put him on monthly pay, but he'd hung around Fort Pierre at times when he wanted to pick up cash from Arnold Diller that usually involved killing.

"Where have you been?" Finlay asked.

"I was negotiatin' with Red Bat Circles Smoke," Candles said.

Red Bat was a Blackfeet warrior who was an outlaw even to his own people. The brave liked stealing horses and attacking small wagon trains. Over the last few months, he'd gathered himself a string of like-minded young Blackfeet braves who were too greedy to stay in the mountains.

"What's Red Bat got to say?" Finlay asked, although he was certain he knew.

"He's ready to trade a lot of buffalo hides for some of those rifles Diller snatched. Says Diller promised them to him."

"Diller didn't tell me that."

Candles shrugged. "Red Bat has been known to lie. Still, we could make some good money with those buffalo hides."

"The rifles are gone," Finlay said in disgust. "That man I fought with, Preacher, killed Diller and brought the rifles back to Chouteau. Didn't you know that?"

"No. I just got back to the fort. I was out takin' care of some business."

That meant there was a wagon train missing horses somewhere. Trading horses to the Blackfeet for buffalo hides was easy money for a man who didn't mind risking a bullet or getting caught out on a bad trade. Candles didn't have a lot of caution to him.

"Every rifle?" Candles asked.

"Yeah."

Candles snorted in displeasure. "That's just stupid." He shifted from foot to foot. He always had trouble standing still. "A man could have gotten a lot of pelts and buffalo hides by sellin' them rifles to the Indians. Red Bat and his braves wanted 'em something fierce. He ain't gonna be happy to hear there aren't any rifles."

Finlay rubbed his hands together in an effort to warm them. He thought through the remnants of the drunken fog that sat heavily on his mind. "Red Bat will have another opportunity. Got a wagon train headed out west in the next day or two."

"Goin' to Oregon?"

"No. Headed into the Sioux lands. Man named Barnaby Cooper supposedly has a deal with a chief named Stands Like Buffalo."

Candles thought for a minute, then shook his head. "Never met him. What kind of Indian is he?"

"Sioux."

"Well, there's at least seven of those tribes out there. I don't know how many chiefs each of 'em has."

"I never heard of him either. I'm thinkin' maybe you can tell Red Bat he can wait till the wagon train is a few days west of the fort, then pounce on it. A bunch of tenderfeet like that ain't gonna be able to put up much of a fight. On top of that, they're carryin' goods out there to start up a tradin' post. I don't know what they have, but it should be somethin' worth Red Bat's time."

"I don't know. Red Bat had himself set for some of those rifles Diller stole."

"Tell him those fellers on the wagon train have got rifles an' they should be easy pickin's. That should brighten his day right up."

Candles nodded. "The wagon train gettin' an army escort?"

"Nope. Goin' on their own. Supposed to have hired Kirkland and Gabbert to do scoutin' for them."

"Gabbert's dead. I ran into him before I came to see you."

"Where?"

"Out to Cherry Creek. That's where I came across Red Bat. Him an' his braves killed Gabbert an' six other men. Told me one man got away."

"Probably Kirkland. He knows the coun-

try, an' he's a damn sight faster than Gabbert was."

"Don't know. Don't care." Candles looked
at Finlay. "What you gonna do when you
get out of here?"

"Gonna be a few days before I do. The
major's throwin' the book at me."

"Could be time you moved on from the
Army an' got on down the road."

Finlay nodded. "I been thinkin' that myownself tonight while I was layin' here near-
to-freezin'. It's temptin' to stay through the
winter, though. I ain't lookin' forward to
campin' out through the comin' winter."

"There's Indians that will put you up for
the cold months. All you gotta do is shoot a
buffalo or deer every now an' again. Squaws
will be right friendly too. You don't have to
pay them like you do them soiled doves over
to the Scalded Beaver."

A time or two, Candles had had his way
with a soiled dove, didn't pay her, and had
escaped the fort till the heat died down.
Women didn't come out to Fort Pierre to
put down roots. They usually came while
escaping troubles of their own.

"I'm gonna think on it some more," Finlay said. "Maybe you can do me a favor?"

Candles looked at him from behind
hooded eyes. "Not for nothin'."

"Of course not. I got some money put back. I'll pay you for your time."

"Let's hear what you want done."

"Preacher did for Diller, an' that sticks in my craw," Finlay said.

"Then put a ball through his head an' be done with it."

"I would, but he'll probably be gone before I get out of here. An' I don't want to go chasin' him through them mountains. Preacher's at home out there as any wild thing you can imagine. It would be easier to get him while he's still here."

"That what you want me to do? Kill Preacher?"

"When I get out of here, I got twenty dollars I can pay you for puttin' him in the ground."

Candles only thought about the offer for a moment. "Preacher's supposed to be as onery as an old he-coon."

"If you take him straight on, maybe he is. I wasn't expectin' you to give him a fair fight."

Candles laughed. "Not after I seen what doin' that got you."

"I was drunk."

"Sure, I heard you say that. Still, might not be a bad idea to have some help. You got another ten dollars, I can get four more men to help me."

"Only takes one ball."

"If I can get the shot, yeah. Ten more dollars gets you four more men."

"You're ridin' with partners? That's not like you."

"Just some saddle pards for the time bein'. We did some business together an' decided to come to Fort Pierre an' drink up a bit of the profits. Found a Shoshone horse breeder out there who couldn't keep his string together. Him an' his boys was probably gonna sell their horses here to the Army. Now me an' my pards are gonna do that tomorrow."

"They'll help you kill a man for two dollars an' fifty cents apiece?"

Candles smiled. "I'm only gonna pay them two dollars. I'm chargin' two dollars myownself for carryin' charges. If I'm gonna be a boss, I'm gonna get paid for bein' a boss."

"I reckon that's fair."

"Of course, it is. So, do we have a deal?"

The price was steep, but Finlay only had to think it over for a minute. He'd been good friends with Diller. The man had made him money, and they'd drunk whiskey together for months. Diller hadn't been like a brother, but he'd been close. A man was supposed to do something when a friend got killed.

Tonight, that meant hiring a killer and his four saddle pards, all of them murderers and horse thieves.

"We have a deal," Finlay said.

Candles spat in his hand and thrust it through the bars. "Shake on it an' spit in the devil's eye."

Finlay took the killer's hand and shook. "First thing in the mornin'. After tonight, Preacher might decide it was best to light on out before I get released."

"In the mornin'," Candles agreed. "But not too early. Got some drinkin' to do to-night."

Finlay released the man's hand, said his good-byes, and stepped back to the hard bed attached to the wall. He laid on it and hoped it didn't spin like it had earlier. When it didn't, he closed his eyes and tried to get comfortable, but the pains and bruises from the fight in the tavern left him restless. He wished he was there to see Preacher get what was coming to him.

More than that, he wished he was the one to give it to the mountain man.

CHAPTER 6

"Why, hello," the pretty little blonde in the hallway of the boardinghouse greeted. Her emerald eyes ran from Preacher's face to his feet as she gazed with bright interest at him.

The sconces on the hallway wall were just bright enough to pick her cleanly out of the darkness.

Her eyes were dulled a mite and her smile was too easy. She wore a long green dress that looked like she'd stepped from a party somewhere. Or maybe it was a fancy nightgown. The mountain man wasn't sure, but it left little to the imagination.

Through the fog of her perfume, Preacher detected the smell of wine on her breath. He halted in front of his door and looked down at her because she was just a slip of a thing. Then he looked to the hallway to see if she was with anyone else, but they were alone together.

73

"Good evenin'," Preacher said and smiled back at her to be polite.

"Is that a wolf?" The woman pointed at Dog.

"No, ma'am," Preacher said. "That's Dog. Me and him travel together."

"He's big."

"Yes, ma'am."

She approached and listed a little as she did. Her footwork was none too steady. "May I pet him?"

"No, ma'am. That would not be a good idea. Dog's not much on bein' friendly."

Despite his words, the woman continued walking toward Preacher. Tentatively, she held out her hand toward Dog. The big cur growled just enough to be heard, and the noise was like a huge bumblebee trapped in his broad chest. Dog didn't have much use for strange folks who had been drinking, and he only put up with it when Preacher did.

Startled, the woman drew her hand back and nearly tipped over. "I guess you're right. He's not all that friendly. I usually get on pretty good with animals. Cats. Dogs. Horses. I even petted a mountain lion one time when Davy Crockett was serving on the United States Congress in 1833, he brought one with him. It was quite the sight.

That was when I petted the mountain lion. Her name was Polly. Davy named her after his first wife, who died most unfortunately. He never got over her. Polly was a splendid animal. Very polite and extremely dainty."

Preacher had never seen a mountain lion like that, and he doubted that this woman had either. Crockett had been a man who liked to tell tall tales, so it was possible she'd heard this one from him. Except she was awfully young.

"He died at the Alamo in '36," she went on. "They say a bear came and carried his body away to bury him in a secret place so no one can disturb him. Can you believe that?"

"No."

"Well, it happened." The blonde pouted and blew a few strands of hair from her face. "I talked to a man who was there and saw it happen."

The story about Crockett and the bear was one Preacher had heard a few times. He didn't believe it then, and he didn't believe it now. He also didn't believe the woman had talked to anyone who'd survived the battle at the Alamo. All of those men had died.

"I cried the day I heard Davy died. I was only a girl when I met him in Washington.

He was a handsome man. I got to meet him because my grandfather, Ludwig Seitz, was interviewing him for the newspaper. My grandfather owned the newspaper. Well, I mean to say, he still does, of course. Why would he sell one of the best-read newspapers in this country?"

Preacher couldn't think of a reason, so he didn't answer. He also wasn't a big reader of anything. He preferred living and learning from what the mountains had to offer in the way of instruction. The things learned there could feed a man and save his life if he paid attention.

"Have you ever read it?" she asked.

"No. Not a big newspaper reader."

She frowned. "Well, you should be. You can learn a whole lot of things from a newspaper. From a *smart* newspaper. My grandfather's newspaper is such a publication."

Preacher felt a little grumpy. He was ready for bed and ached in a few places where he'd been hit and had hit others. The woman was getting in the way of it. Dog pressed in close to his leg. The big cur was probably tired, too.

"Silly me." The woman smiled again. "I failed to properly introduce myself. I've had a little wine to drink, you see. I'm celebrating a new venture my grandfather has bought in to." She offered her hand. "I'm Opaline Humboldt."

Cautiously, Preacher took the small, slim hand in his and quickly returned it. "Pleased to meet you, Miss Humboldt."

"May I have your name? Forgive me if I'm too direct."

"Preacher."

Her eyebrows rose under that hair that looked like spun gold. "Oh? You're a man of the cloth?"

Preacher wondered if that would perhaps make him more appealing to her. It was plain to see she was interested, but he had neither the time nor the inclination to take up with a woman he didn't know in a reputable boardinghouse.

"No, ma'am. It's just a name folks know me by."

Opaline looked at Preacher and smiled again. "Are you as unfriendly as your wolf ?"

"Dog," Preacher said.

"Yes. Dog. The question asked is, how friendly are you?"

"Not friendly enough, miss. Not tonight."

Scarlet colored the woman's face. She tried to slap his face so quick that she almost succeeded. He turned his face to the side and caught her wrist.

77

She shrieked and tried to pull away, but Preacher didn't let go because he didn't want her trying again.

"Unhand me, you ruffian!" she squalled.

"I will," Preacher said, "if you promise to take yourself back to wherever you came from."

"How dare you!" Opaline tried to free her hand again and still couldn't. She set herself and yanked harder.

This time Preacher let her go and she stumbled backward till she lost her footing. Then she fell on her nether regions with an inelegant, sprawling thump.

"What the hell is going on here?" a man roared.

Preacher wheeled toward the voice and spotted a big, beefy man striding along the hallway.

The man wore a suit and looked weathered. His skin was tanned and firm, but he was carrying some extra weight from easy living.

"She belong to you?" Preacher asked.

Dog growled and took a step forward so he was between Preacher and the big man.

"Easy," Preacher said softly, so only the big cur heard.

Hair raised along the back of his neck, Dog locked into position.

The man looked at the huge animal and stayed back.

"Anthony!" Opaline wailed from the floor. "This brute shoved me down!"

"Did you shove my wife down?" the big man shouted. He fidgeted just out of Dog's reach.

Folks stuck their heads out of their rooms along the hallway. Two of them were Lorenzo and Tall Dog. They looked at Preacher with mild curiosity and no little amusement.

"No," Preacher replied. "She tried to slap me, and I put a stop to it."

"Why would she try to slap you?"

"I think she was offended I wasn't interested in what she was offerin'."

"What?" The man looked apoplectic.

Preacher noted the man didn't move to fight him either. Maybe it was on account of Dog being there, or maybe it was because there was a crowd, or it might have been the fact that the man recognized Preacher from the earlier tavern fight because he'd been one of the men sitting with the young man in the D'Orsay hat. The mountain man suspected, given the woman's nature and Humboldt's own controlled anger that wasn't the first time the man had been forced to deal with his wife's improprieties.

"She made it clear she wanted somethin',"

Preacher said. He pointed to the door he stood in front of. "This is my room. I didn't go down to hers. Wherever it is."

"Lies!" Opaline tried to get to her feet and finally managed the task with the aid of the nearby wall. "He called to me, said he wanted to talk to me."

Preacher kept his eyes on Humboldt. "That's not true."

"You're calling my wife a liar?" Humboldt shouted.

"You're the one put a name on it," Preacher said. "I just told you that her accusation wasn't the truth."

Humboldt reached under his coat and revealed the curved butt of what Preacher believed to be a hammerless Belgian Mariette pepperbox revolver with a ring-trigger holstered on his hip.

Preacher hadn't seen that kind of pistol much in his travels, but he knew what it was. Over in Britain, France, and Germany, a lot of men carried them. The hideout guns had been made for civilian use and meant for close-up shooting, but they'd kill a man just as dead as the Paterson Colts Preacher carried.

The mountain man drew one of his revolvers in that manner that had gotten so natural to him that it was hard to follow.

Before Humboldt could free his weapon, he was staring down the barrel of Preacher's pistol.

Preacher eared the Paterson's hammer back and the trigger dropped down into place from where it had been hidden. The clicks echoed in the hallway.

Despite how quickly he could put the weapon into action, the mountain man wished again that the pistol design had been better. Pulling the hammer back with his thumb without a proper trigger guard like on his flintlock pistols was awkward. He only had four shots loaded in the cylinders of each Paterson and left the ones under the hammer empty for safety reasons when he wasn't going to need his pistols for certain.

"Mister," Preacher said calmly, "the discomfort of havin' a wife who causes trouble when she's had a little too much to drink might make you a little raw, but that bit of misfortune is a whole lot better than the mistake you're about to make."

Humboldt stared at the Paterson Colt with wide eyes and slowly took his hand out from under his coat. He held both hands at shoulder level. He glanced down the hallway.

From the corner of his eye, Preacher

noticed that Lorenzo and Tall Dog both had pistols in their hands.

Everybody else in the hallway eased on back into their rooms. They weren't interested enough to pay the freight on seeing what happened next.

That probably made it easier for Humboldt to admit his wife was in error.

"Anthony!" Opaline said. "Did you hear me? That man shoved me —"

"Opaline," Humboldt said in a tight voice, "you're about to get me killed."

For the first time, the woman took notice of the pistol in Preacher's hand. Her eyes brightened with a feverish intensity, and she licked her lips.

Realizing the woman was on the edge of calling for blood, Preacher holstered his weapon. Down the hallway, Lorenzo and Tall Dog put their weapons out of sight, too.

"Maybe it would be better if you saw Mrs. Humboldt to her room," Preacher suggested as calmly as though they were discussing the weather.

For a moment, Humboldt stood frozen, then he nodded and walked to his wife. Without a word, he pulled her from the wall and guided her down the hallway.

"Mr. Humboldt," Preacher called.

Humboldt stopped and cautiously turned.

"Your wife has had a little too much to drink," Preacher said. "It happens to the best of folks on occasion. I'll expect you to remember that. I can see how it might make you angry, but I'm a light sleeper. I don't want to hear you slap-pin' her around when you get back to your room. If she was sober, I wouldn't offer you any counsel, but I still wouldn't care for it. Her not being in her right mind cinches the deal though."

Humboldt just stared.

Preacher nodded. "Good night." He opened the door of his room and entered.

The room was dark, but he could see well enough to find the bed. He placed the flintlock pistols on the floor to one side of the bed and added his bowie knife and tomahawk. He pulled the pistol he'd drawn on Humboldt, placed the hammer once more over the empty chamber, and laid both Patersons on either side of his pillow within easy reaching distance. He crawled onto the bed and laid on his back.

"Dog," Preacher said in a low voice.

The big cur leaped up onto the bed, laid beside Preacher, and placed his big head over the mountain man's stomach.

"Do I have to tell you to watch?" Preacher asked.

Dog snorted.

"This place is gettin' downright inhospitable," Preacher said. "We got to hope tomorrow brings a better day."

He shifted a little to get comfortable and to ease his bruises, then he closed his eyes and dropped right off to sleep.

CHAPTER 7

Hermann Weller managed the boarding-house for Fort Pierre. Like pretty much everything else at the fort, Chouteau owned part of the business. In his late forties, the fastidious little German wore a neat suit and waited anxiously in the dining room where guests received their meals. His short mustache was waxed, and garters held up the sleeves of his starched shirt.

A few of the boardinghouse guests sat at the table and ate their eggs, bacon, and flapjacks. None of them looked in the mountain man's direction, but Preacher knew they were all aware of him.

The food smelled mighty fine, but Preacher could tell by the pained look on Weller's face that he wasn't getting any of it.

Dog licked his chops and Preacher realized the big cur was going to be as disappointed as he was.

"Herr Preacher," Weller said. "I wonder if I might have a word with you."

Without waiting for an answer, Weller waved a hand toward the foyer at the front of the building.

Preacher didn't answer. He just walked over to the small foyer with his rifle in hand. Bright morning light showed outside the curtained windows. Soldiers marched around the open area at the center of the fort to take care of whatever assignments the major had issued.

Frankly, Preacher was surprised that some of those soldiers weren't in the boarding-house to have a word with him, as well. That would have probably been better for Weller. The little German was made of stern stuff, though, and didn't balk at the hard days. He looked up at Preacher fearlessly.

"Herr Preacher, it has come to my attention that you were waving a gun around in the hallway last night."

"Some varmint ratted me out I suppose," Preacher said.

"More than one, actually. That kind of behavior isn't accepted here."

"I don't cotton to it myself. That's why I pulled my pistol."

"I see. There was no report of any other guns in evidence."

Preacher had to allow as that was true.

Weller managed to look stern and apologetic at the same time. "As a result of that hostility, several of my guests have felt . . . inconvenienced."

Feeling a little irritated even though the boardinghouse manager's stance was understandable, Preacher said, "I wasn't the one who started that fandango."

"I understand that the young woman was the instigator of the situation, but you were the one who pulled a firearm."

"I got mine out fast enough that Humboldt didn't have a chance to pull the one he was goin' for," the mountain man said. "I was also fast enough that Humboldt got a chance to think about what he was fixin' to do before he tried it and ended up gettin' carried out of here feet first. Think of how inconveniencin' that would have been."

Weller's eyes narrowed in displeasure. "I have taken that into consideration, and I applaud your restraint. I know you would have been within your rights to shoot Mr. Humboldt."

"I try not to shoot dumb folks makin' dumber mistakes. Otherwise, there's parts of the world that would run short of folks." Preacher was feeling more agitated at the situation even though he'd actually slept pretty well. He'd done nothing wrong. And if a man looked at it right, he'd even saved Humboldt's life.

Weller frowned and looked a little uncomfortable. "Many of the guests also know about the fight at the tavern last night."

"I suppose they were inconvenienced by that, too."

"Some of them concede to some trepidation, yes."

"I have to admit, last night was kind of busy even for me, but at least no one got killed."

Weller sighed. "Yes, I suppose that is a point in your favor. I've heard many stories about you. Be that as it may, and despite the fact that I quite like your company, I'm afraid I'll have to ask you to find other accommodations for tonight."

"I figured as much." Preacher held up his rifle.

Weller shied back a little.

"I already packed," the mountain man said and nodded to the rifle.

"I appreciate you being so understanding, Herr Preacher. I am in an impossible position as you can surely understand."

"If you were in an impossible position, you wouldn't be able to ask me to leave. Guess it's not so impossible."

Weller opened his mouth, started to say something, then decided against whatever it was. He paused for a moment and said, "I wish you a good day, Herr Preacher. I must apologize. Perhaps the next time you come through, things will be different."

"Thanks." Feeling more than a little put out and hungry because the smell of the breakfast setting on that table was so close and so tempting, but not wanting to cause trouble for a man he respected who was only trying to do his job, Preacher headed for the door. He had some jerky and sour-dough biscuits in his saddlebags that would still be good enough. Not what he wanted, but he could make do.

Outside, he looked around. The flag flew from the flagpole, and soldiers stood guard at the gate and in front of the Army building.

At least the morning breeze was cool, and there was a familiar odor that rode on it. Cooked buffalo meat filled his nostrils, and he thought maybe he hadn't missed breakfast after all. Preacher's stomach growled.

Dog turned his nose into the air and yipped.

"Yeah, I caught scent of it," Preacher said. "Smells like some Indians have come callin'. That's fine buffalo meat without all those spices like they serve at the Scalded Beaver. Fresh, not salted over and kept up." He tightened his grip on the rifle. "Let's go have a looksee. Maybe we know somebody who will stand us to breakfast."

Preacher left Horse stabled because Dempsey would see to him. He walked through the front gate. The soldiers standing guard gave him a cursory inspection and let him go uncontested.

He followed the scent of cooking meat around the corner of the fort to the east. Trees had been cleared out to a hundred yards, and stumps stood up from the grass. Part of the reason for the tree chopping was to provide clear fields of fire for the soldiers if they needed them, and the fort had to have wood for heat during the coming winter.

Crews of woodcutters worked the tree line. The thuds as the axes bit into tree trunks echoed over the area. A man yelled a warning and a tall oak fell slowly to the ground, then another crew stepped forward to take the limbs off with their axes.

A wagon partially filled with firewood sat waiting. Getting Fort Pierre through the winter was going to require a lot of wood. Cutting wood was hard, boring work unless a man had his mind set to it. Preacher was glad he didn't have it to do this morning. He was already growing restless, and he'd only been at the fort for a day.

On the east side of the fort, eight tepees stood in an irregular formation. Buffalo hide covered the poles that formed the cone shapes. The smoke flaps hung open at the tops of the tepees, and thin trails of gray smoke floated up to streak the sky.

The Crow and some Sioux often came to trade at Fort Pierre, and their presence was welcome. They brought news of the western lands and shared stories with those at the fort who would listen.

Chouteau traded goods for the beaver pelts and buffalo hides the Indians brought. Each party felt they were getting the better of the deals that were made.

At least forty Indians milled around the tepees. The women tended cookfires, and men cleaned and repaired tools and weapons and groomed their horses. Picket lines held more horses that swished their tails at flies and ate bunchgrass. Children did chores to help the adults and played when their parents weren't looking. Mothers occasionally called to them and put them back to work.

Three white men and two black men in buckskins worked with the Indian men.

Either they were visiting, or they were part of the tribe.

At Preacher's direct approach, one of the white men got up from where he was cutting leather for a bridle and reached for his rifle.

A black man sat on a stone and held a cup of coffee in his hand. He looked up at his companion, then at Preacher, and said, "No reason for the rifle, Caleb. That there's Preacher. I'd know that dog anywhere."

Closer now, Preacher studied the man's features.

The man was about Preacher's age, forty-ish, and built rangy. His dark skin shone in the morning sunlight. His face was narrow and ended at a rounded chin covered by a short, curly beard. His hair was trimmed short on the sides and left a little longer on top. His forehead wrinkled in consternation.

"Preacher," he greeted with a smile. "It's been a couple years."

"Moses," Preacher responded and walked over to join the man. He held out his hand and they shook.

Almost ten years ago, Moses had escaped slavery in Alabama and struck out into the West. Preacher had gotten to know the man while he was trapping along the Snake

River, and they'd spent part of a winter in each other's company, and in the company of others. Moses was a good storyteller, a man who wouldn't let the truth get in the way of a good tale, and he was at home in the mountains. He'd told stories about things in West Africa and the Caribbean Preacher had never heard.

Preacher sat cross-legged on the ground and laid his rifle beside him. He pulled his possibles bag around to the side. "The last time I saw you, you'd taken up with a band of Shoshone on account of some little woman who'd caught your eye."

Moses nodded. "Breeze Upon the Frosty Meadow. For some reason, I caught her eye too. We got a little girl." He held his hand out about two feet from the ground. "I call her Psalm, after my sister who died. Breeze calls our little girl Grasshopper Quick to Jump Away from Bluebird, an' she is mighty quick."

"Psalm would be easier to call to supper."

Moses grinned. "It is. Man could starve to death callin' that girl twice. Sometimes, though, we just call her Grasshopper."

Preacher looked around. "Your woman here?"

"No. I came with Laughin' Coyote." Moses jerked a thumb over his shoulder at

93

the man who'd reached for his rifle.

The man was young and thin. His face was narrow and covered by a short, dark beard. He wore buckskins and a flat-crowned hat that had seen better days. He watched Preacher warily.

The man stretched out his hand and shook. "Name's Caleb Barker. Moses likes to poke fun."

"He's sweet on a Shoshone girl," Moses said. "She's the one who named him Laughin' Coyote 'cause, when she looks at him, that's what she said she sees." He regarded the younger man. "Myownself, I don't see it. Young love, though, it sees what it wants to."

Caleb flushed pink under his tanned cheeks and shook his head.

Preacher looked around. "Most of the other Indians I see out here are Crow, not Shoshone."

"They're not our people," Moses said agreeably. "Me an' Laughin' Coyote just got here a couple hours ago. Saw the Crow an' figured we'd stop in for breakfast. Didn't have nothin' but pemmican with us, an' a man can get tired of it."

"If you got here a couple hours ago," Preacher said, "you were ridin' through the small hours of the mornin' when it was still

94

dark. You runnin' or chasin'?"

"Chasin'. Clouds finally cleared off after midnight an' we could take up the trail of the men we're lookin' for. Knew we were close to Fort Pierre. Figured that was where they were headed, so we pushed on."

A Crow woman carried over two bowls of fresh-cooked meat mixed with scrambled eggs and handed them to Moses and Caleb. The men accepted the food gratefully.

The woman looked at Preacher. "Have you broken your fast this morning, Preacher?" she asked in Crow.

Preacher responded in the same language, and he recognized her. "No, I haven't, Oriole Who Sings."

The woman smiled. "You remember me."

"Of course, I do. I always remember a good cook."

"Complimenting me will not get you fed any more. I will make sure you don't go away hungry."

"Where's Watching Ferret?"

"My man practices the lies he tells to other men somewhere in the trees with his sons while they're supposed to be hunting a deer for my cookpot tonight. Maybe I will get a deer. I do not want another squirrel. Would you like a bowl of food?"

"I don't want to take away from your table."

"There is plenty."

"Yes, please."

"And if Watching Ferret does not come back with a deer, perhaps you will find something to fill my pot."

Preacher grinned. "I'd be happy to."

Oriole Who Sings took a chunk of meat from Moses's bowl and tossed it to Dog. The big cur snatched the meat out of the air and chewed it happily.

"I will bring meat and bones for your dog as well. Everyone eats at my fire. None go hungry as long as I have food." Oriole returned to the cookfire and knelt to reach the pot that hung over the coals.

"Who are you chasin'?" Preacher asked Moses.

"A pack of killers. Did you ever meet Stout Otter? He was a brother to my woman."

Preacher thought for a moment but couldn't call the man to mind. "No."

"You might have met him, but he didn't leave much of a memory. Not a good conversationalist. He liked to listen, but talkin' made him nervous." Moses's dark eyes filled with sorrow, but none of that touched the hard lines of his face. "He was a horse trainer among the Tukudeka Shoshone."

Preacher knew the tribe. The Tukudeka were also known as the Sheep Eaters and tended to live along Salmon River, the Bitterroot Mountains, and the Wind River Range. Like all Indians, some of them tended to wander.

"He's a bit east of his stompin' grounds," Preacher said.

"Some of his people got to fightin' one another. Couldn't decide who needed to be chief. My woman's people settled north of Spearfish Canyon. The Sioux there tend to be tolerant of others as long as there's plenty of game for everyone. Stout Otter made himself valuable to them, too, because he trained horses an' charged fairly for them. He was one of the good ones who broke horses the old way, with a gentle hand, not a whip. The animals he trained are good mounts, the kind of horse you want under you when the way gets hard. He had two wives and three small children of his own."

Oriole returned with a full bowl and another for Dog. She set the bowl between Dog's front paws and gave Preacher his food.

"You may eat," she told Dog.

The big cur dug in hungrily. So did

Preacher. The meat and quail eggs were good. The mountain man thanked the woman, and she returned to the campfire.

Preacher paid attention to Moses, who ate mechanically and with no real gusto. Caleb ate quickly, and his hunger was evident. The two men had been on the trail for a while, and they were deadly focused.

"Stout Otter lived near where the Belle Fourche River meets the Cheyenne River," Moses said. "He built a place where he could raise an' train horses. When he had a string of them to sell each year an' the Sioux couldn't use them, he brought them to Fort Pierre, or took them over to Vermillion if the weather was good an' he was of a mind for a long ride. He was a man who liked to stretch his legs a mite ever' now an' again."

Preacher ate and let Moses tell his story, but he could guess what was coming.

"Folks around here who value horse flesh knew who Stout Otter was," Moses said. "He never had no trouble sellin' those horses he raised and trained. I ride one myself, an' that horse has been as fine as you could hope for." He paused. "Four days ago, five men rode onto his place, murdered him, an' took his horses. His wife walked with her children to where I live with Breeze an' our child. She told us about the men. I

98

couldn't set back an' let it go. So I saddled up. Caleb came with me."

"Do you know who these men were?" Preacher asked.

"No. Stout Otter's wife had never before seen them. The leader was a young man. He wore a necklace here." Moses touched the hollow of his throat. "It was a silver skull with red eyes."

Preacher nodded. "Sounds like a Mexican piece. They like celebratin' the dead an' makin' skulls."

"I thought it was, too."

"The man wasn't Mexican?"

Moses shook his head. "Stout Otter's wife is sure the man was white. All the other men were white, too. By the time she got to us an' me an' Caleb took up the trail, we were four days behind the killers. We got some luck, though, because they had to herd horses an' we didn't. But they set a right smart pace. They're experienced horsemen, I got to give them that."

"You trailed them here?" Preacher asked, because that was the only reason he could figure for Moses and Caleb to be at Fort Pierre.

"Yeah." Moses nodded. "The trail we followed in this mornin' is still pretty fresh.

They probably got here last night some-time."

"I just got here yesterday. I haven't seen a man with a necklace like the one you described."

"He's got to be in there, Preacher. Me an' Caleb done circled the fort. Those horses went in, but they ain't come out."

Preacher finished his meal, long after Dog did, and thought about things. Something worried at the back of his mind.

"How many horses?" he asked.

"Nine," Moses said. "Stout Otter worked his own horses, trained 'em up himself. He had a knack for it like I never seen before."

"A good horseman is hard to find. It's one thing to train your own mount, but it's another to train a group of them."

"You should have seen what he could do, Preacher. Why those horses would have danced an' sang for him if it was possible." Moses sighed. "I sure am gonna miss him. He was a good friend, an' I'm always short on those."

"I know it," Preacher agreed. "If this man decides to leave the fort today, I guess you're gonna catch him out in the woods."

Moses nodded. "I'm not goin' to the Army major an' askin' for help. He'll insist on a trial so he can do things the Army way.

Especially if the men I'm huntin' are soldiers. I don't intend to bring Stout Otter's wife an' her kids all this way to sit in a white man's court. They don't need to go through that. I'm black. They're Indian. I know how things will go. They done lost her husband an' their daddy. No need to get their self-respect beat on."

"Man that did this might not be a soldier," Preacher pointed out. "Might just be a man passin' through. He might not have any friends here. The trial might be more fair than you think."

Moses nodded. "Maybe so, but that's a lot of *mights*, Preacher, an' I ain't got much faith in folks who ain't the same color as me. They don't wear the same evil I do."

The man held out his hands so the sleeves of his buckskin shirt rode up high enough to reveal the shackle scars that ridged the flesh.

"Got scars on my back too," Moses said. "I know how things go." He pulled his sleeves back down. "Besides, I catch them out there in them trees, away from ever'body here, it won't take me long to deal with them."

"You said there's five of them."

"Stout Otter's wife was real certain of

that. Like her man, she's got an eye for detail."

"Five to two ain't good odds," Preacher said.

Moses looked at the mountain man with cold eyes. "I don't intend to let them murderin' bastards see me comin'. Me an' Caleb are good in the woods. We'll have at least two of them down before they know we're on them. Maybe one or two more. When they know you're comin', it's harder. But they won't know."

Preacher stood. "I'm goin' to go have a look-see inside the fort. I'll find out if they're still there an' let you know what you're up against." He resettled his hat. "It's also possible they knew you were huntin' them. They could have sold those horses to the Army, got some fresh mounts, and done lit a shuck for the tall and uncut."

Moses frowned and rubbed his face with a big, scarred hand. "Hadn't considered that. I'm worn thin from ridin' for so long."

Preacher nodded. "I won't be gone long. Should be able to find out what's what pretty quickly. You get some rest."

"I appreciate it, Preacher."

"Ain't done nothin' yet." Preacher told Oriole Who Sings how much he appreciated breakfast, returned the empty bowls, and headed back into the fort.

Fort Pierre Chouteau offered a lot of hope to folks wanting to wander out West, but Preacher was of a mind the fort sure did attract a lot of folks who too easily preyed on others.

CHAPTER 8

"No!" Humboldt roared. He slammed a big fist on the table in front of him. "I won't abide that course of action, Mr. Cooper! There has to be another way!"

Barnaby Cooper controlled his frustration and didn't let it show on his face. That was difficult because he was tired from not sleeping. Bob Gabbert's scalped ghost had haunted his dreams all night long and told him the trading post was a fool's mission.

After a tense, quiet breakfast with the other guests currently staying at the boardinghouse, Cooper and the trading post investors had gathered in the common room. Thankfully, they had the room to themselves. After the debacle of the previous night, Hermann Weller was proving most accommodating.

Truthfully, Cooper faulted Opaline Humboldt more than Preacher, but there was no way he could address that. He didn't want to risk offending the woman or her husband. Not with Ludwig Seitz being such a big part of everything Cooper was planning.

As a result, he found himself on constantly shifting terrain and he didn't like it.

"We need a guide," Cooper said finally into the tense silence that followed Humboldt's outburst. "This man Preacher is supposed to be one of the best guides there is. He's lived most of his life out here in western lands, among the Indians, and he's guided several wagon trains to Oregon. We're not going that far. By all accounts, he's a successful man."

"We might not be going to Oregon, but we're going through lands a lot of white men don't travel," Kent McDermid pointed out. "We know from Kirkland that there are roving bands of Blackfeet in the area around Spearfish Canyon where we expected to only find the Sioux. We need a man who can deal with them and keep us safe. You saw Preacher and his friends fight those soldiers last night. They're men who can handle themselves."

"I got up this morning thinking that very thing," Cooper said. He was happy that someone was taking his side. A little hope dawned in him. He just had to focus the conversation on the pluses of hiring

Preacher and not let it degrade into a discussion of the events of the previous night.

"Why didn't you mention the Blackfeet might be a problem before we set out on this journey?" Humboldt demanded.

"Cooper did mention them, Anthony," Opaline Humboldt snapped. "You weren't listening. You were probably telling one of your safari stories to someone, or thinking about telling one of them to someone. You spend a lot of time thinking about those."

Cooper hadn't been happy about the woman joining the men for the conversation. Women tended to change the parameters of things and put a lot of pride on the line that might not otherwise be there.

But, again, her grandfather's money was footing almost half the bill, and it would be Ludwig Seitz's continued support that would bring in the next wagons filled with trade goods. Cooper wasn't going to be able to do that even if he convinced his own father, and if he had to wait to profit from his trade till he got back in St. Louis, the return trip to the trading post would take too long. A man had to make hay while the sun shined.

Opaline didn't look too healthy this morning. She obviously hadn't slept well and was now hung over. Cooper had never seen such a beautiful woman incapacitated in such a manner. On top of that, he couldn't tolerate women who drank. His grandmother had been one of those. Her presence had put a burden on his family that even he had felt because, after his grandfather died, she had controlled the purse strings for a long time.

Humboldt stalked away and left the woman alone at the table. Opaline ignored his behavior and drummed her fingers on the arm of her chair.

"Are there no other guides in this fort?" Humboldt demanded. "I have seen many men out there. Surely there must be someone."

"None of the other guides want to take us where we desire to go," Cooper said.

"Do you know that for a fact?"

"I had coffee with Mr. Chouteau this morning, before we had our breakfast. He's an early riser and I got up with the dawn. He told me in no uncertain terms that after Kirkland got back with his story of his and Mr. Gabbert's ill-fated journey and bad luck that no one else would take on the guide job."

"Anthony was still asleep this morning," Opaline said. "Probably dreaming of shooting tigers. He didn't shoot Preacher last night."

"It may well be a good thing that your husband didn't shoot that man," Tom Kittle said.

"I certainly dreamed of it!" Opaline folded her arms. "That backwoods buffoon insulted me!"

"Madam," Kittle stated with quiet insistence, "I daresay you had coming whatever disrespect Preacher offered. I saw the events that led up to that embarrassing situation."

Cooper sat in stunned silence. He couldn't believe how direct Kittle was. The man had a reputation for it, but Cooper had never seen that tendency in action at a time so wrong for it. He waited to see who would explode first: Opaline or her braggadocious husband.

"How dare you!" Opaline turned to her husband. "Anthony, are you going to let him speak to me in such a cavalier manner?"

Humboldt turned to her. "Dear wife, I'm still ruminating on whether I'm allowing *you* to speak to *me* so disrespectfully. When I decide which one to address first, I'll deal with it first, then work on the other."

The woman sighed in disgust.

Unflustered by the outburst, Kittle went on, "I see our options as this. Option one:

we go on alone by ourselves. That doesn't seem like a smart idea because none of us have been out in that country. Putting the Indian threat aside, it's easy to get lost in unknown country and winter is breathing down our necks even now if we're to accomplish everything we're setting out to do."

"I have navigated the jungles of Africa," Humboldt said. "I am not an untried warrior, and I know my way around the cardinal points of compass."

"Just knowing which way north is won't be any good. You could walk us into a cliff or canyon or harsh country that we'd have to find a way around. That could potentially involve a lot of backtracking and maybe several lost days. That alone would increase our chances of crossing these Blackfeet Kirkland wandered into."

Humboldt worked his jaw like he was going to argue, but he didn't. Kittle had a good point, and the others in the room knew it.

"Option two," Kittle said, "we wait here at the fort until such time as a suitable guide arrives. Providing one eventually even does, which is not a guaranteed thing, cooling my heels at this juncture is not an attractive answer. We don't have goods that will go bad for a long time. However, keeping them sitting in wagons won't earn any of us a copper penny. On top of that, as I mentioned, we're running out of time. By all accounts I've heard, first frost comes to Spearfish Canyon in October. That's only a few weeks from now. Winter comes hard on its heels. We're going to be hard-pressed to get to Spearfish Canyon and then build that fort so it will protect us through the snowy season."

"I thought we were returning to Fort Pierre after the trading post is built," Opaline said.

"You can if you wish, Mrs. Humboldt," Kittle said, "but I don't intend to leave my goods up in those mountains unattended. You will also be racing the man-killing blizzards that descend upon this hard country. I would wish that on no man. Or woman."

"Anthony and I have someone who will run the trading post for us," she said. She looked at her husband.

"I have hired a man named Rufus Darvis to do that for us," Humboldt said.

Kittle glanced at Humboldt. "He's the man you said would be delivering the balance of the work crew to help us raise the trading post."

Humboldt nodded. "The very same. He's

an engineer. I met him while he was building a bridge in Cape Town. He's also built ships. A trading post will be nothing for him to construct."

Kittle narrowed his eyes. "Why would a man with his background agree to build a trading post?"

"Because we are giving him a percentage of our share of the trading post," Opaline said.

"And Darvis is coming because he's a man who likes challenges," Humboldt stated. "When I wrote him to offer him the job, I explained how the area was infested with hostiles."

"That didn't scare him off?" McDermid asked.

"Real men don't get scared of such things," Humboldt said. "Only two years ago, Darvis fought Zulu *impis* alongside Hans van Rensburg and Andries Pretorius. This was after the Weenen Massacre that led slaughter along the Bushman River in the Republic of Natal. The Zulu king Dingane and his warriors killed almost three hundred Dutch immigrants only days before." He glanced around the crowd. "Believe me, Darvis knows how to build, and he knows how to fight. We became friends while I was on safari. He's a fascinating man."

"He was supposed to be here yesterday," Cooper said.

Darvis's absence was another thing that had Cooper in a tizzy. They'd hired twenty of the local men to join them in establishing the trading post, but that wasn't enough to get the job done in the time allowed. Darvis was supposed to arrive and bring twenty more skilled laborers.

"Don't worry about Darvis," Humboldt said. "He'll be here."

"I hope so. Otherwise, we're paying the men we hired here to sit around and do nothing."

McDermid shifted in his seat and didn't look at Humboldt. "Even if Darvis arrives —"

"He will," Humboldt said.

"— he doesn't know the countryside or those wild lands we'll be traveling through. We still need a guide who knows the area."

"On that, I think we can all agree," Cooper said. He waited a moment and looked around the room. "So, do we reach out to Preacher? See if he wants the job? After last night, there's every chance that he will turn us down flat. Still, I think we would be remiss not to at least ask. Mr. Chouteau thinks highly of him."

"I thought Chouteau was irked at the man over the disbursement of those rifles he rescued," McDermid said.

With his salesman's uncanny instinct, the same instinct that allowed him to become the top seller in his father's furniture store in the months of February and March that very year, Cooper knew he had a chance to strike another point in his favor.

"Mr. Chouteau was aggrieved over the loss of *some* of his rifles," Cooper said. "Preacher was the one who brought them back. Otherwise, those rifles would have all been lost. He also brought them back when no one else could have. Perhaps no one else would have. A lot of men would have been glad to keep that small fortune to be made from selling those rifles. Preacher only took a percentage of the goods he shed blood to take back from the thieves and Blackfeet who had them." He paused. "I think that speaks to the man's resourcefulness and character."

"I'm all in favor of hiring him," Kittle said.

"I'm not," Opaline said.

"I say yes," McDermid put in.

Cooper looked at Humboldt. Even if Humboldt decided to side with his wife, Cooper knew he had the deciding vote.

113

Unless Opaline Humboldt decided to pick up sticks and take her grandfather's investments back to St. Louis.

Humboldt faced her. "Opaline. Last night was a bad night for everybody. We need to understand that and let it go. Cooper has made his case for Preacher. I may not like it, but I think Cooper's correct."

"What if Preacher says no?" Opaline asked.

That gave everyone in the room pause even though Cooper had mentioned that very possibility.

Humboldt said, "I'm going to hope that he doesn't."

"If he does," the woman replied in a voice that was more shrill, "he will have insulted me *twice,* and you will have let him get away with it *twice.*" Her nostrils flared. "That is unacceptable."

"I'll make you a promise," Humboldt stated evenly, "when we no longer need Preacher's services as a guide, that very moment, I will make him regret the callous disregard he has shown to you."

Cooper doubted that, if Humboldt did assay to undertake that task, that he would be successful. Preacher's gun had been out in his hand and cocked in an eyeblink. Cooper had never seen anything like the mountain man's quickness. He wondered if Opaline would hold her husband to such a suicidal promise. Then he decided she probably would.

The woman looked at her husband for a moment, then she gazed at Cooper.

"Very well, Mr. Cooper," Opaline said in a cool, calm voice. "You have my permission to offer Preacher employment." She turned to her husband. "And if he turns that employment down, I expect you to kill him before we leave."

Humboldt paled a little, but he nodded and kissed his wife's hand.

Cooper got up to leave the room before anyone decided to change his or her mind. Finding Preacher might be onerous since he'd been asked to leave the boardinghouse.

As he pulled his D'Orsay hat on, Cooper hoped the mountain man hadn't left the fort.

"Indian horses?" Dempsey the hostler mused. He rubbed a hand over his beard. "Could be. They didn't have any brands on them, but the fella who brought them in allowed as how they're gonna sell them to the Army."

"What did this fella look like?" Preacher asked.

The mountain man walked beside the hostler toward the back of the stable. Horse whinnied for attention and trotted over to the stall gate. Preacher stroked Horse's face, paused long enough to give him an apple from his possibles bag, and kept walking. Dog loped over and briefly touched noses with Horse, then fell in beside Preacher again.

"I've seen him around before," Dempsey said. "Young. Blond hair down to his shoulders."

"Does he wear a silver skull at his throat?"

Dempsey nodded. "As a matter of fact, he does. Got a story that goes with it too, I've been told. Supposed to have taken it off a *bruja* down Mexico way. He claims he took her head too an' burned it in fire so her curses wouldn't stick to him."

When Preacher spotted the nine horses in a small corral at the back of the stables, his excitement grew. He was pretty certain he'd found Moses's missing horses. The murderers couldn't be far away.

"You ask me," Dempsey said, "these horses are mustangs, but they got a little somethin' extra in them. They run to an honest bay color, with a couple of them carryin' chestnut coloration."

"Likely they're mixed with Morgan

blood." Preacher recognized the differences himself because he knew horse flesh.

"For a while folks weren't supposed to sell horses to Indians, but French trappers brought horses in from Canada an' done a little horse tradin' now an' then. Nothin' an Indian likes better than a horse except a new rifle."

Curious, the horses trotted over to Preacher. He reached in his possibles bag again and took out apples he'd purchased at Chouteau's general store in case he found the horses. He twisted an apple in half and offered the halves to the horses that reached out cautiously to him. When those halves were taken, he tore another apple in half.

The horses jockeyed for position to get at the apples. Dog propped his paws up on the gate to say hello by touching noses.

"They're just like little kids," Dempsey said and smiled. "Sure does my heart good to see them young and frisky like that. You don't see them like that often around soldiers. They generally beat their mounts into submission an' use them like any other tool. Like they were a shovel or a tent peg. Wherever these horses come from, they been taken good care of."

"These are the horses I've been told about." Preacher tore another apple in half and held the halves out. He kept tearing apples and tried to make sure each horse got a treat. "The man who had them trained them well."

"He's a good trainer."

"He's dead now." Preacher fed his last couple apples to the horses. "Murdered by the men who brought these horses in."

Dempsey shook his head. "I wouldn't have turned these horses away no matter what, but now I'm not gonna be able to just let them go back to them boys. Don't want to see them go to the Army either."

"We're not gonna do that," Preacher agreed. "They belong to someone else."

He scratched behind the ears of a young filly that searched his clothing for another apple.

"You gonna tell the major about 'em?"

"Think he'd do anything about it?"

"Not hardly. These here horses are supposed to be sold to the Army." Dempsey reached out to one of the horses and stroked its neck. "You ask me, that's a shame. These horses need to go to someone who loves them an' knows how to do right by 'em."

"I agree. The Army's not gonna get them. Not if I have anything to say about it, and I will."

"The major might be perturbed."

"I don't care. These horses were stolen. I'm going to see to it they get returned to the rightful owner." Preacher stepped back from the corral. "Do you know where those men who brought them in are?"

"Probably in them rooms above the Scalded Beaver. They was talkin' about makin' time with soiled doves. Seemed to be the highlight of their trip."

The *click* of a pistol hammer behind Preacher caught his attention. He wheeled around and spotted the group of armed men behind him. There was no reason for them to have their pistols out unless they planned to use them.

Preacher shoved Dempsey to the side. He threw himself to the side into an empty stall. Bullets cut the air over his head where he'd been and whacked into the corral.

CHAPTER 9

Surprised by how fast the mountain man moved, Ian Candles dropped his spent pistol to the straw-covered stable floor and reached for another from the brace of firearms he wore over one shoulder. The young gunman hadn't figured it would take more than one shot to kill Preacher. Instead, a whole salvo had missed him.

Splintered pockmarks showed on the corral rails and the back wall of the stable where the shots had hit. Preacher and the wolf had dived into a stall on the other side of the building. The old man who minded the stables had gone to ground behind a hay manger. The container offered no real defense. Packed with hay as it was, a fired ball would zip right through.

"You're lucky you're still alive, Preacher," Candles crowed. "I wouldn't have put money on that. I most always hit what I aim at. You'd hear more about that, but a dead man can't hear."

Candles laughed at his own wit, but he faulted himself for missing the first time. He blamed it on the whiskey he'd consumed last night and then spending half the night with the soiled doves. He hadn't been able to hold back, though, even knowing he had a man to kill this morning. It had been too long since he'd been with a white woman who gave herself to him. Even though money had changed hands.

The other four men who rode with him were deadly, as well. All the balls had struck where Preacher had been. If he hadn't moved, probably none of them would have missed.

"You can ask those dead men you shot what they thought of your shootin' when we're done here," Preacher said from hiding. "Though, I gotta say I have my doubts that many of them will catch up to you in Hell. I don't think you went out of your way to hunt dangerous men who deserved to be shot."

Stung by the accusation because maybe part of it was true, Candles said, "I've shot plenty of dangerous men."

"While they were lookin' at you?" Preacher snorted. "I don't think that's true."

Lou Kleppe, one of the gunmen in Candles's string, a big man who'd come out of New York when he was younger than Candles, fired his pistol. The ball took a chunk out of a support beam near the stall where Preacher had taken cover. Bright wood stood out against the worn surface of the beam.

"What are you doin'?" Candles demanded.

"Thought I saw him movin'," the grizzled bear of a man said. He dropped his spent pistol and reached for another.

"Hold your fire till we get an honest target," Candles ordered and took cover in a stall. He shooed the horse inside it out into the stable. The horse lit a shuck for the door. "Ain't nowhere that old man can go. We're standin' in front of the only door leadin' out of the stable."

"I know." Lou looked around the stall wall where he hid back to where Preacher was concealed.

As soon as he did, Preacher popped up in a different stall, coolly leveled a pistol the like of which Candles had never seen, and — before Candles could yell a warning — fired. Smoke wreathed the mountain man's head, and a ball caught Lou in the eye and punched through the back of his head. The big man swayed, dead on his feet, and tumbled into the straw.

Candles ducked out from behind cover and snapped a shot at the mountain man, but Preacher was already moving and had gone before the ball tore through the gun smoke cloud.

Figuring it would take their quarry a moment to swap out pistols, Candles drew another pistol, looked at the nearby stall that held a horse, and realized he had another course of action.

"Get the horses out of the stall," he commanded his men. "Use them as shields."

The young gunman moved back a stall to another that held a horse. Preacher popped back up in a different spot behind the stall wall and fired again. Candles's hat flew off and rolled through the hay. The young gunman cursed and swung back behind a support beam.

Preacher kept moving a lot faster than he expected, and the man wasn't backing down.

Candles gripped the horse's halter and pulled the animal from the stall. In the open area, he took shelter behind the horse and leveled his pistol across the horse's back.

Preacher popped up again, leveled two of the strange pistols, and held his fire.

"He won't shoot into the horses," Candles

said and tried not to sound relieved. He glanced over his shoulder. The three men with him held horses in front of them, too. "Stay with me."

Vasco followed Candles. The squat Mexican could barely see over the horse he had in front of him, but he held his pistol steady across the horse's back. Watson and Pithouse shared space behind a horse and forced the animal forward to match Candles's speed. Watson had a pistol in each hand, and Pithouse carried a twelve-gauge shotgun.

Slowly, Candles pressed forward and eased the horse that stood between them forward in a sideways shuffle. The horse pitched her head and fought the grip on her halter, but the young gunman muscled her into doing what he wanted. The distance to the back of the stable melted away.

"I'm comin' to get you, Preacher," Candles taunted.

Lorenzo stood out in front of the boardinghouse and bit back the anger that filled him. With one hand on his hip and the other one around his rifle, he glared down at Hermann Weller.

"You ain't got no call to kick Preacher out of your boardin' rooms. He didn't do any-

124

thing wrong."

"Last night he pulled a pistol on a young woman," Weller declared.

"He did no such thing." Lorenzo was angry, plumb fit to be tied. "I was there an' seen it. Preacher covered that man while that fella was reachin' for his hole card. If it'd been me, I'd have shot him an' put an end to it. As it is, Preacher's gonna have to walk around with eyes in the back of his head as long as we're here."

"Herr Lorenzo," Weller said patiently, "*that* attitude is exactly why I have to ask you to leave. These people staying here aren't used to the kind of violence you and Herr Preacher take for granted. They are cultured people."

Lorenzo puffed his chest up, incensed all over again. "You sayin' I ain't cultured?" he roared. "Just because I know how to save my own skin an' ain't afraid to do it?"

Fear glimmered in the small German's eyes, but he didn't back down. "Herr Lorenzo, I really must insist."

Lorenzo snorted. "Well, me an' Tall Dog ain't done nothin' wrong."

"The possibility that you will exists."

Lorenzo heaved a disgusted breath. He looked at Tall Dog. The young Crow warrior stood silently beside him. Whatever Tall

Dog's thoughts were on their eviction, they didn't show on his impassive face.

"Well I never," Lorenzo said.

"Mr. Weller," a man called out in a Southern accent. "Are you having problems over there, sir?"

Lorenzo wheeled around. A young corporal and two privates stood behind him twelve feet away. They had rifles in their hands and held across their thighs, ready but not threatening.

"You boys mind your own business," Lorenzo growled. "Ain't nobody called for the Army."

Tall Dog eased a step away so they both had room to move should it come to that. Lorenzo liked the young Crow warrior a lot. He was a natural warrior.

"Mr. Weller." The corporal had some bark on him, and he was no stranger to violence. The missing top of one of his ears and a long scar across the side of his neck offered mute testimony to that. He spoke to Weller without taking his eyes from Lorenzo. "Are you having any problems, sir?"

"No," Weller said. "No problems. We are just working out a small disagreement about Herr Lorenzo's continued stay at the boardinghouse."

"You heard the man," Lorenzo said. "Just

126

workin' out some details. Ain't nothin' to see here. Go on an' git."

The corporal's face darkened with blood and his accent thickened into a weapon. "I'm not going to take any sass off you, boy."

"Boy?" That word riled Lorenzo and piled on all those bad years he'd experienced before he'd come West and found Preacher. He took a step down on the short flight of stairs that allowed access to the boarding-house veranda.

The two men beside the corporal raised their rifles, but they didn't quite point them at Lorenzo.

Still, even with the threat before him and outnumbered as he was, Lorenzo found it difficult to stop. Tall Dog's left hand dropped softly on Lorenzo's shoulder.

"We have no fight with this man," the young Crow warrior said quietly. "If that changes, I will fight with you."

Realizing the younger man was correct, Lorenzo stopped two steps up from the street and took a deep breath. A Virginia Southern accent was different than a Texas one. It was still Southern, but the Virginia ones really upset Lorenzo. Wherever the corporal came from had been in the vicinity of Virginia.

"You're right," Lorenzo said. "This fella's

just baitin' the bull an' he knows it. But this ol' bull's too smart for that."

The corporal's eyes flashed. "I was given orders this morning to be on the lookout for any trouble you people and Preacher might cause," he said. "If there was trouble, I was told to escort you from the fort."

"Well that just about tears it," Lorenzo said. "It's one thing for your high-and-mighty major to slip up an' give command to Captain Diller so he can run off with all them rifles an' murder the major comin' to replace him, an' now Major Crenshaw wants to get rid of the men who brought them rifles back. Don't that beat all."

A few dozen men and women crossed the boardwalk and the wide expanse of the fort's center. They stared at the confrontation and gave it a wide berth. They were families who had made homes in the wilderness outside the fort and had come to the fort to resupply.

Horses carrying travelers clip-clopped against the hardpan earth, and buckboards clattered over ruts.

One of the privates nudged the corporal and whispered something to him. The corporal grimaced and narrowed his eyes.

"If you're sure there's no trouble, Mr. Weller," the corporal said, "we'll be on our way.

But we'll be close if you need us."

"I am sure," Weller said. "Thank you, Corporal." The little German switched his attention to Lorenzo. "Mr. Lorenzo, perhaps you would like to return to the boarding-house in the future?"

Lorenzo shook his head. "I'd rather sleep in a tree."

He strode away from Weller and the corporal with his head up.

"This is all on account of that woman," Lorenzo told Tall Dog. "All on account that Preacher didn't take a shine to her while she was throwin' herself at him."

"I did not know that was what happened," Tall Dog said. "I might have gotten out of my room more slowly than you did."

"Naw, you was in the hallway first," Lorenzo said. "Your young bones move faster than these old ones."

"Then how do you know what the woman did?"

Lorenzo eyed his young friend. "You're still wet behind the ears. There's a whole lot about women you don't know yet, an' most of it you can't understand no how. White women can be even harder to understand on account they have different notions than a lot of other women. I know what I know about what happened in that hallway last

129

night because I know I know it."

"This appears to be something I should learn."

"You will. Probably one day sooner than you want to, I reckon." Lorenzo clapped his young friend on the shoulder. "C'mon. Let's find someplace to eat. I'm hungry. It's been too long since supper. My stomach is shakin' hands with my backbone."

"Where will we go? The Scalded Beaver is not yet open."

That was because the boardinghouse operated a restaurant at one end of the building that catered to the morning crowd. Lorenzo didn't like the idea of eating jerky for breakfast. There was plenty of time for that out in the wilderness. Coming to Fort Pierre usually meant getting to eat grub that was fresh-hot off the stove or out of the oven.

However, a scent called to Lorenzo and his nostrils flared.

"Put your nose in the wind an' take a whiff," Lorenzo said. "Unless I miss my guess, that's fresh buffalo meat cookin' on an open fire an' there are probably Indians outside these walls. Chances are good one of us knows somebody who will stand us to breakfast. If not, we'll trade for it."

"What about Preacher?"

"That's where we'll likely find him."

Lorenzo waited till a wagon passed in front of him and headed for the fort entrance.

Several gunshots split the air behind Lorenzo.

Lorenzo crouched and got down low to take the brief advantage of cover provided by a passing buckboard. He tracked the gunshots to the stable and his thoughts immediately turned to Preacher.

More gunshots tore the air.

Lorenzo dodged around the buckboard before it could get clear. "C'mon!"

He ran toward the stable and eared the hammer back on his rifle.

CHAPTER 10

Holding the Colt Patersons in his hands, Preacher squatted behind the stall wall where he sheltered. Dog stayed low at his side.

Ahead, behind the hay manger, Dempsey lay sprawled in the straw.

"Can you shoot?" Preacher asked the hostler.

"Of course, I can," Dempsey said, "but I left my shotgun back there at the door. I don't have anything on me but a pocket-knife."

"Well," Preacher said and grinned, "let's not let it come to that."

"You still there, Preacher?" the young gunman called in a singsong.

"Soldiers are gonna be comin'," Preacher yelled back.

"They're gonna be a minute," the young gunman declared. "Ain't none of the boys here at the fort in a rush to die. By the time they get here, you'll be dead, an' I'll tell them you were tryin' to steal them horses I brought in. They'll believe me because I'll be the only one with a story. Gonna tell them you shot the hostler, too. Major Crenshaw don't particularly favor you none already because you made him look bad."

Preacher ignored the taunt. The young man was screwing his own courage up, and that of his followers. Preacher knew he'd killed one of them, and they'd be thinking about that.

He laid the Patersons down and slipped his flintlock pistols from his sash at his back. Holding the pistols by the barrels, he extended them to Dempsey. The old hostler took the pistols.

"Know how to use those?" Preacher picked up the Patersons.

Dempsey grinned. "Better'n an old hound knows how to lick his own —"

Balls burst through the stall a few inches to the left of Preacher's position and loud thunder filled the stable. Sharp, wooden splinters pricked his face and ricocheted from his hat. Dust danced through the three holes in the stall walls.

"Get ready," Preacher warned. "We're runnin' out of room."

"I know it." Dempsey licked his lips. "Try

not to shoot any of them horses."

"Dog," Preacher called.

The big cur rose to his powerful legs and raked his lips back to expose his fangs.

Preacher removed his hat and peered around the corner of the stall. The nearest horse was twenty feet away. A plan formed in the mountain man's thoughts, born from hundreds of other battles.

He put the Paterson in his left hand on the ground, and tossed his hat toward the end of the stall so that it rose above the railing for just an instant. The gunmen had already fired one volley. It stood to reason they would have another ready.

And they'd be jumpy, ready to shoot.

Shots cracked and filled the stable with thunder. Gun smoke fogged the air around the shooters.

"What the hell are you shootin' at?" the young gunman shouted.

"He was movin'," another man said.

Preacher picked up the Paterson he'd laid down and whispered to Dog. "Hunt!"

The big cur launched himself around the corner on four driving paws that scattered straw in all directions.

"Look out for that wolf!" a man yelled.

Preacher leveled the Patersons. He'd had eight shots loaded in the pistols and had fired twice. That left six charged chambers. He took deliberate aim at the young gun-man's legs showing beneath the belly of the horse he was using for cover.

The .36-caliber ball struck the man in the knee, blood sprayed, and he collapsed. He squalled and cursed.

Dog ran past the felled man and between the legs of a horse. The big cur grabbed the inside of the man's thigh in his wide jaws, sank his teeth into flesh, and rolled like an alligator. Overpowered by Dog's speed and strength, unable to stand on one leg, the man went down.

"Help!" the man yelled. "He's chewin' my leg off!"

The big cur released his opponent im-mediately and fastened his jaws around the man's neck. With a savage wrench, Dog tore the man's throat out.

Preacher ran forward.

Released from the man who had been shot in the knee, the horse ran toward Preacher. The mountain man dodged to the side and took the momentary cover the animal of-fered.

The two men hunkered behind the final horse and raised their weapons. One man held two pistols and the other pulled a shotgun to his shoulder. The man with the pistols squawked in fear and aimed both weapons at Dog.

Seeing the danger, the big cur stopped on a dime and changed directions in a flurry of straw. A jackrabbit would have been jealous of Dog's speed and ability to change direction. Pistol balls slammed into the hard-packed earth of the stable floor where the big cur had been.

The shotgun leveled at Preacher and the mountain man threw himself forward and to his left to escape the blast. Shot shredded the straw several feet behind Preacher and the big *boom!* of the shotgun made him slightly deaf. He rolled onto his side, aimed both pistols, and put two balls into the shotgunner's midsection.

Blood stained the man's shirt as he fell back and sprawled. Dog leaped onto the man who had shot at him with the pistols and tore that man's throat out.

Frightened by the harsh cracks of the guns and the stink of fresh blood, the horses reared and slammed against the stalls all around Preacher. Only Horse remained calm, and he reared slightly now and again, ready to fight.

The mountain man pushed himself up and gazed at the stables through the thick gun smoke haze. Trapped in the building, the air smelled like gunpowder, like it had been pulled from the burning pits of Hell.

Movement behind Preacher alerted him to the threat of the young gunman aiming his pistol. With a slight turn, Preacher eared back the pistol in his right hand and fired a ball into the hollow of the man's throat. The impact drove the silver skull with red eyes into the man's neck. At the same time, Dempsey fired a shot that caught the man in the back of his head. The young gunman slumped limply.

"Told you I can shoot," Dempsey called out. He pushed himself to his feet. Blood streamed down one leg of his dungarees. "Got shot and didn't know it. Ain't that somethin'."

"Need help?"

Dempsey ran fingers over his leg and shook his head. "Barely got me. I've had skeeter bites that have done more damage."

Preacher walked through the battleground and made sure all his enemies were dead.

Dog came over to stand beside him. The big cur licked the blood off his muzzle.

A man dashed through the stable's front door and held a rifle to his shoulder. When Preacher recognized Lorenzo's face tucked into the rifle, Preacher already had his sights on the man's chest.

Preacher lowered the pistol, but he left the hammer at full cock. He wasn't sure where the dead men had come from or why they had been gunning for him. He wanted to stay ready. The day had been full of surprises.

Lorenzo lowered his rifle and gestured to Tall Dog behind him. The young Crow warrior lowered his rifle.

"You all done in here?" Lorenzo asked.

"I believe I am," Preacher said. "Unless there are more of them out there."

Lorenzo shook his head. "Nope. Just the US Army runnin' behind like they do." He walked on into the stable and looked around. "Likely they'll be along directly to arrest us for disturbin' the peace."

"A few minutes ago," Preacher said, "it wasn't very peaceful in here."

"I can see that." Lorenzo knelt beside one of the dead men and studied the man's face. "Do you know who they are?"

"Horse thieves. But I never met them."

Lorenzo stood.

A dozen soldiers posted up around the stable entrance and pointed rifles at everyone inside who was still alive.

"Drop your weapons!" a sergeant ordered.

Preacher laid the Patersons on the stable floor and looked at the sergeant. "I'll want

138

them back once this gets settled."

"We'll see about that."

Lorenzo put his rifle on the ground and added his pistols. "Somethin' tells me we've plumb wore out our welcome here at the fort."

Two hours later, bored and angry and restless, Preacher sat on the floor of the stockade cell where he'd been put after being marched over from the stable. This trip to Fort Pierre was nowhere near what he'd thought it might be, and he wasn't at all certain when he'd be returning to his beloved mountains.

One thing he was sure of though. He wasn't going to sit around in the stockade much longer.

Lorenzo slept on the cell's only bed screwed into the wall. Tall Dog dozed sitting up on the floor with his arms resting on his folded knees.

Dog had stayed with Horse in the stable. The soldiers had wanted to shoot the big cur on sight, but the timely arrival of Lieutenant Kraft had stopped that. Preacher had told Dog to stay with Horse, that he would be back soon. He hoped that was true and would happen before Dog came looking for him because the big cur was sure to get himself shot then.

A foul odor clung to the stockade. It reeked of sweat and desperation.

Only eight soldiers were currently locked up. Five of them, including Lieutenant Finlay, were men from last night's fight at the tavern. Finlay and his group glared venomous hatred at Preacher and his companions. Most of them had knots and bruises.

Preacher ignored them. Even cooped up and separated, none of them were brave enough to try baiting him.

The other three soldiers played cards in a shared cell and talked among themselves quietly.

Even though it was going on midday, the stockade's interior was dark because only three windows about the size of pumpkins allowed in light and fresh air. The breeze barely circulated through the cells, and it was uncomfortably hot. Come nightfall, though, and the cell would be cold.

Preacher didn't know if he was going to melt into a puddle or choke on the heat first.

The big lock on the main door clanked open, then the hinges screamed a little as the door swung inward.

Lorenzo's eyes slitted but he didn't move on the bed. Tall Dog's breathing changed just a touch. Anyone who didn't know the two men would have thought both of them were still sleeping.

"You think maybe it's bread an' water?" Lorenzo asked in a low voice. "Me an' Tall Dog missed out on breakfast, an' I'm thinkin' we're way past dinner now. Don't know if I can make it till supper."

"Doubt it's bread and water," Preacher replied.

Boots striking the wooden floor echoed in the short hallway that ran through the six cells in the stockade. A moment later, a half dozen soldiers followed Lieutenant Kraft to the cell that held Preacher and his friends.

"Major Crenshaw wanted me to ask you why Ian Candles tried to kill you," Kraft said.

Preacher shrugged but didn't bother to get up from the floor. "I don't know who that is. I figure he's one of the men back at the stable, but I wouldn't know which one. They never got around to introducin' themselves before they tried to kill me."

"I was told Ian Candles wore a silver skull here." Kraft tapped a finger against his throat. "A man identified Candles, but we didn't find the skull."

"You're going to have to dig it out of him," Preacher said. "I put a ball into his neck

141

right there. Knocked that skull on inside him."

Kraft frowned. "I thought as much. Mr. Dempsey at the stable said Candles and his men attacked you."

"I just told you that, too. Said that before we were put into here."

"Why did he attack you?"

"I never met the man before today," Preacher said. "I was in the stable lookin' for some horses stolen from an Indian who was murdered for them. I suspect I found the men who did it, too."

"Mr. Dempsey told us you presumed that."

"There's a man outside the fort who's camped with the Crow. Goes by the name of Moses. He's ridin' with a man named Caleb. They came huntin' the killers of Stout Otter, the horse trainer that Candles killed."

"Moses doesn't sound like an Indian name."

"Moses is black. He married into the Shoshone. Stout Otter was his wife's brother. Moses will be able to give you more of the story."

"You know Moses?"

"We've crossed trails here an' there. Talked some. Had breakfast with him this mornin'.

He's a good man."

Kraft looked uncomfortable. "Why didn't this man go to the major and tell him this story?"

"I suspect it was on account he thought he might end up sittin' in this stockade in the heat an' the stink." Preacher locked eyes with Kraft. "Seein' how it's turned out for us, an' these two especially," he pointed at Lorenzo and Tall Dog, "who didn't even have anythin' to do with killin' Candles an' his men, I'd have to say I understand why Moses didn't trust the Army. After gettin' jumped by soldiers last night, an' attacked in the middle of the fort by horse thieves this mornin', which there ain't nothin' lower than a horse thief, I'm feelin' a mite less trustin' of the Army myownself."

Kraft grimaced and looked disturbed. "I have to tell you, Preacher. I've been here almost two years. I've never seen the kind of trouble that seems to have ridden in with you."

"That horse thief was the Army's concern," Lorenzo said. "I heard some fellas talkin' while we was gettin' escorted over here. They said Candles rode scout for Major Crenshaw."

A pained look filled the young lieutenant's face.

" 'Pears to me," Lorenzo went on, "that major of yours has got some learnin' to do when it comes to pickin' folks who work for him."

Kraft looked at Preacher. "Do you think Moses will talk to me?"

"You'll have to go ask," the mountain man said. "I don't speak for that man."

The young lieutenant stepped back. "Major Crenshaw would like to speak to you."

"About what?" Preacher asked.

"He has a proposition for you."

"What about my friends?"

"He didn't say anything about them."

"It's all of us," Preacher said, "or none of us."

Kraft took a breath. "All right." He waved toward the door. "Sergeant, get these men out of there."

CHAPTER 11

With bated breath and his hat in his hands, Barnaby Cooper watched the entourage that walked from the stockade toward the main Army building. Preacher strode in the middle of them, surrounded by soldiers and leading the black man and the Indian who rode with him.

The red, white, and blue flag of the United States fluttered on the pole in the middle of the parade grounds. A few visitors to the fort stopped loading their wagons and buckboards to watch the procession.

Cooper's heart fluttered a little at the sight. So far, so good. The mountain man had agreed to meet with Major Crenshaw. Cooper hoped the bargain would be struck. If the major could get him into the room with Preacher, Cooper was sure he could seal the deal.

"Well, there they go," McDermid said quietly. "We'll know how it goes soon enough."

Cooper, McDermid, and Kittle sat at a corner table in the boardinghouse diner and peered through the windows.

"Preacher will say yes," McDermid said.

"Why should he?" Kittle asked.

McDermid blinked. "Because he has to, that's why. He's the best man for the job."

"That won't matter if he doesn't want a job," Kittle replied.

"He will," Cooper said confidently. "I can sell this. The major has only to get me in front of Preacher."

"I thought the major was going to convince Preacher all on his own," McDermid said.

"The major isn't a salesman," Cooper said. "He's not going to try to appeal to Preacher's finer instincts."

"What *fine* instincts?" Opaline Humboldt demanded. She and her husband sat at the next table. "That man is uncouth."

Since the talk that morning, the Humboldts had separated themselves from the rest of the trading post investors. Cooper had been all right with that — as long as they didn't pull out of the effort altogether.

"Only a few hours ago," Opaline continued, "that man butchered those poor horse traders in that stable."

"That's not what happened," a man at another table said.

Cooper turned to him.

The man was slim, thirtyish, and put together well. His suit was neatly appointed, and his wide face was shaved smooth. He was of medium height, but he had broad shoulders and a ready smile.

"Those five men who are now dead ambushed Preacher in that stable after he discovered they'd brought in a herd of stolen horses. Those miscreants killed the man who originally owned them. Attacking Preacher was their final mistake."

"Who are you?" Humboldt demanded. "And what would you know of the events in the stable?"

"Forgive my bad manners," the man said. "My name is Christopher Carson."

"Kit Carson," McDermid said with reverence Cooper would have thought suited a pious man in church on a Sunday morning.

Carson smiled indulgently and nodded. "The very same."

The young man looked at his companions. "Mr. Carson is a scout and expert trapper. I read about him in the papers."

"I am indeed a scout and a trapper." Carson nodded. "As to how I know what happened in that stable, why at Major Crenshaw's insistence, I went over there and had a look. The major wanted me to verify Preacher's story. After seeing all that was writ upon that stable floor and the environs within, I did. That confrontation happened exactly as Preacher said. Those five men attacked him, and they paid for that sorry mistake with their lives. Saved them from the rope, is what he did. Once the folks around here found out they were horse thieves, those men would have gotten hung from the nearest tree."

Carson looked at Opaline. "Beg your pardon, ma'am. That was downright crude."

Opaline didn't look flustered at all. Instead, she gazed at the man with her emerald eyes glittering. "It's quite all right."

"Anyway," Carson said, "you won't find a finer man than Preacher out here in this wilderness. He'll do what he says he'll do, and he'll do it better than most."

"You say you're a scout?" Humboldt asked.

"I am."

"We're looking for a scout to lead us to Spearfish Canyon to set up a trading post. The men we hired ran out on us and left us high and dry."

Carson frowned. "Going out there is really not a good idea, my friend. Those lands are

148

protected by the Sioux. They're sacred to them. They'll protect them."

"I think we can strike a bargain with the Sioux," Cooper said. "A trading post out that way would be beneficial to them. They wouldn't have to travel to Fort Pierre to get goods they wanted."

"You make that trading post sound attractive, friend."

"Then you're interested in the job?" Humboldt asked.

"I'm afraid I'm otherwise engaged. Only recently, I've accepted employment from Lieutenant John C. Fremont. I met him on a steamboat on the Missouri River and we talked of the Western lands. He had heard of me and wants me along on the expedition from the Oregon Trail into Wyoming Territory. We're exploring new lands. I'm on my way to join Lieutenant Fremont now so we can finish attending to the details."

Carson stood and adjusted his coat. He picked up a rifle that had been leaning against a nearby wall.

"Preacher will only go with you if he chooses to," the man said. "But if he chooses to go, he will stick with you no matter how bad it gets out there. Many of the Indians out that way respect him. That will work in your favor. The Blackfeet have sworn to kill him. That will not work in your favor."

He put his hat on, tipped it in Opaline's direction, and walked to the door.

After he'd gone, McDermid sat back in his seat and said, "That was Kit Carson."

Cooper watched the man go. Carson crossed the parade grounds in front of twenty riders who had just entered the fort.

All the riders were hard men who gazed around warily. They looked weary but ready, as if they'd traveled a long way as quickly as they could. Pack mules with panniers trailed after the horses. The panniers bounced so much they had to be empty or nearly so.

The leader was a swarthy man in his late thirties. His thick, black hair had once been elegantly cut, but it had grown out. His sideburns were neatly edged and trailed down to blend into the short beard that wrapped his chin and lay neatly. His hooded eyes caught everything. A tailor had seen to the fine clothing he wore, but it was dust-covered now and had seen better days.

Two flintlock pistols hung in scabbards on a broad belt around his waist. Scabbards on his saddle held two more. He held his rifle across his thighs. The hilt of a knife stuck out of his right boot. A thin-bladed sword with a looped hilt hung from his belt along his left leg. The sword's scabbard was dark and plain.

The men halted their mounts in front of the general store. The swarthy man talked to them in a language that Cooper couldn't recognize, though it reminded him of the Spanish he'd heard on the docks in Baltimore. He did not understand what was said.

All the men made sure their horses were given feedbags, then they squared away their tack. After several minutes, half of the men climbed the steps to the general store while half of their number watched over the horses.

"Who are they?" McDermid asked.

"Military men," Kittle said. "You can tell by the way they move and the way they watch everything around them.

"The fort needs more soldiers?"

"Those men aren't here for the fort," Kittle replied. "They're not from this country."

"Where do you think they're from?"

"Europe would be my guess. Probably even Spain. That man's boots are cordovan leather, and that's made in Cordoba, Spain."

"Wonder what they're doing here," McDermid said.

Kittle shook his head. "Whatever it is, they're focused."

■ ■ ■ ■

"How are you going to be paying for all this?"

Colonel Luis Yermo Areta, once of the Basque Country, looked at the man behind the counter.

The shopkeeper was short and round, a man who had seen at least forty years, and most of them not easy. He wore an apron over his worn dungarees and a flannel shirt with the sleeves rolled up almost to his elbows. Gray fringe surrounded his bald head. Behind his glasses, his eyes were flat and brown. Yermo's men grabbed armfuls of supplies and brought them to the counter.

As the piles grew, the shopkeeper grew more agitated. He stood close to the counter and tried to watch all Yermo's men.

Yermo suspected the man had a shotgun beneath the counter. The shopkeeper hadn't moved from his spot since the Basque colonel and his men had arrived.

"I will pay with gold," Yermo said easily in English. It was one of a handful of languages he spoke well. "You do still take gold, don't you?"

"All day long," the shopkeeper said, "and twice on Sunday." He smiled hesitantly.

"That last was a joke. I'm not open on Sunday."

"I see."

Around the store, Yermo's men continued stocking up on the necessary staples. They still had many days' travel ahead of them. Over the last three weeks it had taken them to reach Fort Pierre, nearly all their supplies were gone. Game had been good, but there was something to be said for cooked meals that were more than just freshly killed seared meat. Men didn't travel well on empty stomachs.

Yermo had learned that while serving as a captain in General Tomás de Zumalacárregui's army. Zumalacárregui was once called the Wolf of the Amezocoas. Everything Yermo knew about fighting, strategies, and men, he'd gotten from serving Zumalacárregui.

The general was dead now, killed by an infected wound in 1835. Yermo still missed his old friend and leader. The Carlist War that had been fought over the throne of Spain had claimed many lives. It had nearly taken Yermo's life on a half-dozen occasions. He still carried three balls in his body that had been delivered by soldiers fighting for the *isabelinos* who fought to put Isabell II on the throne.

"Are you a Spaniard?" the shopkeeper asked. "The reason I ask, I've heard an accent like that before, but yours is different. And I can tell by those spurs that you're not from this country."

"I am of Basque descent," Yermo declared proudly.

He knew that would raise questions here in this place because it always did. The people who lived in the United States were sadly provincial and lacked a larger world-view.

"Where's that?"

"I am from north of the Ebro River. Have you heard of it?" Yermo knew the answer to the question before he asked it. He wanted to bruise the shopkeeper's ego enough to ensure the man would leave them alone.

The shopkeeper thought for a moment, then shook his head. "I reckon not. I've traveled around a bit, but I've never heard of Basque or the Ebro River."

"Now you have," Yermo said.

"I have." The man nodded.

Two of Yermo's men carried over sacks of flour and beans. They laid them on the floor so the shopkeeper could easily tally them.

"The Ebro River rises in Cantabria and sweeps nearly six hundred miles across the southwest corner of Europe," Yermo said.

154

He wanted the shopkeeper to be impressed. "It ends up in the Mediterranean Sea at the Province of Tarragona. Its waters touch many of the major cities there."

"Spain, right?"

"Much more than Spain, my friend." Despite his dislike of the shopkeeper, Yermo smiled. It was a smile he'd perfected to show confidence, to woo women for a night, and that smile was the last thing his enemies saw in this world. "Men have fought wars all around that river for generations."

"Do tell. Well, Fort Pierre is out of the way for most folks. What brings you here?"

"I come here to seek my fortune. Just as so many of your countrymen do."

"This is a hard place to look for a fortune," the shopkeeper said. "Unless you have a hankering to trap beaver and shoot buffalo. And you'll have to fight Indians to do most of that."

Yermo looked at the glass container of dark cheroots on the countertop. He added a fistful of them to the goods.

"I do not fear a fight, my friend," the Basque declared. "Give me a good weapon and a firm place to stand and I will survive. I have fought men with pistols and swords since I was eleven years old. I am prepared."

The shopkeeper nodded at all the supplies

on the counter. "Well, you buy all this, and you'll be plenty prepared."

Yermo's soldiers stood at the counter and waited patiently.

"How much do I owe you?" Yermo asked.

The shopkeeper poked a pencil at all the goods, toted up numbers on a paper pad, and told Yermo the amount.

Yermo reached into his coat and withdrew a small bag of gold coins that clinked heavily. The shopkeeper stared with open avarice at the bag. If he had known Yermo had that much, the Basque captain guessed the man would have charged more for the goods. As it was, he was sure he was being over-charged, but tolerably so.

He counted out the coins, waited for his change, and got a receipt. He placed the receipt in the bag with the coins he had left and put the bag away. He knew flashing the gold would bring problems if there were any bad men in the fort, but he looked forward to that, too. Hunting game wasn't the same as killing a man.

He kept one of the cheroots out and put the rest in his pocket. He pointed to the small lantern on the countertop and indicated his cheroot.

"Might I borrow a light?" he asked.

The shopkeeper nodded.

Yermo raised the hurricane glass to expose the small flame, leaned in with the cheroot clenched between his teeth, and let it take the flame. He returned the glass to its proper position and nodded his thanks to the shopkeeper. He breathed out and a plume of blue-gray smoke danced before him.

"All right," he told his men in the Basque language, "load the supplies and let's get going. Albion Shaw expects our arrival."

Without a word, his men took the supplies and carried them outside. With economical efficiency and years of training, the men loaded the panniers on the pack mules.

Once the supplies were distributed, the feedbags were removed from the horses and the pack mules.

Yermo stepped into the stirrup and hauled himself lithely into the saddle. His horse was a coal-black Andalusian that had been born in the foothills of El Torreón, a brutal and savage land. The horse was descended from generations of animals that had served as war mounts to kings and royalty. The big black animal had served him during the Carlist War without fail.

When he had left the Basque country after his general's defeat, Yermo had paid handsomely to ship the horse to the United

States. If he was to be a mercenary and an entrepreneur in these new, uncivilized Western lands, he intended to be well outfitted.

His men mounted and awaited his command.

"Ibili," he ordered.

Lieutenant Manu Gayarre, who had served in that position during the last three years of the Carlist War under Yermo, saluted and led the men toward the front gate.

Yermo rode after his men. He puffed on the dark cheroot and glanced behind him.

The shopkeeper stood out in front of the general store and talked to a couple of rough-looking men. When Yermo made eye contact with them, they ducked their heads and looked away.

The Basque warrior turned his attention to his men again and grinned. The trap had been set and it remained to be seen who would take the bait. Mice were always ambitious when they thought they would not be seen.

Yermo looked forward to the coming confrontation. He had not killed a man in almost three weeks.

CHAPTER 12

"You've got all those mountains to roam around in, Preacher," Major Lawrence Crenshaw stated evenly. "I don't know why you think you needed to spend any more time here in Fort Pierre."

The major stood behind his desk with ramrod straight posture and tried to command the room. He was not quite six feet tall and was broad shouldered. He carried about ten pounds above his best fighting weight, but a good tailor hid that. His uniform was clean and pressed, and his saber hung at his side.

Pierre Chouteau sat in a wing-back chair by a small table in one corner of the major's office. The easy way he made himself at home advertised that he was a frequent visitor to the fort. He cycled through pieces of mail and occasionally checked a map spread across the table. He constantly worked at something the whole time Preacher had known him.

Chouteau was an earnest looking man in his early fifties. Tall and dapper, he had a boyish face even at his age. Silver dusted his dark hair, and he was clean-shaven. His expensive black suit fit him well.

"So what you're sayin'," Preacher said, "if I'm to put a fine point on it, is that you're kickin' me out of Fort Pierre on account of you've got some bad soldiers here who wanted my scalp."

"That's not what I said." Crenshaw's face flushed crimson. "And those men who ambushed you in the stable were not soldiers."

"Ian Candles rode scout for you," Preacher said.

Behind him, seated in chairs that had been brought into the office from somewhere, Lorenzo and Tall Dog sat silently. Lorenzo fidgeted and Preacher knew his friend had things he wanted to say, but he was holding his powder while Preacher talked.

Chouteau looked up sharply from his letters at Crenshaw. "Is that true? Did that man serve as a scout for you?"

Crenshaw frowned and looked defensive. "Only now and again, Mr. Chouteau. Mostly to check reports of Indian attacks farther out than I allow normal patrols to range. Many of my men are green, too new to Indian country to trust not to get themselves killed."

"An' too many of them are thieves an' ambushers," Lorenzo commented.

Crenshaw glared at him. "You don't know what you're talkin' about, so you just shut your mouth."

Lorenzo bristled, about to unload, but Chouteau got there first.

"I think Mr. Lorenzo does know what he's talking about," the trader stated evenly. "He certainly knows more than I do, and I own this trading post, Captain Crenshaw. I find that disconcerting. Especially since you and your men are here at my sufferance, and you're supposed to keep me up to date."

"With all due respect, Mr. Chouteau," the major said brusquely, "without us, you wouldn't have anyone to protect you from the Indians."

"I recall a time when there were no soldiers at this fort," Chouteau said. "We traded with the Indians and managed to do quite well for ourselves. Back in 1832 when this fort was built, Preacher helped set some of the posts that make up this installation to this day. We made do then. I only allowed the Army in to see to the defense of immigrants who travel through this land."

Crenshaw turned on the trader. "You need to let me handle this."

Chouteau cocked an eyebrow. "What do you plan on doing? Getting rid of Preacher?"

"It would go a long way toward quieting this fort down. We didn't have all these problems till he got here yesterday."

"This fort," Chouteau said, "hasn't been quiet in some time, Major. Your successor was killed by a man you promoted to his position from ranks you established. That same man stole a shipment of rifles I had bought, and that thievery cost me dearly, not to mention all the innocent lives Diller cut short. The fight in the tavern last night was not Preacher's fault. I have heard testimony to that fact. And I would be willing to wager that I won't have to look very hard or very far to connect this 'now and again' scout Ian Candles to Diller as well. Would you care to place money on that?"

Crenshaw scowled. "I'm just trying to get rid of the problem, Mr. Chouteau, in the best way I know how."

The trader didn't speak for a moment, just let things hang fire.

Preacher sat back and watched. It was almost worth sitting in the stockade a few hours to see Crenshaw get a good dressing-down. The major had gotten sloppy in his command. Maybe he always had been, but that was the case lately. Now all those chickens were coming home to roost.

"Well," Chouteau said finally, "your way is wrong. That may be the way *you* know how to get rid of the problem, but it's certainly not the best way. Certainly not *my* way. I submit that the problems among your troops existed, and only the arrival of Preacher and his friends revealed those at fault that might have continued to be so costly."

Crenshaw shook his head, and opened his mouth to say something, but Chouteau cut him off.

"I have sent a letter to the Department of War, to Secretary Joel Roberts Poinsett explicitly, and requested your immediate replacement and additional troops to replace the ones we have so far lost and will likely continue to lose. Given the preeminence with which this fort is favored in Washington, and the respect given it by companies back East, I anticipate the arrival of that commanding officer and those troops in short order."

The major gawped like he'd been mortally wounded. "You can't do that."

"I own this trading post. I can do that. I did."

Crenshaw struggled to find something to say.

"You may sit down, Major," Chouteau said. "Your theatrics are no longer necessary."

Crenshaw plopped down in his chair and worked his jaw.

"Now, Preacher," Chouteau swiveled his attention to the mountain man, "Mr. Lorenzo, Mr. Tall Dog, the major may be incorrect in how to go about the particular matter of your presence here, but I will point out that, under the present circumstances of us not knowing for sure who Captain Diller's friends were and might yet continue to be, this fort might not be the best place for you to be."

Preacher shook his head. "So *you're* goin' to kick us out?" He smiled coldly. "What if I choose not to go? Although the experience might do Tall Dog some good. He's never been kicked out of town before."

Chouteau grimaced like he'd bitten into something sour. "No, I'm not going to try to force you to leave this trading post. I'm a businessman. I spend my days building compromises that benefit both parties. I have one such compromise for you."

Preacher shifted in his chair. He respected Chouteau, though he and the trader hadn't always agreed on the nature of things. "I'm listenin'."

"You killed five men in our stable only hours ago," Chouteau said. "We know you killing Captain Diller has left you with enemies here at the trading post. Some of them have already been revealed and are currently holding down a cell in the major's stockade. I believe that Ian Candles was part of Diller's organization and a known friend to Lieutenant Judd Finlay. However, we don't know how many more sympathizers to Diller there are. Or, for that matter, how many opportunists still exist in the ranks of the Army soldiers here. If you remain here, you may draw them to you like a magnet draws iron."

"You'd know who they were then," Preacher said. "Get all your rat killin' done at one time that way. I might even take care of some of it myownself."

"Or I would have to bury you and your friends," Chouteau said. "I don't want to do that. Not to demean your abilities, but you — *and* your companions — are not invincible."

"Them killin' us isn't going to happen. You just hide an' watch." Preacher viewed the statement as a challenge.

"I'd rather you accepted my proposition. Would you like to hear it?"

Preacher didn't like the idea of backing down from a fight, but a man didn't get the chance to back down from an ambush. On top of that, staying at the fort and dealing with Diller's friends might get some innocent folks killed.

He didn't want any part of that.

"All right," Preacher said. "Trot it out an' let's have a look at what you have."

"There's a man here at the trading post whose goal it is to establish a trading post of his own at Spearfish Canyon."

"Barnaby Cooper."

Chouteau's eyebrows lifted. "You've heard about him?"

"A man can hear a lot here if he sits still for a minute."

"That's not what you've been doing," Crenshaw said. "Those five dead men today can testify to that."

"Now how're they gonna do that?" Lorenzo asked. "What with them bein' dead an' all?"

"How they got dead says a lot," Crenshaw snarled.

"You mean them ambushin' the wrong fella?"

Chouteau glared at the major and Crenshaw looked away.

"Have you met Mr. Cooper?" Chouteau asked Preacher.

"No," Preacher answered. "He's the man in the D'Orsay hat. I've seen him and his friends. Bumped into a couple of them last night at the boardinghouse."

A small frown bent Chouteau's lips. "I'd heard about that. Herr Weller was afraid you might kill the man."

"If he'd gotten that pistol of his out, I might just have had to do that."

"I have been told Mr. Humboldt, that was the man whom you encountered, was not quite himself last night."

"He'd had a couple drinks, but he wasn't the big problem."

"Mrs. Humboldt was. Yes, I had heard that, too."

"She was drunk as a skunk," Preacher said. "And has her hat set on bein' a gadfly when it comes to makin' trouble."

"Be that as it may, Mr. Cooper has assured me the Humboldts will be on their best behavior in their dealings with you from this point on."

"I never seen the day," Lorenzo groused, "when a man could muzzle a woman set on havin' her say."

167

"I trust Mr. Cooper's opinion on the matter."

Preacher narrowed his gaze. "Are you goin' somewhere with this?"

Chouteau pursed his lips. "Mr. Cooper needs a guide to take him to Spearfish Canyon. He can pay."

"Not interested," Preacher said immediately. "Those are Sioux lands, and they're mighty particular about who goes traipsin' through there. Wagon trains fight shy of them for a reason."

"Mr. Cooper and his band of investors are up against Mother Nature," Chouteau said. "One of the guides they originally had was killed by a Blackfeet band out that way. The other guide returned and quit. Cooper needs an experienced man to take that expedition to Spearfish Canyon."

"He does," Preacher agreed, "but that's not me."

Chouteau paused. "There is another reason I'd like you to agree to the trip, Preacher. There are rumors of a man named Albion Shaw who is rooting around out there in that wilderness for some reason."

"There are lots of rumors out here," Preacher said. "Bored men make up all kinds of stories."

"They do, but I got one of those stories

from Captain Joseph LaBarge. I'm sure you know him."

Preacher had met the steamboat captain a few times while traveling along the Missouri River. LaBarge was a young man, not yet thirty, and had made a good name for himself in the area. He had been one of the first steamboat captains to navigate the uppermost Missouri River ten years ago. LaBarge was tough, hard-nosed, and brave.

"I know him," Preacher said.

"LaBarge has had dealings with Albion Shaw, a few of them not so good. Shaw is an Englishman and fought as a member of the British army during the Second War of American Independence. During those years, Shaw was arming Indians to fight American settlement of the land out there. He helped arm Tecumseh, which, as you know, resulted in several lost American lives."

Preacher thought about that. He'd fought in that war, too, alongside General Andy Jackson in the Battle of New Orleans. The mountain man had been little more than a boy then. During that time, he'd heard about Tecumseh and the Prophet and all the killing that went on around the Great Lakes and in the Ohio River Valley.

The notion that an Englishman might be

out there among the Sioux, riling them up, didn't set well on the mountain man's mind.

"You're sure about Shaw?" Preacher asked. "That he's out there somewhere?"

"Captain LaBarge has it on good authority that Shaw is somewhere out there. I trust LaBarge."

Preacher rubbed his chin thoughtfully. "So do I."

He didn't cotton to the notion of guiding Cooper and his folks out West, but the possibility of finding an Englishman aiming to stir up trouble with the Indians was different. There were a lot of folks heading out to Oregon Territory these days. If something bad took shape out that way, it could cut those folks off from overland help.

"We could go," Preacher said. "Just the three of us. We would be quicker."

"You would be," Chouteau agreed. "But you'd also be more vulnerable."

Preacher wanted to object and point out that Shaw would have to catch him first, but Chouteau lit his powder first.

"Going out there with Cooper and his party might help disguise you," Chouteau said.

"A man doesn't need to be disguised if he is never seen," Tall Dog said.

Chouteau looked at the young Crow war-

170

rior in surprise, as if he hadn't thought Tall Dog could speak English.

"That is true, Mr. Tall Dog," the trader admitted.

"Let's think about this for a minute, Preacher," Lorenzo said. "Suppose me, you, an' Tall Dog ride out there an' Shaw's men see us. We won't be trappin', we won't be shootin' buffalo. We'd be headin' straight at 'em. I don't think Shaw, if he caught wind of us, would believe we were just out ridin' to take in the air. Now if we have to fight our way clear, which we would, that could be a mite harder." He looked at Chouteau. "How many men is Shaw likely to have?"

Chouteau shook his head. "I don't know. Captain LaBarge told me that Shaw went into that area with fifty men. If Shaw has joined up with some of the Indians out there, particularly the Blackfeet, who might prove sympathetic to his cause, you're talking about a considerable increase in their number." A troubled look passed across the trader's face. "Only a few minutes ago, a small group of men stopped at the general store and bought a large amount of goods. Mr. Belkin, the man who runs the general store, told one of my men that those people were Basques."

"What are those?" Lorenzo asked.

171

"They're a group of folks who live in Spain and France," Preacher said. "Prideful folks. Put a lot of stock in themselves. They're fierce fighters. I've known a couple who came out West."

"Never heard tell," Lorenzo said.

"Comes to root hog or die," the mountain man said, "they'll be right memorable. I've seen a couple of them fight. They don't back off."

"These men," Chouteau said, "struck Mr. Belkin as military men by the way they deferred to their leader, a man who carried a military sword, and by the way they were so organized in their gathering of goods. They didn't talk much."

"Belkin wouldn't have understood them anyway," Preacher said. "They've got their own language, an' it's different enough from Spanish an' French that I don't understand it when I hear it. Sounds like it could be either of them, but it's not. I don't suppose your shopkeeper caught a name, did he?"

"Yermo. I've never heard it before."

Preacher shook his head. "Me neither. They headed West when they left the tradin' post?"

"They did."

"To meet up with Albion Shaw?"

"That is something I would like to know,"

Chouteau admitted. "At the very least, it is a sign of ill portent."

"Well," Lorenzo said, "now I'm curious, an' I hate bein' curious because that can get a man killed right quick." He looked at Preacher. "We'll do this the way you want to, but I wouldn't mind havin' a reason for bein' out in them woods that might not make Shaw an' his men so suspicious right off."

Preacher nodded. Much as the idea of dealing with Cooper and his group irritated him, Chouteau and Lorenzo had a good argument. He looked at his two companions.

"I'm interested in seein' what's out there. What about you two?"

"The tradin' post is feelin' a little tight," Lorenzo said. "Lookin' over my shoulder the whole time we're here takes the fun right out of bein' here. I'd rather be out in the wilderness where I can see an enemy comin' at me."

"I have never been to Spearfish Canyon," Tall Dog said. "Nor have I seen many Sioux. I would be interested in learning more about that part of the country. I have heard there are dead lands out there, places where the earth has died and is decomposing like a dead man's body sloughs off flesh."

"It's like that," Preacher said. "There's a place south an' west of Spearfish Canyon called the Devil's Kitchen. The Blackfeet drove buffalo herds over the side to kill them an' take meat. Called those buffalo jumps *pishkun.*"

"Deep blood kettle," Tall Dog said. "I know the term, but I have never seen such a place." He paused. "I would like to."

"May not be that particular place," Preacher said, "but you'll get to see some like it." The mountain man turned back to Chouteau. "All right. We'll do it."

"Wait a minute," Lorenzo said. "This ain't a trade unless we both get somethin' out of it. What are *we* gettin' for our trouble?"

Preacher hadn't been concerned with that. The thought of an Englishman fomenting trouble with the Indians was enough to convince him the journey needed to be taken.

"My goodwill is not enough?" Chouteau smiled.

"Only if it puts meat in the stew."

"Well, Mr. Lorenzo, I'm sure we can come to terms. What do you have in mind?"

"We'll dicker about the rest of it another time. For now, I'll settle for gettin' my bed back at the boardinghouse. Sounds like we ain't gonna get next to a proper bed for a long time once we head out. Last night just wasn't enough to rest my bones."

"I can arrange that."

"An' me an' Tall Dog want somethin' to eat now. We plumb missed breakfast what with gettin' kicked out of the boardin'house an' near' gettin' kicked out of the tradin' post."

"You'll dine at my home, Mr. Lorenzo. My cook is excellent. My wife insists that the food be good."

"Sounds mighty fine." Lorenzo smiled and got to his feet. "You can come with us, Preacher. I wasn't just negotiatin' for Tall Dog an' me."

"I ate this mornin'," Preacher said. "I've got somethin' to see to. I need to get Dog out an' stretch his legs."

"Well, make sure you stay outta trouble," Lorenzo said. "At least until me an' Tall Dog have had a chance to get ourselves fed."

Preacher nodded and turned to Crenshaw. "I'm takin' those horses Ian Candles brought in back to their rightful owners."

"I paid for those horses," the major objected.

"The Army paid for those horses," Preacher said. "You can rob Ian Candles's dead body to get your money back."

"I will not —"

"You will," Chouteau said. "Preacher will have those horses."

Preacher nodded to the trader and turned his attention back to Crenshaw. "Have your men bring our weapons back. With the way things are, I don't want to be wanderin' around out there without them."

CHAPTER 13

Four hours out from Fort Pierre, six men rode the trail taken by the Basque soldiers. The men watched the forest carefully and didn't talk among themselves, which was good and showed some organization, but they smoked tobacco and the scent carried downwind toward the men they hunted.

That was a stupid mistake. Since they hung back from the Basque warriors riding west, perhaps the mistake would not have been so bad had someone not been waiting for them.

Colonel Luis Yermo Areta was disappointed the number of pursuers was so few. He had assumed the gold coins he'd used to pay for his purchases would bring out more greedy men.

Evidently whoever had sent them underestimated the ability of his men, or perhaps the Basques' woodcraft skills in what might be a foreign land was in doubt. Or, it was possible, the men were regarded highly by whomever had sent them. It was also conceivable the men were merely scouts who would report back to a larger force still yet to be sent out from the trading post or who trailed an hour or so behind. The true ambush might be targeted for a later time.

Yermo had seen no signs of other men following. Possibly they were going to wait till the colonel's men made camp for the night.

Any thinking along those lines was a mistake the men in front of Yermo were about to pay their lives for making.

Hidden in the trees fifteen feet off the wide trail blazed through the forest by wagon trains leaving Fort Pierre, the Basque colonel anticipated the coming encounter. The last man he had killed had been weeks ago in St. Louis.

It had been far too long to suit him.

The fight had been over a woman the man had been abusing in an alley. He had been a drunken lout who still had good command of his senses and his reflexes. He had only been lacking good judgment that night, as so many men did who drank too much or too often, or simply who believed themselves to be better than they were. The fight had been fair, except it was over too quickly to satisfy the Basque colonel's desire for blood.

Yermo had opened the man's throat with his sword in that alley, and he'd never learned the man's name. That was a small matter, and one of no consequence to Yermo. The Basque colonel had ended the lives of many men he had not known names of on the battlefields where he had fought.

This afternoon, with the clear, bright sun that he followed to his latest appointment lying partially hidden by the treetops, Yermo would kill more men whose names he would not know.

He smiled in anticipation of the coming battle. He gripped his sword in his left hand and held it so the blade would not rattle through or catch in the brush that surrounded the thick green ash tree where he stood. The tree was native to Yermo's country, unlike many around him, and he was at home under it.

The men rode slowly past Yermo's position. The horses' hooves thudded against the bare soil of the trail and raised small puffs of dust. The horses moved in irregular cadence, and Yermo picked up the awkward rhythm.

He stepped out of hiding behind them without being seen and went silently because whatever noise the horses made covered any sound he might have made. As he moved through the brush and avoided thorny snares and dead branches lying on the ground, he carried his Girardoni rifle in his left hand and ran his right hand over the pistols belted at his waist and the sword at his left hip.

He was ready to kill.

Fifty feet behind the riders now, Yermo lifted the Girardoni rifle to his shoulder. The weapon was thirty-odd years old and had been carried by the Jesuit soldier who had trained Yermo as a boy how to fight and how to use the rifle. The Jesuit had served in the Austrian army against Napoleon Bonaparte and the French. The Jesuit had been a sniper then, and the rifle had served him well. When the old man had died in Yermo's arms fifteen years ago, he had left Yermo his rifle and told him to carry it with honor.

Gustav Hundertwasser would not have approved of all the uses Yermo had for the weapon over the years since. The Austrian had possessed more rules about engagement and killing other soldiers than the Basque colonel had ever felt the need for. That had been a point of contention between them. When fighting for his life, Yermo had argued, a man did not give away any advantage he had over an enemy. Especially out of some sense of honor that belonged to antiquity, if it belonged at all. To let an enemy have a chance that enemy had not taken for himself — or herself, because Yermo didn't differentiate between genders — was to invite death. War was to the death, and honor had no place there.

That was what had gotten Hundertwasser killed in the end those years ago.

This ambush was one such use Yermo's mentor would not have endorsed.

Yermo embraced the air rifle's ability to kill almost silently, and its capacity to fire twenty times before needing to reload. The rifle's air reservoir propelled .46-caliber balls fed by a tubular magazine in near-silence. The weapon could fire thirty balls before the reservoir was empty. Refilling the air tank with a hand pump took hours.

The Girardoni was an ugly weapon, in Yermo's opinion, because it was straight and unadorned, but its function was without fault. The Austrians called it a *Windbüchse*, wind rifle.

The Basque colonel raised the rifle to his shoulder, aimed at the back of one man's head, just above the shoulders where an immediate kill was guaranteed, and squeezed the trigger. The recoil of the fired shot was negligible, and the sound was the equivalent of a small sneeze.

The dead man pitched forward over his horse with his head a bloody mess.

Yermo pulled the transverse chamber bar out of the breech to drop another ball into the chamber. When he released the bar, it snapped back into position with a sharp click that was louder than the expulsion of the ball. He settled the sights over a second man and aimed at the same spot.

The dead man slid from his saddle, dropped to the ground, and only then drew the attention of his road companions. The second man remained a sitting duck.

Yermo's finger tightened on the trigger and another .46-caliber ball was sent on its way. He worked the transverse chamber bar again as the second saddle emptied.

"What the hell?" one of the men said and stared at the second man falling to the ground.

"Somebody's shootin' at us!" another man squalled.

No longer able to be quite so selective in choosing his targets, Yermo seated another ball and aimed toward the center of the third man who was even then turning in his saddle. When the Basque colonel squeezed the trigger, the ball pierced the man's heart and, when the animal turned, he fell backward from his horse.

The men who still lived spurred their mounts and headed into the trees. One of them fired his rifle. A puff of smoke marked his position and the ball whistled by Yermo's ear.

The Basque colonel grinned to himself. He never felt so alive as he did when matched against others who would kill him if they had the chance. He ran into the forest and tracked the men by the hoofbeats of their mounts and their panicked cries to each other. He left the Girardoni rifle by a tree out of the way and drew his pistols from their scabbards. He cocked the pistols and closed in on one of the riders.

"Do you see him?" a man hollered.

"No!" another said. "I lost him in the brush! He killed Nate an' Hayes!"

"I think I got him!" the man just ahead of Yermo declared. "I looked at him over the sights of my rifle! I don't miss!"

Yermo stepped through the trees and spotted the man frantically reloading his rifle while seated on his horse. The Basque colonel aimed one of the pistols at the man and softly called, "You missed."

The man looked up and brought his rifle up at the same time. The ramrod was still in the barrel.

Because he enjoyed the fear and disbelief that stamped the man's features with defeat, Yermo waited a moment too long. He pulled the pistol's trigger just as his target did.

The pistol ball slammed through the man's forehead just above his left eye and tore through the back of his skull. The gun smoke from his rifle obscured his face, and he dropped from the horse.

Something hummed deeply to Yermo's right. There, only a foot away, the ramrod quivered in a tree bole.

Smiling at the near-miss, blood singing within him, Yermo strode forward through the brush like a *mamuak.* When he was a child, his grandmother had delighted in telling him stories about vengeful ghosts. She had been an evil old woman who enjoyed abusing him and taunting him with those stories. At age eleven, after she'd beaten him for the last time he would tolerate such mistreatment, he'd made her a ghost and ran off to join the Basque fighters in the Pyrenees Mountains of his homeland.

The Basque colonel had never met a single ghost, not even his grandmother's, and he didn't fear them now.

"Danny!" a man yelled.

"I think he's done for!" the other man

shouted.

"I'm all for headin' for the tall an' uncut!"

Yermo didn't want that to happen. He wasn't worried that an escaping man might bring more attackers. His troops were battle hardened, so a confrontation against these backward Americans would take no time and offer no real threat.

He would, however, hate to lose a victim.

He headed back toward the trail because that was where a frightened man might first think to run. To get there, the men had to ride past him, and he wasn't going to let them go.

He closed on the nearest hoofbeats and intercepted the man a short distance from the trail. At the last moment, the man spotted the Basque colonel. The man struggled to turn his horse aside and bring his rifle up at the same time.

From fifteen feet away, Yermo emptied his remaining pistol into the man's face. The dying man hung on for a moment, and the horse reached the trail. Before it had gone ten feet, the dead man sprawled to the ground.

The last man rode his horse through the trees and stayed off the trail.

Yermo shoved his pistols into the belt scabbards and whistled. The big black

Andalusian galloped from the trees to the Basque colonel. The horse tossed his head excitedly and his nostrils flared.

Swiftly, Yermo mounted, drew his saber, and galloped after the fleeing man. As they raced through the forest, the man must have heard the Spanish horse's hoofbeats closing in on him. He turned in the saddle and saw in an instant that Yermo was swiftly catching up. The Andalusian was the fastest horse the Basque colonel had ever seen, and the best trained.

The man tried to bring his rifle around and level it. Yermo guided the black stallion to the left to take advantage of the tree line there. The man fired at Yermo, but the bullet struck a tree.

The Basque colonel cut back through the trees and closed on his opponent.

"Don't!" the man yelled and held up the rifle to defend himself.

Leaning forward in the saddle, Yermo easily slid the saber around the man's rifle and opened his opponent's belly. The man's entrails slipped through the broad slash and tangled under the horse's hooves. Blood sprayed and coated the horse and the saddle.

Startled and fearful, the scent of blood fresh in its nostrils, the horse jumped to the side to escape the Andalusian. Dying and already weak from the wound and shock and blood loss, the man toppled and spilled to the ground in a tangle of limbs and intestines.

Weakly, the man lay on his back and struggled to pull his guts back into himself.

Euphoria burned through Yermo. Killing always filled him with joy. Neither wine nor women gave him such bliss. He had tried them all and had found no replacement for the experience of taking an opponent's life or that of any unfortunate soul who crossed his path at the wrong time.

He dismounted his horse near the dying man and looked down at him.

"Do not worry about the pain," the Basque colonel said softly. "It is almost over. But before you go, tell me who sent you. How many more men should I expect to follow me?"

The man's jaw worked, but nothing came out. There was no way to know if he was going to give the answers Yermo sought, or if he was going to curse his killer.

The pupils blossomed within the man's eyes, wiped out his brown irises, and his final breath left him in a ragged wheeze.

Yermo bent for a moment to clean his bloody saber on the man's dungarees. He stood and opened the cartridge pouch affixed to the broad belt he wore. Taking his time, he fished out cartridges and recharged his pistols, all the while death lay around him.

He enjoyed the moment, and he looked forward to more to come. Albion Shaw had been quite clear that there would be more.

Yermo mounted his horse and headed back to reclaim the Girardoni.

When Preacher returned to the stable, Dempsey was spreading fresh straw onto the floor. The hostler limped only a little from his leg wound

The old man paused his work and smiled at the mountain man.

"Well, this is a surprise," Dempsey said. "After those soldiers came an' took you away in irons, I figured I'd seen the last of you for a while."

Preacher grinned. "Not yet." He looked around at the stable. "Looks like you got things squared away pretty good in here."

Dempsey leaned on his pitchfork. "I do. Don't like to work in a mess."

"I was going to give you a hand."

"Don't need it. Gonna need some more straw, though, 'cause all that them bushwhackers bled all over ain't fit for nothin'."

An' the blood stink unsettles the animals. Not to mention folks who want to leave their horses here ain't too happy with seein' it either. Makes 'em think they stepped into an abattoir instead of a stable. Makes 'em a mite uneasy."

Dog loped out of the stall where Horse stood with his tail swishing and his muzzle licked clean. Preacher leaned his rifle against a wall, grabbed both sides of the big cur's head, and roughhoused with Dog for a moment. The big cur growled happily. Then the mountain man went over to Horse and gave the animal an apple he'd brought from the general store.

While at the store, Preacher had gotten Belkin's story about the riders who had purchased all the goods earlier. The shopkeeper hadn't been able to add anything to what Chouteau had told Preacher.

The eagle gold pieces hadn't revealed anything either. They'd been minted at the New Orleans Mint. Preacher knew that from the "O" designation stamped onto the coins. They all looked fairly new, which was no surprise since the mint had only gone into business in 1838, three years ago. That designation on the coins led Preacher to believe the Basques had come in through New Orleans, probably traveled up the Mississippi River to St. Louis, and then headed west.

Whoever the Basque leader was, he'd been secure financially.

Horse ate the apple and nuzzled Preacher for more.

"Another time." Preacher chuckled and scratched behind the horse's ears. Then he turned to Dempsey. "I'm going to take those horses in the back corral to a man who can get them back to where they belong."

Dempsey looked doubtful. "The major's not gonna be happy about that. He bought them horses."

"The major's probably off emptyin' Ian Candles's money pouch to get his money back. I already told him I was takin' the horses."

"I think the major wanted them horses more than he wanted what he paid for 'em."

"The major doesn't get a vote. Chouteau agreed."

A smile crinkled Dempsey's weathered face. "Well, let's get you a lead rope."

Preacher saddled Horse even though the ride to the tepees outside the trading post wasn't far. Horse needed to stretch his legs a little, too. Horse wasn't used to staying in one place too much, and even if he did,

190

there was always something they were doing.

With Dempsey's help, Preacher tied the horses into a string, then mounted Horse and rode out with the horses behind him.

Outside the stable, Preacher got some curious stares, but no one interfered. The lead rope was wrapped around the saddle pommel. The mountain man held the reins in his left hand and his rifle in his right. Dog trotted at the back of the line of horses that followed. The big cur nipped at the horses occasionally to keep them moving.

The soldiers watched Preacher go, but no one said a word.

He rounded the fort and headed out to where the Crow tepees stood. When Preacher was noticed by the camp, Moses and Caleb ambled out to meet him. Preacher reined in and dismounted.

"Those our horses?" Moses asked.

"They are," Preacher assured him. He handed over the lead rope.

Moses took the rope. "How'd you come by the horses?"

"Settled with the man who killed your woman's brother."

"That wasn't somethin' for you to do, Preacher. That was mine." A trace of anger stirred Moses's words.

"I know it," Preacher admitted. "I'd have left him, but I didn't have much choice when that man an' his pards tried to kill me. They picked the time an' place. I just saved my own life."

"We heard a lot of shootin'," Caleb said. "Wondered what it was about."

"That would be it."

"Are all of them dead?" Moses asked.

"I killed five men. They all came together. I don't think anyone was left back."

Moses nodded. "Five men is the number Stout Otter's wife said killed him." He paused. "I appreciate what you've done, Preacher."

"I'm glad of that," the mountain man said, "because I've got a favor to ask."

"If I can."

"I'm about to agree to guide that wagon train out to Spearfish Canyon."

"The one with the men who want to build the tradin' post on Sioux lands?"

Preacher nodded.

Moses took a breath, studied Preacher, and shook his head. "Sure didn't figure you'd be fool enough to try somethin' like that."

"Me neither, but I'm going to be lookin' for an Englishman out that way. A man named Albion Shaw." Since they were heading into dangerous territory, Preacher wanted all his cards on the table faceup.

Moses thought for a moment, then looked at Caleb. The younger man shook his head.

"I haven't heard of him," Moses said.

"Shaw's supposed to be somewhere out there," Preacher said. "Maybe causin' some mischief. There was a group of riders who came through here a short time ago. Twenty men. Not from around here."

"The Spaniards. I saw them."

"They're not Spaniards. At least one of 'em ain't. He's a Basque."

"Never heard of it."

"They're some kind of fierce. I've crossed paths with a couple of them a while back. They done a heap of fightin' in Spain an' France before lightin' over here. Figure this man has, too, 'cause he came up out of New Orleans. Probably on a ship."

"What are they doin' over here?" Caleb asked.

"Might be joinin' up with Albion Shaw." Preacher shifted a little because the thought of an Englishman causing trouble out here in the mountains troubled him. "I was thinkin' you had to make a trip out that way to go home. I was wonderin' if you could hang around a couple days, till I get that wagon train properly squared away, an' we could ride together."

"Watch each other's backs?" Moses asked.

"It's a long way for two men to take a string of horses through lands known to have murderin' Blackfeet wanderin' around in them. An' I don't have much reason to trust the folks I'm ridin' with if it comes down to fightin' somewhere along the way."

Moses grinned. "Together we're stronger?"

"That's how I see it."

Moses extended his hand and Preacher took it. The mountain man felt better at having two more men with him who knew the land they'd be traveling. He just hoped it would be enough, and he wondered what a man like Albion Shaw would be up to that would require the skills of Basque soldiers.

CHAPTER 14

By the time Preacher returned Horse to the stable, brushed him down, and fed him another apple, another group rode into Fort Pierre. Unlike the party of Basques, these men had wagons filled with tools and supplies. Teams of four oxen pulled the three wagons, and the animals were hard used and nearly spent. A dozen outriders flanked them.

The men were a mix of white, brown, and black, but all of them looked capable. They rode warily into the fort and kept their hands close to the rifles they carried.

The drivers headed their teams over to the stable.

"Looks like you're going to be busy," Preacher said to Dempsey.

"I ain't been this busy in a long time," the hostler agreed.

The lead wagon rolled to a stop a short distance from the stable. The wheels and the chains on the doubletree creaked and clinked.

A wide-bodied man sat in the seat. Red hair peeked out from under a wide-brimmed that looked like it had been dragged for a long distance, had the dust knocked off, and pulled on. A short red beard looked like blisters against the tanned cheeks and strong jaw. He wore dungarees with suspenders and a cotton shirt with the sleeves rolled to mid-forearm. His bright blue eyes looked amused and fitted the smile around his pipe.

"Who's the hostler?" the driver asked.

Dempsey stepped forward. "That'd be me."

The man took the pipe from between his teeth and hopped down from the wagon to land on hobnail boots. He strode over to Dempsey and held out a hand. "My name's Rufus Darvis. I'm an engineer. I build things. I don't run locomotives."

Dempsey introduced himself, then jerked a thumb toward Preacher. "This here's Preacher."

"Preacher, huh?" Darvis asked and smiled again. "Don't have a lot of use for a man of the cloth myself, except for consoling parishioners who have gone through bad times. Too many brothers of the faith try to stand between a man and a good drink. Except for the Catholics. I don't mind them so much. They'll tuck into the bar and hoist a tankard with you. When they're drunk enough, arguing with them over stories from the Bible can be awfully amusing. I expect you're a fine fellow, but my soul doesn't need saving. It was lost a long time ago constructing some dam or another."

Amused, Preacher chuckled. The man's accent was interesting, and the mountain man didn't recognize it.

"Preacher ain't a preacher," Dempsey said. "That's just what folks call him."

"In that case," Darvis said, "I'm pleased to meet you before we get drunk together."

Preacher took the offered hand. Darvis's hand was covered in calluses and felt strong enough to bend horseshoes straight.

"Can you take care of my oxen?" Darvis asked Dempsey.

"I got room," Dempsey said.

"You don't have any competition, though," Darvis said. "I looked around on the way in to see if there was any competition. There's not. I like competition. It keeps a fair man fair."

"I'm a fair man," Dempsey said, and he bristled a little.

"Didn't mean anything by that, friend,"

Darvis said. "It's been a long, hard journey, and I've been too long without a good drink."

Dempsey nodded.

"I need two things if I may," Darvis said. "After we square my oxen away and put up my wagons."

"You're gonna need them oxen as they are for a minute," Dempsey said. "Cuthbert's got the warehouse on the other side of the tradin' post. That's where you'll want your wagons if you want them looked over."

"Oh, I'll have my own men watching over them," Darvis said. "I've got too many tools in them not to take care of them myself."

"What kind of tools?"

"Saws, axes, hammers, a couple anvils, wedges, sledges, jacks, hoists, helical wire for cutting stone, gunpowder for blasting tree stumps and rock, stuff that might be in the way, anything a man who wants to chop down a forest and build a city needs."

"You plannin' on buildin' a city?" Preacher asked. He thought of Albion Shaw and thought maybe the engineer might not be so likable after all.

Darvis smiled and shook his head. "Not this time. Built plenty of parts of cities in South Africa and other places. Buildings, bridges, and even a couple of churches. I work in wood and stone and do fine work, even if I have to say so myself. I dig in the ground to make tunnels, and I erect structures to overlook seas and forests. Nothing's ever stopped me."

"What brings you all the way out here from South Africa?"

"My crew and I have been hired to build a trading post by a man named Humboldt," Darvis said. "He's partnered with men named Cooper, McDermid, and Kittle. I was told the location for the trading post would be out in the wilderness, but I didn't expect it to be this far out." He ran a hand through his wild red hair and looked through the trading post gates. "I've got to admit, I've been to some desolate places in my time, but this is about as far into desolation as I've ever been. A lot of pretty country though."

"It is pretty country," Preacher said. Despite the fact that the man was working for Cooper and his business partners, the mountain man liked the engineer. "An' it looks like me an' you are going to see a lot of each other. I'm takin' the job of guidin' you out to Spearfish Canyon."

"That's the name of the very place Anthony Humboldt said we were going," Darvis said. "I'm glad I met you. Do you know where I can find Humboldt?"

"I do," Preacher said. "Over to the boardinghouse. They've set up an office in there. I'm headin' that way myownself."

"Give me a minute to find Cuthbert's warehouse and put my oxen away, and I'll go with you. I'll even stand you for a beer for your trouble later if this place has a pub."

"I'll lend a hand," Preacher said.

It would also give him a chance to get the measure of Darvis and his crew. The mountain man figured he needed every edge he could get.

Preacher's meeting with Cooper and his partners was tense at first, then the mood quickly lightened as a sense of adventure settled in. Opaline Humboldt remained civil, even if she was a bit frosty. The mountain man was fine with that. The woman was trouble, and the farther away from it he stayed, the happier he was.

He worried about dealing with them on the trail though. Kittle looked like a man who could hold his own, but Cooper and McDermid were unproven.

Humboldt probably had some experience, but listening to the man detail the places he'd been and the things he'd done, Preacher got the impression he had been somewhat coddled. There had probably been danger, but others, including Darvis, had protected him.

Rory McClellan was a tenderfoot. This was the young journalist's first trip west of the Mississippi River.

Rufus Darvis was a wild card, a man who had been in some tough scrapes, but his allegiance was questionable because he seemed beholden to Humboldt.

"I'm glad to have you with us, Preacher," Cooper said after the jawing was done. "Real glad."

Preacher just nodded. He was still ruminating everything and everybody he was going to be responsible for. There would be fifteen wagons in all, a couple dozen men with their own horses to act as outriders and hunters when they had the need for fresh meat, and more men who would be common laborers to join Darvis's skilled crewmen. All in all, a combined crew of fifty men, plus Cooper and his investors.

That was a lot of mouths to feed, and a lot of things that could go wrong with that many men who didn't know each other. They were going to be in the wilderness with enemies all around, and they hadn't worked together enough to trust each other.

Lorenzo and Tall Dog sat along the fringe

of the group and listened. Knowing his friends as he did, Preacher was aware that they weren't liking the idea of pushing these greenhorns through dangerous country any more than he did.

After that meeting with Cooper and the others, Preacher insisted on meeting with the laborers and the engineering crew out in front of the boardinghouse. He wanted to get their measure. Lorenzo and Tall Dog joined him for that while Kittle, Darvis, and Humboldt watched. Dog was present, too, because Preacher wanted the men to acknowledge the big cur and not shoot him by mistake during the journey west.

The meeting was short, the information somewhat disheartening, and it broke up quickly once Preacher was done. In a matter of moments, he'd learned all of the men were familiar with guns, but only a few of the men Cooper had hired had fought with Indians. Darvis's men had all fought somewhere, and most of them had been in battle together.

After that second meeting was over, Preacher, Lorenzo, and Tall Dog headed to the Scalded Beaver.

Preacher sat at a corner table in the tavern. Lorenzo and Tall Dog joined him. They all drank beer slowly because there were too many men in the tavern. Most of those men belonged to the group riding out to Spearfish Canyon, but there were a few off-duty soldiers and folks who'd ridden to Fort Pierre to trade.

"You know," Lorenzo said, "after seein' them men out there, lookin' at who knows what an' who don't know, an' that's mighty easy to see if you know what you're lookin' for, I gotta admit I'm a mite uneasy about takin' all of them out there. With all them Blackfeet in the mountains out there, it's likely some of these men in here tonight ain't comin' back."

"We told them that," Preacher said.

"I know it." Lorenzo nodded and sipped his beer. "But they wasn't listenin'. They're all young an' feelin' their oats right now. Don't want to be showed up in front of nobody. Right now, they're invincible. That'll last till they hear the first gunshot an' the arrows fly."

"Darvis's men look good."

"They do. You can tell by the scars they carry. Ain't all of 'em from construction. I seen some scars from knives an' musket balls mixed in there. I figure they're salty enough."

"There is a problem, though," Tall Dog said.

"What?" Preacher asked.

"They do not fit in with the men Cooper and his investors hired. Many of them have different colored skins and they speak different languages."

"I know that," Preacher said. "I don't think much of it. Men are men, an' they tend to come from everywhere in this country."

"True," the young Crow warrior replied. "However, Lorenzo and I do think about it. Even here in this trading post, Lorenzo and I are aware of our skin color because the soldiers and the folks who trade here are aware of it."

Preacher glanced at Lorenzo.

"He's speakin' the truth," Lorenzo said. "There's a reason them tepees are outside the tradin' post, an' a reason those folks wait for Chouteau's traders to come out to them instead of them comin' in. You might not see it as much, an' it might not matter to you, but there's plenty who it matters to."

"The country is changing," Tall Dog said. "East of the Mississippi, a man's color counts more. President Jackson moved the Indians in those lands to lands west of the Mississippi. Black men in the South are chained and whipped and branded like livestock. Lorenzo has told me about that, and I have talked to Cherokee and Iroquois who were moved West."

"It's not the same out here," Preacher protested. He wanted to believe that because it had always been true. The mountains took the measure of a man, and that was all that mattered. "There's plenty of land for anyone who's strong enough to make a home for himself."

"Is there?" Tall Dog locked eyes with the mountain man. "Cooper and his group intend to take part of the land the Sioux call sacred."

"They have an agreement with a Sioux chief," Preacher said.

"Do you know this chief?"

Preacher felt uncomfortable because he hadn't spent any deep thoughts on the matter. Until he'd found out about Albion Shaw, the matter hadn't been his problem. Now, he was more concerned with finding out what the Englishman was doing out there in the mountains.

"No," the mountain man said. "I don't."

"Have you ever heard of a chief named Stands Like Buffalo?"

"I can't say that I have."

"Neither have I." Tall Dog pursed his lips.

"It is possible that this chief is one that is unknown to us. Chiefs come and go sometimes, and tribes war within themselves and split up."

"Maybe so," Preacher said. "I don't think Cooper an' his bunch are gonna make a go of that tradin' post they're plannin' on anyway. It's gonna be a flash in the pan. Just a spark an' no ball through the barrel. Immigrant wagon trains stock up here at Fort Pierre an' go on into Oregon Territory. Likely they won't need to stop again, an' probably won't have any money to spend if they do. We'll just mosey along with the wagon train an' keep a lookout for that Englishman, Albion Shaw."

"Won't be that easy an' you know it," Lorenzo said. "You ain't one to take folks out into the wilderness an' leave 'em high an' dry."

Preacher emptied his beer, and it went down sour. What Tall Dog and Lorenzo said was true. He didn't know enough about Cooper's deal with Chief Stands Like Buffalo, and once he committed to taking those wagons west, he wouldn't walk away from them.

"We ain't havin' second thoughts," Lorenzo said. "Me an' Tall Dog are ridin' with you. We won't pick up sticks till you do."

Preacher looked at both of them and was glad they were his friends. "You may be sorry."

Lorenzo nodded. "That's right. An' that's why you're gonna buy us another round of beers. An advance against the comin' sorriness of it all."

Preacher laughed, picked up the empty glasses, and headed for the swamped bar to try to find a hole to the counter.

Darvis and his men occupied a corner of the bar. They laughed and talked loudly in a handful of languages and dialects that created space between them and the next tables, and they kept a steady stream back and forth to the bar.

The men hired by Cooper had settled around five different tables and bunched up. They had their own ribald jokes and songs they sang with full voices, Irish drinking songs and other tunes Preacher recognized. Men there kept traipsing back and forth to the bar, too.

Someone, Preacher was never sure from which group of tables, said something to the other group, evidently displeased with the amount of noise going on, or maybe the fight started over one of the soiled doves who was trying to drum up some upstairs business while the money was flowing. Immediately, the growing surliness between the two groups exploded into a battle.

A man next to Preacher threw a punch at him. The mountain man ducked and set the glasses on the counter. When the man drew back to strike again, Preacher hit his opponent just above the belt buckle with nearly everything he had.

The man sicked up immediately and fell backward into a group of combatants who threw him back at Preacher. The mountain man sidestepped the man and let him fall to the sawdust-covered floor.

CHAPTER 15

The fights inside the Scalded Beaver broke out in earnest, and Preacher stepped into the middle of them with both fists because he was determined not to get too stove up. He didn't hold back and punched and kicked and fought his way through everyone in front of him so he wouldn't be hemmed up against the bar. He caught a man by the nape of the neck and the inside of his thigh, lifted him, and threw him into a group of men. All of them tumbled down.

"Preacher!" Lorenzo yelled.

He and Tall Dog stood at the outer edge of the group and hauled men out of the fray. The surprised men yelped and hollered as they flew into the wall.

"Get them outside before someone gets hurt!" Preacher bellowed. He at least wanted to thin the herd inside the tavern.

Before the mountain man could properly return his attention to one of Darvis's construction workers in front of him, the big man's blow slid over Preacher's forearm and landed a huge right hand in the middle of Preacher's nose.

Bone and cartilage broke, not for the first time, and Preacher momentarily went blind. Still, being a skilled enough fighter, he seized the man's arm automatically and pulled. He maintained sense enough not to break the arm he held, because that would be one less man to help build the trading post in Spearfish Canyon, and he only used the limb to propel the man attached to it in the direction of the door.

Tall Dog caught the man before he could recover, spun him, and heaved him outside. The man squalled in surprise as he took flight. The young Crow warrior was being none too gentle in his handling of the fighters.

Lorenzo grabbed another man by the shirt collar, hauled him outside, and pitched him on top of the men they'd already tossed from the fray.

Preacher swapped a couple blows with a big mountain man he remembered talking to earlier, then got the man in a headlock and shoved him in Tall Dog's direction. The young Crow warrior caught the addled fighter easily and shoved him out the door.

Outside, a gunshot split the night.

"You boys are gonna stay out here!" Lorenzo shouted through the door. "Party's over! You try to get back in, I'm gonna take your hair!"

Before Preacher could recover from hurling his last opponent, a man dove headlong into him and drove him backward a few steps. He ran into someone behind him. The man shoved a shoulder into Preacher's stomach. Preacher hammered with a forearm across the back and shoulders that knocked him to the ground.

The man behind Preacher moved and he spun to face his newest opponent.

The shock of red hair identified Rufus Darvis immediately. The engineer had a big fist cocked and ready to deliver. He grinned through blood that leaked from both nostrils.

"Tempting to find out which of us would be left standing!" Darvis shouted over the hubbub. "I've seen you fighting!"

Preacher grinned and tasted blood from his own busted nose. "Maybe another time! Right now, we need to get these varmints out of here before somebody gets hurt!"

Darvis nodded. He and Preacher stood back-to-back and shifted as they needed to in order to bust up the fights. They herded the men toward the door where Tall Dog and Lorenzo kept them moving through the door to land outside.

Some of the fights inside the tavern were already breaking up, and the combatants left willingly.

After a few more minutes, the cavalry arrived. Outside the Scalded Beaver, blue uniforms ringed the drunken rowdies.

"Well," Darvis said and swept his red hair out of his face, "I don't know about you, but I needed that. Needed to blow off some steam. Things just got too tense these last few weeks riding out this way."

Preacher nodded. "We've got some attitudes to work on with those boys."

"Can I buy you that beer I promised you?" Darvis asked. "Before the Army bursts in and shuts the place down."

"You sure can. I worked up a thirst."

Ivers, the bartender, stood behind the counter with a club. He'd been protecting his wares, and a couple men lay unconscious in front of the bar.

Preacher and Darvis stepped over the prone men.

"Can we have a couple beers?" Darvis asked. He dropped money on the counter.

Ivers put the club away and drew two beers.

In the mirror behind the bar, Preacher could see Lorenzo stepping through the door. "An' you varmints stay outta the tavern so us peaceable folk can have a drink an' hear ourselves think. Bunch of no-account ingrates."

Darvis laughed. "He's standing there saying that while wearing busted knuckles and somebody else's blood on his shirt. I don't think his innocent routine is going to fool anybody."

"Me neither," Preacher said.

Tall Dog and Lorenzo crossed the floor strewn with unconscious men and broken furniture.

"Two more beers," Preacher said.

Ivers nodded and smiled. "I'll be after havin' one with you, Preacher. Gonna be a hell of a mess to clean up."

Preacher pushed two of the beers over to his companions.

Lorenzo took his beer gratefully and drank half of it in one long gulp. "Two fights in two nights. Lordy, I'm not as young as I used to be."

They all laughed and finished their beers before Lieutenant Kraft stepped through the door.

"You're all under arrest for disturbing the peace," the young lieutenant said.

"Actually, Leftenant," Ivers said, "these men are the ones who broke up the fightin'. Things could have been much worse if not for them."

In disbelief, Kraft surveyed the broken tables and chairs that littered the room and the unconscious men with lumps on their heads lying at the foot of the counter.

"Things could have been *worse*?" Kraft asked.

"Aye," Ivers said. "Much, much worse."

The bartender drew another glass of beer and slid it across the counter in Kraft's direction.

"Have a drink with us, Leftenant. I think we all earned one. An' it'll probably be the last one of the evenin'."

After a moment, Kraft joined them at the bar and hoisted the beer. "I deserve this," he declared, "because all the paperwork to write this up is going to be a headache and a half."

Preacher laughed and the effort caused his busted nose to hurt, which made him laugh again.

Chouteau wasn't amused. The trader stood in the scattered debris of the Scalded Beaver and stared at the damage.

"This," Chouteau stated stiffly, "is inexcusable."

"Yep," Preacher said, because there really wasn't much else to say.

"I should have Lieutenant Kraft throw the lot of you in the stockade."

"I don't think we'd all fit," Lorenzo said with a straight face. At least, his face was as straight as he could make it. His features were a little misshapen from catching a fist or six. "Not if you set your hat on lockin' up everybody involved in this little set-to."

Tall Dog didn't have a mark on him.

Chouteau glared at Lorenzo.

"We didn't start this," Preacher said. "We got them outside as quick as we could manage."

"I don't think your efforts saved much."

Preacher gazed around at the shattered furniture, torn curtains, and broken windows. "I suppose not. At least nobody got killed."

"Which is good news," Chouteau said. "I already have five fresh graves from today's shooting outside the fort. That's not a sight that induces travelers to come in and trade."

Preacher decided to let that comment pass because he couldn't think of a thing he could say that would help.

"Do you know who started the fight?" Chouteau demanded.

215

"Nope. It happened of a sudden. One minute, everythin' was okay, an' in the next, fists was flyin'." Preacher touched his bruised nose. "Those men are drunk enough, I don't think they know who started it either. If you ask them, all they can do is point fingers at each other."

"Then *what* started it?"

"Two different groups of men who know they're gonna have to work together in mighty dangerous country will cause some friction. You remember what it was like when we built this place. We had donnybrooks every now an' again. I think you might even have thrown a punch or two."

"I remember. We worked our way through that. When everyone involved is fighting each other, you can't build something."

"You can," Preacher said and thought back on projects he'd been part of over the years. "We got Fort Pierre built while fightin'. It's just harder to get it done."

"Well, we're going to remove the temptation of alcohol. That's never good to add to the mix."

Preacher disagreed with that because men needed to let off steam, and alcohol was a cheap, easy way to do that. But he wasn't going to argue with Chouteau in the middle of the wreckage of the bar.

The trader drew a long, even breath and pulled at the bottom of his jacket to straighten it. "The bar is closed for the night."

"Ain't no place to sit anyway," Lorenzo observed. "It ain't hardly a bar with no place to sit."

Chouteau glared at him again.

"Just me thinkin' out loud." Lorenzo shrugged and nursed the dregs of his beer. "Probably best you closed it down. There'd be some of them reprobates who'd be just as happy to sit on the floor if they can keep on drinkin'."

"You, perhaps?"

"Well," Lorenzo drawled, "I don't need much in the way of creature comforts."

Chouteau sighed and turned his attention to Preacher. "When are you planning on leaving?"

"A couple days," Preacher said. "Got a few things to tie up before we're ready."

Chouteau looked at the mountain man sternly. "You'll be leaving tomorrow morning. Bright and early."

Preacher hesitated, thought about arguing, then nodded. "That'll do."

"See that it does." Chouteau raised his voice. "Mr. Ivers."

The bartender paused in his efforts to pile

the broken furniture with Tall Dog's help. "Yes, Mr. Chouteau," Ivers responded.

"Lock this bar down and get some sleep. We'll not be in a hurry to open it again. Not until Preacher's wagon train has left."

Preacher thought about pointing out the wagon train wasn't his, but he chose not to. The effort wouldn't have been worth the breath needed to protest. Chouteau had things in his mind the way he had them.

"Tomorrow morning," Couteau continued, "provided you can find anyone sober and willing to work, round up a crew to clean this bar. Get a list to me of whatever tables and chairs you need that you can't find at the general store, and I'll get it out to the carpenters. The Scalded Beaver makes a profit — when the doors are open."

"An' when there's places to sit," Lorenzo said innocently.

That earned another glare from Chouteau.

"Yes sir," Ivers said.

Chouteau clapped his hat back on his head and walked toward the door without a backward glance. "Tomorrow morning, Preacher. Bright and early. I'll wish you good luck with your endeavors now."

Once Chouteau and the Army were gone, and all the wagon train personnel were gone, Ivers reached under the bar and came up with a bottle of whiskey.

"I reckon you lads could use something to wet your whistles back at the boarding-house."

"That we could," Preacher replied. He grabbed the whiskey bottle by the neck. "I appreciate it. You can join us if you're of a mind to."

Ivers shook his head. "Closin' early like this? I'm going to go home and get some sleep. Day's going to start awfully early in the morning, an' it's gonna be none too pleasant."

"Sorry about your tavern."

Ivers smiled. "No worries. You've made the last couple days interestin', Preacher."

Preacher led the way out of the tavern and toward the boardinghouse.

"You realize what just happened to us, don't you?" Lorenzo asked. "What Chouteau up an' did?"

"What?" Preacher asked.

"Chouteau done kicked us out of the tradin' post after he said he wasn't gonna do that."

Preacher looked back at the tavern where Ivers was locking up.

"Well, them varmints sure gave him plenty of reason to. I just hope they blew off enough steam to be ready to go in the mornin'."

"As hungover as they're gonna be, I'll bet you a dollar to a donut that we don't make it outta here before noon," Lorenzo said.

"Come sunup," Preacher said, "we're gonna start yankin' those men out of bed."

The next morning, Preacher got up just before daybreak and felt slightly hungover and bruised. Some of the bruises were in places he didn't remember getting hit in, but there had been a lot of punching and kicking going on during the fighting.

He knocked on Lorenzo's door.

"Yeah, yeah," Lorenzo grumped. "Hold your water."

"Wanted to make sure you're up."

"I'm up." Lorenzo sounded like he'd been poleaxed.

"Meet you in the dining room."

"I'm not gonna miss breakfast. Especially since we're lightin' out."

Tall Dog, neatly groomed and looking none the worse for wear except for a small bruise under his left eye that hadn't been there the night before, stepped out of his room. He had his weapons and, like Preacher, carried his rifle in one hand.

"Good mornin'," Preacher greeted.

"Good morning."

"Coffee?"

"Yes."

Together, they tracked the smell of fresh coffee all the way to the boardinghouse kitchen where Weller's cooks made breakfast.

"Herr Preacher, Herr Tall Dog," Weller greeted warmly, like he hadn't kicked them out of the boardinghouse just the day before. "I hear you are leaving us today."

Evidently Chouteau had put out the word.

"After we've had a big breakfast," Preacher said. "An' coffee. Plenty of it."

Weller turned to his cooks and had them dish up plates of biscuits and gravy, sausages and bacon, flapjacks and eggs over easy.

Burdened with their bounty spread across three plates each, Preacher and Tall Dog retreated to the dining room and sat alone. Weller followed them with cups and a large coffeepot.

They dug into their breakfasts and Darvis and Lorenzo showed up right after.

"You're up early," Preacher told the engineer.

"Some of those men are going to be hard to get up out of bed this morning," Darvis said. "I need to get plenty of coffee in me before I start on that. I planned on starting early kicking doors and pulling them out of bed. I've got to be on my toes. Some of them might get up in the same frame of mind they went to bed in. They've been camping on the trail for the last three weeks. We've worked in rough conditions before, but we usually had beds."

"You ain't gonna have them in Spearfish Canyon," Lorenzo said.

"We'll have them soon enough," the engineer promised. "I can make a bed frame in my sleep, and we'll have plenty of timber out there. Cooper told me Spearfish Canyon has a water source."

"It does," Preacher said. "That's mountain country out there. Got three different falls in the area an' plenty of water."

"That's good," Darvis said. "We'll have reeds to stuff mattresses with. I'll make sure Cooper has plenty of material we can use to make them."

"Well," Lorenzo said. "I like the sound of that. Two nights in a bed here in the fort has plumb spoiled me."

"The long ride out to the canyon will give you plenty of time to recover your lost skill at sleeping under the stars," Tall Dog said.

Lorenzo waved the young Crow warrior off and limped to the kitchen.

"Are you all right?" Preacher asked.

"Finer than frog hair," Lorenzo said. "When I was heavin' them fellas out of the tavern last night, I musta pulled something. It'll sort out."

Lorenzo and Darvis returned with heaping plates and sat. For a time, they ate in silence, but Preacher's mind stayed busy organizing the day and thinking about what might lay ahead of them.

The Englishman and the Basque would be formidable foes. But they were new to the mountains. Preacher hoped that would make a difference.

No matter how he planned it, though, he knew some of the men riding out with him probably weren't going to be riding back. He also knew he'd do everything possible to save all of them he could.

CHAPTER 16

Preacher, Lorenzo, and Tall Dog spent most of the morning rousting the men Cooper had hired as manual laborers to build the trading post. They chased some of them out of Dempsey's stable. The hostler had charged them a dime each to spend the night there. Others had gone out among the Crow Indians to stay with folks they knew. And others slept out in the tree line where Preacher wouldn't have found them if one of the other men hadn't told him they were there.

By the time Preacher got them corralled, they were down to twenty-eight men. And the journey hadn't even started. He worked them on arranging Cooper's wagons to make sure everything was shifted and set right.

Cooper was up early and ready to go. He wore the D'Orsay hat, and it looked like it had been cleaned. The man worked quickly and matched up the cargo in the wagons with the small, leather-bound ledger he carried.

When Cooper was done, he smiled happily. "Most of it is all still there. Lost a few small things, gewgaws for the most part, but nothing we can't live without."

Personally, Preacher had already earmarked some of the cargo as disposable the first time the wagons got bogged down along the way. Even though the land had mostly dried out at the end of summer, there would still be problem areas because they had to travel near to water when they could. The pulling teams and the men would need the water. Water and mud caused problems for wagons, especially if they were loaded heavily, and these were.

Preacher took the time to make sure all the loads were properly packed. When they weren't arranged to his satisfaction, he had the men unload the wagon he was unhappy with, then put everything back the way he wanted.

Some of them got mouthy about his attention to detail, but only one of them said something loud enough Preacher couldn't pretend to ignore it. Without a word, he walked back to Everett, the man who had complained, and stared him down.

"I'm ramroddin' this outfit," the mountain man declared. "Sass what I want done one more time an' I'm gonna knock some of the ugly off you."

The man swallowed hard.

"You don't like doin' what you're getting paid to be doin', you just pick up an' move on down the trail."

"I'll stay," the man said.

"Give me a day's work," Preacher said, "an' you'll get a day's pay from Mr. Cooper. If you change your mind along the way, it'll be a long an' lonely walk back."

"Yes sir."

Preacher returned to checking the wagons. He told himself that things would be better once they got underway.

Just past noon, Preacher had the wagons lined up in the order he wanted. He separated Darvis's wagons and put one of them after every three of the cargo wagons. Many of the construction crew would alternate walking, riding horses, and sitting in the wagons. The loads they carried were heavy, but they weren't as overloaded as the cargo wagons. If push came to shove and one of the cargo wagons got stuck, the construction crew that was behind the stuck wagon could help push. The oxen Darvis used for pulling teams were stronger than horses and could be unhitched to use to help pull those stuck wagons free.

Now and again, Chouteau strode out of his offices and came out onto the boardwalk to watch the progress. He didn't say anything, but Preacher knew the man was ready for them to go. Ivers stepped out of the Scalded Beaver a few times, as well.

As satisfied as he thought he was going to get, Preacher put a foot in his stirrup and swung aboard Horse. The big stallion nodded and thumped his hooves against the hard-packed earth. Horse was picking up the excitement going on all around him and was ready to go.

Lorenzo and Tall Dog sat their mounts near him. Moses and Caleb managed their string of horses alongside the lead wagon where Cooper gripped the reins with eagerness.

"Are you ready, Mr. Cooper?" Preacher bellowed.

"I am, Preacher!" the man cried back. He sounded eager, but his voice cracked and his face was drawn.

Preacher turned Horse toward the trading post gate, glanced down at Dog, and said, "Let's go."

The big cur took the lead toward the fort

gates and Preacher trailed after him as they had done countless times before. Dog would range out a ways and let Preacher know if there were problems ahead.

The wagons creaked and thumped behind Preacher. He adjusted himself in the saddle, but he still had some aches and twinges from the last couple days that he couldn't make comfortable. Served him right for mixing it up the night before a long ride.

Despite the irritating and painful catches, in spite of the danger that probably waited ahead, excitement thrummed inside him. Whatever was out there, he'd take it one day at a time like he always did.

Once on the trail, the wagon train rolled steadily and settled into a rhythm of its own. No two excursions were ever alike in Preacher's experience. Problems differed. Folks differed. The weather differed. It all added up to something new every time.

Preacher and Tall Dog rode up front and remained watchful as they followed the trail. Horse wanted to go faster, but the mountain man kept the stallion reined in. Dog ranged ahead of them, tail up and his nose to the ground, back and forth across the trail. The big cur disappeared time and time again into the dense underbrush and trees.

Lorenzo moseyed along behind them and observed the wagons and the outriders. Some of the younger men Cooper had hired quickly grew bored and wandered out into the woods to galivant around.

"You boys keep them horses gentled down," Lorenzo called. "There's snakes out in them bushes that'll plumb spook a horse. You end up with a broken leg out there, you're gonna walk back to Fort Pierre. An' if you let one of them horses step into a gopher hole an' break a leg, you'll slit its throat to end its sufferin', dress it out, an' eat it till the meat goes bad along the trip."

The young riders settled down, but they grumbled and shot Lorenzo stubborn looks. The rebellion stopped with the looks though. None of them argued.

"Too many of Cooper's men play," Tall Dog said. He never took his attention from the terrain. His paint pony, Skidbladnir, named for a fabulous ship used by the Norse gods in stories told by the young Crow warrior's father, matched Horse's pace like they'd traveled for years together.

"Yeah, I see that," Preacher said. "I think a lot of them grew up around the trading post. They know how to hunt an' fish, an' they know most of what to stay away from that's out in the woods, but they haven't

229

fought any Indians. They haven't been hunted by Indians before. Blackfeet are just a story to them. Nothin' real. That ain't gonna change till they shed blood against a war party."

"That is a bad thing about civilization," the young Crow warrior said. "It dulls a man's senses and makes him forget about all the death that lies in wait for the unwary. In my village, children were allowed to be children, but we were all taught the risks of enemies. We never forgot those."

"Civilization can turn nasty if you forget about the hazards in it," Preacher said. "You get to one of the bigger cities, like St. Louis an' New Orleans, you gotta worry about bad men more than you do regular varmints. At least with a snake or a polecat, you know the kind of trouble you're in. With men, that just ain't so. One of them city folks can shake your hand an' slip a knife in you quick as your back's turned."

"If you do not like the cities so much, why do you go to them?"

Preacher waved at the mountainous terrain around them. "Same reason I come out here an' ride over hills an' down into valleys where I ain't never been. Just to see what I ain't seen. I want to see as much as I can stand of the cities, but I want to make my home out in these mountains."

"Why haven't you built a home out here?"

Preacher thought about that for a minute. The topic wasn't something he paid much attention to.

"I reckon I ain't seen where it is I'm supposed to be," the mountain man said finally. "Or maybe there ain't no place for me. Wanderin' becomes a way of life a mite too easy for me."

"I, too, feel that way," Tall Dog said. "My father says that one day a piece of land will call out to me, and I will know to make my home there. Yet he still travels with the Crow tribe he and my mother have become part of."

"Maybe he ain't a good example."

Tall Dog smiled. "Perhaps not. He claims that the Crow tribe just has a bigger parcel of land than most."

"That's a way of lookin' at it, I suppose."

"My mother says my heart is waiting for a good woman, and that finding her will anchor me the way she has anchored my father."

"Yet she's still wanderin' with the Crow, too."

Tall Dog smiled and nodded. "I listen to them, but I do not point out the lives they live."

"Probably best that way," Preacher said. "Mas and pas always figure they're the ones to be handin' out lessons."

Five hours later, Dog barked sharply almost a hundred yards ahead of the wagon train.

Preacher reined in and took a fresh grip on his rifle. As he scanned the trees and brush for what had caught the big cur's attention, the mountain man canted the weapon across the saddle pommel so it would be easy to level in case of trouble. Beside him, Tall Dog did the same.

Dog barked again.

"Has he found trouble?" Tall Dog asked quietly.

"No," Preacher said. "That's Dog's irritated bark. He's found somethin' he don't like. If it had been somebody dangerous or somethin' dangerous, he would have already killed it or flushed it back to us."

The big cur barked again. A dozen crows lifted into the air with sudden explosions of black wings and angry cawing.

The sight of the birds immediately told Preacher what lay ahead. Now that he was aware of what Dog had found, he detected the whiff of death riding the breeze. He looked at Tall Dog.

"There ain't no trouble," Preacher said,

"but there's been trouble."

"I smell death," the young Crow warrior said.

"So do I." Preacher turned Horse back to the wagon train and rode over to Cooper. He held up a hand to stop the man. Cooper pulled on the reins and halted his team. The wagon creaked to a stop.

"Is something wrong?" Cooper asked.

"There is," Preacher said. "I want you to hold up here for a minute an' let us ride on ahead to look things over."

"What do you think it is?"

"Most likely somethin' you folks don't want to see."

Cooper pursed his lips and looked pensive. "All right, but I don't want to tarry too long. We're already days behind schedule. We've got to find a place to camp for the night."

"You let these folks come up on somethin' they ain't prepared to see, you could lose more men."

"All right, Preacher. Do what you must do."

Three wagons back Darvis called one of his mounted men over. The engineer swapped out the reins to the wagon he'd been driving for the horse his man had. In the saddle now, Darvis held a rifle in one

233

hand and rode up to join Preacher.

"Is this about the crows?" Darvis asked.

"It is."

Darvis scanned the skyline where the crows still flew in circles, and some settled in the branches of nearby trees. "That many crows on the ground only means one thing."

"I know," Preacher said. "There's somethin' dead up ahead. We're going to need to borrow some shovels. We got folks in this group probably ain't seen nobody killed by Indians before."

"My men haven't seen that," Darvis said, "but all of them have seen dead men. Accidents happen during construction that will snuff out a man's life like a sharp breeze taking flame from a candle wick. We've faced Zulu warriors, too. My men will stick no matter how bad it is."

"Good to know," Preacher said.

Darvis wheeled his horse around and called out in a foreign tongue. When he finished, four men disembarked from the first engineering wagon and carried shovels. They also carried rifles and short spears. The men trotted up to Darvis and stood waiting.

All of the men were in their late twenties and thirties. Two of them were black, one was Chinese, and one was white.

"They'll come with us," the engineer said. "They've all been with me through the worst of it. Like I said, I fought Zulus with some of these men, and those warriors traveling with me can put your Indian braves to shame. Whatever's up ahead won't break them."

"All right," Preacher said.

Lorenzo joined Preacher and nodded toward the circling crows. "Well, that don't look good."

Preacher told Darvis, "We're going to ride on ahead, see what's what. Make sure there ain't no ambushes set up. I don't think there is. Otherwise, Dog would have done sniffed it out an' barked to let me know. Keep your men here till we know they'll be safe."

"I'll ride with you."

"Might be better if you stayed here till we make sure the way is clear. This kind of thing is somethin' me an' Tall Dog an' Lorenzo are used to dealin' with. Push comes to shove, we know the land an' how to use it."

Darvis patted the rifle he carried. The weapon was a good five inches shorter than Preacher's Hawken rifle.

"I've carried this Baker rifle around three continents for almost twenty years," the engineer said. "Wellington's rifle companies carried Baker rifles during the Napoleonic War. During the Battle of Cacabelos, a rifleman named Thomas Plunkett shot the French General Colbert at six hundred yards. Maybe more. It's a good rifle, and I'm a crack shot standing, kneeling, or from horseback." Darvis grinned. "You don't have to worry about me, Preacher. I'm no greenhorn."

The mountain man nodded. "All right."

Preacher put his heels to Horse's sides and headed out at a trot. He stayed closed to the tree line to the left so the way ahead would give him a clear field of fire. Lorenzo rode ten feet behind him. Tall Dog rode to the right of the trail with Darvis following him.

Dog barked once more at the top of a small rise.

"I hear you," Preacher called. "What is it?"

The big cur loped over the top of the rise and waited.

As Horse trotted up the hill, Preacher spotted the dead man lying on his side of the trail. He held his rifle up to signal the others. Then he urged Horse forward.

CHAPTER 17

The closer Preacher got to the dead man, the more intense the sickly-sweet smell of death clouded his nostrils. He breathed through his mouth to lessen the stench, but the awful stink made the air thick and was more than he wanted to deal with.

Insects crawled all over the corpse. The birds had been at the man's face and hands, all the parts that were soft and exposed. Ragged pockmarks showed where chunks of bloody meat had been torn away by sharp beaks and teeth.

The worst thing was the pile of exposed guts that lay before the dead man. He'd evidently died trying to hold himself together. His hands gripped his intestines, but they had been strung out several feet in all directions by carrion feeders. Beetles moved through those.

"Somebody purely made a mess of him," Lorenzo commented. "He died hard. Looks like whoever done it took a big knife to his stomach an' opened him up like a water-melon."

"It wasn't a big knife," Preacher said. He raised his gaze from the dead man and scanned the woods. Even though the man had been dead for at least a day, a man never knew who was watching. "Whoever killed him used a sword."

"Like the one Cooper said the Basque soldier was carryin'?" Lorenzo asked.

"Maybe."

Dog trotted ahead and deeper into the trees. He stopped and barked again.

"Looks like he found another one," Lorenzo said.

"That many crows out here?" Preacher asked. "There's definitely more than one dead body. Did you know this man?"

Lorenzo studied the bloody face. "Nope."

"I think I remember him from the Scalded Beaver two nights ago." Preacher pointed to the silver and turquoise bracelet on the man's left wrist. "I saw this. He was sittin' with a group of men."

"You reckon that's who's out here? Them fellas?"

"Yeah."

"You remember how many of 'em there was in that group?"

238

"Five or six."

"If they're all out here, that's a lot of killin'. An' for what?"

"Don't know. All his gear an' his possibles bag are still on him. Whoever killed him didn't take time to rob him. Even left his weapons."

"That don't make sense. Not even if it was over somethin' personal. Weapons would have been took."

"Not if the killer had his hands full an' wasn't wantin' them."

Preacher rode to where Dog waited in the brush well off the trail. Another dead man lay in the undergrowth.

"They're too scattered to have been ambushed by a group," Lorenzo said. "A group would have kept them bunched up an' killed them in the same place. More or less. Made it quick an' easy."

"It was one man." Preacher pointed at the boot prints that still showed on the ground. "All the boot prints where the killer had to have stood to take his shots are all the same size. One man. An' the boots testify to that. You can see the divot in the right heel."

The weather had been hot and dry for the last few days. The ground had taken the boot prints and kept them clear.

"They can't have been dead long," Lorenzo said. "Maybe a day or so." He leaned down and peered at the dead body sprawled in the brush. "Somebody would have found them. If there'd been anybody passin' this way, they would have already been found."

"I reckon."

"Ain't nobody missed them neither, else somebody would have come looking." Lorenzo held a kerchief to his mouth and nose. "How long you think they been dead?"

"Like you said. A day."

"You think they left out of the tradin' post sometime yesterday?"

"Yeah."

"Followin' after that Basque soldier who flashed all that gold?"

"Maybe that's just coincidence."

"Man pulls out that much gold, shows it around, he's lookin' for trouble. He wouldn't have been surprised if somebody come lookin'. Might be he was plannin' on it."

"Because folks would know he spent all that money at the post an' might have more." Preacher nodded. "He could kill one group, make sure a second group's not so quick to take out after him. That makes sense."

"He had enough rifles ridin' with him to turn back anybody who might have wanted to rob him."

"He didn't want to turn these men back. He wanted to kill them."

"Man would have to have him some hard-hearted ways to set this up."

"An' be confident," the mountain man said. "Real confident."

Dog barked again and Preacher rode up to find a third body lying in the tall grass. A bullet hole on the left temple was filled with ants.

"Signs are still the same," Lorenzo said. "I'm seein' tracks left by one man. He was off his horse now, but you can track the horse, too. The shoes are all the same. He mounted his horse here."

Preacher nodded. He'd seen the boot prints, too. The heels had been in fine shape, except for the divot, and left sharp impressions.

"He ambushed them," the mountain man said. "But this wasn't the first place he attacked them. He was chasin' them out here on foot. Came from farther down the trail. Kept to the brush so they couldn't see him comin'."

"Didn't want them to get away." Lorenzo nodded. "I can see that. One man out here in the middle of the woods, him against three others, he was pretty sure of himself."

241

Preacher quietly agreed. Whoever the killer had been, he was thorough and merciless. That was something to keep in mind if it was one of the Basque soldiers. There was a good chance he would cross paths with the man, and that meeting might not be a friendly one. The wagon train would be slower than riders, so that was a positive thing because it let the Basques get on to wherever they were headed.

Unless the Basques waited up ahead to ambush them. That thought soured Preacher's disposition more than seeing the corpses.

The mountain man turned in the saddle and gazed back toward the trail. Through the trees, he spotted three more bodies lying nearby. Two of them lay fairly close together, but a sixth body was nearly twenty feet farther east.

Tall Dog and Darvis rode toward the dead men. Preacher urged Horse forward to join them.

"This was an ambush," Darvis said. He stood near a black stain that had been a pool of blood until it soaked into the earth. Ants and beetles crawled across the stain.

"That's how I read it," Preacher agreed. "Found three more of 'em back yonder."

"Know who these men are?"

242

"They could be men who were hangin' around the tradin' post a couple days ago."

Darvis slowly rode his horse into the area. "Looks like one man did all the killing."

The observation surprised Preacher. Maybe Darvis did have some woodcraft skills.

"This is where the killin' started. With these two men. That's the only way that makes sense for them to fall together. He killed that third man over there right after these two. That third man ran, but he didn't make it far."

"You sure that's how it happened?" Darvis asked.

Lorenzo rode around the site in a circle. "He's sure. So am I."

"These two were dropped almost one on top of the other," Preacher said. "An' it had to have happened pretty damn quick. He killed these two so sudden they didn't have time to react." The mountain man stepped down from the saddle and examined the ground. He gazed around at the torn earth. "The horses were all here when they were jumped." He pointed to ragged places on the ground where the hooves had been. "Riders that were left alive after the initial attack bolted. So did the horses carryin' empty saddles. You can see where the horseshoes bit in."

Darvis gazed around. "Where are their horses?"

"Either they were taken or run off into the wild." Preacher studied the sky and knew they didn't have many daylight hours left. "What bothers me is how one man could get two of these men without them knowin' he was on 'em. He come up on 'em quiet. The first shot was easy, but they would have been movin' by the second shot even if he was usin' both hands an' two pistols."

Preacher backtracked through the signs he found. Fifty feet in back of the dead men, back toward Fort Pierre, he located boot prints that were the right size and had the divot he'd found in the other boot prints. He knelt and traced the boot prints with his finger.

"This is where he come up on 'em. He lighted here an' took a moment to fix in his mind how he was going to take them." Preacher visualized the attack. "The men had been packed together, not suspectin' a thing. Not till after he killed two of them before they knew he was there. He killed the third man right after, then followed the three who survived into the brush. He hunted two of them down on foot. There are hoofprints back by the first man we found. That man was the last one killed. The man who killed them wanted to use his sword and did."

Darvis and Lorenzo remained on their horses a short distance from him. Tall Dog ranged ahead and kept an eye on the woods.

"The man who shot these fellas on his own two feet?" Lorenzo asked. "He wasn't ridin' his horse."

"Not here. He was standin'. Takin' his time."

Lorenzo shook his head. "That don't make no sense. Even if a man had a brace of pistols so's he could keep firin', that takes too long. Maybe he got the first two shots off quick enough, but ain't no way he swapped out a pistol with enough time to get that third man before he got clear. An' a pistol shot ain't so accurate at fifty feet. I wouldn't want to count on it once, much less three times."

"He wouldn't have used pistols." Preacher was sure of that.

"Swappin' out rifles would take too long," Lorenzo said. "Fifty feet wouldn't give him enough time to get off two shots close together like that without those men boltin'. If he needed to drop both of those men so quick, I could see usin' a shotgun."

"Wounds are too clean," Preacher said. "An' they're both precise. He hit each target in the same place." He tapped the back of his skull where the bullet wounds on the dead men were. "Man took the time he needed."

"The dead man just over yonder," Lorenzo pointed to the third body not far off the trail, "got shot in the chest. Put a ball into his lungs, maybe got his heart."

Preacher stood and resettled his hat on his head. "That man was movin'. For the shooter to get him so quick, he'd have had to have a third weapon ready."

"Would have needed a third arm to get that shot off that quick," Lorenzo said. "This is makin' my head hurt. Would be easier to figure if it hadn't been just one man, or if he'd had something like them Colt Patersons you're carryin'."

"I don't think the killer used three weapons," Darvis said thoughtfully. "I think he only used one."

Preacher looked up at the engineer. "What's on your mind?"

"I think he used a repeating rifle," Darvis replied.

"Ain't no such thing," Lorenzo said. "Them pistols Preacher carries are the only ones of their kind that I've ever seen."

246

"I know of a repeating rifle that would allow a man to make shots like these," Darvis said. "If he was skilled enough. This man obviously is. I've seen it done before."

"With what?" Lorenzo asked.

"Have you ever heard of a Girardoni rifle?"

"Nope."

"I have," Preacher said. "When Meriwether Lewis an' William Clark set out to explore the land President Jefferson purchased from France, they had a man with them who carried a Girardoni rifle. Every time Lewis an' Clark crossed paths with Indians, they made sure they put on a show for them with that repeatin' rifle to impress the tribes with the weapons the white men had. To intimidate them. I've never seen a wind rifle, but mountain men I've talked to have told of it. I've always wanted the chance to shoot one an' get a feel for it."

"I've seen a couple of them," Darvis said. "The weapon's construction fascinated me. Austrian troops built sniper units around those weapons back at the turn of the century. They used them in their war against the French and Napoleon. After the Austrians signed a treaty with Napoleon in 1809, they changed sides for a time and took up arms again against Russia. They signed back on against Napoleon in 1813 after he broke the peace with them. Eventually, though, the air rifle was retired as a military weapon because the model took too much training for a common soldier, and the rifle was extremely limited after the air reservoirs emptied."

"Air reservoirs?" Lorenzo asked.

"The reason they call it a wind rifle is because it fires a ball with a blast of compressed air," Preacher said. "I talked to some men who rode along with Lewis and Clark. They liked the rifle because it was smokeless an' didn't make much noise, an' because you could get off a lot of shots quickly."

"Somehow bein' able to hide like that an' not be heard don't seem honest," Lorenzo said.

"Remember that next time an arrow comes your way."

Lorenzo frowned. "Maybe it would even the odds a bit."

"The drawback to the Girardoni was the reload time," Darvis said. "After a rifleman fired ninety balls, he was done. That emptied all three reservoirs he carried with him. It took hours to pump the reservoirs back up to capacity. They were made out of brass, too, and not everybody can work with brass.

It's a persnickety metal. You have to know what you're doing and have time to do it right, because anything less than right isn't going to hold up with all that pressure."

"Ninety balls is a lot," Lorenzo said. "That can make a heap of difference in a battle."

"Yes, but out in the brush, moving across a battlefield, a soldier could drop a rifle or a reservoir and damage it too much to use. Unless he was carrying a spare rifle, he was out of the fight."

Lorenzo looked at the dead bodies. "These men never stood a chance."

"Three of them didn't," Preacher said. "The other three might have held their own if they hadn't gotten spooked."

"He was too good for them."

Preacher nodded. "Not just too good. That man likes killin'. He could have set up back here with a handful of soldiers an' taken all of these men out with a single volley. He wanted to do it himself. It's one thing to go after men for vengeance. He baited these men to follow him out here so he could ambush them."

"That'll be something to keep in mind," Lorenzo said, "if we come across him."

"I reckon that'll happen," the mountain man said. "Whatever they're out here for, it ain't for no good."

"Then we best be ready for it."

"We've hunted mankillers before," Preacher said. "Animals an' men. This man ain't no different. Might be a little more prepared, but he's still flesh an' blood."

A cloud passed over the sun sitting over the trees to the west and reminded Preacher they had to find a place to make camp. He looked at Darvis.

"Get your men up here," the mountain man said. "We'll bury these bodies before Cooper's hired crew gets a look at them. Lookin' at a fresh grave is one thing. This here is another. Ain't no reason to give Cooper's men nightmares."

"If they see this, might not be any of 'em left come mornin'," Lorenzo said. "They'll light a shuck back to Fort Pierre."

Darvis nodded and called to his men.

Preacher walked to the closest dead man, took hold of his foot, and dragged the body off into the brush. They'd plant them off to the side of the trail. He wasn't going to hide the fact of what happened, but he didn't want freshly turned earth so close to the trail to be on the minds of Cooper's laborers.

CHAPTER 18

"Perhaps they prepare for hibernation," Swift Marmot whispered. Thin and wiry, his long black hair bound by a leather strap to keep it out of his eyes, he lay behind the hill that overlooked the creek at the bottom of the shallow defile where the white men worked.

Talks With Toads was sure that the white men weren't planning on hibernation as they dug holes on the bank across the creek, but he didn't know what the men were doing. Eighty-seven men worked in groups of four and five along the creekbank. He kept counting the men and tried to keep track of them because that was what he had been told to do. The fact that they always moved through the underbrush along the creek and were all dressed similarly made that hard, but it was his job to know where all of them were. He did not want to fail. He wanted to prove himself.

The white men's shovels bit into the earth and dumped mud into buckets. The solid impact of the shovels and the plop of mud into the buckets echoed under the broad, leafy branches of the tall trees that stood over their heads. It held a rhythm like that of Woodpecker, only much slower.

A chain of several holes ran along the creekbank till the water disappeared around a bend.

Other men took the mud-filled buckets out into the creek and scooped up handfuls of water to put into the buckets. All the buckets had holes in the bottom because the muddy brown water trickled through almost immediately to plip and plop against the slow-moving current. Although Talks With Toads could not hear the plip or the plop, he knew what noise the drops made, and his imagination filled that in.

Every now and again, the men holding the buckets swirled the buckets around and peered inside as if looking for something they had lost. When they did not find what they were looking for, they reached for more handfuls of water.

"It is too early for hibernation," Crooked Snake said softly. He was heavier than Swift Marmot, and both of them were bigger than Talks With Toads. "Maybe they are cleaning the earth they want to take back to camp with them. Maybe they sleep better on clean earth."

The suggestion was almost logical, but Talks With Toads was sure that was not the answer either. He was the youngest brave among the group of four. He had only seen sixteen summers and knew he still had much to learn. His father, Owl Friend, told him that knowing how much he did not know was a good thing to know. Talks With Toads almost understood that, but he did not say so to his father because he did not want to disappoint him.

"You two close your mouths and watch," Lean Coyote ordered. He was only twenty-two summers, but he was the oldest of the four braves.

Lean Coyote also carried five scars from battles against Blackfeet and whites. He was trim and fit, broad across his shoulders, and when it was warm enough, he walked around the camp without his shirt so every-one, especially the young women of the tribe, could see the marks left by an arrow, knife, and rifle ball. Everyone thought he was so brave.

Talks With Toads believed the other brave to be lacking in stealth skills, and perhaps in the ability to move quickly enough to dodge an arrow, knife, or rifle ball. A true warrior who was good at fighting killed others and never got wounded. Owl Friend agreed with his son. Owl Friend had fought in many battles, killed many enemies among the hated Blackfeet and didn't have a scar on him.

Still, Talks With Toads wanted a scar to show that he had been in battle. So far he hadn't fought against anyone. The thought of doing so excited him and made him feel a little sick. He would never admit that to the other braves.

Across the creek, the digging and the bucket operation continued. The men who shoveled, but were waiting on the men with buckets now, ate jerky or went into the woods to make water and take care of their needs. They had mules carrying panniers of food.

One man made water into the creek a short distance upstream from the men working with buckets. When one of the men with buckets saw what the other man had done, he squalled something in the white tongue that made the man who had relieved himself laugh loudly. Evidently the man with the bucket was angered by the other man's act, and then further angered by the man's lack of contrition.

The man with the bucket reached into the creek and drew up a rock, which he threw at the man.

Before the man on the bank could move, the thrown rock hit him in the head and opened a small cut over his nose. Blood wept down into the hollow of his left eye. The stricken man put his hand to his wounded head, howled in pain, and shouted angry words at the man who had thrown the rock.

Talks With Toads listened carefully. His father believed he could understand things if he listened to them long enough. When he was a child, barely walking, he had wandered through the small woods near where the *Ihánkhunwarj* people lived. His mother and father did not know where he had gone and had searched franticly for him.

When they found him, he had been squatted down near a family of toads that lived in a hollow tree. Until that moment, he had not spoken to his mother or father or anyone. That day, his mother said, he had spoken in the toad tongue, croaking to the toads and listening when the toads croaked back to him. Owl Friend had named him Talks With Toads that day.

If Talks With Toads had ever known the toad language, he no longer remembered it.

He had grown up and lost the ability. Sometimes he wondered what he and the toads had talked about, what secrets they had shared. Other times he thought he had lost some of his intelligence. But his father had always told him he was smart. Maybe one day he would remember the toad language again. Till then, he tried to learn everything he could.

Yelling went on between the two men for a short time. More rocks were thrown in both directions, and both men jumped out of the way and occasionally got hit. The other men drew back. Most of them laughed, but they remained wary because the two men flinging rocks were not always accurate.

Then the chieftain of the white men rode his horse into the clearing and shouted even louder than the two men. He drew a pistol from a scabbard at his hip and looked prepared to use it.

Both men quieted and returned to work.

The white chieftain was an older man, perhaps older than Owl Friend, but less than Talks With Toads's grandfather, Steady Crane. The white chieftain carried himself with a warrior's bearing and sat straight in the saddle. A rifle was slung over his shoulder across his back, and a long sword hung at his side from a sash that crossed his body. His boots were polished and cared for, and his clothing was neat.

The clothes reminded Talks With Toads of the uniforms worn by the Army soldiers at Fort Pierre, but they were different in color and the way they looked. The man's hat stood tall and imposing. A man could hold many things in a hat like that.

"Do you know what the chieftain told the men?" Crooked Snake asked Lean Coyote.

Lean Coyote grunted as though disappointed something so simple eluded Crooked Snake. "He told them to close their mouths and get back to work."

Though Talks With Toads did not say anything, he believed that Lean Wolf could not understand the white tongue nearly so well as he said he did. Talks With Toads knew that the white chieftain had said something like what Lean Coyote even though he had not understood a word the man spoke.

Perhaps that was only his natural skill with the tongues of others, though. Perhaps Crooked Snake could not guess what the white chieftain had told his men.

Talks With Toads counted the white men on the creek-bank again and once more came up with eighty-seven.

Lean Coyote was in charge of the hunting party. They'd been sent by their chieftain, Eyes Cut Like Knife, to take a buffalo so the tribe would not go hungry. Talks With Toads had been excited to go. Owl Friend had made him a new bow for the hunt, this one stronger than the last because Talks With Toads had gotten bigger and stronger over the last few moons. He was convinced he could see himself growing every day.

While tracking buffalo, the four braves had cut the sign of the white men. The whites had left the bodies of three buffalo behind after taking the best meat from the animals. The white men were wasteful and did not use the buffalo the way Talks With Toads and his fellow hunters would have. They had not even taken the buffalo hides, nor had they taken care with their butchering to preserve the hide for use as clothing. They had merely sliced through it to get at what they wanted.

Under Lean Coyote's direction, Talks With Toads and the other braves had taken the hides, even cut up as they were, to be used by the women among the tribe to patch tepees or make leggings.

The *Ihánkhunwarj* were not so rich in good fortune or resources that they could turn up their noses at the scraps left by the whites.

Once the hides were taken in the best shape they could be taken, and the other meat the whites had left, including the tongues, had been cut out, the braves had buried their bounty in the ground so no carrion feeders could get it.

Lean Coyote had directed that they find out what the white men were doing up in lands the *Ihánkhunwarj* people hunted on. So far, Talks With Toads and his tribe only had to contend with Blackfeet bands that prowled the mountains and took what they wanted.

The Blackfeet made survival hard enough, but winter would come soon, and then finding enough food to eat would be more difficult. The old women, including Talks With Toads's grandmother, Silent Like Snow, talked fretfully of what might yet come because the shaman predicted a harsh winter. The summer had not provided as much bounty as it normally did, or perhaps, the shaman said, the *Ihánkhunwarj* had offended the spirits by not defeating the Blackfeet warriors and driving them from the mountains.

Now the whites were in the mountains, in the lands held sacred by the *Ihánkhunwarj*.

Something would have to be done about that. The spirits would grow restless and unhappy.

Talks With Toads chided himself for his inattention and gathered his wandering thoughts. He counted the white men again and immediately noticed the white chieftain, Shaw, was missing from the group.

The tally came to only eighty-one men.

Ill at ease, Talks With Toads watched the men work for a time to see if some of them had wandered into the woods to attend a call of nature, but when none of those missing men returned, he grew increasingly nervous.

The white chieftain had made camp a short distance from the creek in a stone canyon that was easily defensible from attack. When the other men did not return, Talks With Toads ducked beneath the hill and called to Lean Coyote.

"What?" The brave acted angry, but Talks With Toads knew Lean Coyote was anxious and only sought to cover up that weak emotion.

"Six men are missing," Talks With Toads announced quietly.

Lean Coyote's eyes narrowed. "Are you certain?"

"Yes."

"Perhaps they are resting or have gone to prepare a meal at the camp. They have buffalo meat. That will take time to cook."

"This is true," Talks With Toads said. He fought to contain the uneasiness that swam through his body like darting minnows. "Even so, we have seen the white men, and we can tell Chief Eyes Cut Like Knife what we have witnessed."

"We do not know what the white men are doing."

"If the chief wishes to know, he can send us back."

"If we tell the chief what these whites are doing, he will know then and not have do anything but send a war party."

"Does it matter?" Talks With Toads asked. "The whites are here on land sacred to our people. No matter what, Chief Eyes Cut Like Knife will send braves out to chase these men away."

Talks With Toads hoped that was true. Their tribe had more warriors than the whites, but his tribe did not have many rifles. And they would be forced to attack the whites in the defensive position they had improved upon. Many of Talks With Toads's friends and family would die in that assault.

"It matters," Lean Coyote said. "I will not go back to the chief without knowing everything the whites are doing here."

"Six of the whites have gone missing," Talks With Toads stated. His voice quavered. He had failed at his task. This was his fault. All of them were in danger. "We do not know where they are."

"It does not matter," Lean Coyote said. "We —"

A third eye suddenly opened in the warrior's forehead and quickly filled with blood. A heartbeat later, the harsh crack of a rifle filled Talks With Toads's ears. A hammer blow struck his left shoulder and knocked him off balance just ahead of the second gunshot. He was on the ground before he knew it. Blood wept from his wounded arm.

Crooked Snake got to his feet and tried to flee, but at least two balls smashed into his chest, and he sagged limply. His body rolled through the brush, and he landed on his back. His wide, still eyes stared sightlessly up at the trees.

To Talks With Toads's left, gray gun smoke bloomed from a line of brush where several rifles had fired. He was certain he had found the six missing men, and the white chieftain Shaw was among them. The man's hat identified him immediately.

"Run!" Swift Marmot bellowed and leaped from his position on the hill.

Talks With Toads pushed himself up and took a fresh grip on his bow. He ran away from the whites and plunged into the surrounding forest. Branches and brush clawed for his eyes, but he knocked it all away and ran faster.

Swift Marmot lived up to his name and quickly drew abreast of Talks With Toads.

"Run!" Swift Marmot yelled again.

Talks With Toads ran and tried to even out his stride, but he was scared and the way was treacherous. He skidded, fell, caught himself on his hands, and shoved himself back to his feet to run again.

Another volley of shots, this one fewer in number, split the noise of the forest. Birds took wing from the trees.

Swift Marmot stumbled, then he reached for his throat where a ragged wound poured blood down his chest. In the next instant, eyes wide with fear, he fell.

Talks With Toads took shelter behind a tree and glanced back at the fallen brave. Swift Marmot clawed at the ground and tried to get to his feet, but another ball struck him in the head and he went limp. He jerked and shuddered like a broken-backed snake for a moment, then was still.

Terrified, Talks With Toads pushed away from the tree and ran with death at his heels.

CHAPTER 19

Major General Albion Shaw, once of Her Majesty the Queen's Royal Army, a man who had seen war and soldiers dying around him for more than two decades on battlefields around Europe, calmly reloaded his rifle and watched the young Indian brave disappear into the forest on the northern edge of the creek he and his men had been exploring.

A familiar black rage seethed inside the general. He and his men had been spied on. His lookouts had been lax. He cursed them. His operation in this misbegotten wilderness had been discovered by the Indians. Again.

Now his enemy wouldn't stand and fight.

Those were the same ignoble tactics the American revolutionaries had used in both wars against the sovereign nation of Great Britain. Those *Americans,* labeling themselves so proud and fierce, had learned

264

those tactics from the natives and employed them ruthlessly.

Those cowardly tactics had gotten Shaw's father, Willard Shaw, captain in the 41st Regiment of the Foot, killed in 1813 during the Battle of the Thames. Captain Shaw had served under Major General Henry Procter, but the battle had turned unexpectedly against the British troops. Captain Shaw and Tecumseh, the leader of the Shawnee tribe fighting with the British against the so-called Americans, had died in that engagement. Afterward, even though dead, Major General Procter had been court-martialed for his poor leadership.

Private Albion Shaw, then only fourteen years old, had been fighting the French during the Peninsular War. When news of his father's death had reached him, Shaw had been stationed in Spain and served under the Marquess of Wellington.

Though he was part of the army that broke Napoleon's hold on Spain and threw Joseph Bonaparte off the Spanish throne, Shaw discovered he was a pauper by the time he reached London. His father had overextended his credit to buy his elevated commission in the Queen's Army and had the ill misfortune to die in battle. As a result, creditors had stripped the family home of its assets.

That old anger at the wicked whims of fate stirred in Shaw now. The war against the United States had been lost. *Twice.* The upstart country had doubled in size thanks to the land Napoleon sold them to finance his own efforts to hold onto France.

If his father had fought against the French, the Shaw name and title would have remained venerated instead of being dragged through the gutter as it had been. That loss had spurred Albion Shaw to leave England, where he had no future, and seek his fortune elsewhere.

Shaw banked those embers and concentrated on the skirmish ahead of him. He didn't know how long the Indians had been spying on him. He didn't know what the Indians knew or suspected. That vexed him. He didn't want them underfoot. He thought he was closing in on his objective, a means to strike back at the United States' westward expansion.

"What is the status, Mr. Rapp?" Shaw demanded.

Lieutenant Oscar Rapp stood at Shaw's side and peered at the countryside through a spyglass. Rapp was slightly taller than Shaw's six feet in height, and he was two full stone heavier than his commanding officer's slim build. His dark hair and tan contrasted with Shaw's fair blond hair and pale complexion that only burned and never darkened in the miserable sunlight.

Rapp had been Shaw's second-in-command of his mercenary forces since that bitter bit of business in Veracruz three years ago. Lieutenant Emerson, his previous second, had died in that bloody confrontation. Emerson had been buried with less ceremonial pomp than Antonio López de Santa Anna's amputated left leg, which had been awarded full military honors.

The loss in the Pastry War, as it had been called because it had started over the complaints of a French pastry chef who said officers in the Mexican army had looted his shop, had been unpalatable. France had used that chef's appeal for redress, and other complaints of the same stripe by other Frenchmen, to launch a fleet against Mexico.

"Mister Rapp," Shaw called again. His rifle was reloaded, and he was ready to proceed.

"Three of the Indian spies are down, General," Rapp replied. "A fourth has disappeared into the trees."

"How many were there?" Shaw itched to pursue the fleeing Indian.

"Only the four I told you about, sir."

When Shaw had dressed down the two men who had been fighting, he had spotted the Indian spies and quickly rounded up a squad to accompany him to eliminate them. Rapp had confirmed the Indians' number. After Shaw had withdrawn with his men from the creek bank, he had crossed the creek in the shallows around a bend that took them from the sight of the Indians.

"All right then," Shaw said. "Let's proceed."

"Of course, sir." Rapp turned to address the other five men who had followed them and barked orders in full voice. "Advance together. Rifles ready."

The line marched forward. All these men had served with Shaw for the last few years. When he had quit Mexico and come to the United States, into the young nation's western lands, they had come with him because they believed he would lead them to fortunes. If the legend Shaw followed turned out not to be true, they would be glad of the chance to kill and loot.

They were mercenaries, trained killers with greedy hearts. Shaw kept them in line because they knew he wouldn't hesitate to shoot dead anyone who moved against him.

Shaw led the men with Rapp at his side.

Over forty now, he'd led a life of action and remained nimble and strong. His senses on the battlefield were acute, and he'd spent almost thirty years fighting one war or another.

And he was still without a proper fortune that would allow him to return to England and buy back the family estates that had been lost when his father's star had dimmed.

He would not be stopped now, though, and he would deal the Americans a mighty blow before he left their country.

Shaw strode quickly and kept his eyes moving. The line of men at his sides were straight and focused. He took pride in how skilled they were. He had drilled them, trained them, and made them what they were. They had all been killers, but he had made them professionals at that trade.

A few feet farther on, the body of the Indian Shaw had shot lay facedown on the ground. Shaw called for the line to halt.

"Turn him over," Shaw commanded his second.

Rapp leaned down, caught hold of the brave, and flipped him over. Dead eyes stared, wide and vacant.

"Between the eyes, sir," Rapp enthused. "Beautiful shot."

Shaw briefly nodded in acknowledgement.

"Thank you, Leftenant." He raised his voice. "Forward."

The line advanced again. One of the young braves was still alive and breathed laboriously. When he saw Shaw and Rapp standing over him, he tried to move, but he was too weak from the three bullets that had struck his body.

Shaw drew a slim blade from his left boot, knelt with the rifle across his knees, and slipped the blade between the Indian's third and fourth ribs. The young Indian shuddered and died.

"Timmons," Shaw called. He cleaned his knife on the dead Indian's buckskin shirt.

"Sir?" a man responded.

"Take Baudin into the brush and find that last Indian for me. Flush him out of whatever hole he's hiding in."

"Yes sir."

Two men trotted forward and vanished into the trees.

"Phillips," the general called.

"Sir?"

"Tell me about these Indians." Shaw returned the knife to his boot and stood. "Who are they?"

Phillips had experience with the Indians in this area. Before the man had signed on with Shaw in Veracruz, he had lived in these

Western lands and Canada. For a time, he had lived among the Indians.

"They're Sioux, General," Phillips said.

"Not Blackfeet?"

"No sir. The beadwork on their buckskins is definitely Sioux. One of the tribes that live in this area."

That wasn't good. Shaw would have preferred the Indians to be Blackfeet. Those Indians didn't live out here. Roving bands of them hunted in the lands and warred with the Sioux and other Indians native to this area, but they laid no claim upon the land.

"Remind me, Sergeant," Shaw said. "The Sioux are the ones who hold these lands sacred, correct? They believe they are serving the Great Spirit."

"Something like that, sir," Phillips replied. "Their beliefs get a little muddled. The upshot is, they will fight for this place where the Blackfeet will not."

That really wasn't good. Shaw had fought zealots before, and the experience had been harsh, filled with dangers. Someone who believed in a cause, and that surrendering that cause would doom him, was hard to fight. Simply spilling blood wouldn't drive a man like that away. He would have to be killed.

Shaw had no qualms about doing exactly that. But it would take time and considerable resources to ensure that endgame. He needed to find what he was looking for before things became so costly.

A rifle cracked in the woods, and gun smoke lifted through the treetops.

Shaw tracked the report, but the forest masked and bent sounds and made identifying the point of origin difficult. He hoped the shot meant that the fourth Indian was now dead, but he wouldn't believe it until he saw it for himself.

"All right, soldiers," Shaw said, "forward."

Again, he led the way.

A moment later, another rifle report rang out and Shaw knew that things hadn't gone as well as he had wanted.

Talks With Toads fought to keep himself steady. The men following him had spotted him and were after him. The first shot had whistled by his head, missing by inches, and he'd taken cover behind a tree. He could not stay there, but he did not know what to do. Running would expose him to their rifles. They would not keep missing.

He breathed a silent prayer to the spirits.

For a moment, the white men had held their positions in the brush, in cover of their own. They didn't know if he was alone or how he was armed. Their indecision wouldn't last long, and more of them were coming.

Although the wounded arm hurt, it wasn't disabled. Talks With Toads slipped a goose-fletched arrow from the quiver at his waist and nocked it.

He didn't want to get shot. Not again. He didn't want the scars that Lean Coyote would no longer wear so proudly. He wanted only to live.

He also wanted to kill the men who had killed his friends.

Talks With Toads hardened his heart and chased the fear and hesitation over killing another man from his body. He could not harbor those feelings. He had to be cold and skillful. He concentrated as his father had shown him to do.

One white said something to the other. The other spoke something back.

Talks With Toads wished he understood their tongue. He didn't, but he sensed that the men were worried and conflicted about what to do next. The young brave made himself breathe calmly and slowly. He slowed his heart and focused.

Branches cracked behind him. The whites were on the move again. From the noise they made going through the brush, they had split up and planned to close in on him from both sides. He could not allow that to happen or they would have him.

Talks With Toads moved smoothly and drew the arrow back. He turned around the tree like he had all day to complete the maneuver, and he searched for the man on his right.

The man spotted Talks With Toads at the same time the young brave found him. The man tried to raise his rifle into position. Talks With Toads already had his bow bent, the arrow back, and his forward hand steady. He aimed and released the arrow.

The shaft leaped from the bow and hissed across the thirty feet that separated the two combatants. An eyeblink later, the arrow ripped through the white man's throat just above his breastbone and penetrated the soft flesh there.

The man jerked the rifle trigger, and the ball struck the tree over Talks With Toads's head. Bark splinters rained down over him. He slid behind the tree again and reached for another arrow.

The white man dropped his weapon, reached for the arrow in his throat, and fell to the forest floor.

The other white called to the dying one.

Talks With Toads couldn't be certain what was said, but the cry was enough to give the man's position away.

This time Talks With Toads spun around the tree in the opposite direction with an arrow nocked to string. The second man dragged his attention from his partner and tried to focus on Talks With Toads. He swung his rifle up.

The young brave loosed his arrow, and the goose-fletched shaft flew true, higher than what Talks With Toads had meant. The flint head plunged through the white man's left eye and sank into his brain. The rifle fired and gun smoke obscured the horrible sight of the man with the arrow through his eye.

Knowing he had bought himself only a little time and he had to make the best of it, Talks With Toads ran into the forest and away from the white men who dug mysterious holes in the ground.

CHAPTER 20

Six days west of Fort Pierre, with little more than a week of hard traveling left to reach Spearfish Canyon, Preacher strode through the forest ahead of the wagon train and tracked a young, three-hundred-pound elk he had first spotted an hour ago. The elk had remained elusive, though, and trailed after the main herd. Preacher hadn't been able to get downwind of his intended prey and between the elk and the herd to lay up a good shot. He was determined to take the elk to make meat for the crews.

The elk was a spike bull, one of the young males of the herd with antlers that had not yet forked. Long scratches on the animal's muzzle bled slowly and blended in with the dark brown fur that covered his head to his front shoulders.

This time of year was mating season for elk. The young bulls hadn't yet learned the proper courtship manners the herd females expected, and they ended up annoying the females. After a time, when the aggravation got too large to ignore, the older herd bulls fought the spike bulls and drove them off for a while. That had happened to this one.

Preacher had watched the young elk's bad luck, and the mountain man knew the animal's misfortune was about to get worse because the elk might not have been a suitable mate, but he carried plenty of meat the men on the wagon train could use.

The supplies carried in the wagons would only go so far. Preacher didn't want to be strapped for meat while they holed up to build Cooper's trading post. When game was present, he and Lorenzo and Tall Dog had been supplementing the stores the wagons carried. Fresh meat, whether venison or wild turkey, was always appreciated at the cook-fires come suppertime.

The elk lumbered through the woods and warily looked around. He was no longer as trustful of the world as he had been that morning. He kept pace with the rest of the herd, kept them in sight because he didn't want to lose them, but he wouldn't go back to them until almost sunset because the older bulls wouldn't allow it. Daybreak was only a few hours gone.

Dog stayed low and back from Preacher.

They had the wind coming at them, but this morning the direction had shifted now and again, which had caused further problems. A hundred yards from the young elk, Preacher angled off a direct route and moved more quickly on a roundabout approach that would give him a better shot.

When he had the position he wanted, he sidled up to a tall oak tree and knelt on one knee. He pulled his rifle to his shoulder, eared the hammer back, and laid his sights over the elk's chest just behind the foreleg. He wanted to kill it with the first shot. Even a mortally wounded elk could run for miles before its heart gave out.

Preacher squeezed the trigger slightly, took up slack, held his breath, and waited for the right moment.

Two rifles cracked to the east, back where the wagon train was a half-mile away.

The young elk jerked up his head. The elk herd two hundred yards away broke into a staggered run to the west. Seeing the herd leaving him, the young elk bolted forward.

Unwilling to lose the elk even though the rifle shots had come from where the wagon train was and possibly meant trouble, Preacher adjusted his aim. He had to trust Lorenzo and Tall Dog could handle things till he got back. The travelers still needed meat.

Preacher led the elk a short distance, breathed out, and squeezed the trigger. As distant as he was from the wagon train, he'd be too late in returning to help by the time he got there. The meat was here to be had. It wouldn't be later.

A cloud of gun smoke blocked Preacher's vision. He pushed up and away from the tree and trotted toward the running elk. Blood showed on the big animal's side. He'd definitely hit it, and it looked like he'd hit it where he'd intended. It would mostly likely soon die, but he didn't want to leave that to chance.

Skillfully, even though moving, Preacher pulled a cartridge from his possibles bag, tore it open with his teeth, and poured the powder into the rifle barrel. Keeping his gaze on the elk, he shoved the ball still in the now empty paper cartridge into the barrel. He slipped the ramrod free, and the elk stumbled and fell. He trusted the animal wouldn't get up again and stopped long enough to properly seat the ball and return the ramrod to its position beneath the barrel. Taking a percussion cap from his possibles bag, he pulled the hammer back and fitted the cap onto the nipple.

Dog ran forward and stood near the downed elk, watchful in case anything tried to take it. Since the elk weighed over three hundred pounds, that would be almost impossible, but the big cur maintained his position.

No more shots came from the direction of the wagon train. Preacher took that as a good sign. He thought one of Cooper's hired hands might have happened on a skunk or a snake and blazed away at it. A lot of those men hadn't been out in the true wilderness like where they were headed up in the mountains. Living within easy proximity of the trading post had taken away a portion of their good sense.

Darvis's crew had shown a lot of gumption. Maybe the Dakota Territory was a foreign country for them, but they knew how to act out in the wilderness, in uncertain and dangerous lands, and they traveled with practiced care. After seeing them move and take orders, Preacher had wished he had twenty more just like them. Out here around the Blackfeet and the Sioux, men who knew how to take care of themselves and follow orders were valuable.

When Preacher reached the elk, the animal was dead. The mountain man laid his rifle on the ground and told Dog, "Watch."

The big cur moved a few feet away and lay on his belly. He kept his head up and moving. The elk herd had disappeared into the woods and probably wouldn't stop for a good distance. They'd be skittish now, too. Getting close enough to take another of them would be harder. That wasn't something he was wishful of at the moment. He'd have enough on his hands trying to get his present kill back.

Preacher took out his bowie knife and cut around the elk's anus to free the colon. He rolled the elk over so it was on its back, then shored it up with nearby rocks so it stayed in that position. He split the elk up the middle, severed the windpipe, and yanked the organs out in a bloody train. Scarlet fluid spilled onto the ground. With a few swipes of the blade, he cut the heart and liver loose from the mass and tucked those back inside the elk.

He cleaned his knife and his hands in the grass as best as he could, and he whistled for Horse.

Less than a minute later, the stallion galloped up with the pack mule tethered to the saddle.

Getting the gutted elk off the ground and onto the mule was hard, but Preacher got it done because he wasn't going to chance leaving his kill behind. Too much could happen in the time he was gone. The meat was here now and he intended to take it.

He used rope to tie the elk onto the mule so the carcass wouldn't slide. The mule shifted and acted put out at the burden and the blood, stamping and snorting, but it had no problem carrying the weight.

Preacher retrieved his rifle, stepped up into the saddle, and turned Horse back toward the wagon train.

"Let's go see what all that fuss was about," he told Dog.

Eagerly, the big cur loped ahead of him.

The wagon train had stopped in a clearing near Cherry Creek. Preacher knew the place because he'd stopped there himself a few times. Many trees grew along the waterway, and it hadn't changed much from the last time he'd seen it the previous year.

Lorenzo stood arguing with Humboldt at the front of the wagon train. Moses stood at Lorenzo's side, not too close, but close enough that he and his intentions couldn't be missed. Caleb lounged nearby and quietly watched. As Preacher rode up, the young man nodded.

Humboldt had gotten more aggressive during the trip and now leaned into Lorenzo so that he almost touched him. Over the last six days, every chance Humboldt got to step forward and throw in his two cents during decision-making, he took. He walked around, proud as a banty rooster. Most days, he also reeked of whiskey.

Preacher had had about enough of the man and made an effort every day to stay away from him.

Moses and Caleb walked over to join Preacher. The mountain man swung down from Horse. Eighty yards away, Tall Dog sat mounted on his horse on a hill that gave him clear visibility around the wagon train.

"You got back just in time," Moses said quietly. "I think Lorenzo's 'bout ready to punch Humboldt in the mouth, an' I ain't sure how that would set with the rest of his crew."

"I'd pay to watch it done," Caleb admitted sourly. "I've gotten mighty tired of that man an' his braggin'. If you listen close, you'll see most of whatever he *accomplished* was done for him."

"You will lead us out of here," Humboldt thundered at Lorenzo. "That's what you were hired for. Do your damn job."

Lorenzo just leaned on his rifle and looked at the big man like he was bored.

Preacher dropped Horse's reins. Horse

wouldn't move again until he was headed somewhere, and then only with Preacher. The mountain man glanced around to take stock of the situation.

Darvis sat on a nearby fallen tree, puffed on his pipe, and watched with mild interest and a hint of vexation. Evidently, he'd decided to take no part in the argument.

"We're gonna stop," Lorenzo said finally. He spoke slowly, like Humboldt had trouble understanding what was said. "At least long enough to do what's Christian."

Cooper stood beside Humboldt and looked pained. He glanced up at Preacher and quickly averted his gaze.

"If we stay here, what's been done to them is going to get done to us!" Humboldt roared. "Those dead men prove that we're in danger!"

Lorenzo's hands knotted into fists. "Go on if you want to go. I ain't gonna stop you."

"You're the guide. One of them. I don't know where to go, and splitting up is a bad idea."

"Just follow Cherry Creek there," Lorenzo advised. "Keep headin' west. Right now, since it's still mornin' an' ain't noon, that means you're headed *away* from the sun." He pointed west. "*That* way."

"I'm not going without you."

"Good. That makes things simpler. We'll be safer stickin' together."

"Our safety is what I'm concerned about. We can't stay here. We need to move on, and you have to lead us."

Lorenzo ignored the man and turned toward the creek. He hadn't yet seen Preacher. "While I'm busy, you tend to your livestock. They could always use waterin', an' we got plenty of it right here. They've been workin' up the mountain all day today. That grade is hard on 'em. They could probably use the rest."

"We're not staying here!" Humboldt reached for Lorenzo.

Lorenzo dropped a hand to the knife at his belt. He wouldn't take chances since the man was bigger than he was and close to thirty years younger. He'd cut him and gut him if he had to.

"Humboldt!" Preacher shouted to save the man's life.

The big man spun around and glared at Preacher.

"There you are!" Humboldt yelled. He crossed the distance to Preacher with long strides. "Get your man moving! While you were off galivanting around, he decided we were going to stop here. This is the *last* place we should stop."

285

"If Lorenzo thinks we need to set for a spell," Preacher said, "we'll set."

He wouldn't undermine Lorenzo's authority, and, in this case, Lorenzo was right. Probably even being more polite than Preacher would have been able to.

"No, by God, we will not stay here one minute longer!" Humboldt glared menacingly and leaned toward Preacher.

The man's breath smelled of whiskey. He'd been drinking of an evening, *every* evening, but Preacher hadn't said anything about it because the drink had kept the man quiet for the most part.

"We're out in dangerous country!" Humboldt snarled. "This proves it!"

Preacher met the man's gaze, and he didn't move. "We've been out in dangerous country since we left Fort Pierre."

"This is different! We need to move on! Now!"

"We're not goin' anywhere until Lorenzo says we are," Preacher stated calmly.

Humboldt roared angrily and swung a fist at Preacher's head. The mountain man slid back a half-step, leaned away from the blow, and let the fist sail on by his chin.

"Mister," Preacher growled, "this here's the only warnin' I'm gonna give you."

Opaline Humboldt stood beside Cooper's

wagon and watched with bright eyes and a half-smile. "Don't let him tell you what to do!" she called.

Rory McClellan stood only a short distance away and watched everything with anxious eyes. Preacher still hadn't gotten the young journalist's story.

"I've had it with you!" Humboldt shouted. "You're an obnoxious, stubborn fool! I'm sick of your high and mighty opinion of yourself, and with what you're doing out here!"

The confrontation at the boardinghouse in Fort Pierre had festered. Whatever was going on in Humboldt's mind now wasn't just from whatever had happened while Preacher was gone hunting this morning. This was a rotting canker that needed lancing.

Humboldt swung again. Preacher shifted slightly, and the wind from the blow kissed his cheek. Humboldt stepped forward to close the distance. Before he got his foot down solidly on the ground, the mountain man kicked it over in front of his attacker's other foot. Humboldt tripped over his own feet, tried to right himself, and prepared to swing again.

Tired of the man's attitude and knowing Humboldt wouldn't quit because his anger was driving him on and the whiskey had removed the brakes, Preacher threw a solid right cross to the big man's jaw. The impact sounded like an ax biting into wood.

Humboldt's eyes turned up so only the whites showed. His knees sagged from under him, and he dropped backward to the ground.

Darvis's men cheered. Even a few of Cooper's hired laborers celebrated.

Over by the wagon, Opaline stared spitefully at Preacher for a moment, then she turned and walked behind the wagon. Evidently, she wasn't much in a nursing mood. McClellan was writing in a small journal he held in one hand.

"What have you done?" Cooper yelled. He dropped to his knees and looked Humboldt over.

"As much as needed doin'," Preacher said, "an' a whole lot less than that windbag deserved."

"You didn't have to hit him!"

"If he'd had any good sense, I wouldn't have had to," Preacher agreed. "Seems like that man keeps a mighty short supply of good sense on hand. He'll be fine. Should wake up soon enough. When he comes to, you'll want to make sure he don't get any ideas about shootin' anybody. If I have to,

I'll kill him. You let him know that, and you keep that thought in mind."

Cooper stared up at Preacher. "You're supposed to protect us."

"When I get up in the mornin'," Preacher said, "the first person I protect is me. An' I tend to look out for me all day long after that. If I can look out for others along the way who need help, I do."

Still, it didn't set well with Preacher that he'd hit Humboldt. He could have stayed away from the man, dodged him until Humboldt's temper had cooled. Of course, with the frustration chafing away at Humboldt, the man could have made matters worse by reaching for that pistol of his again. That would have been a lot worse. Preacher would have killed him and been done with it.

The mountain man walked over to Lorenzo.

"You saved him from me killin' him," Lorenzo acknowledged. "Won't allow no man to put his hands on me in anger. Never again." He swallowed. "An' him drunk an' carryin' that pistol, I wouldn't have taken no chances."

"I know. You want to tell me what started all this?"

Lorenzo nodded and frowned. "Did you

289

know Cooper hired a man named Bob Gabbert before he hired you?"

"He hired *us*," Preacher said. "And no, I didn't know that."

"Well, he did. Gabbert an' another man named Hiram Kirkland were supposed to come out here an' meet a Sioux chief Cooper made a deal with for some land out to Spearfish Canyon where he could build his tradin' post. Then, after that, Gabbert an' his men were supposed to guide Cooper's wagons out to Spearfish Canyon like we're doin'."

The story about the Sioux chief didn't sound any better to Preacher than the first time he'd heard it. He still had his doubts.

"After comin' out here, Kirkland made it back to Fort Pierre," Lorenzo said. "He was the only one of the group who did. That young journalist, Rory McClellan, told me Kirkland drew his pay an' quit on the spot. The chief they were supposed to meet didn't show up. But they ran into a Blackfeet war party followin' a brave named Red Bat Circles Smoke."

Preacher shook his head. "Never heard of him."

"Me neither."

"What does that have to do with what happened here?"

"Trouble happened when one of Cooper's men found what was left of Gabbert an' the other men that came out here with him." Lorenzo paused. "You need to take a look."

He walked toward the creek and Preacher followed.

CHAPTER 21

The mortal remains of Bob Gabbert dangled from a rope tied to a tree branch over the creek. Anyone who came to take water would see the corpse, but until that time, the thick underbrush hid it. Most of the stink of death had gone away, as it did after a time, but a faint hint of it remained.

The dead man had been exposed to the elements for a couple weeks. Varmints and insects had been at him. Most of his face was gone, and a lot of the flesh from his hands and fingers was missing too. His bare feet, nibbled down to bone, hung just out of the slow-moving water.

"You sure this is Bob Gabbert?" Preacher asked. He studied the tracks at the base of the tree and saw possum and bobcat paw prints.

"Cooper identified him at the start of the hooraw. He was the one who found Gabbert, and he wasn't none too happy about the experience." Lorenzo nodded at the corpse. "Gabbert had powder burns on the right side of his face from his eye to his jaw. Left that black tattooin' behind."

The tattooing stood out against the parchment-like skin probably more now than it had when Gabbert had been alive and in good health. Losing all that blood had turned him pale. The skin was slack, empty of soft tissue.

"Said Gabbert was missin' part of his right ear, too," Lorenzo went on, "because a bear caught him up once an' gnawed on him some."

Both the dead man's ears, and his nose, were missing.

"Knowin' that don't much help for identification now," Preacher said.

"No, it don't," Lorenzo agreed. "Gabbert was also missin' the baby finger on his left hand. Lost it to a beaver that wasn't quite as dead as he'd thought when he went to claim its pelt."

Preacher studied the corpse's left hand and saw that the little finger of the left hand was missing. "Cooper tell you that?"

"Got another man in Cooper's group, Murray, one of the hired men, who did some drinkin' now an' again with Gabbert an' Kirkland in Fort Pierre. Murray told me about the finger. Said him an' Gabbert swapped stories while they was drinkin', an' the one about the finger was one of them stories."

Preacher looked farther down the creek. Six more bodies hung from the trees on both sides of the creek. Half of them hung by their ankles upside down.

All of them had been scalped.

"What about their horses an' gear?" Preacher asked.

"Gone," Lorenzo said. "Ain't hide nor hair of it left. Red Bat and his braves took it all."

"Did you figure out which way the Blackfeet war party went?"

"North. While I rode herd on that mess you seen back there, Tall Dog an' Moses followed tracks. Only just got back before the fracas busted out. Before that, it was just a buncha mullygrubbin'."

Preacher considered the information Tall Dog and Moses had brought back. "There's only wilderness north of us."

"Yeah." Lorenzo nodded and tilted his hat back with a thumb. "Plenty of places for them Blackfeet to hide out an' come again when they're ready."

"We'll keep the wagons bunched up, not let them stagger out, and we'll put Darvis's men out as guards. I don't want to trust

294

Cooper's men to do that."

"Nope. Me neither. We'll all end up missin' our hair. Unless we get attacked by dead men."

Preacher looked at his friend.

"You heard them two shots?" Lorenzo asked.

"I did. Almost lost me that elk I brought in."

"That was a fine-lookin' elk."

"Tell me about the shots," Preacher said.

"Cooper an' two of his men, Gunther an' Ellmann, reached this spot first an' went to water their horses. When they got down close enough to the creek, they spotted ol' Bob here, that's what Murray says he called Gabbert. Murray said he thought ol' Bob was climbin' down out of that tree to get 'em."

"Ol' Bob's dead."

"I know it." Lorenzo nodded. "That's what scared 'em most. A dead man, one of 'em said, purely ain't got no good intentions." He frowned and nodded at the body. "I got to agree."

"So they shot a dead man."

"They did. I looked ol' Bob over. Looks like they both missed, though, but he's gone soft in places, an' he's all out of blood, so could be I just didn't see any new holes.

295

Maybe you want to take a look."

"No," Preacher said. "I don't."

He shook his head and banked his anger at the situation. The folks in the wagon train would be riled up for a bit. Hitting Humboldt had helped Preacher calm somewhat, but he was still feeling mean about things. He didn't want to be out there with Cooper and his party. If it hadn't been for Albion Shaw somewhere out in the wilderness, Preacher would have just passed on the opportunity.

Maybe. He didn't like the idea of tenderfeet, and a woman on top of that, out in the mountains so close to the winter.

And he'd needed something to do.

"I'll get some shovels an' a few of Darvis's men," Preacher said, "an' we'll bury ol' Bob an' his friends."

"Darvis's men do know their way around a shovel an' excavatin'." Lorenzo looked at the dead man swinging gently in the breeze. "An' buryin' them is the only Christian thing to do. If that don't touch his heart, I 'spect knowin' gettin' on with this buryin' will get us movin' sooner might do the trick."

"I agree, but those men back there are going to be mighty worried now. That's twice we've left graves behind. Ain't like we can cover over their worries, too."

"Good thing is, we ain't buried none of them."

"So far," Preacher said.

The next morning, six miles from the new graves that had been dug along Cherry Creek, Preacher stood watch on a hill that overlooked the camp the wagon train had set up the previous night. He held a cup of coffee that he'd brought up from the cook-fires. The coffee had gone cold, but he'd nursed it along until it was now almost empty.

The day was still early enough that the coming sunlight hadn't chased all the shadows out from under the trees. Some awfully dark places still existed along the trail leading back to Fort Pierre.

That darkness was almost enough to hide the men fleeing the campsite. They led saddled horses out as quickly and as quietly as they could.

"You saw them?" Tall Dog asked.

When he wanted to, the young Crow warrior moved without making a sound. Preacher only heard him about half the time, and that was a trifle unnerving. He was glad he and Tall Dog were friends.

"I did," Preacher said.

"Are we going to let them go?"

Preacher considered the situation and how he felt about things. The men leaving was one thing, but taking horses with them that didn't belong to them was another. It also set a bad precedent for any other men who might want to follow such a notion.

As he deliberated in his own mind, the men kept sneaking away. Tall Dog didn't move and maintained his own counsel.

Finally, Preacher reached his decision. "We're not going to force them to work for Cooper," the mountain man said. "And we're not going to make them ride any farther to Spearfish Canyon before cuttin' them loose, but we're not lettin' them skedaddle with four horses neither. Those horses don't belong to them. Can't allow those men to take the horses."

Preacher tossed the dregs of his coffee into the brush, put his cup back in his saddlebag, and carried the saddle over to Horse, who stood and dozed near a copse of pine trees. Dog lay nearby and chewed on an elk bone he'd saved from last night's supper and this morning's breakfast.

Tall Dog melted into the woods.

By the time Preacher had Horse saddled and put his foot in the stirrup, Tall Dog returned riding his horse.

"We are going to take back the horses?" the young Crow warrior asked.

"Half of them," Preacher said. "I won't leave a man afoot out here in the wilderness with Blackfeet around liftin' hair, but I'm not going to let those men take all four horses neither. Cooper will need them to build his tradin' post. Those men can double up on their ride back."

"What if they don't want to return two of the horses?"

"They don't get a vote." Preacher looked down at Dog. "Let's go."

The big cur left the bone, stood, and arched his back in a long stretch. He lifted his tail and loped forward.

Preacher headed through the forest and angled away from the men. Dog stayed nearby. Cherry Creek cut back south about a half-mile up. Preacher planned on intercepting the men there where they'd be far enough away from the wagon train in case things turned violent. He didn't want anyone else getting confused in the heat of things.

Only a few minutes later, the creek's surface caught sunlight and gleamed brightly ahead of Preacher. He rode over to a large elm tree growing at the base of a tall hill and dismounted. He left Horse ground tied and carried his rifle in both hands.

Tall Dog climbed down from his mount and carried his rifle, too.

"No firin' till I fire," Preacher told his companion. "Ain't no sense in hurtin' them boys because they're feelin' a mite skittish about things after ol' Bob an' his friends were found hangin' in the trees."

Tall Dog nodded.

"If they display bad judgment," Preacher went on, "we'll empty those saddles an' not take chances on gettin' ourselves hurt. Right now, those men have signed on as horse thieves, and you have to work hard to find a varmint lower than that."

"If we let them have two horses they do not own," the young Crow warrior said, "does that not make us horse thieves?"

It was a way of thinking about things.

"No. We're just bein' generous. We make them leave out of here on foot, it'd be the same as murderin' 'em. Me and you and Lorenzo are going to earn our keep with this little folderol. We'll be worth those two horses Cooper and his partners will lose to see those men safe."

"When those men quit the wagon train, their safety was no longer something we had to protect."

300

"I agree, but we're going to do it anyway."

"Why?"

"Because I won't leave them out here afoot on account of them bein' stupid."

"All right." Tall Dog was quiet for a moment. "This is not a chance every man would give them, but I agree with you."

A few minutes later, the four deserters came into view, riding their mounts at a quick trot. They had followed the bend of the creek. That way through the woods had taken longer, and they'd probably taken it because they were afraid of getting lost.

When they were fifty yards away, Preacher stepped from behind the elm and dropped his sights over the lead man. Tall Dog fell in beside him like he'd been doing it for years and aimed his rifle. Dog took his place in front of Preacher, bristled up, and growled menacingly.

"You need to stop right there," Preacher said loud enough the men could hear him. They hadn't yet seen him. He eared the rifle's hammer back to emphasize his point.

The men drew rein and looked uneasy.

"What are you doin', Preacher?" one of the men asked.

He was jowly and had a cocked eye. His beaver hat was bare in places and looked ill-used. After a moment, Preacher remembered the man's name was Tomlinson.

"Came out here to shoot some horse thieves," the mountain man said. "Myself, I thought it was a mite early for foolishness like this, but you can't always know when horse thieves will strike."

"We're not horse thieves," Tomlinson protested.

"Those ain't your horses," Preacher said. "When nobody back at the camp was lookin', you took 'em. That's horse thievin'. If you want, we can ride on back an' see what Cooper an' his friends think of it. Maybe they'll see it differently."

"No," Tomlinson said. "I'd rather not do that."

"All right."

Tomlinson wiped at his mouth with the back of his hand. "Didn't mean to be horse thieves. Just can't stay here no more. Not after seein' what them Blackfeet did to Bob Gabbert an' his crew. We talked last night. We just want to get on back to home. We took the horses because the fort is too far to walk back to. An' there's Indians out there."

"You signed on to do a job," Preacher said.

"Can't do it if we're dead."

"You'll have a better chance of gettin' out of here alive if you stay with the wagon train. You go off by yourself, just the four of you, you're takin' a mighty big risk."

"Me an' you are of two different minds regardin' that," Tomlinson said. "We signed on to build a tradin' post, not to end up buried out here. Cooper was supposed to have permission from the Indians to build his fort."

"From the Sioux. Not from the Blackfeet. The Blackfeet killed those men we found yesterday."

Tomlinson shook his head stubbornly. "I ain't takin' no chances."

"I'm not going to stop you from leavin' since you're set on it," Preacher said. "This is a free country. But them horses ain't free."

Tomlinson hardened his voice. "We're four men to your two. You might want to consider the odds."

"I have," Preacher said. "Here's how you and your friends goin' for your guns would play out: I'll empty your saddle. My friend here," the mountain man nodded slightly in Tall Dog's direction, "will take his pick of the other three. That gets it down to two really quick. That big cur in front of me will take one of those two left over before that man has time to blink. Then it'll depend on whether Tall Dog or I shoot the last man with a pistol. Might not be that easy, but I suspicion it will be. Either way, you're not going to be here to see it."

Tomlinson looked at his companions. They looked away from their leader. None of them wanted to buck Preacher's idea of how the situation would be resolved.

"We don't have a chance getting out of here afoot," Tomlinson said. "You've got to know that."

"I'll let you take two of the horses," Preacher said. "You can ride double all the way back to Fort Pierre, and I wish you good luck. When you get to the fort, you turn those horses over to Dempsey at his stable and have them looked after and held till Cooper and his folks get back there."

"Two horses!" Tomlinson growled.

"Best offer I can give you," Preacher said, "and it's more than you deserve. Now get on to decidin' what you're going to do. I haven't had breakfast yet, and it smelled good. I sure don't want to miss it."

Tomlinson looked around at his companions, then he said, "Frisco an' Pete, you boys climb on down an' mount up between me an' Matthew. Give your horses to Preacher."

A brief argument ensued, but neither of the men whose names were called was much in favor of putting up a fight. They dismounted and led the horses toward Preacher.

"Tie them to that tree there," Preacher said. He waved his rifle to a lone white spruce.

The men tied the horses to the tree and mounted up behind the other two men. Without a word, Tomlinson and the other man headed their horses farther along the creek.

Preacher settled back into the trees and watched them go.

"We'll give 'em a minute to get good and gone," the mountain man said. "I don't think they'll be back, but I'd rather be sure."

Tall Dog nodded and leaned against a cottonwood. "Cooper's not going to be happy."

"I expect not," Preacher said.

"You let those men take our horses?" Cooper stared at Preacher in disbelief.

"Two horses," Preacher said. "They took four. We brought the other two back."

"They were *our* horses," Humboldt said. The big man kept his distance and stayed on the other side of the cook-fire where Cooper and his companions had settled for breakfast. The left side of his jaw had turned an impressive eggplant purple. "You had no

305

right to give them away. They were ours."

"I didn't give them away," the mountain man said. He allowed some of his irritation to seep into his words. Humboldt wasn't going to learn. "Tall Dog and I stopped Tomlinson and those others from takin' all four horses. If we hadn't caught them, they'd all be gone."

"You *lost* two horses," Humboldt said. "There's no excusing that."

"Maybe you'd like to ride after 'em and bring those horses back," Preacher said. "I wouldn't recommend it. Those Blackfeet that killed Bob Gabbert and the men ridin' with him are likely still out there lookin' to take more scalps. I warned Tomlinson an' those other men about that, too. They rode on, but I'll bet they'll be mighty skittish. If you set out now, it probably won't take you long to catch them."

"That's your job!"

"No," Preacher said coldly, "it's not. I signed on to take you to Spearfish Canyon, not chase down horse thieves. I intend to take you there. Unless that's not what you want me to do anymore."

Tom Kittle rose from where he'd been sitting on a small milking stool near the fire. While Humboldt struggled to figure out what to say, Kittle set his cup on the stool, stepped up quick, and put a hand on the man's chest to back him off.

"Preacher," Kittle said, "you're right. You were hired to guide us to Spearfish Canyon and help us get started on the trading post. That's what we want you to do." He turned his attention to Humboldt and spoke in a low voice that didn't carry past Preacher. "You had better get hold of yourself, Anthony Humboldt. If you drive Preacher away, do you really expect these men we hired at Fort Pierre to follow us through hostile country without him?"

Humboldt worked his jaw fiercely and winced.

"On top of that," Kittle continued, "if Preacher and Tall Dog had set those men out on foot, or had killed them, do you think the rest of the men following us would remain with this wagon train?" The man paused. "Because I don't."

Finally, looking angry and frustrated that he'd lost the battle, Humboldt turned and walked toward his wife, who had been standing at the side of Cooper's wagon. Before he reached her, she spun from him and walked away.

The relationship between Humboldt and his missus was going to be a problem. Preacher didn't care for it and decided he'd keep his distance even farther back than he had already been doing. He couldn't wait to get shut of them.

Kittle reached for the coffeepot sitting on a small pile of banked coals and took it up. He looked at Preacher.

"I expect you've got a cup somewhere?" Kittle asked.

Preacher stepped back to Horse and got his cup from the saddlebag. When he returned to Kittle and the coffeepot, the man poured him a steaming cup full.

"I'm not going to advise you on how to handle Humboldt," Kittle said. He put the coffeepot back on the coals and stood to face Preacher. "I think you're doing a fine job so far. I would have handled yesterday the same way you did. Don't want to kill a man until you're sure you have to. I might not have stopped with just hitting Humboldt the one time. I probably couldn't have held myself back once I got started."

Preacher sipped his coffee and didn't say anything.

"Humboldt talks a good game," Kittle said, "but he's only ever bought men. He's never led them. I expect he doesn't know the difference."

"Probably not," Preacher allowed.

"The other problem is, Humboldt let his

wife come out here, too. I can't, with a clear conscience, just leave her out here. I suppose I can't leave him either if it came to it. Not as long as she insisted on staying with him, and right now I think that's probably what she'd do. I don't think you would leave her out here either. For the same reason you gave Tomlinson and those other men those two horses. You couldn't stop them from going, so you gave them the best chance you could without cutting too deeply into what we need."

"Two horses or four horses, it won't matter. As long as they don't have bad luck, they should get on back to Fort Pierre in one piece."

"I hope so." Kittle gazed around at the campsite. "It'll be hard for morale if they don't."

All the men were busy getting the teams hitched, squaring the loads, putting their bedrolls into one of the wagons, and finishing their breakfasts or a final cup of coffee.

"The good thing is," Kittle said, "we're halfway to Spearfish Canyon. You might want to hang onto that thought."

"I'm countin' down the days," Preacher said.

He finished his coffee and went to check on Lorenzo, Moses, and Caleb. The moun-

tain man had an itch between his shoulder
blades that he couldn't ignore. Something
was in the wind.

CHAPTER 22

Talks With Toads rode his paint horse only a short distance from Chief Eyes Cut Like Knife. Forty braves, half of the warriors in Talks With Toads's tribe, rode in a staggered line through the forest toward the creek where the white chieftain Shaw had killed Lean Coyote, Crooked Snake, and Swift Marmot four days ago.

Alone, feverish, and hungry because he hadn't dared stop to hunt, Talks with Toads had walked back to his tribe's camp and finally reached his people two days ago. Once the guards had recognized him and realized he wanted to talk to Chief Eyes Cut Like Knife, Talks With Toads had sat in the chief's tepee, had his wound bandaged, and recounted the tale of how the others had been killed.

Eyes Cut Like Knife listened quietly and asked only a few questions. By nature, the chief watched quietly while others talked and made decisions. He did not brag like some of the warriors did, nor did he have to beg for attention as others sometimes did.

The chief was a great hunter and a mighty warrior. All the braves respected him because he kept them safe and cared for. Hunting was good in the lands that Eyes Cut Like Knife chose for them to make camp. He followed the old ways and led them to buffalo within the sacred lands by reading the stars. He watched the skies and knew when the weather was going to turn bad before it did.

He kept his people safe from the Blackfeet and he kept his people fed, even the old and the sickly.

After he had heard Talks With Toads's story, Eyes Cut Like Knife had selected many of his best warriors to ride out with him to seek the white chieftain Shaw.

Talks With Toads took pride in the fact that his chieftain had told him to come along, but he feared the whites and their rifles. Only a few warriors among his tribe had rifles, and they seldom used them. Gunpowder and lead were too hard to acquire.

Owl Friend, Talks With Toads's father, remained behind with the other warriors to defend the tribe against any who might attack. Before Talks With Toads had left, his father had given him his best bow.

"If you should have to, my son," Owl Friend had said, "shoot straight and live."

Hooves beat against the ground ahead of them and drew Talks With Toads's full attention.

Eyes Cut Like Knife held up a hand to stop his warriors where they were. The braves vanished into the trees in a ragged line. Then the chief sat with his bow in one hand and held an arrow nocked to string in the other. The quiver over his shoulder was filled with many more arrows.

The chief had seen forty winters, but he was still broad shouldered and powerful. He wore his thick black hair in braids. Hints of silver caught the morning sun. His face was sharp and hard, like it had been cut from flint. His eyes were black and could see into a man to his most secret self.

At least, that was what Talks With Toads had been told by his father and his uncle. When Eyes Cut Like Knife looked at a man, all that man's defenses were laid to waste and his secrets were exposed.

When he had told his story two days ago, Talks With Toads had felt like that — like his chieftain stared into the depths of him.

That was why he had told Eyes Cut Like

Knife how scared he had been that he was going to die during the battle with the white chieftain Shaw. Talks With Toads had determined not to speak of that to anyone. Yet he had opened up and even wept during the conversation with his chieftain. That weakness had embarrassed him the most.

Chief Eyes Cut Like Knife had reached over to Talks With Toads and placed a hand on his unwounded shoulder. The chief had gazed into his eyes and restored his spirit. The tears had stopped, and the young brave had felt strong again.

Talks With Toads locked onto that strength again now. He held an arrow nocked to string and took a fresh grip on the bow his father had given him. Around him, the warriors spread out so they would not be clustered and easy prey for the whites' rifles if they should chance upon them in the wooded hills.

A moment later, Hawk Strikes rode up to them and addressed Eyes Cut Like Knife. Hawk Strikes was the tribe's best scout and tracker. When deer and buffalo were difficult to find, Hawk Strikes could find them.

"The white chieftain and his men are gone," Hawk Strikes said.

"Do you know in what direction they went?"

"There are tracks of many riders. They will be easy to follow."

"What of our dead?"

"They lie where they fell."

Eyes Cut Like Knife nodded. "They have not been savaged?"

"No."

"The holes in the earth are still there?"

"Yes."

The chief was quiet for a moment. "We will go there. Our braves need proper burials. That must come first. Then we will have our revenge."

Eyes Cut Like Knife urged his horse forward. The other braves and Talks With Toads followed. They wound steadily through the trees toward the creek. Dread built up in Talks With Toads but he kept it tightly covered.

Only a short time later, Talks With Toads stared down at Swift Marmot's swollen body. Small, relatively bloodless wounds showed where animals and insects had been at the dead flesh.

Talks With Toads pushed away the pain and confusion that roiled within him at the sight of his friend. He didn't think a warrior was supposed to feel such weakness. His newly cut hair swept across the back of his neck. He had shorn it himself on his walk back to the camp of his people to show his grief. He had hoped to cut away his grief with it. That had not happened.

"Did my son die slowly and in pain?" Brave Bear asked.

The man stood on the other side of Swift Marmot's body. He was Swift Marmot's father. Brave Bear had three daughters. Swift Marmot had been his only son. Brave Bear's hair was cut in a ragged angle. His face was impassive, but his color was lighter than normal.

"No."

Talks With Toads believed that was true. For Swift Marmot, he hoped that was true, and for his father. Knowing his only son died in pain would be a hard burden to carry. Talks With Toads knew about such burdens now.

"The white men's rifles roared." The thunder crashed in Talks With Toads's mind again and his voice cracked. From nowhere, winter blew its breath across the young brave's neck and his scalp tightened. "Swift Marmot and the others died quickly. There was nothing I could do but run. Lean Coyote perished where he stood, without knowing the attack was coming. Crooked Snake, Swift Marmot, and I fled because we were outnumbered and we had no defensive position. They came upon us before we knew they were there."

The image of Swift Marmot falling to the ground played again and again in Talks With Toads's mind. He wished he could shut it out. More than that, he wished it had never happened.

Brave Bear placed a hand on Talks With Toads's shoulder. "You did the right thing. You had to run. If you had stayed, you too would lie here now. No one would have brought the story to us or told us where to find my son and the others so quickly."

"I put arrows into two of the white men. I think I killed one of them. Maybe both." Talks With Toads had trouble remembering. Everything had happened so fast, and he had been in pain from his wound.

"You did well."

"I did not kill enough of them."

"We will find the rest of the whites," Brave Bear promised. "We will take our vengeance and those men will all die."

The grieving father opened the burial blanket he had brought for his son and laid it over Swift Marmot's body.

Other braves around them worked to build platforms in the nearby trees where they could place the other two bodies. As they tied branches together to create a proper burial spot, the shaman, Dream Keeper, burned sage and made good medicine to send the dead on their way along a clearly marked path.

Dream Keeper sang the old songs, the ones that promised the *Ihánkhunwarj* would live in peace and harmony with plenty to eat and warmth in the winter. They filled Talks With Toads's heart and kept him whole.

Talks With Toads helped Brave Bear place Swift Marmot into the burial blanket. When they had the body laid properly, they carried it to one of the trees that had been prepared. The other braves helped Brave Bear lift his dead son into the tree.

"May I have gifts to supply my son properly that he may begin his journey?" Brave Bear asked the gathered warriors.

The braves passed up pemmican, a few arrows, and Swift Marmot's bow, tomahawk, and knife. Brave Bear laid those items with his dead son.

Talks With Toads took his necklace off and held it up. Sunlight caught the obsidian flint and turned it pale gray and translucent. The piece of flint was a treasured thing. He had found it along the Knife River where the ancient peoples had lived and quarried the stone for tools. Swift Marmot had been with him. The oval shape with edges keen as a blade had captured their attention.

During that trip, Talks With Toads's father had helped him cut the hole through the stone's center so the leather thong could be worked through it. He had worn the flint for six winters and always been proud of it.

Talks With Toads handed the necklace up to Brave Bear. The brave knelt in the tree beside his son.

"For Swift Marmot," Talks With Toads said.

Brave Bear allowed the stone to dangle from the leather thong. "I remember this. This is a precious gift. Are you certain?"

"Yes," Talks With Toads replied. He would not have it any other way.

"Thank you." Brave Bear placed the necklace on the blanket beside his dead son. "He will wear this in the next life and remember you."

"I will also take the scalps of three white men for Swift Marmot," Talks With Toads said. His voice was strained, but that was a promise he meant to keep.

"Why do you think the white men dug these holes?" Eyes Cut Like Knife stood on the edge of one of the holes along the creekbank

319

and peered down into it.

Nothing could be seen in the holes. Talks With Toads had already peered into three of them. He'd climbed into one of them to search further, but he'd found nothing and only gotten his moccasins muddy. The bottom of the hole was soft and held water.

Dream Keeper, who was older and wiser than Eyes Cut Like Knife in the ways of white men, stood beside the chief and looked angry.

"This is bad medicine," the shaman said. "This is part of the craziness of the white men. They seek the yellow metal."

"There is no yellow metal here," Eyes Cut Like Knife said. "This is a holy place. Where our people came into the world. The spirits would not put the yellow metal here to tempt the whites."

Dream Keeper opened his hand to show the chief. "I have found this in one of the holes."

On the shaman's callused palm, a tiny kernel the color of fresh corn caught the bright sun and gleamed.

"There are stories," Dream Keeper said, "of hunters who found the yellow metal around here." The shaman closed his hand over the small object, and Talks With Toads felt relieved when he could no longer see it.

Dream Keeper waved his fist to indicate the mountains. "In those days, they found it and hid it at the bottom of a river so none of the white men traveling through the mountains could find it and become crazed."

Several of the warriors who stood watching growled in dismay and displeasure.

Talks With Toads's mouth turned dry. He had heard the stories about the yellow metal and the way it made white men feel. They often sought the yellow metal even though it cost them their own lives. They did not hesitate to kill anyone who stood in their way.

Rides Far Traveler, a brave known to many in the area, had brought up stories of the white men and their evil ways from the lands to the south. The Comancheros were some of the worst. Those men traded women and children to get their hands on the yellow metal.

"Is there more of that cursed rock?" Eyes Cut Like Knife asked.

"I have seen no more," Dream Keeper said.

"They could have taken all the yellow metal except that piece," Brave Bear said.

Eyes Cut Like Knife thought for a moment, then shook his head. "Either they did not find this, or they found only a little and have decided to dig somewhere else."

"The whites knew Talks With Toads escaped them," Bent Goose said. He was one of the older warriors and, when he spoke, men listened. "It could be that they left because they knew we would come."

"They have rifles," Eyes Cut Like Knife said. "They have shown a love of killing. I do not think they left because they feared our retribution." He waved to encompass the creekbank. "Look at all these holes. These men are greedy. I believe they left because they believed they would have better luck somewhere else." He paused. "Still, they may have found the yellow metal here, so they may return one day. They will come to believe they missed what was here. I have seen the white men do this."

"The whites cannot be here," Dream Keeper said. He flung the bit of yellow metal into the creek and it plipped as it sank beneath the water. "These are sacred lands. Our people were born here and spread out into the mountains from these lands. No one except the animals are supposed to live here. The spirits have made that plain."

"I know," the chief said.

"We must drive this white chieftain Shaw from these mountains."

"We will." Eyes Cut Like Knife urged his horse north, in the direction Hawk Strikes had said the whites went.

Talks With Toads took his place among the warriors and rode with them. He didn't look forward to facing the white men's rifles again. If he fell in battle, he hoped he lived long enough to honor the promise he'd made to Brave Bear and to Swift Marmot.

He would take three scalps.

CHAPTER 23

Hunkered in the cool, dark shadows beneath the trees that speckled the tall, rocky hill overlooking the game path running alongside the creek twenty feet below his position, Red Bat Circles Smoke watched the four men riding double on their horses.

His scout had cut their sign an hour ago. It was immediately evident that the men didn't know the country and were following the creek. Their destination had been easy to guess, so Red Bat had gotten ahead of them and set up the ambush in this spot.

The men talked in their accursed white tongue, and their voices cracked and strained from the fear that filled them. Nervously, they glanced around. They sensed they were being followed. All the birds in the area had left, and even the frogs had quieted. A few fish and turtles surfaced in the water but quickly headed back into the depths.

A pair of red-winged blackbirds broke from the cattails that grew along the creek and skimmed the water for a moment before they disappeared around a bend. Their outraged cries vanished with them.

One of the whites riding behind another raised his rifle and pointed it in the direction the birds had come from. The white holding the reins grabbed the rifle barrel and yanked it down.

"Don't be a fool, Parsons! That was just birds!" The anger in the voice of the white controlling the horse was naked and hot. "You shoot an' you'll have every one of those red devils down on top of us."

"They're out there, Tomlinson." The other man lowered his rifle reluctantly. "I can feel them watchin' us."

"Shut up!" Tomlinson ordered. "If they were out there, they would have attacked by now."

Red Bat smiled to himself. The Blackfoot warrior was rangy and strong, at home in the woods. He had seen twenty-six winters. He wore his black hair long and braided down his back. Scars from abuse, bad luck, and vicious men marred his face. Still, even with those scars, he considered himself a handsome man. Girls looked at him, and women did, too. If he belonged to a tribe, he could have had his pick of available women.

That was impossible, though, because his life had not run true. He was a warrior of his own making despite the harsh path the Sioux had put him on so many years ago. He hated them, but he hated the whites even more than the Sioux. The Sioux had killed his father and older brother during a raid the Blackfeet committed. Those losses were understandable, because the Sioux sometimes warred with the Blackfeet, but those deaths were not desirable.

White men, though, had found his tribe's camp, then shorn of so many warriors in the battle with the Sioux. The whites had used their rifles to kill the few remaining Blackfeet warriors. Their bodies had hit the ground, and the thirsty earth drank down their life's blood.

Afterward, the whites had killed the small children and used the women. When the whites were done with the women, they kept a handful of them to use again later, took a few of the young boys, and forced them to walk south where they planned to trade them to the Comancheros, who in turn would sell them to the Spanish.

The way had been long and hard. Red Bat's older sister, one of the unlucky few young women who had been chosen to serve the whites, finally, just before they reached the land of the Comancheros, succeeded in killing herself. She had tried twice before but the whites had saved her. The men had delighted in her efforts to free herself through death, and had taken joy in denying her that. She had feared the rough handling of the Comancheros, and the white men had spurred on that fear.

When the whites rode on, they left her body in the open for the creatures to take. Red Bat had never wept since that day.

In the Comanchero lands, Red Bat had been captured and later sold to a man named Tobit Moon Deer. The Comanchero traded with the whites and the Blackfeet. He showed no favorites.

For seven years, Red Bat had labored for Mexican ranchers in lands that were now part of Texas. He had endured the whip, harsh treatment, and unending work in the horrible heat that filled the South. He had grown taller and stronger surviving those hardships, and he had waited until he could escape.

In the end, he had won his freedom, taken a horse and weapons, and rode north till he returned to his home. He had learned Spanish and English, and he had learned how to battle man and beast. He was known as a warrior, and as a brave who would brook no trespass by any man.

Upon his return to a tribe that had kinship with his own lost people, Red Bat had been unable to temper his hate for the whites. He hunted them wherever he found them despite the chief's warning, and he dared go as far as Fort Pierre to kill more. As a result, he had drawn the Army into more confrontations with his adopted tribe, to the point that the chief had moved the camp to less hospitable lands to avoid the vengeance-seeking whites.

Eventually, the chief blamed Red Bat for the move and drove him from the tribe. Twenty-six of the tribe's young warriors who had often followed Red Bat to hunt the whites rode with him. They had been hunting and raiding for two years. Red Bat didn't want to face another harsh winter without the proper supplies and a good location. He raided now to gain the things he needed.

The wagon train headed west drew him because it was wealth on wheels, possibly enough for him to build and equip a larger war party, but he didn't have enough warriors to take it by force. Before he rode directly against them, he wanted to winnow their numbers, and he had a plan to do that. He would instill fear in them, and they would look to saving their own lives and abandon the cargo they protected because it could not be moved so quickly.

The nine Blackfeet warriors he had assigned to this ambush peered down on the whites along the creekbank. The Blackfeet held arrows nocked to bowstrings and waited with anticipation that their leader could feel.

"Do not kill the men," Red Bat commanded in a low voice that was masked by the creek's slow current where the riders were. He wanted them alive. For now. "Do not injure the horses."

The horses were invaluable.

His warriors said nothing, but they heard what the riders said.

"We need to run these horses for a while," Parsons complained loudly. "We need to get out of this place."

"The horses are tired," Tomlinson said. "If we push them, they'll pull up lame an' then we'll be afoot. If you want, you can climb down an' run on ahead."

Red Bat loosed the arrow he held nocked and the shaft sprang from the bow with a liquid hiss. The sharp flint point struck Tomlinson in the leg, punctured the flesh, slid around the bone, and pierced the saddle pommel.

Tomlinson yelled in pain and surprise, and he dropped the reins he'd held, but he put his boots to the horse's sides and the animal bolted. Another arrow lifted Tomlinson's hat from his head.

Caught unprepared, Parsons fell backward off the horse and thumped to the ground. A quivering arrow protruded from the man's right shoulder and, when he rolled to his feet, it snapped off to leave a jagged end only a couple inches long. He raised his rifle and stared into the trees.

"Indians!" Parsons bellowed.

Another arrow sank into his left thigh, and a third pierced his left calf. He fired the rifle and the ball ricocheted through the trees.

Unwilling to allow Tomlinson to get away, Red Bat abandoned his bow and ran along the hilltop through the trees. He matched the horse's direction and overtook it. From a standing start, a fleet-footed man could outrun a horse over a short distance. He couldn't permit the animal to get up to its full speed or he would lose his prey.

Once Red Bat was ahead of the horse and rider, the Blackfoot warrior angled down the steep slope. When Red Bat was eight feet from the horse, the animal came adjacent to him. He leaped forward, flew through the air for a moment, and slammed into the rider hard enough to take Tomlinson from the saddle.

Slightly dazed and the wind knocked from him by the impact, Red Bat rolled and got to his feet. His mind spun for the blink of an eye, and he gasped for his breath. He stood and drew his tomahawk in one hand and his knife in the other. The steel of both weapons gleamed in the sunlight.

Tomlinson floundered, coughed, and struggled for his breath. His rifle lay several feet from him. When the white man spotted the weapon, he threw himself forward, lifted the rifle, and tried to swing it around.

Red Bat knocked the barrel aside with the tomahawk. The clang of metal on metal filled his ears. Fear filled Tomlinson's eyes and he scrambled back to free the rifle. Steel rasped, but Red Bat maintained the block against the weapon and followed the man so the rifle could not be used. Desperate, Tomlinson kicked at Red Bat. The Blackfeet warrior blocked the kick with his left forearm and drove his knife blade into his opponent's thigh.

Tomlinson screamed in pain, and the noise blended with the screams of his companions.

Red Bat drew the knife out of the white man's leg and drove it home into Tomlinson's right shoulder. Blood spread down the white man's shirt.

Still backing away, Tomlinson tripped over a loose stone and fell on his back. Before he could get up, Red Bat jumped on top of him, planted a knee on the other man's chest, and held his knife against Tomlinson's throat.

The white man stopped moving and swallowed with care. He released the rifle and turned his hands palm-down against the grass-covered earth.

"Don't kill me," Tomlinson whispered. The knot in his throat worked against the knife and a bright line of red blood appeared through the thin beard.

"I won't kill you," Red Bat said in English. "Not yet."

A figure darted through the brush ahead of Preacher. The mountain man rode a half-mile in front of the wagon train. Preacher had come to scout out the terrain because the mountains made it hard any distance ahead, and to possibly take a deer or pronghorn if fortune smiled on him. He'd cut signs of both animals, so herds were in the area. If an elk or a buffalo had presented itself, he would have taken that, too.

Dog trotted back from the brush and looked up at Preacher. The big cur growled lowly, and the noise vibrated in his big, furry chest.

"Yeah, I know," Preacher said softly and kept riding along. Horse's ears perked up. "We ain't alone out here. They were here and we rode into 'em."

The mountain man took a fresh grip on his rifle.

If there had only been one man out in the brush, Dog would have settled for him on his own. The fact that the big cur had returned to Preacher told the mountain man there were a few hostiles out in the woods.

The chittering pip of a downy woodpecker, which only nested in this part of the mountains during the winter months and was now out of season, reached Preacher's ears and let him know Tall Dog was aware they had company. They'd agreed that the birdcall would be their signal for when things went wrong. The young Crow warrior rode sixty yards or so to the mountain man's left, out of sight now below the hill and behind the trees.

They'd stepped into somebody's trap. Now they had to step back out. Or spring the trap, catch the trappers unaware, and hope to survive.

Preacher balanced the rifle across his saddle and lifted his hands. He cupped his hands together by lacing his fingers, put his mouth to his thumbs, and blew a chittering pip of the downy woodpecker to let Tall Dog know he was alive and was aware of the danger they were in.

"Dog," Preacher said softly. "Hunt."

The big cur loped forward and disappeared into the brush. Whoever was hiding out there would watch the mountain man more closely. That would be a mistake.

Horse plodded along, but the stallion turned his head to the sides and twitched his ears. He was tracking movement around them as well.

Preacher sat tight and waited. He was a mighty appealing target sitting on Horse, but nobody had taken a shot at him, so that was something in his favor. They probably wanted to take him quietly and not alert the wagon train.

A moment later, a man howled in agony and Dog growled fiercely.

Immediately, Preacher threw a leg over his saddle pommel and dropped to the ground in a crouch. He held his rifle in one hand and his other hand over his possibles bag to keep the contents safe.

An arrow hissed through the space where he'd been sitting.

"Hyah!" Preacher bellowed to Horse. He slapped his mount on the hindquarters.

The big stallion galloped forward through the brush toward where Dog fought an unseen opponent.

Preacher remained crouched and ran. Three more arrows zipped through the air and clattered against branches. One of them plucked at the mountain man's buckskin shirt. He watched the brush and he listened to everything around him. Leather-clad feet scraped the ground to his right only a short distance away. He fetched up against a thick chokecherry tree and brought the rifle to his shoulder. He kept his breathing slow so his pursuers wouldn't hear him.

Dog's growling faded and the man he'd fought no longer screamed. One of them was done for and Preacher would have put money on the big cur.

A man spoke quietly in the Blackfeet tongue a short distance away. "I have lost the white man. He no longer rides the horse."

"Maybe he was so frightened he fell off the horse," another man said. "I have seen this happen."

"Get the horse," a third man said. "And kill the wolf."

"Maybe the wolf will kill the white man," the first Blackfoot warrior said.

"It rides with him," the third man said. "Take no chances. Kill it."

Preacher tracked the voices and remained framed by the chokecherry tree so the Blackfeet warriors hunting him couldn't easily see him. Tall Dog hadn't fired a shot and that worried Preacher a little.

The downy woodpecker pip that reached him removed those worries, though. Preacher perched his rifle on a branch, put his hands together, and responded with a pip of his own.

Another chorus of cries came from the brush, followed immediately by Dog growling.

"Quickly!" the third man said. "The wolf has Spotted Elk. Kill it before it gets away."

One of the Blackfeet warriors broke cover and raced in the direction of Dog's unseen battle.

CHAPTER 24

Preacher tracked the Blackfoot brave's movements through bare patches that allowed him to see between the brush. Preacher led the man slightly, timed his opportunity in a bare spot, then squeezed the rifle's trigger and put a ball into the Blackfoot's temple. The rifle shot cracked loudly in the still air.

No longer in control of his arms and legs, the dead brave tumbled to the ground and dropped the bow he carried.

Already moving to his right because he knew the gun smoke fog marked his position for the other Blackfeet warriors, Preacher reached into his possibles bag and took out a cartridge. He bit the cartridge open, poured the powder into the rifle barrel quickly, fitted a new percussion cap to the nipple, and watched another Indian break cover. With the trees and brush around, the mountain man wanted to depend on the rifle's .54-caliber ball to get through the branches rather than the lighter .36-caliber loads in the Paterson Colts.

The three Blackfeet who came out of the brush at him were skilled warriors. They moved silently and quickly, and they were almost on top of him before he knew they were there.

Spinning to meet the three Blackfeet warriors, Preacher lifted the reloaded rifle, ran at his three attackers to throw off their attack, and fired point-blank into the chest of the man in the middle. A hole opened in the buckskin shirt over the warrior's chest and blood bloomed around it. The warrior stopped running and looked down at his chest.

Without breaking stride, Preacher ran into the dead man, knocked him back with his forearm, kept his balance through sheer stubbornness, and spun to face the remaining two warriors before the dead man landed in a heap a short distance away. Both Indians were young and fast. Tomahawks and knives filled their fists.

They ran at Preacher, and the mountain man ducked beneath a tomahawk blow. He stepped forward and slammed his rifle butt into the forward knee of the second brave. Bone cracked, and the Blackfoot crumpled to the side on a knee that would never work the same again. Still, on his way down, the Blackfoot warrior slashed at Preacher with his knife and caught the mountain man in the thigh.

Pain burned across the outside of Preacher's thigh. The knife had caught flesh as well as the buckskin breeches. He ignored the pain for the moment and trusted that the wound wasn't too bad because the leg still moved fine and supported him. None of the tendons or muscles were sliced through.

The first Blackfoot warrior leaped at Preacher and swung his tomahawk. The mountain man held his rifle in one hand and blocked the blow with the weapon's barrel. When the weapons met, metal squealed. Preacher drew his own tomahawk from behind his back, drove his attacker backward and blocked with the rifle again, then he brought his tomahawk down in an overhand blow that split the Blackfoot's skull.

Leather scraped the ground behind Preacher. The mountain man yanked his tomahawk and dragged the body of his vanquished foe around as the dead man fell. The third Blackfoot reached awkwardly over the falling body of his comrade and thrust his knife at Preacher's face.

Preacher shifted sideways and the blade almost missed him. Pain burned along his jaw just below his ear and warm blood trickled through his stubble. His tomahawk slid free of the dead man between him and his newest opponent.

He dodged the next knife thrust and held off killing the brave because he wanted to keep one of them alive to question. Knowing who they were and how many of them there were in the woods would help him figure out what to do with Cooper and his folks. They were in bad country to set up a proper defense.

He was also conscious that he was a half-mile from the wagon train. It would take him a few minutes to get back there if they needed him. He dodged the blade and the tomahawk in quick succession, and swung his tomahawk to catch that of his opponent. The wooden shafts met with a harsh crack as Preacher had intended.

The head of the Blackfoot's tomahawk snapped off and flew into the brush. Immediately, the warrior set himself again and thrust his knife. Preacher blocked the blade with his tomahawk, lifted his rifle, and drove the butt into the Blackfoot's face. Knocked unconscious, the brave dropped.

Working quickly, Preacher rolled the warrior over, cut a strip from the man's buckskin shirt, and used it to bind the brave's wrists behind his back. Then he cut another strip and bound his prisoner's feet. He picked up his rifle, listened intently, and reloaded while he headed for Tall Dog.

A moment later, Preacher stepped out of the brush into a small clearing beneath overhanging trees. Four Blackfeet lay sprawled on the ground. Some of them were missing limbs. One had been eviscerated. All of them bore grievous wounds dealt by the deadly *espada ancha* the young Crow warrior fought with.

Two Blackfeet warriors faced Tall Dog, but they gave ground before Tall Dog's powerful thrusts and swings with the Spanish sword. Metal rang as tomahawks and knives clashed against the sword. Even as powerful and as skilled as Tall Dog was, fighting with the sword required time and space.

In desperation, one of the Blackfeet left his companion's side while he was engaged in holding off Tall Dog. A few feet away, the brave hurled his tomahawk and the weapon spun end over end through the air.

Preacher lifted his rifle to his shoulder, but Tall Dog was between him and the

Blackfeet.

The young Crow warrior yanked his sword free of his latest vanquished foe and got it up in time to sweep the tomahawk out of the air. Before he could recover from the defensive move, the Blackfoot rushed him, closed on him, and thrust his knife.

Tall Dog dodged to his left, only partially got out of the way, and fell backward. His left arm swept under the Blackfeet's knife and arm, trapped the arm and weapon, and took them both over in a controlled roll. Tall Dog came up on top of his foe, planted his knees on the Blackfoot's chest, and reversed his sword. The young Crow warrior drove the blade into the Blackfoot's chest.

Breathing harshly, Tall Dog forced himself to his feet and turned to Preacher.

"Is that all of them?" the young Crow warrior asked.

"I didn't stop to count," Preacher admitted. "Things got pretty excitin' there for a minute. All told, at least a dozen."

"Perhaps they were just a scouting party or a group of hunters."

"Maybe. They ain't wearin' paint. Could be we surprised them as much as they surprised us."

Tall Dog glanced around and took a moment to clean his sword blade on the shirt of one of the dead men. He took a couple steps to his right and recovered his rifle from the ground.

"Who are they?" Tall Dog asked.

Preacher shook his head. "Blackfeet. That's all I know. I left one tied up back there. Thought maybe we'd ask him so we'd know what we're up against."

Dog loped out of the brush and stood beside Preacher. The big cur's muzzle was covered in blood. He licked his chops and settled down.

"That would be all of them," Preacher said. "Otherwise, Dog would have found them an' flushed them out. Or he'd still be out there huntin'." He paused. "If you're ready, we'll go back there an' see what that prisoner has to say."

"I am Lone Badger." The young Blackfoot warrior glared at Preacher and Tall Dog. "I fight with Chief Stormcaller. He will find you and kill you all. We will be avenged."

Unimpressed because threats from a prisoner didn't pack much powder and tended to be all noise and smoke, Preacher asked, "Where's your chief?"

"To the south. Our tribe camps near *Hinhán Kága.* Go to him if you dare. Tell him Lone Badger sent you."

"*Hinhán Kága* is Sioux land," Preacher said.

Lone Badger grinned mirthlessly. "Let the Sioux come and try to take it. They will die. Chief Stormcaller has many warriors. The Sioux are too divided to hang onto those lands. If they come, their bodies will feed the coyotes and their spirits will wander forever. We look forward to killing the Sioux."

The daring of the Blackfoot chief surprised Preacher. Making camp on *Hinhán Kága* was a bold move and would doubtlessly cause friction between the Blackfeet and the Sioux once the trespass was discovered.

Hinhán Kága was Sioux for "owl-maker." It had been named that because the formations along the top of the mountain looked like roosting owls. Only a few white men had ever seen those lands. Preacher had only seen it once, and he'd been passing through in a hurry while avoiding a Blackfeet war party some years back.

Tall Dog was listening, but the young Crow warrior didn't say anything. He and Dog kept watch. The young Crow warrior hadn't been to this part of the mountains, so he likely didn't have much reference for it. He'd come with Preacher to explore more of the mountains, and he was getting to see quite a lot of the country.

"*Hinhán Kága* is four days' ride from here," Preacher said. "What are you doin' this far north?"

"We came to fight the white men," Lone Badger snarled. "To take their guns and their horses. We killed many on our way to this place. We killed some before we found you." He glared at Dog, who watched him with disdain. "If you had not had that furred demon with you to warn you, we would have killed you, too."

The part about killing other white men only a short time ago was probably a lie. Only a few mountain men would be out in this area. Some would come for the beaver and the buffalo, but most would respect the Sioux's claim that these lands were sacred because the Sioux would fight to keep it clear of outsiders.

But there were other white men in the area who passed through. Some of the immigrants headed to Oregon Territory came this way.

And somewhere out there, Albion Shaw was doing whatever he'd come to the mountains to do.

"You came huntin' wagon trains,"

Preacher said.

"It is easier to find white men that way," Lone Badger said. "With the wagons, they travel slow and take the easiest paths. After we kill them, we can take the goods that they carry in those wagons."

That explained the wagon trains Crenshaw and Chouteau had reported missing. Evidently Stormcaller and his Blackfeet tribe had been preying on them.

"How long has your tribe been at the *Hinhán Kága*?" Preacher asked.

"Many moons," Lone Badger replied. "It is our place now."

"Then that means the Sioux don't know that you're there."

Lone Badger hissed angrily. He rocked in place as though he couldn't contain his frustration and hatred. "We do not fear them. One day they will come, and then we will kill them."

"Reckon we'll see about that. The Sioux can be hard to kill."

Having somehow freed his hands, the Blackfeet warrior sprang at Preacher like a wildcat unwinding. A small blade glimmered in his fist. The mountain man realized Lone Badger must have claimed it from one of the dead Blackfeet lying around him.

Preacher stepped forward, grabbed his attacker's knife wrist, and kicked the Blackfoot in the crotch to take the starch out of him. Groaning in pain, the warrior folded, but he stubbornly tried again to stab the mountain man. Preacher yanked his rifle up by the barrel, swung the butt up, and rammed it into Lone Badger's throat.

Bone crunched.

Gasping for breath that would no longer come, the Blackfoot warrior dropped to his knees. His throat was ruined and swelling rapidly to finish closing off. Rather than let the man die a long, hard death, Preacher twisted the Blackfoot's captured arm and forced him to slit his own throat.

With the man on the ground and bleeding out, Preacher plucked the knife free of the warrior's hand and flung it into the brush. He wasn't going to leave the Blackfoot alive anyway because the brave would have returned to his tribe with news of the wagon train, so this way worked out fine.

Preacher glanced at Tall Dog. "Did any of the warriors you fought have rifles or pistols?"

"No," the young Crow warrior replied. "There was nothing they had that was worth taking."

"Good. Means we still have an edge on them."

"Not if there are many of them."

"If many of them come, we can hear them," Preacher said.

"Getting caught out here would be bad."

"It would. We need to get on back to the wagon train." The mountain man put his fingers in his mouth and whistled sharply.

Horse galloped up and stopped nearby.

Preacher hauled himself into the saddle and kept a weather eye peeled for more Blackfeet. Years of traversing the mountains told him there could be more roving bands covering the area. With the trees and brush as thick as they were, they could possibly be on top of the wagon train in minutes.

An uneasy itch crawled along the back of Preacher's neck.

Tall Dog retreated into the brush and returned quickly mounted on his own horse. Preacher took a moment to tie a bandage from his saddlebag around his injured leg to stop the bleeding. The wound wasn't serious, but he didn't want to leave a blood trail for as long as the slash would take to stop on its own.

Together, the mountain man and the young Crow warrior rode back to the wagon train.

■ ■ ■ ■

"Heard shootin'," Lorenzo said. He sat astride his horse and cradled his rifle in his arms.

"There was some," Preacher allowed. He joined his friend at the head of the wagon train. Horse matched stride with Lorenzo's mount. "Me and Tall Dog done it all."

Tall Dog patrolled a short distance ahead and took advantage of the ridge line to watch for trouble.

"I don't see any game," Lorenzo said and looked past Preacher in the direction he'd ridden from, "an' it ain't like either of you to miss somethin' you're shootin' at, much less both of you."

"We hit what we were aimin' at," Preacher said.

Lorenzo narrowed his eyes and glanced at the dried blood on Preacher's face and leg. "Looks like you ran into trouble out there."

"Blackfeet. Looked like a hunting party, but there were plenty of them."

"Red Bat an' his warriors?"

"No. Blackfeet chief named Stormcaller."

"Never heard of him."

"Me neither. He's supposed to have made camp at the *Hinhán Kága.*"

"That owl place?"

Preacher nodded.

"Thought that was Sioux sacred lands."

"It is."

"Well, there's gonna be hell to pay when the Sioux find them Blackfeet nestin' in that place."

"Yeah, but those aren't our troubles. We've troubles of our own." Preacher glanced at the western sky where the sun was sinking. "I figure three, four hours of good daylight left."

"Probably."

"We need to push on as close to dark as we can, put as many miles between us an' this place as we can."

"Cooper was talkin' about makin' camp early tonight. Him an' his friends are feelin' a little peaked from all this travelin'."

"They're gonna have to get over that," Preacher said.

CHAPTER 25

Red Bat walked among the dead warriors scattered in the brush. They hadn't perished long ago, and the carrion feeders were only now trying to gather. Most would come during the night, and by morning the bodies would be ravaged. When Red Bat's warriors had ridden up, they'd scared away a brown bear who had only torn open one of the bodies.

"Whose warriors are these?" Red Bat asked. He studied the dead eyes of a brave who stared into the trees.

"They belong to Stormcaller," Copper Wolf said. He pointed to one of the dead braves. "This one I know. He was Painted Crane. When we were boys, we stole horses from the Sioux together. He had ridden with Stormcaller for many winters."

Copper Wolf was a scar-faced warrior who had seen nearly thirty winters. He was the oldest of Red Bat's warriors. Broad and strong, he followed Red Bat's lead and served as second in command. He had been driven from his own tribe for killing the chief's son over a woman he had wanted. She hadn't wanted him. When he had tried to take her, the woman slashed his face from his ear to his chin with a skinning knife twice before he had killed her, too.

It was said that Chief Eagle Flight still hunted Copper Wolf.

Red Bat shifted his gaze from the dead men to farther west. The wagon train rolled over the next mountain and trailed dust after it. Soon the wagons would disappear. He had thought about attacking the wagon train, but it was far larger than he had thought it might be. Fifteen wagons were a lot. There were several white men, and all those men had guns. Some of them, according to the white men he had taken prisoner, were warriors from a far-off land who had fought in wars and would be skilled.

Attacking the wagon train with only the number of braves he led would have been foolish, but Red Bat hated the idea of not taking the goods that were even now rolling out of sight up the shoulders of the next mountain range.

"How many dead warriors are here?" Red Bat asked.

"Twelve," Copper Wolf answered.

"Are any white men among them?"

"No."

Red Bat nodded because, while circling the battleground in the woods, he had counted the same number of dead and had seen none that were not Blackfeet.

"How many warriors does Stormcaller lead?" Red Bat asked.

Copper Wolf was a scout and spoke with the other Blackfeet bands more than Red Bat did. Copper Wolf would have knowledge of those numbers.

"Almost eighty. His tribe has grown during the last two years."

That was a large number to have to live off the land as the Blackfeet did. Winter would come soon, and the Blackfeet would have to be prepared for it. Surviving would be even more difficult. That was why Red Bat had kept his band only as large as it was.

"He has less than seventy now," Red Bat said. "This was a band of hunters. Their loss will be felt."

"What are you thinking?" Copper Wolf asked.

Red Bat stared in the direction the wagon train had gone. It was out of sight now, but the haze of dust that drifted over the mountains marked their path.

"The whites are too many for us," Red Bat said. "They have more rifles than we do." He kicked the dead warrior at his feet. "These bodies prove that there are men among them who can fight."

"Or maybe it only proves these warriors could not fight." Copper Wolf spat in disgust.

Red Bat strode to where four bodies lay dismembered. He didn't know the kind of weapon that would do that. "They fought. They stood their ground and they died. They did not run." He shook his head. "We do not have enough warriors or weapons to take the wagon train."

"You think we should turn away from it?"

"No." Red Bat smiled grimly. "I think we should find out if Stormcaller would like to share in our good fortune. Especially since so many of his warriors have died because of it."

Copper Wolf frowned. "I would rather keep all of the goods on that wagon train."

"So would I, but that is not possible. I would rather have part of it than none of it though. Greed will kill an unwise warrior. We will not be that. We will offer Stormcaller an alliance."

Grudgingly, Copper Wolf nodded.

"Leave five warriors to follow the wagon train. They are not to engage, and they are not to get caught. You and I will backtrack these dead men and find Stormcaller. I will make him agree to my terms."

"It will be as you say."

Red Bat peered at the ridge. The last wagon disappeared over the top behind the thick trees.

"When we return," the Blackfoot chief said, "we will kill all the whites and take all their goods."

After their release from the stockade, Judd Finlay and his cohorts met Lieutenant Kraft in the stockade's office. The young officer looked grim. So did the four soldiers standing alert and ready behind him.

"Somethin' I can do for you?" Finlay asked. He and Kraft were of equal rank, though the younger man had the major's support. That was something Finlay had always resented.

"Lieutenant Finlay," Kraft stated in a cold voice, "Major Crenshaw asked me to take a moment of your time."

The statement was more demand than request. Finlay had been expecting it, though maybe not so quick. Or late. He'd actually anticipated having this conversation while still locked up.

Controlling his anger because he didn't want another stay in lockup, Finlay scanned the small office. With himself and his six men, Kraft and the four men that backed him, and the stockade's quartermaster filling the space, not much room was left over.

The tension in the office was thick enough to cut with a knife.

"Whatever you've got to say," Finlay said, "you can say it here."

"I thought we might do this in private."

Finlay shook his head stubbornly. "I'm not gonna hide anythin', an' I ain't some little body to cower behind my momma's skirts."

Kraft nodded. "As you will, Mister Finlay."

The address, without the *lieutenant* that should have preceded it, hit Finlay squarely, but he refused to show anything of what he felt. He'd always hated Kraft. Hated the man's prim and proper attitude and his by-the-book way of operating.

"Major Crenshaw is unimpressed by your service," Kraft said, "especially in light of your relationship with Captain Diller."

Unable to stop himself, Finlay took a step toward the younger man and raised a beefy hand.

Kraft held his ground but dropped a hand to his holstered pistol. The four soldiers behind him spread out to give themselves room to shoot if things came down to that.

Corporal Dave Mullen stepped up alongside Finlay and grabbed him by the shoulder. He put his bearded face next to Finlay's and peered at him with watery blue eyes. "You keep yourself wrapped," Mullen whispered harshly. "We're about two minutes away from bein' shut of this place. Let's take that as a win."

Finlay knew there was wisdom in his friend's words, but he had a hard time acknowledging it. Finally, he nodded and forced a fake smile.

"You step lightly," Finlay told Kraft. "Arne Diller was a friend of mine. A *good* friend. Kept Indians from liftin' my hair a half-dozen times out in them mountains. I won't tolerate any besmirchin' of his name."

"Understood," Kraft said. "Let me get to the point then. The major is considering bringing you up on conspiracy to commit murder in the deaths of Ian Candles and his gang."

"You can't prove nothin'."

"Should it come to a military court case," Kraft said, "I think I can. You and Candles were friends. He came to see you the night before he tried to assassinate Preacher. Only Preacher's fighting ability prevented Candles from carrying through the action you put into motion."

Finlay shook his head. "I'd like to see you try."

Kraft's features hardened. "The major is offering you a choice, Mr. Finlay." The lieutenant flicked his gaze up to Mullen and the five other men behind Finlay, then back to Finlay. "You can end your service to the Army today or face those charges."

Finlay clenched his fists. Mullen stepped a little more in front of Finlay and held onto him more tightly.

"We're leavin'." Mullen spoke to Finlay more than Kraft. He leaned his head in and spoke more forcefully. "We're . . . leavin'. Ain't nothin' here worth fightin' for."

Finlay took a breath, let Mullen's words sink in, and nodded slowly. "We're leavin'."

Kraft turned his attention back to the stockade quartermaster. "Their weapons are unloaded?"

The quartermaster nodded.

"Give them their belongings." Kraft met Finlay's gaze. "Get your things. Leave your weapons unloaded till you pass through the gates. Should you, or any of your men, load those weapons, you will be arrested or shot.

358

Is that clear?"

Finlay stilled a curse that was on the tip of his tongue.

"It's clear," Mullen said. "Now give us some room."

"We got horses," Finlay said. "Those are ours. Don't belong to the Army."

"Mr. Dempsey has readied them," Kraft said. "They're waiting outside."

Finlay took his rifle and his pistols from the quartermaster. He took the uniform blouse off, wadded it into a bundle, and threw it into the corner of the room.

"I won't be needin' the hat that went with that," Finlay said.

Kraft said nothing.

When all the belongings were sorted, Finlay led the way out of the stockade. As Kraft had promised, their horses were saddled and tied to the hitching post in front of the building.

A few of the other soldiers lounged in front of buildings. Even Chouteau peered out one of the windows of his building.

"I also had your saddlebags filled," Kraft said. He stood out on the porch in front of the stockade. "Two weeks' of provisions. You've got water and food. I won't send a man out into that wilderness unprepared."

Finlay thought about emptying the saddle-

359

bags onto the ground, but that wouldn't have proven much.

"Didn't need your charity," Finlay said. "I've been makin' my own way since I was nine." He glanced at Kraft. "I'm a lot more able out in them mountains than you'll ever be."

Kraft remained silent.

Mullen hauled himself into the saddle and peered at Finlay. "Let's go. It'll be like the old days. We been civilized way too long."

Finlay unwrapped his reins, walked around to his horse, and stepped into the saddle. He turned his mount and headed for the gate. His men followed him.

Outside the gate, away from the fort and Kraft's disdain, Finlay felt more free, but his anger still burned within him.

"Got the whole world opened up to us," Mullen said. "Which way you wanna go? I ain't been to St. Louis in a coon's age. I 'spect we could make ourselves some good cash money there doin' one thing or another. St. Louis sounds good to me."

"Not St. Louis." Finlay reached into his pocket and found a cigar. He clamped it between his teeth and wished for a light, but he had none. "Preacher's the one what started all this mess. He killed Arne Diller, an' I can't abide by that." He glanced back

360

at the tall walls of the fort. "Ended things for us here, too. We coulda hung on through the winter."

"I ain't scared of winter," Mullen said. "Every last one of us is a curly-haired wolf. We'll make out just fine."

"I know." Finlay glanced up at the morning sun, then at the wagon ruts that led away from the fort. "Preacher's leadin' that wagon train loaded with goods to Spearfish Canyon. Them folks probably got money with 'em. We're gonna follow them an' see what we can do about evenin' the score with Preacher, an' puttin' together a nest egg for after winter. Come March or April, I'm gonna ride back to this fort an' put a ball through Kraft's head."

He put his heels to the horse's sides and followed the wagon tracks. He had a destination and a plan. He banked his anger and held onto it.

CHAPTER 26

Nine days after the fight with the Blackfeet, and after a bitterly cold, heavy rain turned the ground to mud and stalled the progress of the wagons for a day and a half, Preacher rode over the top of the last tree-covered ridge in front of him. He'd expected yet another mountaintop in the distance, but discovered he'd reached the summit over-looking the stream he was searching for. He reined Horse in and peered down into Spearfish Canyon.

The chasm was deep and narrow. The mountains stood tall to the south and west. Immense tree growth, thick and vibrant and only now turning to reds and burnished golds with the approach of fall, covered the craggy landscape. A few narrow runs of the earth were visible and marked game trails frequented by varmints wanting the water. Tall grass and brush covered most of the exposed land.

Water spilled down the incline to Preacher's right, created white water in places, and splashed on down to a shallow creek that ran north until it disappeared into the mountains. Somewhere out there, the stream joined the Redwater River. The rushing water created a constant low gurgle that clambered against the incline and whispered to Preacher.

A small herd of white-tailed deer stood drinking their fill at a wide point in the stream. A buck stood proud and alert on a nearby boulder and had already marked the arrival of Preacher, Dog, and Horse. Ears pricked, watchful for danger, the buck surveilled them intently.

For a moment, Preacher drank in the scene and considered the deer. Meat was always good to have, but a fresh kill wasn't yet necessary. Yesterday he and Lorenzo had taken two buffalo while on the scout, and Moses and Caleb had brought down a third. For the moment, their larders were full and taking more would be a sinful waste of good meat.

Preacher wanted to make sure they stayed well provisioned. Winter was coming, and it looked like the constant cold would arrive earlier than usual like it sometimes did. That wouldn't help the folks trailing after him who were intending on building. Darvis had voiced his concerns to Preacher. Every day brought more uncertainty about the trading post construction. The weather was unstoppable and unforgiving. Once winter dug into the mountains, it wouldn't let go.

Seeing the deer there in the canyon meant there would be more deer later when he needed them. Preacher took that as a good omen. Game lived between the tall shoulders of the surrounding mountains that would block off some of the northern winds. They'd found safety there.

The buck lifted his head and snorted. His little band raced along the creekbank and disappeared into the woods. He followed them.

Relief lifted some of the mountain man's fatigue, but only slightly and only for a time. Those worries and tiredness would return. The wagon train crew had a lot of work to do just to make sure they could survive through the winter. Sickness might claim some of them. Ill luck would take others.

Preacher pushed those thoughts out of his head. There was only so much he could do, and he was savvy enough to know Cooper's dream was probably doomed. For Preacher to ride up into the high country by his lonesome or with a few friends was one thing, but doing that while leading a group of greenhorns new to the mountainous terrain was another.

His mind lingered on the threat offered by Albion Shaw, and he wondered for a moment what the Englishman would do when winter arrived. The mountains might take care of whatever threat Shaw posed. Preacher wished he knew what Shaw's timetable was like, what the man was up against. That would make planning for the man a mite easier.

He didn't, though, and that was why Chouteau had sent him out into the mountains. Discovering that would take time. Preacher had to remain patient. He needed a base of operations while he explored and searched for the man.

Somewhere along Little Spearfish Creek would be a good site for a trading post, though, provided the Sioux were truly amenable. If the Sioux allowed the establishment to happen, they would trade with Cooper and his investors. The Easterners would probably turn a profit quickly. Plenty of tribes traveled through the area, and word of mouth would draw in plenty more.

As long as Cooper and his associates had things the Sioux wanted.

Spearfish Canyon was a place known to

guides who led wagon trains to Oregon. A few wagon trains that had started out late and gotten caught by bad weather had wintered there and moved on in the spring. Preacher had done that a couple of times.

No one stayed there, though, because the Sioux didn't permit it. In the winter the Sioux allowed immigrants to pass on through, but they made sure they kept passing come spring.

Preacher wondered again if Cooper's dealings with the Sioux chief was as good as he'd said it was. He reckoned they'd know the first time they crossed paths with local Indians.

The Blackfeet in the area remained a possible problem, though. They hadn't given up. A small group of five or six still followed the wagon train. Preacher and Tall Dog had occasionally dropped out of the wagon train and looped back around to find their abandoned campsites. The Blackfeet had tried to hide their presence, but Preacher and Tall Dog were certain about the number.

They still didn't know why they were there.

Preacher had glimpsed them again this morning with his spyglass. There couldn't have been over four or five in the group, not enough to do much against the guns carried by the wagon train, and the Blackfeet had given no sign they were willing to engage.

They hadn't gone away either.

That bothered Preacher even more than if they'd attacked. If the Blackfeet chose not to pursue aggression, there was a reason. They were waiting for something. Or someone.

With a scrabble of hooves on the hard earth loaded with rock, Lorenzo rode up and halted his mount alongside Preacher.

"Mighty pretty country," Lorenzo commented. He pushed his broad-brimmed hat back with a thumb and let his mount blow.

"It is." Preacher took a deep breath of the clean air, and the late-morning chill that foreshadowed the coming winter bit into his chest.

"It's a shame to think of buildin' a tradin' post here an' seein' folks moseyin' on out this way to find it. They'll destroy a lot of this an' never see it for the blessin' it is."

"Just because Cooper sets the tradin' post up doesn't mean it'll stay. Got too many things workin' against it. Gettin' enough of it built to survive the winter is going to be one of them."

Lorenzo rubbed his stubbled chin. "I was thinkin' that myownself. Wasn't for Chouteau, an' me bein' curious about this Shaw fella, I'd not be out here with this wagon train. I'd rather you an' me an' Tall Dog see what we could do over the winter our ownselves. Get us a mess of beaver pelts an' ride out high, wide, an' handsome come spring." He twisted in the saddle and gazed back at the wagons creaking up the incline. Chain links in the traces clinked. "Could be these folks survive this one winter, *if* they do, they'll see how hard it is, sell ever'thin' they got, then cut bait an' go on home."

"That's not our lookout." Preacher shaded his eyes with a hand and looked out over the valley. "We need to find Albion Shaw if we can, see what he's up to, then report back to Chouteau and Crenshaw."

Over the last week, Preacher, Tall Dog, Lorenzo, Moses, and Caleb had taken turns scouting out around the wagon train. They'd taken game and trailed tracks while looking for Albion Shaw.

On three occasions, Preacher had cut sign left by the horse ridden by the man who'd ambushed the men from Fort Pierre. Preacher had ridden carefully around those places and thought about the possibility of the air rifle the man had used. Death could come silently and without warning. However, the tracks had been two and three days old each time he'd found them.

Still, the fact that the killer and the wagon train were all headed in the same direction was nettling. But it led Preacher to believe the Basque murderer, and there was no other way to think of the rifleman, was headed on out to find Albion Shaw. Preacher wondered what had pulled the Basque into the mountains.

The mountains were big, but Preacher felt certain he'd cross paths with the Basque and Shaw soon enough. When that occurred, he wasn't sure what would happen.

"Reportin' back to Chouteau might be hard to do if we get caught up in bad weather," Lorenzo said. "Could get snowed in till spring. Winter's gonna come fast an' smack hard when it does. I got old bones that's grumblin' an' tellin' me that."

Rattling from tack and curses from men came from the other side of the mountain.

Preacher turned Horse around and rode forward a short way to peer through the trees and back down the mountain.

Along the incline, red-faced from effort and anger, Cooper whipped his team. Worn out from the long haul over the past days, the horses balked at the final, steeper incline and shifted in their traces. The grade wasn't too much for them, but they weren't of a mind for it now.

"Ease off those animals," Preacher ordered. "Give them some time to blow. When they catch their breath, they'll come on up."

"How much farther?" Cooper demanded.

Preacher judged the distance separating him from the lead wagon. The other wagons had halted behind Cooper's.

"Thirty feet," the mountain man said, "give or take, but the incline here is a mite harder. If the horses were still fresh, they'd handle it. You get to where I am, you can look down into Spearfish Canyon. Got a gentler grade on this side."

Cooper whipped the horses again. The animals stutter-stepped and leaned into the traces, but they ended up milling around.

"Keep it up," Preacher growled, "you'll make those horses bolt. Then you'll have nine kinds of Hell to deal with. If that wagon gets away from you, it'll cause problems for all of those behind you. You'll get some folks killed."

Frustrated, Cooper threw the whip away and glared at Preacher.

"This is your fault," Cooper accused. "You could have found an easier way."

Preacher grinned coldly at the man and banked the anger inside him. To give himself a minute, he adjusted his hat. He was tired, too, but allowing himself to get angry at Cooper wouldn't do any good. It might feel good, though, and he was tempted for a minute.

"These are mountains," Preacher said. "Some of the biggest mountains in this country. None of 'em come easy. You wanted to come out here. You should have known the way would be hard before you got here."

"I knew that," Cooper fussed. "I hired you to get us here the easiest way. There had to be a way easier than this."

"Ain't just about easy," Preacher said. "Time's a factor, too. All that bad weather and the cold we been havin' tells me winter's gonna come easy this year. Goin' another way would have cut into time we don't have. We still have to build shelters for us, the livestock, and your goods. This was the best way we could come and get where you wanted to go in the time we needed to get here."

Cooper glared at Preacher and looked like he didn't believe what he was being told.

"If you think this is hard," Lorenzo said, "you should see Ash Hollow. Folks have to rope their wagons down the other side of the mountains there because it's so steep. At least you ain't lookin' at that. Do what Preacher says an' let them critters blow a mite. They'll make it."

Two wagons back in the irregular line, Rufus Darvis pulled his team of oxen to one side of the wagons ahead of him. The few men resting from walking for a moment clambered out of the wagon and strode alongside. Creaking and cracking, the wagon rolled along. The ponderous beasts hooked to it clambered up the grade steadily.

A moment later, the wagon gained the summit and rocked to a stop.

Darvis looked around and grinned. "A horse is a fine thing to ride, I'll give you that, but when it comes to pulling a load, you want an ox."

"Maybe," Lorenzo allowed. "Just wished they tasted as good as a cow or a buffalo."

Darvis hopped down from the wagon and looked down the slope. "It's going to be easier getting down than getting up. The slope is gentler on this side." He turned to the men beside his wagon and spoke in one of the languages Preacher didn't understand.

Immediately the men set to work taking ropes from the wagon bed and unhooking the harnesses.

"We'll hook up to the wagons that have trouble making the summit," Darvis said.

"Sounds good," Preacher said. "Me and Lorenzo will go have a look around. See if we can find someplace to camp for the night. The animals need to rest."

"It'll do us all good," Darvis admitted. "Tomorrow morning, if you'd be willing, I want to ride along with you to find a spot for the trading post."

"All right," Preacher said.

"I mean no disrespect," Darvis said. "I trust your judgment, but you and I look at things differently. I'm sure you've built houses and fortifications before, but I'm an engineer. I'll want some place where we can take timber and stone to get this fort started. We have to build fast and build right, so we'll need plenty of it close by."

"No disrespect taken," Preacher said. "That's your lookout."

"I'm going to depend on you to keep my men and me fed and safe," the engineer said.

"That I can do," Preacher said. "Let Tall Dog know that me and Lorenzo will be back soon."

"I'll do that," Darvis said. He walked to the back of the summit and helped his men carry the ropes down to Cooper's wagon.

Preacher adjusted his hat, put his heels to Horse's sides, and rode down into the canyon. Lorenzo followed.

Seated atop one of the horses the engineering crew had brought with them, Darvis surveyed the forest standing before him. Little Spearfish Creek ran wide and steady, deep enough now that crossing would be a problem. To the south and east, a great wall of shattered limestone soared up at least fifty feet. On the other side of the creek, another wall of rock stood. Together, they almost formed a generous bottleneck that partially closed off the area.

The engineer tilted his hat back and smiled a little.

"You were right, Preacher," Darvis said. "This is a good spot. We can build here."

"This is the best place I found yesterday while I was scoutin'," Preacher agreed. "Thought you might agree. There are other places farther on you might like better, but this one's got plenty of stone and timber and water."

"Farther on will take us farther away from that summit we came up yesterday," the engineer said. "Everyone who comes to the trading post will have a hard time making that ascent."

"Hard times don't stop folks wantin' to come out West," Lorenzo said. He stood at the creek's edge.

"I know that," Darvis agreed. He took a deep breath. "Given time, I can improve on that grade. I can make it more accessible. I've got blasting powder that we can use. Blow it out and reshape it." The engineer rubbed his bearded jaw. "I'll probably work on that next spring if we make it through the winter and this project still seems viable."

A large rainbow trout broke the creek surface twenty feet away and took a dragon-fly out of the air.

"This place has ever'thin' you're lookin' for," Lorenzo said, "an' the fishin' looks promisin', too. This river moves too fast to freeze solid in the winter. Only the bottom freezes, so we can fish the whole time we're here. When it ain't too cold."

"I've always been partial to fishing," Darvis said. "It takes the kinks out of a man's back after a long day of hard work."

"That it does," Lorenzo agreed. "Ever caught rainbow trout?"

Darvis thought for a moment. "Can't say that I have. I've caught and eaten many other things. Dusky kob, hottentot, squid, mackerel, and hake out in the ocean. I'm partial to kingklip."

"Never heard of it."

"It's an eel, but it's one of the finest tasting things you can get from the sea. They'll grow to thirty pounds."

Lorenzo shook his head. "That's a lot of fish. You'll get catfish up here sometimes that go a hundred pounds, but you'll never see a rainbow trout that big." He gazed out at the creek. "I got some fine fishin' stories I can tell you."

Darvis grinned. "I'll bet I can match you, mate."

Preacher shook his head and didn't say anything. When it came to fish stories, the first liar never stood a chance. His thoughts weren't on fishing though. Now that Darvis was happy with the building site, it was time to deal with those Blackfeet warriors that had been trailing them.

CHAPTER 27

Hunkered in the darkness on the east side of the incline that led up to Spearfish Canyon, several yards away from the cut-up path and bent brush left by the wagons, Preacher pulled his buffalo robe a little tighter and husbanded his warmth. He stared down the mountain to where the Blackfeet warriors had camped.

Because they believed they were observed, they'd laid two false sites and moved under the cover of night, but their efforts hadn't mattered. Preacher tracked them easily enough by sight, sound, and smell. If he hadn't been able to do it, Dog would have. The big cur lay stretched out at his side and paid attention to the night and the creatures in it. Preacher ran a soothing hand along Dog's back.

The smell of fresh coffee filled his nostrils. He glanced over his shoulder and spotted Tall Dog moving gracefully through the shadows. A tin cup in the young Crow warrior's hand trailed faint fog into the chill air.

"I brought you coffee." Tall Dog sat on his haunches and handed the cup to Preacher.

The mountain man took the cup in both hands and enjoyed the warmth for a moment. "Your horse?"

"He's back there with yours." Tall Dog gazed out at the woods at the foot of the mountain.

"That animal moves as quiet as you do."

Tall Dog smiled. "Yes. I trained him." He was proud of his horse and his skill. "Are the Blackfeet in the same place?"

The young Crow warrior had kept watch over them till a couple hours before sundown. Then he'd swapped places with Preacher and gone to get his supper.

"They've been moving around," Preacher said. "Not going far. Sometimes they split up, wander a little bit, but they're together now."

"That will make what we need to do much easier."

Preacher sipped the coffee. It had cooled somewhat and he drank it down. "Did you get any sleep?"

"Some."

"That's good."

"Darvis's men worked until sundown."

"Noisy?"

"Yes."

Preacher nodded. "I heard the axes." The noise had subsided with the coming of night.

"They work rapidly," Tall Dog said.

"I saw that. They had tents stretched quick enough. You can see they've done this before."

"They set palisade stakes until they lost the light. The walls will be over ten feet tall. They'll probably have enough trees cut down and set into the ground by the end of the week."

"Good. We need strong walls." That eased Preacher's mind a little. "Darvis knows the Blackfeet are out there, and he knows we're in dangerous country."

"I have listened to him talk to you. He has lived in hazardous places like these mountains for much of his life."

"He's a man who knows what he's doin'."

Tall Dog hesitated for a moment. "I would like to learn what he and his men do. They are clever with their axes and tools."

Preacher eyed his young companion. "Not much call for woodwork in a Crow village, is there?"

"No. We travel with tepees and support poles. We take down our dwellings, transport them, and set them up again. My father is clever with an ax, too. The braves in our tribe respect his abilities. He has built small houses for my mother at times, when we lived apart from the Crow and had not yet found a tribe my mother wished to belong to. Those houses were strong and watertight, big enough for us and our horses in the winter."

"Your father's a Swede. I've seen men like him in the Territory of Wisconsin."

"My father is from there."

"Those men," Preacher said, "build houses and barns and boats and ships with just an ax, no other tools. All the joints are tight and the timbers are made strong. I learned a little from some of them. They work hard, and they've kept the skills their ancestors have passed down to them."

"So my father tells me. You stayed among them?"

"Not so long. They tend to gather and build towns. Got a little too crowded for my likin' right quick."

"My father likes company. He enjoys telling stories and working with other men. I am not so much that way."

"You want to get out and see things."

"Yes. My mother wishes that were not so. My travels make her unhappy."

Preacher nodded. "You've got to be true to yourself."

Tall Dog grimaced. "Doing so gets . . . confusing."

"It does. Until you figure out for sure what you truly want."

Tall Dog took a breath. "When will that be?"

Preacher smiled. "At the worst time you can imagine, and probably there'll be a woman involved."

A frown pulled at Tall Dog's face. "I will not do a woman's bidding."

"Maybe not." Preacher chuckled. "I didn't, and still don't."

"You haven't settled down with a woman."

"No, I ain't. Found a lot of good women along the way, but none of 'em I'd give up traipsin' through these mountains for, and I wouldn't drag any of them through this. None of them have the same appreciation for them that I do."

"Perhaps when you are older." Amusement lighted Tall Dog's dark eyes.

"At one time, I thought that might happen," Preacher admitted. "These days I know I'll be buried somewhere up in these mountains, and that's just fine with me."

"I will ask the ancestors to watch over you."

"You do that, and you might take a minute to ask them to look over us right now, too."

Preacher placed the cup in the grass near a rock he would find on his way back up the mountain. He gave Tall Dog a moment, then the mountain man curled his rifle into the crook of his left arm, rose to a crouch, and headed down the mountain.

"Hunt," he told Dog.

In order to come up on the Blackfeet quietly, Preacher and Tall Dog had to circle around a bit. Getting upwind of them might have carried even a slight noise to the Indians. If the Blackfeet were alert, even Preacher and Tall Dog's scent could have given them away.

The mountain man lay in the grass thirty feet from where three Blackfeet lay wrapped in buffalo robes on the ground. A thin gray haze leaked from an underground firepit that had died down to coals. Fed judiciously to keep from creating flare-ups, the residual heat would carry on till morning.

The Blackfeet had dug Dakota fire holes in their campsites, used them to cook their supper and for heat during the night. The method produced only a little smoke that was quickly lost a few feet away. Even the meat smell of the venison they'd eaten was only faint. While backtracking the group, Preacher had discovered the warriors always filled in the holes and laid sod they'd cut out to cover their sign. They were careful.

If Preacher hadn't been looking for the fire holes, he wouldn't have found them. He knew to look for the firepits because he'd used them himself, oftentimes for the same reasons.

Ignoring the chill that hovered over him, he sat quietly and stared into the darkness. Even under the best conditions, a man couldn't see well at night by looking ahead. He had to use the edges of his vision to find things. It took a moment to discover the two warriors hunkered twenty feet from the campsite on opposite ends.

Both guards only moved a little as they kept watch.

Preacher looked at Tall Dog and signed quickly. He and Dog would take care of the guards. The young Crow warrior had to deal with the sleeping warriors. Preacher would arrive as quickly as he could.

Tall Dog protested, but, when Preacher refused to budge on his plan, the young Crow warrior quickly gave up and nodded.

No guns, Preacher signed. He didn't want

to alert anyone else who might be in the vicinity, and he didn't want to worry the wagon train. There were too many greenhorns there and someone might get hurt.

The young Crow warrior reached over his shoulder and drew the *espada ancha* from its scabbard. The steel hissed quietly against the leather. He nodded.

Preacher put a hand on Dog's shoulder and shoved him off to the left. The big cur vanished into the brush without a sound. The mountain man filled his hands with his tomahawk and his bowie knife and slid through the brush quickly. Dog wouldn't wait long to take out the sentry on that side of the enemy camp.

Shadowed by a pine tree ahead of Preacher, the Blackfoot sentry squatted on the ground and held his bow in one hand. He clasped an arrow nocked and ready, but didn't pull the string. His head moved steadily, but the movement was too slow to pick up Preacher's approach. The warrior wasn't as attentive as he could have been.

Preacher crept to within six feet of the Blackfoot. Just as he readied himself to attack, a howl of fear-filled pain tore through the night. Dog had reached his target.

The sentry in front of Preacher shoved himself to his feet, dropped his buffalo robe to the ground, and whipped around with the arrow fully drawn. His gaze caught Preacher charging forward and he shifted his aim.

Lurching to his right, Preacher narrowly escaped the arrow that was released. Its passage produced a sibilant hiss and plucked at his sleeve. The Blackfoot reached into his quiver, drew another arrow, and fitted it to his string as he backed away.

Preacher righted himself, continued his charge after his quarry, and, when he was upon his opponent, swung the tomahawk. The tomahawk's broad blade caught the bow and knocked it aside. The released arrow sang by the mountain man's head. Another stride brought Preacher into the Blackfoot.

The warrior threw away the broken bow. Still backing away, he reached for his tomahawk, drew it from his waist, and swung the weapon in a savage upward blow at Preacher's head.

With a quick shift, Preacher dodged his enemy's tomahawk and blocked the man's arm with his own arm. He took another step forward, slid his tomahawk forward to catch behind the Blackfoot's head to halt the warrior's retreat, and thrust the bowie knife's point into the Indian's throat. Fearful and in pain, with blood spilling down the front of his shirt, the warrior tried again to back away.

This time Preacher brought the tomahawk down in an overhead blow that split the warrior's skull. The Indian's eyes rolled to the back of his head, and his knees sagged. He dropped bonelessly to the ground.

Knowing the Blackfoot was dead, Preacher turned back to the camp. The other sentry's cries of pain had quieted.

In the camp, the three Blackfeet warriors gathered their weapons and stood. Tall Dog appeared out of the darkness and sprinted into them. The young Crow warrior collided with one of his enemies and knocked the man sprawling. The other two Blackfeet closed on the young giant and held blades in their fists.

Preacher sprinted toward the battle.

Tall Dog stepped to the right and dodged a knife. With the Spanish sword, he blocked the tomahawk wielded by the other warrior and recovered quickly. He whipped the sword around again and slashed open the man's stomach, then turned his attention back to the first man he'd evaded.

The Blackfoot who had been knocked to the ground shoved himself to his feet and reached for his bow only a few feet away.

He pulled it up and nocked an arrow smoothly.

Unable to reach the archer in time, Preacher pulled his tomahawk back and let fly while on the run. The weapon spun end over end and struck the Blackfoot in the chest. Although the sharp edge didn't sink into flesh, the impact was enough to knock the warrior to the side and leave him off-balance. It also let the warrior know Tall Dog wasn't alone.

As the Blackfoot recovered and turned his attention to his new attacker, Preacher ran into him and knocked them both to the ground. They sprawled and fought to re-cover an advantage. Both separated and went in different directions. The Blackfoot came up with his knife and tomahawk in his hands.

"White Wolf," the warrior snarled. His breath came rapidly, and he moved warily. "Some say you are unkillable, but I have watched you for several days. You eat, you sleep. You are only a man." He narrowed his eyes in disgust. "A lucky man so far, but that luck ends tonight. I will kill you and hand your scalp to Red Bat Circles Smoke when he returns."

Preacher stepped toward his enemy and thrust his knife at the Blackfoot's face. The warrior dodged back and slashed with the knife in his left hand. Preacher ducked under the blow and stepped forward at the same time to hook his opponent's left foot with his own. He raised his tomahawk to block the Blackfoot's weapon, and the handles clacked.

Leaning into the trapped weapon, Preacher put his head behind the warrior's left elbow to trap it. He drove the bowie knife to the hilt between his opponent's third and fourth ribs. The keen blade pierced the Blackfoot's heart, and he shivered.

For a moment, to make sure of the kill, Preacher held the knife in place and kept the man pressed against him. He twisted the man around to check on Tall Dog.

The young Crow warrior thrust his sword through the chest of a Blackfoot warrior who already bled furiously from a freshly severed arm stump. The other man lay still a few feet away and showed no signs of getting up again.

When the Blackfoot's strength fled and life left him, Preacher slid the knife free, relaxed his hold, and stepped back. The dead man fell on his face. Preacher knelt briefly and wiped the bowie clean on the warrior's breeches.

"He is dead?" Tall Dog asked.

"Yeah." Preacher stood and slid his bowie back into its sheath. He studied the campsite.

In the distance a couple of horses whickered.

"Is the sentry dead as well?" Tall Dog asked.

"Yeah."

Dog trotted up, sat near Preacher, and licked his bloody chops.

Tall Dog looked at the three dead Blackfeet warriors and the big cur. "Then we have no one left to question. I do not think the one Dog went after remains alive. Perhaps we can find answers among their possessions."

"The sentry I killed told me he was going to give my hair to Red Bat Circles Smoke," Preacher said. "I think it's safe to say they were with him."

"I have heard of that man, but I have not met him." Tall Dog walked among the dead men and turned them to peer more closely at their faces. "Perhaps he is here."

"Not here," Preacher said. "From what Lorenzo and I were told, Red Bat leads a couple dozen warriors. The numbers are small enough for them to survive on the run and stay hidden, and large enough for them to take down a wagon train passing through here. This is only part of that group."

"They were ordered to track us."

"Seems right. A couple dozen braves is enough to take what they wanted from small wagon trains and hunting bands crossin' through here."

"But not enough to confront our wagon train." Tall Dog stood and peered around. "So Red Bat has gone somewhere."

"Probably to get reinforcements would be my guess."

"Then we will have to face them again."

"Probably. So you and me need to help Darvis and his men as much as we can. I've got a feelin' we're going to need that palisade wall they're puttin' up." Preacher gripped his rifle. "Let's go get the horses tied up out there and get on back to the camp."

He strode toward the horses. Tall Dog joined him, and Dog raced on ahead on the scout.

"I do not like the idea of waiting to be attacked," the young Crow warrior stated quietly.

"We're going to help Darvis, but we're going to see what we can find out in the meantime. We're not going to be caught unawares."

Preacher hoped that was true.

CHAPTER 28

With morning light barely lifting the gloom left over by the night, Red Bat Circles Smoke resented riding with Chief Stormcaller. Not far away, as the crow flies, a wagon train sat waiting to be taken. He had five warriors watching over it. All Red Bat needed was a few more warriors that would help him secure the cargo.

Only Stormcaller had forced Red Bat to accompany his own strike against enemies. Red Bat had almost rejected the idea, but too many of his warriors had been pulled in by Stormcaller's description of goods and weapons that could be taken from the men he pursued. Getting their minds off those things would prove difficult.

For now, Red Bat held his venom and bile and rode alongside the chieftain.

The Blackfoot leader was only a few years older than Red Bat, and Stormcaller acted like he could smell the stink of the Comancheros that had taken Red Bat as a prisoner those years ago.

Even though they had never met, Stormcaller knew about Red Bat, knew what he was doing now, and the chieftain knew what had happened to him when he was young. Although Stormcaller hadn't said as much, the man despised Red Bat for being weak enough to get captured and taken away. The fact that Red Bat has escaped and returned to the mountains didn't matter to Stormcaller.

The renegade chieftain was like most other Blackfeet and had no use for Red Bat.

Only Red Bat's knowledge of the wagon train filled with cargo had gained Stormcaller's goodwill. There was no promise that goodwill would remain, or that Red Bat wouldn't be betrayed in the end.

Those thoughts tramped through Red Bat's mind as he trailed Stormcaller's braves along the twisting gully that ran between the short mountains. Even sitting on his horse, Red Bat couldn't see over the surrounding walls. The ravines here looked like they had been chopped into the land by the Great Spirits when times were just beginning. Even crossing the land left a traveler cut off again and again from the rest of the mountains.

Red Bat hated the trapped feeling of unease that twisted through his stomach like a lizard clawing for purchase on stone. While they traveled in the gully, there was little chance of them being seen. The horses' hooves didn't even raise dust because rock and stubborn green grass and brush covered the narrow strip of ground that formed the gully floor. The air held a chill to it, the threat of winter coming.

A trickle of water ran through the gully and turned the ground soft in places. Past floods had carved earth away from large rocks and created islands. Some of them stood as tall as the towering ravine walls and others were large, flat disks that held pockets of water. Small lizards sunned themselves on the rock.

The horses' hooves rattled and thudded against the rock and the earth. The noise probably traveled a long way down the gully. If the men Stormcaller hunted were alert, the Blackfeet war party could be found out and violence would break out in the gully.

This would be a bad place for them to get caught because there was no place to run. The gully provided a good hiding place, but it could also swiftly become a death trap.

Red Bat wanted to ride up the side of the gully and look at what was around them.

He hated feeling vulnerable, and it had been a long time since he'd felt this vulnerable.

Silently, he cursed the wagon train for being so large, and at the same time knowing it was there and carrying so much made him desire it even more. Stormcaller should have set aside his own goals. They should have gone after the wagon train before the people there had a chance to settle in. But the chieftain refused, and Red Bat had risked his life in trying to make an argument against the choice of action.

Stormcaller's younger brother had been one of the warriors who had been killed by the white men they hunted in an earlier encounter. The Blackfoot chieftain was determined to eliminate all of his brother's killers.

Red Bat searched the surrounding walls and pushed away his thoughts of abandoning his agreement with Stormcaller. Every so often, narrow ledges led up the gully walls to the high ground. Stormcaller's scouts rode up there and kept watch over the hundred braves who rode through the ravine.

If Red Bat left, he wasn't certain that all his warriors would follow him. If Stormcaller accepted them and made a permanent place for them, they would leave. Many of

Stormcaller's warriors carried rifles, and many of them had pistols as well. Those weapons, and the cache of supplies they had at their camp, offered mute testimony that Stormcaller's leadership was profitable for his braves.

Stormcaller rode ahead of Red Bat. Four of the chief's guards rode near him and watched over him.

Red Bat was jealous of the chief's success, and it galled him to think he had reason to be thankful for it now. Without Stormcaller's warriors, though, taking the wagon train would be impossible. When Red Bat balanced losing the things aboard those wagons with sharing them with Stormcaller, there was no choice. Winter would be easier for his men if they were better supplied.

Copper Wolf rode to Red Bat's left. Like Red Bat, the brave held his rifle in the crook of his arm.

"This will be all right," Copper Wolf said quietly.

"I do not trust Stormcaller not to turn on us." Red Bat hated that he had to talk so softly, but voices carried in the gully. "His warriors outnumber ours. If he decides not to share, they are too many."

"Those wagons have many things. Even all of Stormcaller's warriors will not be enough to carry it all away."

"I will not take what is left like some old wattle-faced buzzard too crippled and afraid to take prey."

"They number more than us, this is true, but Stormcaller knows he would lose men if we fought him. He does not want to lose warriors. He fears us a little, and he needs us a little because the whites have many men. Otherwise, he wouldn't have made an agreement with you."

"Stormcaller is greedy," Red Bat said.

"We all are greedy. If we were not, we would forget about those wagons and find an easier prey."

"Greed is not what compels me," Red Bat growled. "This is my land to hunt in. That wagon train is rightfully my prey. I found them. I want those things the whites carry, and I am brave enough to take them."

"I spoke badly."

"There is truth in what you said, but I do not wish to walk away from what is there."

Red Bat looked at the dark sky to the north. The coming storms were a long time off, but they would be here soon. Winter would come early, and it would be fierce.

"We can use the goods that wagon train has," Red Bat said. "With those things, we can rob the teeth from the winter and wait for the warmer days. By spring, our warriors will be strong and ready."

"I know."

Red Bat guided his mount around a tall stone spire in the middle of the gully. "What do you know of these men Stormcaller hunts? Have you learned anything more than we were told?"

"They are white," Copper Wolf said. "Their leader is English. Those men killed Stormcaller's son and the small band of hunters with him. The chieftain wants revenge."

"They are British like those who betrayed the Blackfeet in the years when they warred with the Americans. The British promised guns and warriors, and gave us not enough of either."

"The British were fighting the French then. They no longer fight those people."

"The English are friends with those who have invaded our lands. They no longer seek control of this place. Even if they did, they would not be any better. We would still have to fight. We will no longer believe their lies."

"No, we will not, but Stormcaller believes the man he hunts is different."

"Have you learned anything more of this Englishman Albion Shaw. What has brought him here?"

"He hunts the yellow metal that drives white men insane."

"There is none of that here."

Copper Wolf shrugged. "Perhaps he has heard some of the stories the whites like to tell. I, too, have heard white men talk about the yellow metal that can be found here."

"That is more reason to kill these white men," Red Bat said. "If they spread their lies to other white men, more of them will come. For the moment, my goals are aligned with those of Stormcaller. We will kill these whites, then we will kill the ones with the wagons. We must drive them from these mountains."

Ahead, the warriors slowed. One of Stormcaller's chieftains rode back to Red Bat.

"We must go quietly from this moment on," the warrior said. "The whites have camped just on the other side of this mountain. Chief Stormcaller wants us up on the eastern ridge. The rising sun will be behind us, and we will use that to our advantage."

"What are the whites doing?" Red Bat asked.

The chieftain smiled. "There are caves in that mountain. They dig in them like prairie dogs." He wheeled his horse around. "We will line up and, when Chief Stormcaller gives the signal, we will ride down and kill them."

Red Bat nodded. Some of the irritation within him died away. He focused on the killing that lay ahead of him. That would be a good place to start, and once Stormcaller's battle was finished, then they could focus on the wagon train.

"You've lost the vein?" Holding aloft the lantern he held, Major General Albion Shaw stared at the scarred surface of the cave wall.

A slight golden gleam, no larger than a shirt button, caught the light. Shaw touched it with a callused finger and scratched at it with his nail. The small nugget popped free of the earth and dropped to the pile of earth at the bottom of the wall.

He swallowed the flood of anger that vibrated within him. His men operated on the information that he had given them. However, he had been certain that this cave would lead to the treasure he hunted.

Corporal Carmichael, who had dug coal in Lancashire before signing on with the Queen's Royal Army, shook his head. He was a short, stocky man with blue-black beard growth that showed even in the morning hours after a fresh shave.

"I don't know that it was a vein, General,"

the corporal said. "I think it was just a pocket of color. They come up now and again. And if you look at that rock, you'll see that it's iron pyrite, not gold."

The corporal knelt briefly and picked up the nugget. He set his pick aside and dropped the rock into his weathered palm.

"Looks like gold," Carmichael said, "but it's practically worthless. Men who don't know metal wouldn't know the difference."

Shaw peered at the stone. His first experience with gold mining had been the little they'd managed since reaching these mountains, and with the time they'd spent along the streams following the map he had. He considered grubbing in the earth beneath him. A man could use gold to build an empire. He intended to do exactly that.

"How can you tell it's not gold?" Shaw was reluctant to let go of the idea he'd found the mine he was looking for. That lost fortune had to be out here somewhere, and he was certain he was close to it.

"Gold is soft," Carmichael explained. "Pyrite is hard. It has a lot of iron in it."

Holding the stone between his thumb and forefinger, he quickly scraped it against the wall.

Sparks flared and drove back some of the darkness that filled the tunnel. Then they died. Shaw's hopes that they'd found his fortune waned as well.

"Gold won't strike sparks, sir," Carmichael said. He sleeved sweat from his heavy brow.

Despite the coming morning, a chill lingered, and in the tunnel that chill proved dank and thick. Around Shaw, more of his men worked with pickaxes and shovels. Others pushed primitive wheelbarrows on wooden wheels. Noise filled the space, and the undercurrent of voices threaded through it all.

"This doesn't mean we should give up on finding what you're looking for, General," the corporal said. "Gold and iron pyrite aren't mutually exclusive. They can be mixed in together. From the little true gold we've found, I believe we'll find more if we keep looking. As long as you're sure this is where we should be digging, we'll keep it up. If it's here to be found, we'll find it."

Shaw hid his anger and his disappointment behind the professional soldier's face he had built throughout years of war and commanding men. But he clung to his belief that the lost gold mine he'd been told about was in this very cave.

"I know you will, Corporal. Carry on."

Shaw stepped back from the new tunnel

and returned to the main cave this tunnel branched out of. Two men pushed wheelbarrows filled with rock and earth toward the wide cave mouth a hundred paces distant.

Scouts had found the caves only nine days ago. When he'd first seen the site nestled in at the foothills of one of the tallest mountains in the area, Shaw's hopes had risen. He'd followed that tale of lost gold, and the old map, straight out of Mexico into some of the most inhospitable land he'd ever seen. Still, that landscape hadn't dissuaded him from his quest as much as it had reinforced the idea that the gold yet remained to be rediscovered.

Once Shaw had the empire he desired, he could return to England to reclaim his ancestral lands, but he would come back to the United States and enlarge his holdings in these mountains. With Queen Victoria's blessing, and the young royal would have no choice but to give it, Shaw would stake a new claim on the lands Napoleon had sold to the United States. The English had defeated the French. By rights, the "Louisiana Purchase" negotiated by President Thomas Jefferson should have been relinquished as well. It was supposed to be part of the spoils of that war.

At the end of the Napoleonic War, King George III had been decrepit, blind with cataracts and barely able to move. He had chosen to let the peace with the fledgling United States stand when he should have returned to the war there with all true vigor.

As it was now, the joint occupation by the British and the Americans of the Oregon Territory was at risk because of all the American immigrants rushing out there to settle. Even the Russians still held a large fiefdom in Alaska.

Shaw would stand as the bulwark in the mountains. He would turn those would-be American settlers back and keep them from taking all the rich lands available here and out to the west coast. England's power would once more swell, and it would be because a Shaw had rescued the empire that was almost lost.

The thought warmed him despite the chill, and thoughts of failure dissipated. He would succeed because he would allow nothing less.

Morris, one of the Englishmen who had survived Mexico with Shaw and Rapp and some of the others, entered the cave at a dead run. He was wiry and quick to react, a true fighting man.

"Where's the general?" Morris demanded

breathlessly of a man pushing a wheel-barrow through the entrance.

"Here, Mr. Morris," Shaw called. Seeing the agitation plain in the man's body language bothered the general. The corporal wasn't a man to easily become untethered.

Morris ran to join Shaw. The corporal carried his rifle in one hand and rested his hand on the butt of a pistol at his waist. "General, Lieutenant Rapp sent me to get you. He and Sergeant Phillips think we have a problem."

"What problem?" Shaw demanded.

"Indians, sir."

"The Sioux?" Although the encounter with the Sioux along the river was days ago, Shaw had instructed his scouts to be watchful.

Marshaling his thoughts, Shaw strode toward the cave entrance.

"No sir." Morris fell into step beside him. "I saw them myself. They're Blackfeet. All along the rim to the east of our position."

"I thought after the drubbing we gave them weeks ago they'd know not to come near us again. We're far better armed than those savages were."

"Indians aren't always smart," Morris said. "They can be prideful and stubborn. As far as weapons go, these are carrying a lot of rifles. And they're wearing warpaint. They've come here with an agenda."

"Take me to the lieutenant."

"Yes sir." Morris lengthened his stride and took the lead.

Outside, Shaw adjusted his tall hat and followed the corporal. Lieutenant Oscar Rapp and Sergeant Phillips stood in the shade under a copse of pine trees and peered up the mountain to the east. Shaw blinked against the harsh morning light that now splintered across the ragged mountains.

Across that ridge, only two hundred yards distant, and Shaw knew that because he'd stepped it off himself to be certain, Indians on horseback gazed down on them with sharp intent.

Shaw joined Rapp. The lieutenant studied the Indians through a spyglass.

"What is the situation, Mr. Rapp?" Shaw asked.

"We're still trying to deduce that, sir." Rapp took the spyglass from his eye and handed it over to the general.

Shaw fitted the spyglass to his eye and trailed it along the ridge. Sunlight caught him again and again with blinding intensity. His eye throbbed. Frustrated, he lowered the spyglass.

"Do we not have guards along that ridge?"

Shaw asked.

"We did, sir," Rapp answered. "Three men."

"And no one gave a signal?"

"No sir."

"Then those men are dead." That was a plain fact and Shaw stated it as such.

"Or taken prisoner," Rapp said.

"Then they'll be dead later, probably in a most unpleasant fashion." Since Shaw had been in the mountains, he'd seen some of the Indians' handiwork torturing prisoners.

"Yes sir." Rapp pointed to the left and right of the cave entrance. "I've taken the liberty of sending out troops."

His eye still smarting from the light, Shaw raked the spyglass over the mountain's incline. His men lay prone among the scattered trees and brush. Most of the trees had been trimmed to provide a sight line, and all the fallen branches had been gathered up for firewood. They'd taken wood from the woods to the south, and they'd felled a few trees for use in the event they were trapped by the weather in the mountains. They were also laid to provide positions for them to fall back on if necessary.

Shaw had never faced winter the like of which happened in these mountains. He knew it would be difficult, but he had no doubt they could survive it. They had stores they'd gotten from passing wagon trains. All the immigrants were dead. Some of his soldiers used bows and loosed arrows into the wagons. When those luckless individuals were found, if they ever were, they would look like victims of the Indians.

Two wagons, taken only recently and from not far away, occupied space to the left of the cave entrance. Both wagons held food-stuffs they'd gathered from the passing immigrants. Shaw hadn't believed they could easily transport those goods through the mountains in the event of another move, but he had hopes they were in the right place. They wouldn't be able to continue searching. They would have to lay up for the winter soon.

Picket lines held their horses and pack animals in small groups under trees a short distance away. None of them were saddled, but they wore bridles so they could be mounted quickly if needed.

"Very good, Mr. Rapp." Shaw collapsed the spyglass and handed it back to his lieutenant.

"I told them they were to fire at the first sign of an advance, or upon my signal."

"Do you think those Indians are up there

just building their courage, Sergeant Phillips?"

The sergeant rubbed his jaw and squinted at the ridgeline. "It's possible, but I don't think that's all they're here for."

"We have snipers, Mr. Rapp."

"We've also got the sun in our eyes."

"Still, those snipers are crack shots. If we draw first blood, show those Blackfeet we're ready to fight, and we knock a few of them from their saddles, perhaps they'll find somewhere else to spend their day." Shaw turned to Morris. "My long gun, Corporal Morris, quick as you can. Tell Taylor, Wilson, and Pohl to saddle the horses. In case we need some mounts to harry these devils. Bring my horse to me when you bring my rifle."

"Yes sir." Morris took off.

"Sergeant Phillips," Shaw said, "go into the cave and get those men ready. Nearly half our forces are in there unawares. Assign Burleson, Farrell, and Stadlen to help with the horses. Split the rest of those men to the groups Mr. Rapp established. Let's be prepared."

"Yes sir." The sergeant trotted toward the cave.

"What do you think the Indians are waiting on?" Rapp asked.

"What would you be waiting on?" Shaw countered. He was always a teacher, always demanding officers around him to learn how to think. Until it was time to think for them.

"The same as we're doing now," Rapp said. "To see if they choose to fight, or they're going to ride off."

"I agree. So, we'll hurry that choice along a little. We'll put spurs to them."

"They've got the sun to their backs as an advantage."

"And we have rifles, Mr. Rapp, and men trained how to use them under fire. We'll fare fine." Shaw was convinced of that.

CHAPTER 29

Cautiously, aware that hostile guns could be around him in the tall grass and the trees in the mountains, Preacher swung down from the saddle and led Horse down into the ravine where the tracks he'd followed since early this morning had disappeared. Going down a steep incline while on a horse was trickier than coming up one.

He and Tall Dog had been on the scout to take meat. Now that the building of the trading post had begun in earnest and the men were working hard every day, they were going through supplies faster than Barnaby Cooper and his group had planned for.

Preacher had known keeping enough food on hand was only going to be part of the challenges facing the group. They still had winter coming, and it was coming quickly.

On top of that, there were the Blackfeet war parties that Preacher, Lorenzo, Tall Dog, Moses, and young Caleb Barker had found while hunting. So far, none of them knew about Albion Shaw and his group.

Or the Basque sharpshooter and his group.

To Preacher's way of thinking, this stretch of the mountains was awfully crowded. He wasn't certain what he was going to do about that, but he knew his solution would probably be rendered in powder and lead. And plenty of it.

The path Preacher followed down the mountainside was steep and treacherous, but it was possible to travel with a sure-footed mount. Horse picked his way with care with never a misstep.

Dog trotted down the trail ahead of Preacher and kept watch on everything. The big cur's paws didn't disturb a pebble and he moved silently as a shadow. Tongue lolling, Dog kept his ears pricked and remained watchful.

The ravine was at least ninety yards wide and probably just as deep. Four tall pillars cut out of rock stood in the bottom forty feet below. The pillars reached the height of the walls on either side. Striations in the stone showed where moving water in the past had stripped the mountains of soil down to its bones. A gleaming stream trickled through the belly of the ravine.

Dog ran over to the pile of fresh horse

apples that had caught Preacher's eye from the ravine's rim. The big cur sniffed intently for a moment, then sneezed and looked at the mountain man.

"Yeah, I know," Preacher said. "They came along only a short while ago."

He dropped Horse's reins and left the big stallion on his own, then the mountain man walked around the line of horse apples. One of the hoofprints had the divot of the man who'd laid up outside of Fort Pierre and ambushed the men who'd followed him.

Dropping to a crouch and gazing around, Preacher pressed his fingers to the center of the track. The ground was still soft and moist around the impression. It cleanly held the impression. The rider couldn't be more than an hour or so ahead of them.

Preacher wasn't sure how close he wanted to get to them. Whoever the Basque rifleman was, he was deadly accurate and had a thirst for blood. At present, the Basque and the men riding with him had skirted the trading post, but those men knew about the wagon train. Their curiosity had shown in the way they'd been around Little Spearfish Creek. Thinking it was time to find out what they were up to, Preacher had found their tracks and trailed them here.

The Basque had a mission though. That

was plain enough to see. He was hunting someone. The half-dozen cold camps his group had left behind testified to that.

Glancing up to the ridge, Preacher spotted Tall Dog just over the top. The young Crow warrior and Preacher had spent the last four days felling trees and cleaning up timber to help build the palisades around the trading post. The defensive barrier and the rough walls of the main building were coming along nicely. Darvis and his men worked surprisingly quickly and competently. The engineer knew the stakes they were facing and he made sure he got a good day's work from all of his men and from those who had been hired at Fort Pierre.

"Dog," Preacher called.

The cur had followed the trail of the horses seventy yards away and had almost disappeared around a curved wall. Dog hesitated, glanced back at Preacher, then at the gully around the corner. The dog's behavior indicated that he was curious, but he hadn't seen anything.

"Let's go," Preacher said. He took up Horse's reins, climbed into the saddle, and rode back up the mountainside.

Dog galloped up the incline and reached the top first.

Preacher reined Horse in, swept the surrounding countryside with his gaze, and glanced at Tall Dog. "Those tracks belong to the Basque and his men. Couldn't have passed through here much more'n an hour ago. Looks like they're followin' the ravine."

"They have circled the trading post several times," Tall Dog said.

"Yeah, the Basque knows the tradin' post is there. You and I have found his tracks. He's only travelin' with twenty men. He wouldn't have wanted to tangle with us unless he had to. He's out here for a reason. Maybe he's lookin' for somethin' and ain't found it yet. Whatever that is, it's close by. He's stayin' in the area."

"Perhaps to meet up with Albion Shaw."

"That's the likeliest thing I can think of."

"What do you want to do?"

"We're still going to take meat where we can. Those men back yonder have got to eat." Preacher gazed at the horse. "But I want to see where these tracks take us. We'll ride out farther than we've been ridin' out. The more we know about what's going on, the better." He urged Horse into motion along the ravine. "We'll just try not to get shot while we do it."

Shaw balanced the heavy Brunswick rifle across a thick pine branch. He stared down the thirty-inch barrel, noted the wind speed by the passage of a leaf that slid through the foothills of the mountain where the mine was, and sighted on one of the Indians on the mountain ridge who wore feathered headdresses.

The major general wasn't sure which one of the men was the leader of the Indians around them, but killing one of them at this distance would let them know they would find no easy prey in the mountains this morning.

"Mr. Rapp," Shaw said.

"Yes sir."

"On my signal."

The lieutenant hesitated for the barest second. Probably Rapp would have made the correct response, but Shaw wasn't willing to allow even the slightest equivocation. The time to strike was now.

Shaw spoke more forcibly. "Lieutenant."

"I was just considering our options, sir. The Indians haven't attacked yet."

"No, they haven't, and I'm not going to wait for them to do so. Those misbegotten heathens are nuisances at best, and dangerous at worst. They showed up here in numbers that suggest they're all for using force. Over this last couple months, we've left enemies among them."

416

Rapp nodded grimly. "That we have, sir. Among the Blackfeet and the Sioux."

"If we're going to dance, and I think we are, I'd rather call the tune myself," Shaw said. "Either we strike preemptively, bloody their noses, and dissuade them, or we cut their numbers down before they reach us. No matter. I'll not tolerate them sitting on that ridge watching us like carrion fowl."

Rapp drew one of the pistols belted across his shoulder. "Yes sir."

"Now . . . on my signal."

"Yes sir."

Shaw stood straight and pulled the rifle butt into his shoulder to handle the recoil. The Brunswick rifle fired a .704 belted round ball with a girdle that neatly fit the grooves in the barrel. During a reload, the girdle required extra attention and time, but when the rifle discharged, the ball spun along the grooves and flew straight and true out to three hundred yards. That accuracy was why the major general had chosen the weapon.

Calmly, Shaw flicked the leaf rear sight up. He set it for two hundred yards, the distance to the mountain ridge. He tightened his finger on the trigger, made a final sight adjustment, and pulled through smoothly.

Boom!

The rifle thumped solidly against Shaw's shoulder. He dropped the weapon butt first to the ground and gripped the barrel with one hand.

On the ridge, the Indian wearing the head-dress he'd aimed at slumped backward and fell over the hindquarters of his horse. The warriors nearest the stricken man milled about in obvious consternation.

Shaw reached into the wooden ammunition box at his feet, selected a cartridge, and tore it open with his teeth. He poured the powder down the barrel, patched the girdled ball, fitted it into the grooves, and rammed it home.

"Here they come!" Rapp shouted.

The Indians left the ridge in a rush. Their ponies galloped down the mountain and looked like a falling wave coming in off the ocean. The clamor of thundering hooves spilled over the camp near the mine.

"Ready rifles!" Shaw roared. He stepped forward, took the ramrod from the rifle, and pulled the weapon to his shoulder. "Stand steady!"

The men rose from the brush and aimed at the Indians.

"Steady!" Shaw commanded. He was certain many of the Blackfeet had never faced the debilitating concentrated fire his men could deliver. The Indians were riding into the fires of Hell and didn't yet know it.

The major general's men held their ground. The Indians closed to within a hundred yards. Shaw took aim at another Indian wearing a headdress. Only three were left now. The savages closed another forty yards and were now at almost point-blank range.

"Fire!" Shaw roared. He squeezed the trigger, and the rifle thumped against him.

Beside him, Rapp discharged his pistol to signal the soldiers ranked in front of the invading horde to fire their first volley.

This time, Shaw's ball only cut feathers from the Indian's headdress because the warrior ducked low over his pony.

Rifles cracked and black gun smoke filled the air around Shaw's men. Several of the Indians tumbled from their mounts, but others kept riding. They didn't turn and run. They rode straight into the soldiers and the horses knocked several of them into the grass. The bone-jarring impacts reached Shaw and echoed around him. Men's yelled curses, and screams chased them.

"Reload!" Shaw roared and followed his own order. *"Reload!"*

Some of the soldiers tried to obey, but the

Blackfeet warriors slid free of their ponies with tomahawks and knives in their fists. Sharp metal images splintered the sunlight and turned bloody. Bodies of soldiers and Blackfeet hit the ground and spilled their life's blood into the hard earth. Other Indians bent their bows and loosed shafts into the soldiers.

The line fractured and became milling groups of desperate creatures fighting for survival. Over the years, Shaw had seen the tableau again and again.

Shaw sighted on one of the Indians who rode past the engagement line. He fired a ball into the Indian's chest. When the warrior slid lifelessly to the ground, hit, bounced, and flopped to a stop, satisfaction filled the major general.

Five Blackfeet warriors spotted Shaw and rode at him. Their war-painted faces barely showed over the ears of their mounts. Rapp stepped forward, leveled his rifle, and fired.

Blood blossomed on the chest of the lead horse. The animal stumbled, slid down, and took another horse with it. Both Blackfeet hit the ground hard and only one of them got up.

Shaw dropped the rifle and drew one of his pistols. Once the weapon was level, he fired it into a mounted warrior's face from a dozen feet away. Features torn and bloody, the Blackfoot toppled from his horse. Shaw sidestepped the panicked animal and tossed away his spent pistol. He had no remaining loaded firearms.

Rapp shot a fourth Indian from his horse, dropped his pistol, and reached for another.

The last mounted Blackfoot yelled and rode at Shaw. The major general drew his saber, stepped to the side to avoid the pony so the galloping animal would miss him, set himself as it passed, and swung his blade. The keen edge sliced through the pony's back legs. The animal crashed to the ground and whinnied in terror.

Dazed from the fall from his mount, the young Blackfoot warrior pushed himself to his feet and took a fresh grip on his tomahawk. Before Shaw's opponent could set himself, the major general strode forward and thrust the blade into the warrior's stomach. Flesh parted with a spray of blood. Shaw yanked his weapon to the side and opened the wound even larger.

The warrior looked at the horrific wound and died. He fell forward onto his war-painted face.

Shaw shook the blood from his weapon and looked at the two lines on either side of the mine entrance. The Blackfeet outnumbered his men at least two to one, and the driving force of the charge had broken all hope of the soldiers holding their positions. Most of them fought for their lives in clumps.

The realization that they couldn't hold this position hit him like a sledgehammer.

"Damn them!" Shaw swore. "Lieutenant, with me."

Shaw ran for the horses. Rapp had two more charged pistols and emptied both into Blackfeet warriors.

Seated on a horse and riding low, Morris held the reins to two other horses and approached Shaw at the gallop.

"General!" Morris squalled.

Still holding the saber naked in his fist, Shaw turned and ran in the direction the horses were headed.

Morris pulled up a little and slowed the horses slightly.

"Keep going!" Shaw ordered.

Morris nodded and put his heels to his mount.

Shaw caught hold of the saddle horn on his horse, took two long strides to set himself, and swung up into the saddle. He thrust his boots into the stirrups and got his balance.

"The reins, Sergeant," Shaw said.

Morris tossed over the reins to Shaw's horse. The major general caught the leather straps easily in his left hand and leaned low in the saddle.

Rapp caught up to the other mount, caught the saddle horn, and effortlessly hauled himself up. He caught the reins when Morris tossed them to him, took control of the horse, and drew one of the two pistols holstered on his saddle.

"With me," Shaw said. "We can't let them get organized."

CHAPTER 30

"Looks like we found Albion Shaw," Preacher observed.

"Only the Blackfeet found him first."

The mountain man lay on his stomach on a northern promontory and watched the battle four hundred yards down the mountain through his spyglass. Gunfire had alerted him to the danger only moments ago, but he'd been curious enough to find out what was going on and had found a way to slide up onto the scene unannounced.

Dog and Tall Dog lay beside him in the tall, blue grama grass under a ponderosa pine. Their position afforded Preacher a good view of the fighting.

"The soldiers will lose," Tall Dog said. "There are too many Blackfeet."

"They'll lose if they try to stand and fight," Preacher agreed. He centered the spyglass on the rider in the middle of the fight who was slashing with his saber. "I don't think Shaw, if that is Shaw, is going to stay on this mountain just to die. He'll build as much of a line as he can out of those troops, and I'll lay odds that he heads to the bottleneck to the west if he knows about it."

"If he is a good soldier," Tall Dog said, "Shaw will know about that bottleneck."

"I think so, too. It's the only chance he's got."

"That lies in the same direction as the trading post. If Shaw knows about it, he might go there to replenish the supplies he will surely lose here."

That thought had settled uneasily in Preacher's mind, too. Even after the losses he'd taken, Shaw still had a lot of trained soldiers. Even though Darvis's crew was pretty salty, the folks at the trading post weren't professional killers.

"Maybe we need to get on back that way," Preacher said.

"We cannot go through the bottleneck," Tall Dog said.

"We can if we get there before Shaw does." Preacher collapsed his spyglass and shoved it into his possibles bag. He took up his rifle and edged back from the promontory.

Horse whinnied then, something the big

stallion wouldn't do unless there was cause, and the only cause up in these mountains that appeared probable this morning was the presence of Blackfeet warriors.

Standing on all four feet, Dog's hackles lifted, and he bared his fangs. A low growl hummed deep in his chest.

Preacher had a warning on the tip of his tongue, but Tall Dog was already sliding to the side. The mountain man rolled over onto his back and brought his rifle up.

Two arrows buried in the ground where he had lain. Four Blackfeet warriors stood revealed beside the trees that covered the promontory. Preacher laid his sights in the center of one Blackfoot's chest and squeezed the trigger. The large-caliber ball caught the Indian just below his throat and knocked him backward.

Tall Dog's rifle boomed, and the Indian on the right dropped where he stood.

Preacher rolled again and came to his feet behind a tall ponderosa pine. A boulder jutted up from the ground to the left and almost reached the mountain man's waist.

Dog ran in a zigzag pattern through the patchy scrub that covered the ground under the tall trees. The Blackfeet poured through the trees, and there were enough of them for Preacher to realize a pincer movement intent on circling the soldiers' position from the north had stumbled over Tall Dog and him.

Arrows whipped through the trees and caromed from branches. Several of them narrowly missed Preacher. Others shattered against the boulder and struck sparks against the flint.

Dog popped up like a jackrabbit and took down one of the Blackfeet. The scrub brush hid their battle, but from the Indian's hoarse screams, the big cur was winning.

Preacher placed his rifle against the tree trunk and drew the Patersons. He rolled the hammers back. This morning, since they were headed out into hostile territory, he'd loaded all five cylinders in each revolver.

Pistols in his hands, Preacher pivoted around the tree and aimed at his targets. At least fifteen Blackfeet still closed on Tall Dog and him. One of the young Crow warrior's pistols barked, and a Blackfoot jerked and went down.

As swiftly as he could pull the hammers back and drop the triggers into place, Preacher fired at a target, moved to the next, and fired again till all ten rounds had been dispatched toward his enemies.

Eight Blackfeet dropped, but two remained to continue the charge. Preacher slid behind the tree again, holstered his weapons, and drew the two pistols behind his back. He cursed his luck. He should have figured the Blackfeet would have been canny enough to attempt to surround the soldiers and cut them off from the bottle-neck. They would know this area, too.

He eared the hammers back, then stepped around the tree. Another wave of at least nine Indians — too many for his pistols — ran at him.

He took aim.

When Red Bat Circles Smoke recognized the White Wolf hiding in the trees and watching the battle with the soldiers instead of partaking in it as a warrior would, the Blackfoot chieftain couldn't believe his luck.

Of course, since all of this was watched over by the spirits, the luck was good and bad. He'd thought his scout had spotted a group of soldiers that had fled from the battle farther down the mountain, or who had been returning from a hunting or exploring expedition.

The good luck was that Red Bat was lead-ing his warriors, and the White Wolf only had one companion, a traitorous Crow war-rior from the looks of him. There were no other men to fight. Red Bat felt certain the battle would only last a few heartbeats.

Then the bad luck happened. The White Wolf had stepped from hiding with pistols the likes of which Red Bat had never seen. The White Wolf fired again and again, something that Red Bat had not known was possible, and the Blackfoot chieftain's warriors fell dead because the man's aim was so lethal.

For a moment, the White Wolf had stepped back behind the tree, then he had returned with two fresh pistols.

The Blackfoot chieftain pulled his rifle to shoulder, aimed at the White Wolf sixty feet away, and squeezed the trigger. The wind must have caught the ball, though, or perhaps the White Wolf's evil magic protected him, because a branch bent down just enough to deflect the ball.

The pistols in the White Wolf's hands boomed, and two more of Red Bat's warriors tumbled loosely into the scrub.

Red Bat reloaded.

"Tall Dog!" the White Wolf bellowed. "We can't stay here!"

Good. Red Bat took pride in the fact that he was causing the White Wolf to turn tail.

"I am ready," the young Crow warrior called.

"Horse!" the White Wolf yelled.

The Crow whistled shrilly.

Hooves thundered to Red Bat's left. A moment later, two horses charged through the trees and scattered the Blackfeet. The big gray stallion raced for the White Wolf and the other to the Crow. Both men paced their mounts, then hauled themselves into the saddle so the horses didn't have to slow.

"No!" Red Bat screamed.

With his rifle reloaded, he ran back to where he and his men had left their own mounts after his scout had found the White Wolf.

"Come to me!" Red Bat ordered his men. "Come to me! The White Wolf must not get away!"

His men followed him to their ponies, and they mounted. Then they galloped in pursuit of the White Wolf and his companion. Red Bat would not allow the old Blackfoot enemy to escape. He would take all the glory for killing the man for himself.

Breathing the acrid gun smoke around him, Shaw wheeled his horse and the big animal faltered for only a moment. It regained its footing and headed to the line on the mountain that his soldiers hadn't been able to hold. He didn't fault them. The advantage had belonged to the Blackfeet attacking out of the east and to their greater numbers.

He wanted to save as many of those men as he could. A major general wasn't worth much if he didn't have an army to command.

The stiff fletching of an arrow cut his cheek below his right eye, but he didn't turn from his course. He rode at a Blackfoot who fitted another arrow to his bow from less than ten feet away.

Standing in his stirrups as his horse lunged forward, Shaw swung the saber with all his strength. The heavy blade slammed into the Blackfoot's bow, shattered the wooden weapon, and crunched into the Blackfoot's face with an impact stout enough to vibrate up Shaw's arm. Bleeding profusely, the Indian silently fell from his mount.

Mercilessly, Shaw rode into the disorganized fray and swung the saber again and again. He chopped into the Indians' arms and legs and bodies. He swung indiscriminately and hit foe after foe in passing. He'd killed at least three more of their foes, wounded others, and still they were coming.

Several soldiers lay unmoving on the ground. Others limped away only to have arrows strike them and drive them to the earth.

Shaw glanced back at the picket line where the horses, some of them saddled, stamped their hooves and shook their manes anxiously.

"To the horses!" the major general roared. "Retreat!"

He swung the saber again and slapped aside a bow. His follow-up swing opened the Blackfoot warrior's throat.

The soldiers abandoned the broken line and ran for the horses. The Blackfeet pursued on foot and on horseback.

Shaw guided his horse toward the Blackfeet and struck at every opportunity. His arm grew tired and was soaked in blood and gore. His horse breathed like a bellows. Rapp rode at his side and fired a pistol he had managed to reload. An arrow protruded from the lieutenant's thigh and blood wept down his horse's side.

As he watched some of his men go down to enemy arrows and blades, Shaw realized they weren't going to make it. The odds were against them. There were simply too many Indians.

The major general cursed the fates and God and everyone he could think of. His fortune lay within his grasp, and he was going to be denied.

A Blackfoot with a spear rode at Shaw from his left, in a position that the major general couldn't easily bring the saber around to defend himself. The Indian smiled coldly in anticipation.

A hole opened above the Blackfoot's eyes, and the Indian's head snapped back. Silently, the warrior slid from his mount, and the horse turned aside.

In quick succession, three other Indians dropped in front of Shaw, and a dozen rifles cracked. A way cleared to reach the horses. In the trees, fifty feet away from the horses, at least ten riflemen stood their ground. Gun smoke curled over their heads.

Among them, Basque colonel Luis Yermo Areta stood at the forefront with the Girardoni to his shoulder. The man fired again and again, pulled his weapon up, and fed a new magazine of balls into it. Then he resumed shooting.

Shaw had first seen the weapon used in Veracruz. Until that time, the major general had only heard of the Girardoni. The wind rifle, in the hands of the skilled marksman who held it, had changed the course of some of the battles they'd been in together.

Yermo's rifle company were all trained marksmen and had been blooded in Spain and Mexico. They stood their ground around their leader, fired, reloaded, and fired again.

When confronted by the withering rate of accurate fire, the Blackfeet warriors wheeled about and galloped out of rifle range. That strategic retreat wouldn't last long, and Shaw and his men couldn't hold the mine.

"Mount up!" Shaw roared. "Take what you can carry and ride to the west!"

Shaw had scouted various staging areas around the mine in case of disaster. A good military man always did.

A bottleneck that could serve as a defensive position lay between those tall mountains. They could hole up there, and he could take stock of his situation.

His soldiers mounted, and there were wounded among them.

"General," Rapp called. He held a rifle and a brace of three pistols.

Shaw sheathed his saber. Rapp tossed the rifle across the distance and Shaw caught the weapon, then the leather sling that held the pistols.

"The rifle's loaded, sir," Rapp said. The arrow remained in his thigh, and he busied himself reloading his rifle. "I didn't have time to reload the pistols."

"Thank you, Lieutenant." Shaw slung the

rifle over his shoulder and drew the first pistol. He reached into his saddlebags for pistol cartridges and took one out.

The Blackfeet pulled back two hundred yards and milled about. The three surviving chiefs rode among their warriors and formed them up.

"General Shaw," Yermo yelled.

Shaw continued reloading pistols as best as he could and rode over to the Basque. "Colonel Yermo, it is good to see you. Your arrival couldn't have been more fortuitous."

A small, grim smile lit the Basque's face. "Only for the moment." He nodded toward the Blackfeet. "The leaders of those men will whip them back into a frenzy. They will return, and we will not be able to hold this position. They will overrun us."

"I know." Shaw slid another charged pistol into his brace and completed those three. He reached for the first of the pistols holstered on his saddle. "There is a bottleneck in the mountains only a mile to the west."

Yermo nodded. "My men and I have scouted it on the way to this place. We came through that bottleneck while searching for you. We can take defensive positions there."

Shaw holstered the first saddle pistol and reached for the second. "We'll head there, Colonel, and catch our breaths."

435

Yermo swept the surrounding terrain. "Did you find it, General? The gold you told me of back in Veracruz?"

"I believe I did."

Greedy fire lit in Yermo's dark eyes. "Then it is there for the taking."

"It would be, if not for these damned savages."

"We cannot hold this position," Yermo declared.

"No," Shaw reluctantly agreed. There were no grounds to even begin a rebuttal to that statement.

"I have every confidence we can turn the Indians back at that bottleneck," Yermo said, "but they will take everything you have here. There will be nothing left. We cannot mine for the gold while we starve."

Shaw studied the supply wagons and knew that was true. The Blackfeet would take the foodstuffs and the powder and lead they couldn't carry.

"True," Shaw replied, "nor can those murderous Blackfeet remain here. They don't care about the gold. They'll get their fill of being killed, then they'll take the supplies and ride away. We'll do what we can and hope for another wagon train of immigrants headed for Oregon. Then we'll take what we need. We'll just need to survive till then."

Yermo stroked his mustache. "Only a few hours from here, beyond the bottleneck, there is a group of men who hope to build a trading post."

"Out here?" Shaw couldn't believe it.

"Foolish men are everywhere," Yermo said. "They spend their lives chasing foolish dreams. You and I have seen this on three continents."

On the mountain, the Blackfeet grew more restless. Around Shaw, his surviving soldiers were mounted now and were charging their weapons.

"Those men will have supplies we need," Yermo said.

"How many men?"

"Fewer of them than the Indians we now face."

Shaw took only a moment to consider. He wheeled his horse around and faced his men. "To the west! Ride and we'll live!"

Behind the trees, Yermo and his riflemen saddled up. They all rode en masse for the bottleneck.

And, after a moment, the Blackfeet once more galloped down the mountain at them.

CHAPTER 31

For a moment, Preacher was certain Horse and Skidbladnir ate up the distance through the trees and drew away from any possible Blackfoot pursuit. The gray stallion and the paint pony ran like they'd been looking forward to the opportunity.

The easterly way they were headed bothered the mountain man though. The direction left them cut off from Little Spearfish Creek and the trading post. The mountains here were treacherous, and he only had passing knowledge of the area. They had ridden this way this morning because he'd wanted fresh hunting grounds.

He hadn't counted on running into Albion Shaw and a large Blackfeet war party.

Something caught the brim of Preacher's hat and he instinctively dropped forward in the saddle and reined Horse to the left toward a thick copse of white spruce trees to take advantage of the nearby cover.

The crack of a gunshot, followed by a half-dozen others, rolled over Preacher. Gun smoke fogged the trees ahead.

Preacher reined Horse up and peered through the trees. He set himself to reloading his weapons while in the saddle.

"You got lucky, Preacher," a man roared. "I figured my ball would have smashed that smug look right off your ugly face."

While his hands were busy going through the familiar task of tamping down balls in one of the Patersons, Preacher peered through the trees and spotted a group of men and horses seventy feet away. They'd spread out along a line of boulders that jutted up a couple feet away. He realized he recognized the man's voice.

"Is that you, Finlay?" Preacher demanded.

"It is," Finlay yelled back.

"Crenshaw let you out of the brig?"

"He did. Me and my men came on out here because you and me have some unfinished business."

Preacher shook his head and tamped down his final load. "You came a long way to die, Finlay."

"The way I look at it, I came a long way to kill somebody who needs killin'."

The rapid drumming of the Blackfeet ponies' hooves filled the trees and raised a line of dust to the west.

"Well," Preacher said, "today it looks like you're going to have to stand in line for the privilege of killin' me."

Tall Dog turned to face the approaching Blackfeet. He and his paint dropped back into some trees, but there was no real safe ground.

They were in a hard place, and it looked to get harder.

"What the hell?" Finlay squawked.

"You butted in," Preacher said. "Us and the Blackfeet already had our party goin' on. You interrupted our getaway. You can ease on out if you'd like. Maybe those Blackfeet haven't seen you yet."

Finlay cursed. "There's no way we're gettin' out of here without bein' seen."

"Probably not," Preacher agreed.

A second passed and the Indians rode closer. They still hadn't spotted Preacher or Tall Dog and were continuing at a rapid clip.

"Come on over here," Finlay said. "We set camp behind these rocks an' were just gettin' up to be about when we heard you ridin' in hell for leather."

"How do I know you're not going to shoot me?"

"Because it looks like I'm gonna be busy

shootin' Indians."

Preacher considered the situation briefly and didn't like any of it. The only thing he trusted was that Finlay might recognize they were stronger together against the Blackfeet.

Of course, that would change as soon as the Indians were no longer a threat.

Preacher glanced at Tall Dog.

The young Crow warrior nodded. "We do not have much of a choice," he stated quietly. "Our odds are better with them."

"Only till Finlay figures he doesn't need us anymore."

Tall Dog smiled. "We will no longer need him either. We are faster and better."

Preacher held his rifle and urged Horse into motion. Dog trailed beside him.

"Comin' in, Finlay," Preacher called.

"Hurry up. Those Indians are almost on top of us."

A moment later, Preacher dismounted near the picket line that held Finlay and his men's horses. He left Horse untethered, and Tall Dog did the same for his paint. They held their rifles and walked over to join Finlay and his men.

Preacher grabbed Dog's scruff and positioned the big cur between himself and Finlay.

"Watch," Preacher said, and he pointed to Finlay.

Dog growled his understanding.

The seven soldiers kneeled in a line behind the boulders and sighted down their rifles. Preacher and Tall Dog did the same.

"On my mark," Finlay ordered. "We let them get close enough to make sure we hit them. If you don't knock down an Indian with your shot, he's gonna be right in the middle of us before you can reload."

Preacher counted at least twenty-two Blackfoot braves riding toward them. They never slowed as they galloped through the trees.

"Ready," Finlay said.

Preacher had to admit the man had nerve. Finlay held his men from shooting longer than the mountain man had expected.

"Now!" Finlay roared.

He fired, and the other soldiers fired, too. Seven saddles emptied as the Indians spilled from them.

The Blackfeet fired a volley of their own, and balls smashed against the boulders, ricocheted off, and found flesh in Finlay and his men. Three soldiers went down, two of them with bloody faces.

Preacher and Tall Dog fired a moment later.

Two more saddles emptied, and the Black-feet charge wavered slightly, but on they came. Fifteen howling braves on horses jumped the boulder barricade.

One of them sailed over Preacher and the mountain man swung his spent rifle into the horse's back legs. Off-balance, the horse fell and rolled over the top of its rider. The slack way the Indian lay there afterward told Preacher he was dead.

Fourteen Blackfeet slid from their horses and scared their mounts back toward the soldiers.

Preacher held onto his spent rifle and dodged a horse that was driven at him by a Blackfoot. A brave came from behind the animal and swung his tomahawk at the mountain man's head. Using his rifle, Preacher blocked the blow and shot the warrior in the head at point-blank range with one of the Patersons.

Even as the dead man sank and the horse leaped back over the boulders to gallop away, Preacher rolled the Paterson's hammer back and took aim at another Indian who had speared Finlay through the stomach. The mountain man shot the Blackfoot in the head and dropped him.

Back against a boulder, Finlay sat with the spear jutting out of him and held a pistol. Blood leaked from the corners of his mouth.

Another soldier fell to a tomahawk between the eyes.

Preacher killed that warrior and stepped toward others. The Paterson barked twice more, and two more Indians went down. Dog grabbed the ankle of yet another Blackfoot, ran under the man to bring him down, then jumped on him. His flashing jaws closed on the back of his opponent's neck. The Blackfoot squalled in pain and fear, then he ceased making noise.

Ten feet away, Tall Dog stood with the *espada ancha* naked in his fists. The young Crow warrior stepped in a measured cadence as he dueled with three Blackfeet.

Preacher trusted his young companion could carry his own water and swept the battleground with his gaze. He holstered the first Paterson, swapped hands with his rifle, and drew the second revolver.

A soldier shot a Blackfoot warrior in front of him but took a flint knife through the eye that pierced his brain. Holding his wounded stomach, the brave stumbled back.

Preacher shot the Blackfoot in the face and turned his attention to another warrior who used his pony as cover. The brave stood twenty feet away and leaned out to loose an arrow at Preacher's head.

The mountain man dodged to his right so the arrow slid by, then aimed at the Blackfoot's exposed leg and squeezed the Paterson's trigger. The ball knocked the warrior's leg out from under him and he crashed to the ground still holding his bow with a nocked arrow.

Preacher fired at the man but was ducking the arrow at the same time. The shaft cut through his hair, and his ball flew wide of the mark. He rolled the hammer back again and put a follow-up shot into the downed man's throat.

Movement to Preacher's right alerted him to an attack. He blocked a war spear with his rifle but was knocked back and down by the weight of his attacker. The Blackfoot lay atop him and trapped the pistol against the mountain man's side with his body.

Holding Preacher down with an arm under his throat, the Blackfoot released the spear and freed his tomahawk.

"I am Red Bat Circles Smoke, White Wolf, and I will be your death today."

Preacher headbutted his attacker in the face and drove him back. He flipped Red Bat over, pulled his long knife, and shoved it into the Blackfoot's throat.

"Not today, varmint," the mountain man

snarled. "You're going to have to circle somewhere else."

Red Bat shivered and went still.

Preacher got to his feet and looked around. There were no more Blackfeet and no more soldiers. Tall Dog stood over three corpses with long cuts that bled out swiftly. The young Crow warrior held his sword at his side and crimson dripped from the edge.

Dog barked a warning, but he was still fighting an opponent that held one of his legs. His fangs sank into the man's throat.

A pistol hammer locked back into the firing position. Ten feet away, Finlay sat holding onto the spear that pierced him. He also held a pistol pointed at the mountain man.

"You've got to be the luckiest man I've ever seen, Preacher," Finlay snarled, and he grinned. "But that's —"

Preacher twisted the Paterson up and fired from the hip. The ball smashed through Finlay's confident grin and snapped the man's head back.

The mountain man drew a deep breath and stared around him. He looked at Tall Dog.

"Are you hurt?" Preacher asked.

"No," the young Crow warrior replied. He knelt and wiped his sword clean on a dead man's shirt. There weren't many places free of blood, but he found one.

"Then we'll ride." Preacher reloaded his weapons methodically. "We'll have to find another way back to the tradin' post. I don't want to follow Shaw and his men through that bottleneck — in case those varmints double back. We can't go back to the mountain where Shaw and the Blackfeet fought because they'll be takin' whatever supplies out of there that they can fetch for a while." He peered to the south. "Ain't no way we're going to beat Shaw back to the tradin' post, if that's where he's headed."

"That is where he will go." Tall Dog reloaded his rifle and pistols, too. "He has no choice. If he hopes to stay out here, for whatever his reasons are, he must have supplies. The Basque and his men know about the trading post."

"I know." Preacher strode toward Horse. "We'll have to see what's still standin' when we get there."

CHAPTER 32

Fatigued, but filled with anger and frustration, Major General Albion Shaw glared down at the trading post that nestled into the mountain beside Little Spearfish Creek. He hadn't even known the place existed. The location wasn't on the maps he'd gathered for his campaign.

"The trading post is bigger than it was the last time I saw it," Yermo said. "These men have been very busy. They must be highly motivated."

"It's because winter is coming," Lieutenant Rapp said. "They know they can't get back out of here in time to be safe. They have to make preparations to stay. As I have said, General, the winters here are most harsh."

"We have winters in my country," Yermo said.

"Not like these." Rapp's tone was harsh.

Instinctively, Yermo's hand stole toward

his saber.

"Forgive my young lieutenant's lapse in respect," Shaw said. "As you can see, his wound is aggravated and has stolen away some of his hospitable mien."

In truth, Rapp looked sickly and feverish. His eyes were glazed and, despite the chill in the air, he was sweating profusely. His wounded thigh had been bandaged, but it had bled through the cotton.

"I did not mean to speak so forthrightly," Rapp said.

That wasn't true, and Shaw knew it. Rapp was taking his cue from his commanding officer. Rapp had never cared much for the Basque even though the man had proven quite useful in Veracruz.

The three of them stood in the shade of trees on the ridge looking down into the canyon.

"It is forgiven," Yermo said. "I do hope, my young friend, that those goods down there contain medicines that will help infection. I fear that your leg needs attention, and it would be a shame for that injury to kill you or cost you a leg."

Maybe, Shaw thought, the trespass hadn't been forgiven so much as banked for another time. The alliance still remained somewhat uneasy, but the truth was that

Shaw needed the Basque and his riflemen.

Especially after today. Today had proven that.

Ten-foot walls surrounded the trading post on three sides. The fourth wall was the stone mountain behind it. Rock had been quarried from the mountain and used to build three fireplaces with another three underway.

The walls had been constructed of thick timbers taken from the surrounding forest upstream. Men poled more floating logs down the creek toward the building site.

Inside the trading post, carpenters and loggers worked. They cut beams for the roofs of buildings, and a large structure had taken shape in the center of the area. To the north, observable to Shaw because he stood above it, a stable ran half the length of the wall. Horses and wagons stood in the stable. Men threw in armfuls of long grass cut from the surrounding woodlands.

Hammers banged and saws ripped, and timber was fashioned into dwelling places, shops, and a warehouse that doubtless held the goods that Shaw coveted. Men shouted good-naturedly at each other, and they cursed one another, as well.

"Taking the trading post by force," Rapp stated, "if we can achieve that objective, would be costly."

Shaw silently agreed. Even with Yermo and his eighteen men — two of the original twenty had died during the running battle to escape the Blackfeet before the Indians had turned back to focus on the goods they'd captured — the major general's forces had been cut by half.

But there was an advantage Shaw had seen due to his long years of commanding men through hellish situations.

"Perhaps that would be true, Lieutenant," the major general said, "if we faced a *unified* force. However, that camp is divided."

"What do you mean?"

"Some of those men have distinct engineering and construction experience. Many of them are the black and yellow ones. See how they work at the more skilled tasks?"

Shaw pointed to where the more knowledgeable men worked at the saws and the hand-built forge.

"The other men," he continued, "some of them white and some of them black, are assigned menial and labor-intensive work. Given a few more weeks, this trading post might well implode under a lack of true leadership."

"I don't see what good that will do us," Rapp stated.

"Weak command is always a problem," Shaw said. "I intend to exploit that weakness. We've got a gold mine to find and we'll have to dig our fortunes from it. We'll need laborers as well as men with rifles. We can get both here."

Yermo smiled in understanding. "That is a bold move, General. One that might work."

"I'm going to ride down there," Shaw said, "and see if anyone is interested in signing up with us."

The argument escalated before Barnaby Cooper decided how to handle it. The friction had been building all morning and everyone knew it. This wasn't something Cooper was versed in. He wished that Darvis was there, or that Preacher was back from his hunt. Those two could keep things rolling smoothly.

"You can't tell me what to do!" Ernie Hillman roared at Nkosi.

They stood only a short distance from each other, and Hillman glared like he was as fierce as they came. Nkosi sighed and looked mildly irritated, not angry.

There were a handful of Nkosi sprinkled among Rufus Darvis's engineering corps. One was a blacksmith. One was a stone mason. Another designed the pitch and fall of the roofs and the trading post walls. Still another handled the blasting powder used to remove stone and tree trunks from the trading post's ground.

This Nkosi was a sawyer, and was built like a bull. He had a deep chest and thick arms and legs. He and his team took charge of the logs floated down the creek and cut them into planks and beams. He worked hard every day, and even though the temperature was cool today, he was dappled in sweat.

Ernie Hillman was from Texas, didn't care much for black men, and didn't mind telling folks about it. He stood holding a crowbar and thrust his jaw out like a petulant child.

Nkosi placed his end of the long saw on the ground and walked over to Hillman.

"You will do as I say," Nkosi the sawyer said in accented English. "You and your men are dawdling. We need the finished planks moved quickly so we can continue our work. You are putting us behind schedule. I will not tolerate that."

Hillman's crew stood behind their straw boss and urged him not to take Nkosi the sawyer's guff.

"To hell with you!" Hillman roared and

readied his crowbar to swing. "You're not gonna —"

Nkosi swung a big fist and caught Hillman on the ear. The Texan went down like he'd been poleaxed. When the man hit the ground limply, the crowbar slid from his unconscious fingers. The ear Nkosi had hit him in looked like it had been ironed flat and bled.

The other sawyers laughed aloud.

Glaring at Hillman's cronies, Nkosi gestured to Hillman. "Pick up this lazy man and lay him somewhere. Then come move these planks — quickly — or I will be having words with you."

Hillman's associates decided it was better to do as they were told. Gripping the unconscious man by his arms and legs, they carried him to a place beside the porch of the main building and left him there. They hurried back to the planks Nkosi and his crew had cut.

Relieved, Cooper continued looking out the open space in the main building that he hoped might one day hold a fine window that advertised COOPER'S TRADING POST. He hadn't finalized the name with the others, but he hoped it would be acceptable. After all, this whole venture was his idea.

"Hey," one of the lookouts posted on the wall bellowed. "Got a rider comin'."

The man held a rifle and stood on the catwalk Darvis and his carpenters had built along the wall and over the double gate that was the trading post's entrance.

Darvis trotted out of the small forge that had been one of the first things they'd built. The building stood thirty feet from the main building and was a hub of production. The hammers rang from sunup till sundown. Darvis and his men smithed the beam braces they used on the main building there. The engineer grabbed a rifle that stood beside the forge.

"Who is it?" Darvis yelled and ran to the wall.

"Don't know," the lookout said. "Man on a horse. Looks like he wants to talk to someone."

Tom Kittle, also carrying a rifle, followed Darvis up the stairs.

Feeling safe enough with the others armed, Cooper followed them up the steps. He was surprised by how firm and stable they were in light of the fact that they hadn't existed until a few days ago.

On the catwalk, Cooper stood and peered over the stockade wall. The posts were dulled but showed edges where the axes had

455

cut them to size. Mud filled the gaps between the posts. Hillman and his crew had done that work, as well, and complained about it. The work was shoddy and Darvis had dismissed them from it until he trained men who could suitably replace his men.

The man was in his late forties. His hair was blond, and he sat his horse in a fine fashion.

Anthony Humboldt, already somewhat drunk even though the day was young, plodded up the steps to the catwalk. He carried a rifle and Cooper remained mindful of it because he didn't trust the man. In hindsight, inviting Humboldt had been a mistake, but the man had come with all his wife's money, and that had been necessary.

"What's going on?" Humboldt demanded.

"We're waiting to find out," Cooper replied.

Humboldt leaned blearily over the wall and roared, "State your business."

The man on the horse smiled and nodded. "I am Major General Albion Shaw, lately of Veracruz and previously from England."

"Don't want no Englishmen here," someone shouted inside the trading post grounds.

"I have come with a business proposition," Shaw continued. "I have recently discovered a gold mine not far from here. I was given a map by a man in Veracruz who had mapped out some of these mountains. He told me of the gold mine he found."

"So why ain't he diggin' it an' gettin' rich?" one of Hillman's cohorts asked.

"He was unfortunately killed in the war against the French before he had the chance," Shaw replied. "I, myself, nearly died this morning fighting Blackfeet who want to drive me from this mountain."

"We're not interested in your proposition," Darvis said.

Unperturbed, Shaw smiled. "Come, come. Surely there are a few brave souls who would be willing to dig for gold."

"I'll dig for gold," someone said.

"So will I," someone else said.

"I'm tired of takin' orders from these people," another said.

Opaline Humboldt dashed up the steps to join the men. The reporter, Rory McClellan, followed her. Both appeared to be somewhat disheveled, and it was known that they'd been keeping company while Anthony Humboldt had his own, separate, sleeping arrangements.

"You'll find no one here interested in such a venture," Opaline said. "These are men whom I have hired to help build this trading post. I have already spoken for them."

"You ain't spoken for me," someone below growled.

"Or me," another said.

Opaline glared around but didn't see the offenders.

"My dear madam," Shaw said, "I'm afraid you don't understand the lengths to which I am prepared to go to get what I wish. If needs must, I will attack this trading post and take what I desire."

Lorenzo climbed the steps and talked to Darvis in a hurried tone that Cooper overheard.

"He ain't alone," Lorenzo said. "He's got men up along the canyon wall. Me an' Moses an' Caleb seen 'em."

Cooper shaded his eyes, squinted, and made out a dozen men along the canyon wall.

"How many men?" Darvis asked and frowned.

"More'n we might be able to handle," Lorenzo said. "With these fine walls you built, we can make a fight of it to keep them outside, but we can't count on ever'body inside these walls helpin' with that. Or maybe not even to not shoot us. Some of those men from Fort Pierre don't care for you or your men."

Cooper glanced at the men gathered below. They'd already formed two groups for the most part, and those groups were exactly what had been building over the last couple weeks.

All those men had guns.

The trading post, Cooper realized, was a powder keg waiting to blow. All it would take was one spark.

"Mighty hard to fight a war on both ends," Lorenzo said.

"I know," Darvis replied. "I've done some of that."

"What about it, gentlemen?" Shaw asked. "Shall we put it to a vote?"

Darvis didn't say anything, and Cooper knew things were dire.

Someone cried out in pain, and something hit the catwalk hard enough to vibrate it under Cooper's feet.

A pistol cocked.

"I'm voting," Anthony Humboldt declared.

Cooper turned to the man.

Humboldt held a pistol pressed against the back of Opaline's head. Rory McClellan lay at their feet with a bloody face and scared eyes.

"Humboldt!" Tom Kittle roared. He pointed his pistol at Humboldt. "What the hell do you think you're doing?"

"Divorcing this unappreciative, trouble-making harpy I married," Humboldt said. "Lower your weapon before I put a ball in her head and save myself some aggravation."

"Anthony!" Opaline squalled. "You can't —"

"Can't what?" Humboldt demanded. "Stand up for myself? I promise you I can, though you've tried your damndest to shame me in front of everyone by taking up with that scrawny-necked boy who can't even defend you. Now you shut up or I'll end your life just so I never have to hear your voice again." He glanced back at Kittle. "I said, lower that weapon."

Slowly, Kittle dropped his pistol to his side.

"Good." Humboldt peered over the catwalk at the men below. "Now, how many of you want to go gold hunting with me and give up this trading post foolishness?"

A resounding cheer came from below.

Humboldt looked back over the stockade wall at Shaw. "Well, General, looks like you got yourself a crew. Some of you men down there open those gates."

Cooper watched in dismay as his trading

post was so easily surrendered. He only hoped he lived through it.

Chapter 33

From his hidden observation point on the other side of the canyon, Talks With Toads watched the blond-haired general oversee-ing the removal of the supply wagons from the trading post. Talks With Toads had been there for the whole standoff.

While hunting meat for the war party still hoping to kill the general and his men, Talks With Toads had discovered the trading post and the general lying up in wait above it. Chief Eyes Cut Like Knife and the main group of the braves were only a few miles away.

At first during the encounter at the trad-ing post, Talks With Toads had thought there would be bloodshed, but he didn't really care because it would have been men who were not Sioux killing men who were not Sioux. Given their insistence on invading the mountains used by Talks With Toads's tribe, that would not have been a bad thing.

He had mixed feelings about the woman. In his tribe, women could be fierce and stand up to men who were wrong.

This one didn't seem strong.

The general and his men remained outside the trading post. The white man who held the woman captive oversaw the removal of the supplies. He and the men who followed him took all the food and drink, and they left all the tools. Except for picks and shovels and wheelbarrows. Those they took and piled into the six wagons.

Violence threatened again and again as the men shouted at each other, but the whole affair remained bloodless until one of the men leaving with the general attacked one of the black men.

The black man defended himself, but he didn't return the attack. A moment later, the general pulled out his rifle and shot the white man dead. Then he warned the men riding out with him that he would not allow any insubordination.

Talks With Toads wasn't sure what that word meant, but he got the idea. No one else attacked anyone.

The wagon train crept up the side of the mountain and disappeared in time. Talks With Toads hated to see them go. So far, the white general had had too many men for the Sioux to fight. They would have died. Now they were getting desperately short on food and winter was coming.

Talks With Toads didn't want to lose the trail. He didn't want to fail in his vengeance promise.

He didn't know how long he sat there, but when that time passed, he spotted two riders coming over the mountain. They rode down into the canyon and a wolf trotted beside them.

It was the wolf who identified the man for Talks With Toads. He had never met the man, but had heard stories of him. They were all good stories. Tales mixed with bravery and cleverness and an accounting for those who had wronged the man.

And there were other stories of the man's wrath against the Blackfeet. It was said that Chief Eyes Cut Like Knife and Hawk Strikes had fought alongside the man called Preacher in the past. Even Owl Friend told a tale of hunting buffalo with Preacher when the tribe was hungry.

As Talks With Toads watched the man ride toward the trading post, a desperate plan formed in his young mind. It was scary, but he had to try.

"They took all the food, Preacher," Lorenzo

said. "With Humboldt holdin' a pistol to his wife's head, with all them men inside the tradin' post turncoatin' like they done, wasn't nothin' we could do."

Anger burned in Preacher as he looked over the looted trading post. Wagons were gone. Oxen were gone. Horses were gone.

The food was gone.

They couldn't make it through the winter without it. There were too many of them to feed.

And it wouldn't be safe to try to go back to Fort Pierre.

Still, things were better than Preacher had expected them to be. He would have put money that many, if not all, of the folks at the trading post would have been killed.

He stood with several of the others in front of the framed main building. The planning was thin, but they had to think of something.

"We shouldn't have let them go," Lorenzo said. "As it is now, we ain't got what we need."

"If you'd fought then, sounds like a lot of folks would have been killed. Maybe all of you." Preacher dropped a hand on Lorenzo's shoulder. "I'm glad you're alive."

"Me, too, but that ain't gonna help in the middle of winter when I'm out here gnawin' on my own foot."

"It's not going to come to that. And as long as we're alive, we can change the way things are." Preacher looked over at Rufus Darvis. "You said your men could fight."

"They can," Darvis said. "And they can fight as hard as they can work. Not like most of those layabouts Shaw took with him."

"How many of them would be willin' to fight if there's a chance to get those supplies back?"

Darvis grinned coldly. "All of them. They don't take kindly to betrayal. The problem is, Humboldt's still got his wife prisoner." He frowned. "I expect things won't go well for her. They won't want to risk a woman's life. Me neither."

"I might sound unkind," Preacher admitted, "but she's got some of that hardship comin'. I wouldn't wish her dead, so we'll work to prevent that. If we can." He looked at Lorenzo. "How many men did you see?"

"Shaw's men?" Lorenzo shook his head. "I had to guess from the tracks me an' Moses found when we went lookin', maybe fifty, but that Basque with the wind rifle was with him. I seen him a-settin' up there smug as all get-out."

"We've never seen him."

466

"I have," Cooper spoke up. "I saw him, as well."

"I recognized him by that rifle," Lorenzo said. "With that straight-out stock fittin' what you an' Rufus described, I'd know it anywhere. It was him."

"I guess he was out here lookin' for Shaw," Preacher said.

"Guess so," Lorenzo said. "Found him, too. They were lookin' thick as thieves."

"That's because they ran off with all our goods," Tom Kittle said. "They *are* thieves."

Preacher looked at Cooper. "How many of the men you hired at Fort Pierre stayed behind?"

"Six."

"Will they fight?"

Cooper shook his head. "Most of them are ready to take their chances on returning to Fort Pierre. They want no part of this."

Preacher couldn't blame them. This was a lot more than any of those men signed on for. He glanced at Darvis. "How about your men?"

Darvis grinned coldly, and dark lights gleamed in his eyes. "I've got twenty-seven men who can fight."

"Will they?"

"Rather than starve to death in a foreign land?" Darvis hiked an eyebrow. "You're damn right they'll fight. Most of them have been fighting their whole lives."

"Do they have weapons?"

"Shaw didn't try to take personal weapons," Darvis said. "We've got those."

"Shaw sure packed out ever'thin' that wasn't tied down though," Lorenzo said. "Took a lot of gunpowder and lead, too."

"He did," Darvis agreed. "But he didn't get it all. I've got a supply set aside in a powder magazine I had my men build into the mountain. I wanted to keep it safe from everyone."

"I know what you're thinkin', Preacher," Lorenzo said. "Trust me, I want to get me some hide over this thing, too. Especially a piece of Humboldt's an' them other traitors. Coulda held our own if they hadn't done what they done. Problem is, you got about half the army you need to take them on."

That, Preacher knew, was true.

"We can tilt the odds a little in our favor with some strategies I've used over the years," Darvis said. "My men and I have fought before, and we've come up with some explosives that have helped turn the tide a time or two. We can mostly empty kegs of nail, leave some nails in, and repack those kegs with gunpowder. Set them off with fuses when you're ready, and you've got some hellacious blasts in confined areas. Those nails will rip a man to shreds."

"We have to tilt the odds more than that," Preacher said. "Shaw and his men outnumber us."

"Short men or not," Tom Kittle said, "Shaw and his men left us without food. We'll never make it through the winter."

That truth quieted the talk for a moment.

Caleb hailed them from the catwalk. "Preacher, you might want to come have a look at this."

Preacher carried his rifle with him to the catwalk. Dog loped at his side. The others followed.

Peering over the palisades, Preacher studied the young Sioux brave standing in front of the trading post.

"Where'd he come from?" Preacher asked Caleb.

"Don't know. One minute he wasn't there. The next he was."

"Is he alone?" Preacher studied the creekbank and the mountain sloping down into the canyon.

"I would have thought we were alone," Caleb said.

Preacher raised his voice and called out. "What do you want?"

"I am Talks With Toads," the young brave said.

Judging by his voice, he was little more than a boy.

"I come to speak to Preacher," Talks With Toads said. "It is about the white general who raided your house. My tribe and yours share a common enemy. My tribe and I wish to destroy him with you."

Four hours later, after the Sioux had explained his thoughts and his history with Shaw and his men, and after Preacher had made plans with Darvis and his men, Preacher, Lorenzo, Tall Dog, Moses, and Caleb rode with Talks With Toads to his tribe's camp. Although Talks With Toads had a general idea of where the Sioux band would be, it took an hour of riding to catch up with them.

A line of Sioux warriors met Preacher and his group in a small clearing, and they stopped at a respectful distance. The other Sioux warriors were spread in a half-circle around the arrivals.

"I will ride on ahead and explain things," Talks With Toads said. "That way they will know what is going on."

"That's fine," Preacher responded. "Make sure your chief knows that striking tonight, while Shaw and his men are worn out from their previous battle this morning, would be best. They might expect retaliation in the morning and be better prepared. Tonight, we will have an advantage."

"I will." Talks With Toads urged his pony forward.

The Sioux warriors separated long enough for the boy to ride through, then closed immediately.

One of the older warriors looked at the mountain man. "I know you, Preacher. It has been a long time."

"I know you, Bent Goose," Preacher said.

"The last time we fought together, we fought the Blackfeet."

Preacher nodded. "I hope we fight together again."

"As do I." The old Indian looked at the riders with Preacher. "Your companions are fighters?"

"Every one of them," Preacher said. "We have more. They are preparing for our war now."

"That is good," Bent Goose said. "The white general must be killed."

"I think so, too."

Riders came from behind the line of Sioux warriors. Talks With Toads rode with Chief Eyes Cut Like Knife and Hawk Strikes.

Preacher knew both men.

The warriors separated. Eyes Cut Like Knife reined in his pony and stopped in front of Preacher.

"We have a common enemy," the chief said.

"We do," Preacher agreed.

Eyes Cut Like Knife took the measure of the men with Preacher. "The white general searches for the yellow metal that drives white men crazy."

"I was told that. Shaw rode to the trading post and recruited men from us with that story. Then he took all of our food."

"The spirits have foretold this will be a hard winter. Those who have not prepared will not live to see the return of spring."

Preacher nodded and waited impatiently till the chief had his say. The mountain man knew more was coming.

"Has the white general found the yellow metal?" Eyes Cut Like Knife asked.

"I don't know," Preacher said.

The chief paused. "And if the white general has?"

"The yellow metal has never interested me," the mountain man said. "If he has found it, news of the yellow metal will draw more folks here. I don't want that any more than you do."

"Yet you guide wagon trains across these mountains."

"*Through* them," Preacher said. "I take them through these mountains to Oregon and to the big water there. They are going to go no matter what I do. The best I can do is guide them through these mountains so they keep going."

"Talks With Toads tells me of the trading post. It is not allowed."

"Those people don't know what they're doin'," Preacher said. "Little Spearfish Creek isn't a place where many wagon trains go. I'm bettin' those folks will be gone come spring. The woman who invested the most in this venture has been taken by her husband, a man who is now workin' with the white general. If she lives, she'll be gone as soon as she can."

"If that does not happen," Eyes Cut Like Knife said, "we will force them to leave."

"That's not my problem," Preacher said. "I was out here to get the white general. Those folks were just a way to disguise that."

The chief took a deep breath and looked around at his men. "We will ride with you, Preacher, against our common enemy."

"Did Talks With Toads explain to you that we have to attack them tonight? Before they get a chance to dig in?"

Eyes Cut Like Knife nodded. "He did. I have talked with Hawk Strikes."

The other Sioux warrior nodded.

"He agrees that your plan is a good one," the chief said. "My warriors are gathering their gear. We can be ready in minutes."

Preacher glanced at the setting sun. "That's good, because we're runnin' out of time."

"Have you ever noticed how shiny and bright gold is?" Major General Albion Shaw asked Yermo.

Inside the main cave, lighted by several candle lanterns, Shaw sat across from the Basque colonel at a large water barrel he was using as a table. The major general opened his left hand slightly and let the small nuggets of gold he held in that hand trickle into his other hand.

"I have," Yermo said.

The colonel picked up a lantern from another water barrel that was also used as a table for the men in the common room. He raised the hurricane glass, ducked his head, and lit one of his dark cheroots.

"It is pretty," the Basque said. "Women like the way it shines against their skin." He smiled. "Sometimes I like to see it on them."

Shaw nodded. "It is pretty, but it is heavy,

too. Heavier than would be expected after seeing it." He held out his fist with the gold. "Feel it."

Yermo held out a hand.

Shaw dropped the dozen nuggets into the man's hand.

Yermo weighed the nuggets in his hand. "It is heavy, my friend." His dark eyes glittered. "How much do you think there is?"

Shaw shook his head. "I have no way to know. My mining expert, Carmichael, thinks he may have found the mother lode with his latest efforts. We'll know more in the morning."

Yermo smiled. "Then we will all be rich men."

"We will," Shaw agreed. He pulled the cork from one of the whiskey bottles they'd taken from the trading post and poured them each a drink in tin cups. He put the corked bottle away and raised his cup. "To your health."

Yermo picked up his cup and raised it, as well. "And to yours."

When Shaw emptied his cup, the whiskey burned the back of his throat, but it was a good burn. A burn a wealthy man might become accustomed to. He looked forward to that day, and to returning to London to take his rightful place.

"Do you think this man, Preacher, will try to make things difficult for us?" Yermo asked. "While I was riding out this way, I heard stories about him. He seems to be an incredible man."

"I've heard some of those stories, as well." Shaw waved the thought away dismissively. "In this country, these people tell big stories about their heroes. I have listened to all the tales about Davy Crockett, Mike Fink, and Daniel Boone that I care to hear. There might be some truth in there, but much of it is utter balderdash."

"Those three men are dead," Yermo said. "Preacher is very much alive."

"One day Preacher will be dead, too," Shaw said, "and the stories will probably only get bigger and more outlandish." He shook his head. "You can worry about him if you want to, but it'll amount to nothing. We have a small army here. We're well-armed and well-fortified."

Shaw poured another drink for them.

"Even if Preacher dares to show his face here," the general said, "I have you to shoot it right off, don't I?"

Yermo smiled. "You do indeed." He lifted his cup. *"Salut."*

"Salut," Shaw said.

Outside, the woman screamed again.

Humboldt had taken her to a tent near the outer edge of the campsite in front of the mine. Humboldt had taken his wife there to abuse at his leisure.

"That will be annoying," Yermo said and frowned.

"She is sounding weaker," Shaw said. "I don't think she'll last much longer."

"Pour us another drink," Yermo suggested. "We can toast the coming silence."

Shaw poured and they drank.

Opaline Humboldt yowled again.

Irritated himself, Shaw glanced toward the cave mouth. Outside, men labored by lantern light to carry away the dead soldiers and Indians that had been left by the earlier battle.

The Blackfeet had emptied the supply wagons and gone hours ago. All of the dead soldiers had been scalped and otherwise slashed and hacked to the point they no longer looked human. Maybe that made the disposal of the bodies easier for the men who carried those bodies to a small ravine a hundred yards away. In the morning, they would burn those bodies, and the mountain would stink of it for a day or so, then it would be gone.

All that would remain would be the gold.

CHAPTER 34

Opaline Humboldt's scream ripped through the night and rendered the cold-blooded scene taking place on the mountainside below even more grotesque.

Lying in brush fifteen feet from the top of the mountain, Preacher scanned the campsite around the cave entrance with his spyglass. He was far enough down that the hunter's moon blazed bright yellow amid all the silver stars. No clouds hung in the sky, and some of the darkness was torn away by the moonlight and starlight.

"That woman's screams are causin' my back an' shoulders to knot up somethin' fierce," Lorenzo whispered to Preacher. "I've heard butchered hogs after they been kissed by the knife that didn't wail so."

"Humboldt's not killin' her," Preacher said.

He focused the spyglass on the tent where Humboldt held his wife captive. Humboldt

478

had stepped out of it a few minutes ago and sported long scratches on the side of his face and neck. Evidently Opaline Humboldt was determined to give as good as she got.

"He might not be killin' her," Lorenzo said, "but listenin' to that caterwaulin' is gettin' on my nerves."

"At least it's a distraction, and we know she's not dead." Preacher shifted the spyglass around and studied the rest of the camp.

Several tents occupied the south side of the mine entrance. Shaw's men had cleared most of the dead from that side of the cave. Men rolled the dead onto thick quilts that would never wash clean of the blood soaked into them, then they carried the bodies to a ravine north of the mine and dumped them.

A dozen cookfires lit the night where men warmed themselves and ate late suppers despite moving the bodies. All the soldiers and the recruits from the trading post glanced around anxiously and looked tired. The soldiers still hadn't recovered from the battle earlier in the day, and the recruits were fatigued from working on the trading post. Thin tendrils of gray smoke curled up to the sky and vanished in the bright starlight.

Opaline Humboldt screamed again, and

Lorenzo cursed quietly.

Preacher almost wished the woman was dead. Attacking Shaw and his men would be simpler if she was. He didn't feel guilty. He didn't owe her anything, and she'd done her best to get her husband to kill him.

Still, she was a woman in trouble, and not helping her wouldn't set right with some of the men in Darvis's group who had notions about protecting womenfolk.

Letting Opaline die wouldn't be agreeable to Tall Dog either, come to think of it. The young Crow warrior still had his head full of ideas from those old Norse fables his father had told him.

Preacher put his spyglass in his possibles bag and picked up his rifle. He raised slightly and Dog got closer to him. A short distance away, Tall Dog got to his feet, too.

The two of them planned on sneaking down to Humboldt's tent and freeing Opaline Humboldt. Then the attack on Shaw and his men could begin.

"Preacher," Darvis called. The engineer held up a small canvas bag. "The slow match is on the outside pocket. You've got two explosives inside the bag."

Preacher accepted the bag and pulled it over his body. The slow match burned steadily inside the small pocket sewn to the bag and a thin string of gray smoke lifted into the air.

The smoke wasn't enough to mark Preacher in the night, so he ignored it. However, he couldn't stop thinking about the damage the two explosives would do if the bag caught fire and set them off.

Back at the trading post, Darvis had demonstrated the fist-sized ceramic pots he'd filled with nails and gunpowder. He'd topped them off with wooden disks and sealed them with tallow. A short fuse protruded from each one.

The explosives couldn't be thrown because of the fragile natures of the ceramic containers, but once the fuses were lit, they could be rolled toward opponents. Preacher doubted any of Shaw's soldiers or the traitors from the trading post had ever seen the like.

Tall Dog took a bag of his own, slung it, and together Preacher, the young Crow warrior, and Dog crept down the mountain. They skirted the campsite by a wide margin and stayed in the shadows and the brush.

The men gathered around the fires drinking coffee and tea from tin cups. The odor of both beverages slipped through the night air and thankfully leached away some of the stink of the dead. The men didn't talk much, and only then briefly and quietly.

In due time, Preacher fetched up behind a tree fifty yards from Humboldt's tent. Opaline screamed again.

Tall Dog tensed.

"Easy," Preacher said. "We'll get there. She's still alive."

Three groups of men carrying bodies passed on the other side of the tent. Preacher waited till they were safely away and weren't glancing back. He slipped his long knife from his moccasin and walked to the back of the tent as quickly and quietly as he could

Flesh struck flesh and Opaline Humboldt screamed again. Her voice had grown ragged, but she wasn't going to quit on it.

"Stupid sow," Anthony Humboldt growled. "You'll take what's coming to you. I'll teach you to scratch me."

Another meaty blow echoed inside the tent.

Preacher shoved his knife in near the top of the tent and swept it down through the slit canvas. Quick as a wink, he stepped into the tent. The lantern hanging from the center support illuminated Anthony Humboldt's handiwork.

Bruised and bloody, Opaline Humboldt lay on the earthen floor and cowered from her husband's next blow.

Aware that they were no longer alone in the tent, Anthony Humboldt jerked his head up and spotted Preacher.

"You!" Humboldt snarled. He snapped his hand out and the small derringer popped out of his sleeve into his hand.

Unwilling to shoot the man and raise hob in the campsite, Preacher crossed the floor in a single stride, swung his rifle, and knocked the small pistol flying out of Humboldt's hand before he could fire it. Then the mountain man sank his knife up under his opponent's sternum and pierced his heart. Humboldt died with a look of surprise.

Satisfied, Preacher released his blade and caught the dead man by the shirt before he could fall. He lowered Humboldt to the ground.

A pistol cocked behind Preacher. He threw himself to the side and turned.

Opaline Humboldt held her dead husband's derringer in her fist. She pointed the weapon at Humboldt and pulled the trigger before Preacher could reach her. Flame spat from the small barrel, and the ball struck Humboldt's surprised face. Blood wept over his features and the *crack* of the shot filled the tent.

"What the hell was that?" a man yelled.

"Came from Humboldt's tent," someone else said.

"Reckon he killed her?" another asked.

"You damned woman," Preacher growled. "He was already dead."

He tore the derringer from Opaline's tight grip, threw it away, then pulled the woman to her feet and shoved her toward the opening he'd cut.

Opaline screamed, but this time it was in fury, not fear. "Don't you touch me!"

"Tall Dog," Preacher called.

The young Crow warrior reached into the tent, grabbed one of Opaline's arms, and yanked her outside. She screamed again. Preacher paused just long enough to grab his knife from Humboldt's body, then he slipped through the opening in the tent as well.

Outside, the camp was now in a furor. Men carried lanterns and shined them in all directions. Many of them were directed at the tent where the Humboldts had been.

Tall Dog dragged Opaline after him into the trees. She squalled the whole time until the young Crow warrior slung his rifle over his shoulder and clapped a hand over her bloody lips. Tall Dog lifted the woman and carried her into the trees.

"Over here!" a man yelled. "Somebody's over here! It ain't Humboldt!"

Preacher ducked behind a tree and reached into the canvas bag Darvis had given him for one of the explosives. Now seemed as good a time as any to use one of them. A cluster of men closed on Humboldt's tent. All of them carried rifles.

Opaline's decision to shoot her dead husband had knocked Preacher's plan into a cocked hat. He hoped that didn't turn Eyes Cut Like Knife away from the battle.

Dog snarled at the mountain man's side.

"Easy, Dog. Me and you, we been through harder times with less than what we have now."

Preacher took out one of the explosives and opened the pocket to get at the slow match.

The men gathered around the tent.

"You men!" Shaw called from the entrance to the cave. "What's happening over there?"

"Don't know, General," one of the soldiers said.

"Humboldt's in there dead," another man yelled. "The woman's gone."

"She didn't get out of there on her own," Shaw bellowed. "Otherwise, she'd have been gone hours ago. Find her."

Preacher blew on the slow match until it

glowed dull orange. He touched it to the fuse in the center of the explosive. The fuse sputtered to life and burned quickly. Darvis had said they would burn fast.

Wheeling around the tree where he took cover, the mountain man rolled the explosive across the ground. It jumped over a high spot, spun end over end, and rolled to a stop near the men.

They didn't notice because they opened fire at where they had seen him. The mountain man ducked back to cover. Balls whizzed into the tree and around Preacher. He filled his hands with the Patersons and waited.

"He's over here!" a man squalled.

"It's that mountain man! Preacher!"

"Kill him!" Shaw commanded.

More shots followed and more rounds smacked into the tree.

Boom!

Light flashed over the immediate area like a stroke of heat lightning. Dirt and rock and dust flew into the air. No more shots were fired.

Preacher glanced around the tree.

Only ragged pieces of canvas remained of the tent. At least six bodies lay strewn and ripped in the vicinity.

"Kill Preacher!" Shaw roared. "I'll reward

the man who brings him down!"

Preacher glanced over his shoulder for Tall Dog and found the young Crow warrior only a short distance away behind another tree.

"Where's the woman?" Preacher asked.

Rounds clipped the trees around them.

"I tied her up and gagged her and left her a short distance away," Tall Dog said. "I could not fight while carrying her. That would only have gotten both of us killed, and it would have left you on your own. I think together we might still escape this."

Preacher wasn't so sure of that. Shaw's men weren't running toward them, but they were clustering mighty thick.

"Stay behind me," the mountain man said. "We'll be movin' quick."

He stepped back into the trees and let their pursuers come after them. If the Sioux decided not to attack, Lorenzo and the others wouldn't be enough to stand against Shaw and his men. Running and hiding was the only chance Preacher and Tall Dog had.

"Over here!" someone yelled. "They went thisaway!"

Preacher paused and spied the lanterns carried by the men. The lights marked them as targets. He stood his ground for a moment and fired all ten shots into the group that followed them. Bodies dropped in the trees and brush.

A man cursed, hit or scared or confused, Preacher didn't know. He holstered the Patersons and drew his tomahawk and knife. He saved his last two pistols and his rifle.

Tall Dog kept pace with him, a shadow almost lost in the shadows. Dog was there, too. Although Preacher didn't see the big cur, he knew his companion was there.

A line of explosions lit up the upper ridge of the mountain. A moment later, boulders and rock tumbled down the mountainside toward the campsite. Then Sioux warriors and Darvis's men rode toward the campsite. With all the dust in the air, the rock tumbling down the mountain, and his night sight ruined by the bomb flash, Preacher barely glimpsed the riders.

The pursuit behind him and Tall Dog pulled up in a cluster, probably gathered for mutual protection. Preacher reached for the bag Darvis had given him because now would be a good time to use the other one.

Tall Dog leaned out of the darkness and threw one of his explosives underhanded toward the group. The fuse sparked, and the explosive rolled through the darkness and landed in the middle of the soldiers.

The men spotted the device, must have

guessed at its nature, and tried to flee in all directions.

Preacher turned from the coming destruction and put away his tomahawk and knife.

The explosive detonated with a thundering basso boom.

CHAPTER 35

Preacher drew one of the Patersons and reached into his possibles bag for cartridges. Working as swiftly as he could, he reloaded the cylinders, and shoved percussion caps onto the nipples.

"Reloadin' my pistols," Preacher said to Tall Dog to let the young Crow warrior know. It took longer to reload the Patersons than a rifle, but the revolvers were fierce in combat.

"There is no pursuit," Tall Dog said. "They have withdrawn toward the camp. You have respite."

The mountain man holstered the pistol he'd finished and drew the other. He reloaded it, as well, then peered back at the camp a hundred yards away.

Shaw stood in front of the cave and tried to form up his men, but half of them were men who'd come from the trading post and didn't know what they were doing. They kept getting in the way of the professional soldiers.

The Sioux swept through Shaw's men. Arrows pierced targets and left screaming, frightened, and angry men in their wake.

"All right," Preacher said, "let's go."

He raced forward in the darkness and didn't use his straight vision. Instead, he used the corners of his eyes, where a man could see more clearly in the night. He'd memorized some of the way they'd come, and he returned to the camp in the same direction. He dodged and weaved around the tents and stayed away from the still-burning campfires so they could partially hide in the shadows.

Shaw stayed within the cave, and the Basque sharpshooter stayed with him. A knot of soldiers stood with their general. Coolly, the Basque tracked the Sioux warriors and dropped at least two of them with his rifle.

Sixty feet from the cave, Preacher pointed the Patersons at the cave mouth and fired all ten rounds. Balls tore into flesh and screamed from the stone walls inside the cave.

Six of the men with Shaw dropped to the ground. The general and the sharpshooter withdrew into the cave.

Preacher hunkered behind a boulder on the south side of the cave entrance. He reloaded the Patersons automatically and gazed out over the campsite.

Chief Eyes Cut Like Knife and his warriors had the battle in hand and were tracking down the scattered pockets of soldiers. Darvis and his men rode into the mix as well.

Lorenzo, Moses, and Caleb hid behind cover on the other side of the entrance.

"Thought I seen you up here, Preacher," Lorenzo said. "Me an' Moses an' Caleb thought we'd come see how you're doin'."

"Things are goin' better than I thought they would," Preacher admitted.

"Lost some good men," Moses said. Blood gleamed high up on his right shoulder.

"We knew that couldn't be helped," Preacher said. "Only other choice was starvin' over the winter."

"I know," Moses said, "but it makes me want to be sure none of these men escape."

Preacher put percussion caps on the nipples of his second pistol. He nodded to where Darvis and the Sioux slew Shaw's men and recruits. Several skirmishes still lit up the night.

"I don't think that's likely," the mountain man said.

"Where's Shaw?" Lorenzo asked.

"Back in the cave," Preacher said.

"Ain't many places to go in there," Lorenzo said.

"Rats," Tall Dog said.

"Yep," Lorenzo said, "makes me downright sad, too."

Preacher knew Tall Dog wasn't talking about the general's temporary evasion of the justice headed his way though.

"I am not sad," Tall Dog said. "Rats always have a place to run." He nodded toward the cave. "Wherever this goes, there will be a bolt hole that Shaw plans to use to escape."

Preacher glanced around the entrance, saw the way was clear, and plunged into the cave. He holstered his left-hand pistol and scooped up a lantern from one of the water barrels in the main chamber. Three tunnels branched off from the chamber.

A quick shine of the lantern into the one on the left revealed a short tunnel that dead-ended quickly. He moved on to the next, but the long run was filled with darkness.

"Can't see the back end of this one." Lorenzo shined his lantern down the remaining tunnel.

"You three take that one," Preacher said. "Me and Tall Dog will take this one."

"You be careful, Preacher," Lorenzo said.

"You too. If you find that varmint, kill him. And watch out for that Basque and his wind rifle." Preacher shoved his lantern into the tunnel and followed the light.

Dog loped along at his side.

The narrow tunnel trapped the noise their moccasins made across the rough surface. The scraping sounded louder.

Gunshots echoed behind them, and men yelled in surprise and anger.

Thinking that Lorenzo and the others must have found Shaw and the Basque sharpshooter, Preacher almost turned back.

Except there was a patch of fresh blood on the right wall.

"You wounded someone," Tall Dog said. "They came this way."

"Lorenzo and the others ran into somebody," Preacher said. "Could be they split up and Shaw went the other way."

"Perhaps they found another group of men who hid in the tunnels," the young Crow warrior reasoned.

Preacher nodded. "What matters is we got blood here. Dog. Hunt!"

The big cur bounded forward, and Preacher was hard-pressed to keep up with him. In a few more feet, Preacher stepped out of the tunnel and into a long, narrow cave.

A sharp, acrid scent tickled the mountain man's nose, and it took him a moment to recognize it.

"Bats," Preacher said. He looked around the ground and spotted the white smears that covered the floor and marred the walls. He lifted the lantern and shined it against the roof.

Several brown bodies with wings clustered together a few feet overhead. Disturbed by the light, some of the winged varmints lit a shuck farther down the cave.

"If there are bats," Tall Dog said, "then there is another way out of this tunnel. We saw no bats until we reached this place."

Hearing Dog barking excitedly, Preacher lowered the lantern and ran forward.

At least a couple hundred yards farther on, moonlight glared down through a crack in the top of the long cave. A few of the bats flew through the opening.

Dog stood under the opening and stared up because he couldn't negotiate the handholds carved into the wall. The handholds were old, worn smooth by years of use.

Preacher holstered his pistol and handed Tall Dog the lantern. Unencumbered, he climbed the wall a few feet and stuck his head through the opening.

Sixty yards away, moonlight gleamed from a metallic surface that shifted and a ball left a gray smear on the stone surface around the opening. There was no sound of the shot.

Preacher dropped back into the cave. "Them varmints are settin' up there and waitin' on us to stick our heads out. The Basque almost got me. Next time I try to go up, he will get me." He thought furiously. "If we wait here, or try to make our way around, they could be long gone before we get them."

"There is another way." Tall Dog rummaged in his explosives bag and held out his last one. "You have another. We could throw them outside and let them be a distraction."

"All right." Preacher took out his explosive, pulled out the slow match, and blew on it.

He and Tall Dog held their fuses to the slow match and they quickly lit. They held them for a brief moment, then hurled them through the opening at an angle that, hopefully, guaranteed they wouldn't roll back into the cave with them.

Preacher readied himself at the handholds. When the explosions, first one and then the other, flashed outside the opening, he swarmed up the handholds and threw himself out on the rough ground. He unslung his rifle and held it ready. He wanted the accuracy now more than the firepower of the revolvers.

Tall Dog followed just behind him. They split up and sought shelter in the trees. Rifles cracked and balls struck the trees around them, but the thing Preacher worried about most made no sound.

In the cave, Dog howled forlornly because he couldn't accompany Preacher. The mournful cries echoed over the mountain and sounded like something supernatural.

A soldier fired his rifle ahead of them and Tall Dog put a ball through his head. Even as the dead man fell back, the young Crow warrior rolled to the side and took a fresh cartridge from his possibles bag.

Preacher studied the trees and used the edge of his vision to better penetrate the shadows.

Dog howled again, and another soldier stepped out for a quick shot. Preacher fired a ball into the man's throat. The soldier collapsed and tried to stem the blood that rushed from his neck.

Preacher slid to the side and reached for a fresh cartridge.

This time the Basque slid into view just long enough to fire two silent rounds that cut through brush around Preacher. The mountain man knew the marksman probably could have at least a dozen rounds left before he had to reload. Perhaps more.

When Preacher's rifle was reloaded, he hunkered behind a rocky outcrop and waited for the Basque to reappear.

Two more soldiers fired into the trees, and Preacher thought maybe they were ordered to do it, because they didn't come close to hitting him or Tall Dog. Calmly, the young Crow warrior picked one of the soldiers off and slid away.

This time, though, the Basque grew over-eager and tried to follow Tall Dog. The sharpshooter kept in tight to cover. From his vantage point, Preacher could only see the man's shoulder.

And he could see the air tank that was the wind rifle's stock.

Preacher adjusted his aim and fired. The ball sped true and struck the air tank. The highly pressurized device exploded and blew off several chunks of metal that turned into shrapnel. Several of those shrapnel pieces struck the Basque, and the man cried out in pain.

Wounded, maybe dying, the Basque tumbled from hiding. He struggled to recover and get to his feet. He clawed at the pistol holstered on his hip.

Preacher slid his rifle over his shoulder and drew the Patersons. He advanced through the brush and shot three soldiers on his way to the Basque. Tall Dog shot twice, once with his rifle and once with one of his pistols. Both times soldiers fell behind the trees.

The young Crow warrior drew his sword and advanced beside Preacher.

When Shaw was flushed from the shadows and pointed his pistol at Preacher, Tall Dog took off the man's outstretched arm with his sword and the mountain man shot the general between the eyes.

As Preacher closed on the Basque, the man raised his pistol. Before he could fire, Preacher put a bullet into the bottom of the man's jaw that exited through the back of his head.

The Basque dropped his pistol and stared sightlessly into the night sky visible in patches between the trees.

A quick search of the area showed that no one remained alive on the mountain. Only a few shots were fired in the campsite down below.

Preacher reloaded his weapons and

headed back to the cave where Dog still
howled.

CHAPTER 36

"You sure you want to do this?" Rufus Darvis asked.

Tired and a little chilly in the cold breath of the morning, Preacher studied the cave entrance in the mountain that had been the cause of so much trouble in his beloved wilderness. Gold had been found on Shaw's body, and there was little doubt that it had been mined there in that cave.

Bodies still littered the land in front of the cave. All of them were Shaw's men and the men who had left the trading post. A few of the Sioux and a few of Darvis's men had died in the fight, too, but their bodies had been claimed and taken away. Those who remained were banquets for the varmints.

Chief Eyes Cut Like Knife sat on his horse a short distance away. His braves, including Talks With Toads who had three fresh scalps hanging from his spear, had watched Darvis and his men drill blasting holes around the cave entrance. They'd put in more around the opening at the back end of the long tunnel where Shaw and the Basque had tried to make their escape.

"I'm using a lot of blasting powder here," Darvis said. "There's enough to bring down a sizable chunk of that mountain, too. Whatever's in that cave, if it is gold, will never be found again."

Preacher didn't say anything. He wasn't sure Shaw had really found the gold he was looking for, but he'd announced it to everyone at the trading post. It didn't take much to set up a bad case of gold fever that could get folks killed. And just a whiff of it brought varmints running from all over everywhere.

Bruised and battered, Opaline Humboldt sat in a buckboard back in the tree line. Rory McClellan, the young reporter, sat beside her. She'd cleaned herself up, but it was going to take a while before all the bruising faded.

She hadn't said a word about her dead husband's body. Nobody had volunteered to bring Anthony Humboldt in for a proper burying.

"Get your men out of there," Preacher said. "I want you to take that mountain down."

Darvis grinned. "Happy to do it. Back in South Africa, there are men enslaving men to dig in mines for gold and diamonds. I've never been a fan of riches. Give me work and the health to get it done, and I'm a happy man."

"My husband employed you," Opaline called from the buckboard. "You can't just blow up that mountain if I don't wish you to."

"Mrs. Humboldt," Darvis said, "your husband put a pistol to your head and threatened to kill you to get us to do what he wanted done. That effectively ended our working relationship."

"I can pay you to leave it alone."

"You do that," Darvis said, "and I suspect there are folks here who will make sure none of us make it out of these mountains." He puffed on his pipe. "Nope, I'm going to bring this mountain down." He grinned. "I haven't had a job this big in years. Least-ways, not one where I got to blow things up like this."

Opaline frowned and quieted.

"You know that woman's gonna be a problem," Lorenzo said. "Her an' that young whippersnapper sittin' with her. They got stories to tell, an' they're newspaper folks. They'll tell this one because it's too good not to tell."

"I know," Preacher said. He'd considered trying to convince Opaline to leave the story alone, but he knew he couldn't.

"Might even be a good enough story to draw folks out here," Lorenzo warned. "If I was a man who prized gold above all else, I sure might want to sneak out here and have a gander."

"In the end, whatever they say in her father's newspaper ain't going to matter," Preacher said. "There are already stories travelin' around that talk about lost mines and treasures up here. This one will just be one more."

"Sure hope you're right. What did Chief Eyes Cut Like Knife say about the tradin' post?"

"He's going to leave them alone for now," Preacher answered. "He's bankin' on them pullin' up sticks in the spring."

"I ain't bankin' on it," Lorenzo said, "but I don't see how they're gonna survive out here on their own. Anybody who needs anythin' stops at Fort Pierre. Ain't enough business left over to keep them alive."

"We have to get them through the winter first," Preacher said.

"You figure on stayin'?"

"If we don't, Darvis and his men might

not make it through either. We got back those supplies Shaw and his men took, but that won't hold them through the winter. They'll need somebody to show them how to make it. After what Darvis did to help us against Shaw, I owe him."

"Thought you might see it that way." Lorenzo folded his arms. "I ain't set up in the high country durin' a winter in a while. I'm kinda interested in seein' if I'm still tough enough to get it done."

Preacher grinned at his friend. "You are."

"Besides that," Lorenzo said, "sittin' up here tellin' lies an' stories Darvis an' his men ain't never heard will help me sharpen my skills. You know a man who can spin a yarn that can hold a man's attention will never have to buy himself another beer."

"Maybe not."

Darvis looked over at Preacher. "Ready?"

The mountain man nodded.

The engineer lit his tangle of fuses, and sparks skittered through the grass and brush up to the mountain. It took a while to span the distance, but the resulting series of explosions cracked rock, shifted rock, and buried the cave in a thundering rumble that filled the valley.

Dusty haze hung over the area. When it cleared, there was no sign that a cave had ever been there. A mass of tumbled and jumbled rocks ran across the mountain like the thick seam of a scar.

Preacher knew the stories about the gold would persist though. They always did. If there was gold in this mountain, or any other mountains in this wilderness, men would one day find it.

Then everything would change.

The wilderness would be beaten into submission and all the beauty would be chased away.

Preacher hoped he never lived to see that day because he liked the rough country and the critters hardy enough to survive in it. Especially the ones that tasted so fine.

Until that day, though, he'd make his home in the mountains and enjoy that life he loved so dearly.

HISTORICAL NOTE

Thirty-four years later, the Gold Rush Preacher predicted came about, as thousands of fortune-seekers flooded into what was, by then, known as the Black Hills of Dakota Territory. Although the trading post established by Barnaby Cooper was long gone, a new settlement known as Queen City came into existence at the head of Spearfish Canyon, a settlement known today as Spearfish, South Dakota.

Less than ten miles south of there, lay the center of the Black Hills Gold Rush, the hell-roaring camp that came to be known as Deadwood. Not surprisingly, Preacher lived to see that. In fact, he was in Deadwood in August 1876, when Jack McCall went looking for Wild Bill Hickok . . .

But that's another story.

ABOUT THE AUTHORS

William W. Johnstone is the #1 bestselling Western writer in America and the *New York Times* and *USA Today* bestselling author of hundreds of books, with over 50 million copies sold. Born in southern Missouri, he was raised with strong moral and family values by his minister father, and tutored by his schoolteacher mother. He left school at fifteen to work in a carnival and then as a deputy sheriff before serving in the army. He went on to become known as "the Greatest Western writer of the 21st Century." Visit him online at WilliamJohn stone.net.

J. A. Johnstone learned to write from the master himself, Uncle William W. Johnstone, who began tutoring J.A. at an early age. After-school hours were often spent retyping manuscripts or researching his massive American Western History library as well as the more modern wars and conflicts. J.A. worked hard and learned, later going on to become the co-author of William W. Johnstone's many bestselling westerns and thrillers. J. A. Johnstone lives on a ranch in Tennessee and more information is at WilliamJohnstone.net.